D0338920

Linda O. Johnston loves to write. While honing her writing skills, she worked in advertising and public relations, then became a lawyer… and enjoyed writing contracts. Linda's first published fiction appeared in *Ellery Queen's Mystery Magazine* and won a Robert L. Fish Memorial Award for Best First Mystery Short Story of the Year. Linda now spends most of her time creating memorable tales of paranormal romance, romantic suspense and mystery. Visit her on the web at lindaojohnston.com.

Books by Linda O. Johnston

Harlequin Nocturne

Alpha Force

Alpha Wolf

Alaskan Wolf

Guardian Wolf

Undercover Wolf

Loyal Wolf

Canadian Wolf

Back to Life

Harlequin Romantic Suspense

Undercover Soldier

Covert Attraction

Visit the Author Profile page
at Harlequin.com for more titles.

Linda O. Johnston
and
Linda Thomas-Sundstrom

CANADIAN WOLF
AND
SEDUCED BY
THE MOON

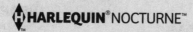
HARLEQUIN® NOCTURNE™

ISBN-13: 978-0-373-60176-9

Canadian Wolf and Seduced by the Moon

Copyright © 2015 by Harlequin Books S.A.

The publisher acknowledges the copyright holders of the individual works as follows:

Canadian Wolf
Copyright © 2015 by Linda O. Johnston

Seduced by the Moon
Copyright © 2015 by Linda Thomas-Sundstrom

Printed in U.S.A.

HHARLEQUIN®
TM www.Harlequin.com

CONTENTS

CANADIAN WOLF

Linda O. Johnston

My special thanks to my wonderful agent,
Paige Wheeler of Creative Media Agency, and to
my delightful Harlequin editor, Allison Lyons,
who have been so fantastic in helping to keep
the stories of Alpha Force an ongoing miniseries.

Thanks, too, to writers Leslie Knowles
and Ann Finnin, who read my manuscript
and gave me some great revision ideas.

And as always, thanks to my amazing husband,
Fred, whom I always acknowledge in each of my
books because he inspires me.

Like my other Alpha Force Nocturne novels,
Canadian Wolf is dedicated to shapeshifters
and the readers who love them.

Chapter 1

"I'm still so jazzed!" said Lieutenant Rainey Jessop, clasping her hands under her chin. "Working with Mounties. This'll be so much fun!"

Lieutenant Selena Jennay sent a wry smile toward her aide. Rainey had been excited from the moment the two of them had first been given this assignment—yesterday. As for herself, she was skeptical. She'd reserve judgment until she better understood the players in this new mission.

She took a seat across from her aide at the table in the small meeting room with gray wallpapered walls, the secluded area to which they'd been shown after arriving at the Royal Canadian Mounted Police's northwest Vancouver facility. Her cover dog, Lupe, a canine who resembled a mix between a wolf and a husky, lay beside her.

She glanced at Rainey. "Do you think it's more fun than working with shapeshifters?"

Rainey looked momentarily shocked, a rare occurrence for the outgoing and chatty young woman. "Hardly. But I'm going to get to work with both Mounties *and* shapeshifters. Amazing!" She paused, and her smile morphed into a frown as two men in white shirts and blue pants walked into the room. "Although I'd hoped that we'd get to work with Mounties in their gorgeous dress uniforms and tall hats," she added under her breath.

Selena and Rainey rose to meet the men, smoothing down the camo uniforms of Alpha Force, the highly covert US military unit to which they belonged. Selena's light brown hair and Rainey's darker brunette locks were both pulled back tightly into clips.

"Good morning," said the first man to enter. He appeared middle-aged and had short white hair. Walking around the oval wooden table to where Selena and Rainey now stood, he held out a veined, long-fingered hand. "I'm Anthony Creay, deputy commissioner of the RCMP's general policing services."

Then he was the head of the group who'd contacted Alpha Force, Selena reasoned. "Hello, sir," she said, shaking his hand. She introduced both Rainey and herself. Then she let her gaze drift to the other man.

"Sergeant Major Owen Dewirter," he said, proffering his hand for a shake, too. "Also with general policing services."

And most likely the man with whom they'd be working over the next few weeks, Selena figured. The other guy was his superior officer and probably just wanted to make sure things got started well.

"Which one of you is the shapeshifter?" Owen asked. The sergeant major had a distinctively handsome face, with brilliant blue eyes beneath strong brows that matched his short, wavy black hair. His nose was aquiline, his chin broad with just a hint of a beard shadow.

Yet judging by his unreadable expression, Selena

had the impression that he wasn't overly fond of shifters. Did he even believe in them? That wasn't clear, at least not yet.

"That would be me," she said in as mild a tone as she could muster, considering her initial bout of irritation. She could be wrong. She didn't know the guy, let alone how RCMP members thought or acted. He might be attempting to impress his superior officer by remaining emotionless.

"How fascinating!" Anthony did indeed appear fascinated. He stood behind a chair at the opposite side of the table, his eyes wide, his mouth slightly open. "I'm pleased that you're here to give us a close-up demonstration."

"Yes. About that." Rainey drew their attention as she sat down again. Her movement caused Lupe, who'd stood up as the humans did, to sit as well. "We've discussed that and are not sure about the best way to handle it. You see, we need a bit of privacy. Actually, Lieutenant Jennay needs a bit of privacy," she amended. "I'm her aide, and I'll be with her, but a shift requires that someone, er—"

"I'll be nude," Selena interjected. She remained standing for now, her arms crossed. "That's why I have a female aide. We use a special proprietary elixir, and we will make some available to the shifters you have recruited into the new RCMP team that we're to train. When the rest of our Alpha Force team arrives tomorrow or the next day, they'll include a male shifter or two. They may be more amenable to being observed by men when they change. But although you can definitely see me once I've shifted, you unfortunately can't watch me shift." She found herself looking straight into Owen

Dewirter's still-unreadable gaze. "Too uncomfortable for me. And I don't like to feel uncomfortable."

"I see." The words were drawn out slowly by Anthony Creay as he sank down into a chair across from the two women. And clearly, to Selena, the point was that he could *not* see. Not everything. "Nude? I didn't consider that—but I believe that observing a shift was part of our understanding. So we would be sure of the genuineness of the help we're getting." As he scowled, his fleshy lower lip protruded.

Owen took a seat beside him, then exchanged glances with his superior officer. When he turned back to Selena, he had a decided frown on his face, too. "We need to work something out here," he said. "We have to watch the process to be sure you're a real shifter and not just trying to put something over on us."

His pronunciation of the word *out*—with an almost long *O* sound—emphasized that he was Canadian. But his accent wasn't the only difference between them. He wanted her to get nude in front of him for her demo shift? Not gonna happen. Even though he was one great-looking guy. The thought of him observing her body as she stripped sent waves of heat through Selena that made her feel as if this meeting was on the hottest summer day in the US South instead of a cool evening in the Canadian West.

Was this whole thing primed to be a fiasco? Selena hoped not. She and Rainey were here representing Alpha Force and, since they had been in the western United States and were therefore the closest of those in their unit who had been selected to help the RCMP form their own similar unit, they'd been ordered to Vancouver to give a small and limited demonstration.

Limited being the key word.

Even Lupe must have sensed the tension in the room since she stood beside Selena and whined. Selena reached out and hugged the wolf-dog closer to her.

"Here's the thing," she said to the men in as reasonable a tone as she could muster. "Let me introduce you first to my cover dog. Lupe, this is Deputy Commissioner Creay and Sergeant Major Dewirter." She scratched Lupe behind the ears in a manner that caused the dog to turn her head toward the two men, not that Lupe, a genuine canine, could understand her words. "Gentlemen, this is the canine who looks a whole lot like me when I'm shifted. The way I figured we'd do this demonstration is for Rainey and me to go into another room. You can keep Lupe with you and lock the door to the room. With Rainey's help, I'll shift. Then when you unlock the door there'll be Rainey inside with a canine who looks a whole lot like Lupe. Voilà! That'll be me, shifted. There'll be no other person in the room. With doors locked and all, there's no way we'd be able to do this without it being the real thing." The very suggestion that they'd try to pull a scam on representatives of a national police department that had requested their help really peeved Selena.

"But we understood we could see the actual shift take place." Creay's tone was icy.

Selena glanced toward Rainey, who looked uneasy and bewildered. Well, she needn't be. Selena was in charge here, at least for now.

"I understand your wish to see the process, gentlemen," she said. "Maybe you'd have been able to if you hadn't requested Alpha Force's presence so urgently. You said you needed at least our initial representation within one day. We were the closest team members available. So here we are."

"I recognize that," Creay retorted. "But we don't have any extra time, either, to wait—or to deal with a situation where things aren't as represented to us."

"Are you accusing us of lying?" Selena hated to be confrontational, but their attitude was forcing her into it.

"We're not accusing you of anything." Owen's voice sounded placating, but his expression remained unreadable. "We just want to ensure we've got what we were promised by the US military."

Selena wanted to make good on that promise, too, for the sake of Alpha Force. She took a deep breath, then said, "Look, we want to cooperate with you—but certain things are nonnegotiable. If you don't feel you can trust us, if you think we'll play some kind of hoodwinking, magical game even when you can watch to make sure the room stays locked—well, maybe we'd better just leave right now."

Selena saw Owen glance once more into the angry face of his commanding officer. Then Owen looked directly toward Selena. "Okay," he said. "We understand your concern, and I hope you understand ours. Our mission is highly important. And…well, it's probably no surprise to you that not all people believe in shapeshifters. We just need—"

"Do you believe in them?" Selena glared as if daring him to say that who she was, what she did, wasn't real.

"Yes," Owen said quietly, planting his arms on the table in front of him and leaning toward her. "I do. But this is all new to Deputy Commissioner Creay and he has his doubts."

Interesting, Selena thought. Creay's position was that

of the majority of regular people. But the sergeant major was a believer. How did he know the reality?

Well, if he was the one who'd be working with them, maybe she would find out. Or not, if things continued to deteriorate.

He leaned in closer toward Selena, and his confrontational posture made Lupe tense up and growl. Glancing at the dog, he backed up slightly. "We seem to be at a stalemate. I'll be with you at the headquarters of the new team we're forming. But Deputy Commissioner Creay won't be with us. He's going back to our headquarters in Ottawa when we're done here. I may be able to watch some of the male shifters change then, but he needs to see you shift now." His expression changed then from demanding to something Selena couldn't interpret at first. Challenging?

Could be, considering his next words.

"I'll tell you what, Lieutenant Jennay. If you strip and show us your change, I'll strip right along with you. That way we can both feel uncomfortable, not just you. Although I have to admit that I'm just a normal human being."

Selena blinked in surprise at his outrageous offer.

Normal? She doubted that. The idea set her body on fire, and it was all she could do to prevent herself from letting her gaze slide down his fully clothed body toward the area she really would like to see nude.

But was he serious? Or was this some kind of additional challenge? "That's not—" she began.

"Not necessary," Deputy Commissioner Creay interjected. Selena drew her gaze away from Owen and focused on Creay. His expression had calmed a bit. "I trust the people I spoke with at Alpha Force, and I'll trust them more after one of us gets to observe a shift. But that's apparently not going to happen now, so why don't you do your shift, as you suggested, inside a locked room. We'll check out the room before you enter and then monitor the shift from the outside. For now, that should be fine."

Selena gave a sigh of relief that the face-off had now been averted, even as she continued to watch Owen Dewirter. Now his eyes, too, were unreadable.

What would he do if she told him that she accepted his offer to strip bare?

No matter how much she liked the idea on some level—like, deep inside her now-blazing body—she wouldn't agree. Handling her shift the way she had already described was the best way to go. It should satisfy them. This was an RCMP facility. Where would Alpha Force find another dog that looked like Lupe and be able to sneak it in?

Besides, she was aware that others in Alpha Force sometimes used this method of shifting in a secured room to prove to nonshifters who—and what—they were, and she hadn't heard of any problems resulting.

But all she said was "Fine. So…shall we get started?"

Owen Dewirter observed Selena from across the table—for the moment, at least—as she stood.

Maybe he'd been way out of line with his suggestion. It had been impulsive. But it had also been born out of irritation and a need to end their impasse.

Owen hadn't wanted to strip here—although the idea of seeing Selena Jennay nude definitely stiffened a certain part of his body. But he also knew Anthony Creay well enough to be certain that his superior officer didn't like to be denied anything he believed he was entitled to.

This way, Anthony wound up making the decision—a good thing, and probably the only way to make the superior officer stand down. And now what Lieutenant Selena Jennay had proposed had become acceptable. She would shift without a male audience.

She would shift, though. He didn't actually doubt that she was a shapeshifter.

Although he believed—no, knew—they existed, he had major concerns about shapeshifters.

But this one was also a gorgeous, sexy woman—even dressed in the sexless camouflage uniform of US soldiers.

She was slender, moderately tall, with full lips and high cheekbones. Her light brown hair seemed most unusual, with highlights that shimmered in even the low artificial lights in this conference room. Her amber eyes flashed with emotion as she spoke—like now, as she conversed softly with the other woman, glancing occasionally toward the two men.

Owen rose, too, as did Anthony. "Do you know of any suitable room?" his superior asked in a low voice.

"Why not in here?" Owen asked. "We can leave." As he spoke, he scanned the small chamber, furnished only with the table and chairs. They were two stories up, so their visitors couldn't slip Selena out and a dog in—especially since the window overlooked the parking lot and the station's inside guard post. Whoever was on duty would no doubt see any shenanigans.

"I suppose that would work," Anthony said, also looking around.

As they spoke, Lieutenant Jennay speared them both

with a sharp gaze that gave no quarter. Owen had no doubt that if her demeanor was typical of the US military's Alpha Force, that explained how the covert group accomplished its sometimes impossible missions.

He looked forward to this assignment.

He'd been one of the very few members of his division within the RCMP's general policing services who hadn't immediately scoffed when Anthony asked in his interview whether he believed in shapeshifters. Owen knew they were real.

He just didn't happen to like them. Experience had taught him to mistrust them.

And yet, it was in his country's best interests for a group of shifters from the States to help the RCMP to form its own covert unit, similar to Alpha Force, but a police unit instead of a military one.

Owen was all about helping his country. He would head the team. The fact that he'd previously worked with canines at the RCMP's police-dog service training center wouldn't hurt, either.

"So what do you think?" Selena eventually asked, her hands on her hips and confrontation in her expression.

"We'll lock you right in here," Owen said with no inflection, as if he had no interest in continuing the confrontation. "This is as good as any place. Maybe not the most comfortable location to get naked, but you won't be aware of it for long anyway."

"Not true," Selena snapped back. She clearly hadn't lost her attitude. "You may believe in shapeshifters, but you don't know anything about Alpha Force and our elixir if you think we lose awareness. For your information, the elixir developed by members of Alpha Force allows us to shift without a full moon and to keep our human awareness when the moon isn't full, and neither is the case with other shifters."

"Sounds like a useful concoction." Owen had understood there was something that made Alpha Force members different from other shapeshifters, but hadn't known what it was.

She seemed to relax a little after that. "But that's okay for now. You'll learn more as we help to train your RCMP shapeshifters." She drew out those words as if to rub the concept back in his face.

He realized that he was smiling—wryly perhaps, but genuinely. She wasn't only lovely. She amused him.

Even though she was a shapeshifter. Or so she said.

She was right. He knew little about Alpha Force, its elixir or anything else related to the unit. But if she could genuinely shapeshift now, when the next full moon wasn't due for a couple of weeks, it would tell him a lot.

"There aren't any security cameras in here, are there?" Selena asked. He watched as she scanned the walls.

"No," said Anthony Creay. "This room is usually used for secure and private meetings."

"Okay, then we're on." Selena looked around a little more as if she didn't trust what he said, but there were no places that Owen saw, either, where equipment could be hidden.

"Fine," he said. "Now, what would you like us to do?"

It was her turn to grin. "If you'd like, you can go ahead and get naked anyway." She let her eyes scan Owen's body up and down, and he felt himself start to respond. Not a good idea. Not here, and not ever.

But since they were going to be working together,

should he call her bluff after all? He gave it a second's thought before he knew the answer. No sense in angering his commanding officer. "Nope," he said. "I think this is your cue, not mine."

She shrugged one shoulder, as if she had no interest in whether he kept his clothes on or not. Too bad, he thought. But it was better that way.

"So what would you like us to do?" he asked her.

"Leave." She began walking around the table, holding out the leash attached to her dog's collar. "Just watch out for Lupe. She's a great dog—but like me, she's got quite a bite if you rile her."

He assumed she was still just teasing. Even so, he gingerly grabbed hold of the leash's looped handle. It was his responsibility, not his superior officer's. The furry wolf-dog looked up at him with eyes that did indeed appear a similar amber shade to Selena's. Her cover dog. The way she would appear while shifted, she'd indicated.

A fine representative of the wolf species, albeit with some traces of other canine stock, like, perhaps, Siberian husky.

"I bite, too, Lupe," he said, although the way he petted her furry head belied his words—justifiably. He liked dogs. A lot.

It was their shapeshifting counterparts that he didn't trust.

Was Selena different? He'd see, as time went on.

"Well, don't bite my dog," Selena said.

She turned around, waving her hand. "Right now is a good time for you gentlemen to leave." She glanced over her shoulder. "After you lock the door you can stand in the hall to make sure we don't slip out and play the games that you apparently expect. Rainey will knock for you to open the door when my shift is complete."

"Fine." Owen waited until Anthony had cleared the doorway, then followed.

He turned back for an instant, just long enough to notice that Selena was already preparing for what would occur after he locked the door. Her head was bent as she started unbuttoning her shirt.

Too bad he really couldn't stay and watch. Maybe some other time.

The other woman, Rainey, had crossed the room and picked up the large backpack she'd carried inside before. She studied its insides, and before Owen left, he saw her extract some kind of bottle. Was that the elixir Selena had mentioned?

He figured he would find out, if not today, then in the days to come, when he was with the Alpha Force members who had promised to help instruct the new RCMP members he had assisted in recruiting.

Those new members were also shapeshifters—or so they'd claimed—and had their claims confirmed by reputable friends and family, including others within the RCMP. He hadn't yet had a chance to watch them shift, either, since they did so only under a full moon—so far.

"Hey, haven't you left yet?" That was Rainey, who'd looked toward the door after handing the bottle to Selena.

Selena had stopped moving and was also watching him suspiciously.

"On my way." He gave a small yank on Lupe's leash. The dog obeyed and preceded him out the door.

Owen shut the door behind him and took the key from Anthony's hand. He turned it in the lock.

"So," he said, "I guess now we just wait."

* * *

Moving her erect ears, inhaling deeply to further stimulate her sense of smell, Selena stared at the door.

Her shifting had finally ended. As always, there had been discomfort.

Also as always, she had finished taking off her human clothes before imbibing the elixir and waited while Rainey shone the special battery-operated light on her that resembled the glow of a full moon. But this time she had also turned to stare at that closed door.

Maybe the distraction had helped, since the discomfort hadn't seemed as bad as usual. Even now, shifted, she couldn't help wondering what it would have been like if Owen Dewirter had actually removed his clothes, too.

"You okay?" *Rainey asked as she always did.*

In her wolfen form Selena couldn't shrug and say, "Of course." *Instead, she just gave a soft growl and lowered her head.*

"So, you ready to show off to those doubting Thomases?" *Rainey asked next.* "Why would they even invite Alpha Force to help save their Mountie butts if they didn't believe that our abilities—your abilities—were real?"

That wasn't something Selena could respond to, either. Not now, in any event. And in fact she had no answer.

But she'd definitely gotten the sense that the smart-alecky Owen Dewirter believed in, but did not appreciate, shifters.

She would find out why. Eventually.

For now, she padded over to the door and listened. Even as a human, her hearing surpassed that of normal people, but it was particularly enhanced after her shift, as were her senses of smell and taste.

She sensed that Lupe was still outside. The men were talking, perhaps joking a little.

The older man clearly did not know what to expect.

She lifted her paw and touched the door frame, which cued Rainey, who knocked to summon the two Mounties.

Selena heard footsteps on the hallway floor. In seconds, she heard the sound of the key in the lock. The door was pulled open, and Owen stood there, looking in.

On one side of him was Anthony Creay. On the other was Lupe, who pulled on her leash.

Selena walked forward and traded nose sniffs with her cover dog.

"Care to come in and look around, gentlemen?" Rainey sounded smug.

"Yes," said Anthony, and he strode through the open entry.

Owen just stood there, looking into the room and down at her. She could not read his expression. It wasn't admiring, but neither was it full of scorn.

"It is real," she finally heard the older man say. "No Selena here, just the dog. The wolf. Whatever."

"Yeah," Owen agreed. "It's real. And that's a good thing, since our guys have a lot to learn to accomplish our underlying mission."

She might help to teach them a lot—but she needed to know exactly what that mission was. And soon.

Chapter 2

It was morning, the day after the three Alpha Force members, including the dog, had arrived in northwest Vancouver.

Now Owen was ready to drive them up to their new headquarters, where he—and they—could get to work.

For the moment, he had parked his SUV in front of the hotel where both he and the visitors had spent the night. He settled back in the driver's seat, waiting for them.

Last night, when their sort-of demonstration had ended, it had been too late to head out. Besides, Selena had looked tired after what she had been through. Once Anthony acknowledged that she must indeed be a shifter—Owen hadn't doubted it by then—she, her aide and her dog had remained in that conference room while Anthony and he went back into the hall.

Owen hadn't locked the door that time. He'd figured Selena, changing back from a wolf-dog into a human— a naked human—might have wanted that option, but she hadn't asked for it before shifting back, and neither had her aide.

Of course neither he nor Anthony had attempted to

peek. Even so, Owen, who never considered himself to have much of an imagination, had still somehow visualized what her slim but curvaceous body might have looked like without any clothes on...

Well, he could imagine anything he wanted, including sexual attraction to a female shapeshifter in human form. That fantasy would remain far from reality, for a whole lot of reasons, not the least of which was that she was a professional colleague...and—oh, yes—she was a shifter.

The good thing was that Anthony now believed—which meant their operation could move forward.

Plus, Owen hadn't had to strip to get the dispute resolved. It had been a dumb offer on his part. He knew that. He'd recognized it even as he'd suggested it, Anthony's attitude notwithstanding. Worst thing now was that it might negatively affect his professional relationship with Selena. He'd have to be careful and treat her with total respect from now on.

And keep his clothes on.

Before they'd adjourned last night he'd called this hotel and made reservations for them and himself for the night. His current home was in Ottawa, since he'd been most recently stationed at the RCMP main headquarters there—until now. But he would become a resident of West Columbia as soon as they got there.

He scanned the front of the hotel and saw the trio emerge. He got out of the car to open the doors for them.

The women rolled suitcases behind them and carried bags over their shoulders. Rainey seemed in charge of the dog.

As they got closer, Selena blatantly looked him up and down. Interesting. Did she approve of what she saw?

"You're not wearing your Mounties uniform," she said. "Not even the casual kind you had on last night— although someday soon we're going to insist on seeing you in one of those classic and formal red jackets and rounded hats."

She had a smile on her face. She looked well rested and seemed clearly in teasing mode. Good. Maybe things weren't as bad as he thought.

"Only if you earn the right to see me that way," he said, keeping his face expressionless. "I have to admit that I like you in the civilian clothes you're wearing today a lot better than the camo uniform." The jeans and T-shirt she wore hugged her curves.

Why was he noticing such things? Especially after cautioning himself to resist any sexual attraction to her.

He quickly opened the rear hatch and helped them load their suitcases and backpacks, then watched as Rainey ushered Lupe into the backseat and followed the dog inside. Lupe was obviously a well-trained dog, one he'd enjoy working with, given the opportunity.

He doubted that the humans, while shifted, would be as well behaved.

By the time he closed the door after the woman and dog, Selena was already buckled in the front seat. He hurried to the driver's side and got in.

"So where, exactly, is our destination?" Selena said as he turned the key in the ignition.

"West Columbia."

"How far is it?"

Owen maneuvered the car away from the curb. It was his own vehicle. Even though this was an official mission, the whole operation was to be done undercover. Plus, he was moving to this area to be in charge of the new covert team. He would not drive his prior on-the-job vehicle, an RCMP sedan, around here.

"About an hour from here," he finally answered as he pulled into traffic. "It's a somewhat remote, moderate-sized town where tourists come and go, so we won't stick out as being intruders. It abuts some forested mountains and seems like a good location for our new detachment, but we'll see. The location is also part of our experiment. The new RCMP members who are part of my team are already located there, and to everyone they talk to they're on vacation but considering moving there. That's what all of us are to say, if anyone asks."

Owen drove north toward Highways 1 and 99, the Trans-Canada Highway nearest to where they started out, although it would turn into the Upper Levels Highway and Sea-to-Sky Highway before they reached their destination.

"Sounds good," Selena said. "Since you're national police and not military, you shouldn't need something like Ft. Lukman, which is Alpha Force's headquarters. It's an actual military facility in Maryland and has units stationed there besides ours. We'll tell you more about it, if you'd like, as we undertake our training sessions. By the way, what's your new team to be called?"

"It's the Covert Special Services Group. Our nickname for the group, at least for now, is the Canada Alphas, or CAs."

"That works," Selena said. "At least it's somewhat compatible with Alpha Force."

He glanced at her yet again and saw that she was smiling, and that lovely expression was aimed toward him.

"Now all we need to do is to get your shapeshifting team whipped into shape," she said.

* * *

Staring out the window at the lovely, forested Canadian countryside with vast mountains in the background, Selena couldn't help wondering how hard their assignment would be. From the little she'd learned when ordered to hurry to this area, the shifters Alpha Force was going to assist in training had only just been recruited into the RCMP. They probably had no experience in law enforcement or the military. Their shapeshifting backgrounds probably hadn't even allowed them to consider the possibility of shifting outside of full moons, let alone keeping human cognition while in shifted form.

Bless you, Alpha Force elixir, she thought.

Yet she had a sense that this man, who'd be in charge of the RCMP contingent, could make her job even harder.

She needed to figure him out.

What did he really think about shapeshifters?

And the idea of his offering to get naked…? *Stop thinking about that, Jennay*, she ordered herself silently.

She glanced into the backseat. Lupe lay down with her ears up but her eyes closed, and Rainey watched the view out the window, as Selena had been doing.

Yesterday, they'd been in a car most of the day—a rental vehicle they'd picked up hurriedly in Seattle and dropped off in Vancouver.

Good thing they'd had adequate ID with them to get into Canada—their passports and military identification. But Alpha Force members were always prepared for anything. It was part of the job.

She hoped she was prepared for the man beside her.

Turning to Owen, she asked, "I gathered that you believed in shapeshifters even before you got the assignment of working with them, right?"

"That's right."

Along with his bland acknowledgment, she watched Owen's physical reaction. There was none. At least none that she could see. He didn't look at her, and his handsome blue eyes didn't blink as they stared at the road ahead of him. His strong chin remained at the same level as before. He continued to drive at a speed compatible with the flow of traffic, watch the road and not say or do anything that would indicate his attitude toward shifters.

But she was curious. She wasn't sure why it mattered, but she hoped he not only believed in shifters, but also liked them, at least a little. Might even be interested in them as more than strange aberrations in the world of human beings. Maybe one of them in particular.

Not that she would encourage anything between them but a good professional working relationship. He might be attractive and hunky, and her human hormones might be tweaked just by looking at Owen Dewirter, but she knew far better than to get involved with a nonshifter. She had learned her lesson, and learned it well.

Besides, this nonshifter seemed to have an opinion, one she couldn't interpret.

But with him, or despite him, she intended to do all she could to make sure that the Alpha Force mission here was a complete success for both the US military and the Canadian Mounties.

Of course, she'd have help when the rest of the Alpha Force contingent arrived.

When Owen didn't follow up his acknowledgment with anything else, Selena decided to push him for more. "Most people don't believe in shapeshifters. Why do you? Have you met any? Seen any shifts?"

"Some members of my family knew a shapeshifter."

He didn't look at her, but his icy expression as he regarded the road suggested he didn't want to say anything more about it.

Not that that would deter her.

"Knew? They don't now?"

"No," he said shortly.

"I gather that the experience wasn't a good one. But even if they told you about it, if you didn't see it yourself, why did you believe?"

"Let's just say I saw and heard enough to convince me. So how about you? What made you join Alpha Force?"

She must have hit a nerve. But surely the man must have realized that if he was about to work with a bunch of shapeshifters, they'd want to know his experiences with others of their kind.

For now, though, she'd go along with him.

"I grew up in Wisconsin, in the same area as the commanding officer who first developed the elixir. He helped to form Alpha Force, and his cousin's a member, too." That was Major Drew Connell and recently promoted Lieutenant Jason Connell. "I heard they were looking for new recruits, so of course I had to jump in."

Not to mention how the timing had worked. She'd needed something then to help her get over a bad romantic relationship.

The divorced guy she'd been dating then, and cared for a lot, hadn't known she was a shifter. His cute but sneaky young son had unfortunately seen her ending a shift once before her aide moved her away. The kid gleefully told his father that Selena was a werewolf. Her boyfriend had responded to his son that shapeshifters existed only in stupid stories and he wanted his kid to be realistic and smart. He had told Selena about it. Laughed about it.

So she'd left him and her teaching job and hurried home—only to find this position where shapeshifters were revered and treated well.

But she didn't want to talk about it. Not now and not ever. Like she'd done with her questions to Owen, he'd pushed buttons with his that really bothered her. It was time for a change in subject.

"I've always heard such wonderful things about the RCMP," she said. "How long have you been a member? And do you like it?"

He glanced over at her. Now those gorgeous blue eyes of his actually had an expression in them—pride, if she read it right. "Ten years, and I love it."

She asked more questions, and Rainey leaned forward to join in the conversation. For the rest of the ride they were regaled with tales of undercover adventure in trapping bad guys, enjoyable training sessions with those horses that the Mounties rode and antics of the K-9s Owen had worked with. He apparently liked canines, even if his feelings about people who shifted into wolves weren't quite so warm.

Selena realized that, if she wasn't careful, she might actually come to like sexy Owen Dewirter. And that could really be bad news.

By the time they reached West Columbia, Owen could almost believe this was a pleasure ride instead of an official diplomatic mission of sorts: the Canadians requesting US assistance for a particularly touchy situation.

One he hadn't yet discussed with his new best friends. Friends? Heck. Under other circumstances, he'd have seduced Selena, or at least attempted to, with more than an irreverent yet necessary offer to take his clothes off. She definitely attracted him that way…at least as she was right now, all sexy human female.

The glances they sometimes shared, brief as they were, suggested she might be attracted to him, too. That was fine here, in the car, when neither could act on any inappropriate appeal.

Later, he'd pretend those glances had never happened.

He drove through the residential area and onto a driveway that rose a short distance through a forest and into the hills.

Up that driveway was the small enclave of two homes that had been acquired to become the CAs' hidden head-quarters—assuming everything worked out.

Owen parked on the paved area between the homes and was met by the four new recruits for the CAs who had rushed out of the smaller of the two houses. The one-story white wood-frame building would be used as the meeting place for the US and Canadian teams as the CAs learned how to use their shifting skills for the good of their country.

The group had clearly been watching for their arrival.

"Hi, Owen." That was Constable Sal Emarra, the youngest of the new recruits, only nineteen years old. Like the others, he didn't wear an RCMP uniform; instead he was dressed in casual civilian clothes of a tourist. He held out his hand for a shake, even as he peered past Owen into the vehicle.

It was too late for him to see the passengers since they had exited at the other side. In fact, they were already being greeted by the other recruits even as Owen hurried to open the hatch and extract the luggage.

"Where should we put our things?" Selena asked, joining him.

"I can handle them all."

"But—"

Before she could grab any, Owen hefted the backpacks over his shoulders, then took hold of the suitcase handles.

Selena shrugged and said, "Just be careful with the backpacks."

"Of course."

He put the luggage in the larger of the two homes, a two-story that would be used as the Alpha Force barracks. Then he joined the group for pizza in the other house.

Before eating, though, he stood and looked at each and every member of the group. "Let's go around the room and introduce ourselves."

"Better yet," said Selena, also standing now, "don't just give your names but tell us whether you're a shifter and if so, what you shift to."

She gave him a small, smug smile, as if she'd somehow shown him who was boss.

He didn't contradict her, though. That information did need to be shared.

Selena went first and then Rainey introduced herself as another lieutenant and Selena's nonshifting aide.

The others went next: Constables Sal Emarra, Tim Franzer, Craig Neverts and Andrea Willburn. The men informed everyone that they all shifted into wolves, too.

However, Andrea, a pert young woman with short black hair and a long nose, said, "I shift into a falcon— and that's really fun. But tell us, Selena. How do aides work—and what's a cover dog?"

"Oh, you're all going to have fun learning what Alpha Force is going to teach you," she said, grinning.

Owen didn't miss the way her smile lit up her face or the way her amber eyes sparkled like twin topaz gemstones.

Oh, yeah, this was going to be fun, indeed.

Chapter 3

Selena couldn't start teaching anything until her fellow Alpha Force members arrived. She might have the teaching credentials and some experience with the unit, but Captain Patrick Worley was the commanding officer on the American side of this operation.

That was why she decided to excuse herself, leaving Rainey with the others who were peppering her with questions about how someone who wasn't a shifter worked with Alpha Force. There were things, of course, that Rainey could not reveal about their covert military unit, but Selena trusted her not to mention them. Right now, she needed a little time to herself.

"Where are you going?" Owen called to her from the porch as she walked across the lawn with Lupe beside her.

From there, Owen appeared even taller. Even sexier. She caught her errant thoughts. "Nowhere in particular."

"Well, then, why don't I show you where your sleeping quarters will be?" He pointed toward the other house as he walked down the steps. "You can choose which room you want."

Selena liked that idea. In fact, as much as she loved being part of a large, close-knit outfit like Alpha Force, she hoped to find a room that would give her some privacy.

In fact, maybe she could just pick out a room and chill out there for a little while.

Although it would be hard to chill at all with a hot guy like Owen around. And if she didn't stop thinking about him that way, she was going to have one really tough time working with him on their training assignment.

She started toward the larger house and Owen walked beside her. "Ever been to Canada before?" he asked.

"No, this is my first time. Have you ever been to the States?"

"A few times." His tone suggested he might not have been impressed with her country, but when she glanced at him his face had gone to that neutral, unreadable expression she couldn't interpret.

She had to keep a lot of secrets as a shifter and member of Alpha Force, but she had a sense that Owen Dewirter might have an even greater number of his own.

The front of the other house was similar to the one they'd just left. They climbed stairs onto the broad wooden porch, Lupe following. It was empty, but Selena imagined sitting out there with the entire group one of these days, holding one of the lessons she intended to provide.

After he unlocked the door, she walked through the five upstairs bedrooms, but it was the one downstairs that called to her. It was an understated room with a narrow white dresser with a mirror on top, a small chair and a single bed that was not much larger than a cot. The bare essentials. There was even a private bathroom—small but convenient.

Feeling a presence behind her, she turned and realized Owen was in the room with her. She was in a bedroom, all alone with Owen. Why had she noticed that? And why did it make her feel so warm inside? In fact, the lower part of her body seemed to ignite.

She chilled it immediately. "I'll take this one."

"Somehow I thought you would." He looked at her with an expression that seemed heated—as if he also recognized they were alone in this house in a bedroom.

Then, clearing his throat, he said abruptly, "I'll leave you to unpack. See you back at the other house." And with that, he left.

That was a good thing, Selena told herself, though she felt suddenly bereft.

Instead of unpacking, though, Selena called Captain Worley. When she got his voice mail, she left a message, asking him to call with his expected arrival time.

Then she quickly opened her suitcase and pulled out a few items that she hung in her closet. Almost everything was civilian casual, to maintain their cover.

She next went to the entry and got both of the backpacks. She unpacked the remaining bottle of elixir stored in an insulated container and secured it at the back of the refrigerator.

Then she said to Lupe, "Ready for a walk, girl? When you're done we'll go back to the others."

But as eager as Selena was to get started, she had a feeling it would be a long afternoon.

Owen had returned to where the constables who now reported to him still surrounded Rainey in the small and crowded living room. They were asking her questions about Alpha Force.

Too bad he hadn't stayed around to listen to her answers. The more he knew about the group that would be helping to train these raw new candidates, the better.

Instead, he had gone off to spend time with Selena. Not that he regretted it.

He felt more than saw her enter the room a short while later. His nerve endings tingling, he looked up as she and her dog joined the group. But then he noticed that Tim Franzer seemed to sit up straighter. He even moved over on the sofa and waved at the empty spot for Selena to sit down.

The guy wasn't especially tall or muscular, and he didn't appear particularly good-looking to Owen, not with his round face and prominent nose.

Even so, Selena gave him a big smile as she joined him.

Which irritated Owen.

If she ever smiled at him that way… She wouldn't. But it was definitely hot. *She* was definitely hot—no matter what else she was.

"So, Selena," said Craig Neverts, getting her attention. He was a nicer-looking guy than Tim, with dark hair, a wide mouth and prominent chin. "I'm finding all the stuff that Rainey's told us to be amazing. She said you guys shift when the moon isn't full and you're going to teach us how."

"Soon," Selena said. "When our other Alpha Force members arrive. But maybe tomorrow we can give a brief demonstration of what I'm like while shifted even if they're not here yet."

She glanced toward Owen, her expression challenging as if she expected him to say something about how she had done the same for him and his commanding officer—shifting remotely. Not demonstrating the actual shift.

He remembered the demonstration and his lame offer of getting naked with her. Feeling those stirrings again, he banished the images that the mere thought brought to mind.

"Well, I, for one, don't appreciate just hanging around here like this," said Andrea Willburn. But she must have sensed that Owen, her new commanding officer, was glaring at her. "Sorry." She appeared somewhat chastised. "But if it's okay, can we maybe…well, go into town now rather than waiting till later? Party a little, as part of our cover? I mean if we're not accomplishing anything useful today?"

To Owen, she somewhat resembled a falcon, the kind of animal she apparently shifted into, with her cap of dark hair and large, beak-like nose.

He thought about her suggestion. It might be the best thing to give everyone the afternoon in town. He'd stay behind, alone, and get some much-needed distance from the woman who was getting under his skin. He looked at Selena as he said, "Why not? Go ahead."

That was fine with Selena.

As everyone left the room, she sat there. She had no particular interest in shopping or partying. Besides, she needed time away from Owen. Time to get her mind away from X-rated fantasies and back on the assignment. She took Lupe out on the porch, where she planned to sit and rest.

"You're still here."

At the sound of his voice, she turned to see Owen. Why was *he* still here? "Why didn't you go with your troops?" Selena challenged him.

"Why didn't you?" he countered.

"I—I need to take Lupe for a walk." Not that she hadn't, just a little while ago.

"I'll go with you."

He wasn't her commanding officer, and she could have responded in the negative. But what the heck? Nothing would happen on a little walk in the woods.

There were worse things than hanging out a little more with Owen, her inner voice said.

Yeah, like not getting to be with him at all...

Now, where did that come from? She liked the guy, sure. But only as a temporary colleague. And if he truly didn't like shifters despite believing in them, as he'd hinted before, that was even more reason not to spend much time with him.

So was the fact that she was sexually attracted to him.

Without looking at Owen, she grabbed Lupe's leash and started out. The woods behind the houses smelled rather like citrus from the fir trees that formed a tight canopy, which nearly blocked out the sun. A carpet of downed needles crackled beneath their feet.

"Good area for shifters," Selena told Owen, wanting to hear his reaction to her touch of goading.

"Glad to hear it." She looked up to find him grinning down at her. Grinning? He now accepted the idea of her being a shifter?

Heck, that was what she was and why she was here.

Lupe didn't have much to do except explore, sniffing the ground and air. They nevertheless stayed in the woods for twenty minutes or so.

"Ready to go to town, too?" Owen asked as they headed back.

"Sure," Selena said, glad she'd survived the walk unscathed. Then she tripped over a branch and Owen grabbed her arm to steady her.

She found herself smiling in thanks up into his handsome, rugged face and saw that there was more than concern in his eyes. Not just casual heat, either.

More like lust.

She opened her mouth just a little as she attempted to thank him…and Owen's lips came down on hers.

The kiss seemed to ignite the cool forest, especially when his arms went around her and pulled her close. She held him tightly, too, tasting him with her tongue as his teased hers.

Her eyes closed, and for a moment she was aware only of Owen. And herself. Here. Together, in the wilds, where anything could happen.

Before she could conjure any steamy scenarios, he pulled away. His breathing was hard and irregular, as was hers, and his expression was still full of heat, but his words were just normal and friendly, as if nothing had happened.

"Let's drive into town, shall we?"

"Right. Sure. That sounds fine."

Selena put Lupe in the kitchen of the house where they'd be staying, then joined Owen at his car.

Neither of them mentioned that kiss or where it had come from—let alone how inappropriate, yet suggestive, it had been.

Maybe it was just an act of closure after their initial

discussions of nudity. Something they just had to get out of their systems. Now it was over. At least she hoped so.

Why, then, did it leave her aching for more?

Owen drove them carefully down the hill, then parked along the main commercial street and led her into the Yukon Bar. It was crowded, but even so, there were a couple of available tables. At his urging, Selena chose one—the one closest to the door and therefore the farthest from the noisy bar.

"Is this all right?" she asked.

"Definitely."

She ordered a glass of red wine; he ordered a beer. When their server left, he asked, "Is it okay— I mean, you're all right drinking alcohol?"

She laughed. "You mean…people like me? Yes, when we're like this, all usual activity is fine."

He smiled at her. She liked his smile and the way it raised his hint of dark beard ever so slightly. "I think I have a lot to learn about people like you."

"And I have a lot to learn about the Mounties. You've told me a bit about your background, but how did you wind up here, in this kind of assignment?" One he didn't seem to relish. "And when are you going to tell me the main reason for the formation of the CAs unit? I gather it's something important."

"It is." He moved a little closer and spoke softly. "It's actually a bunch of serial kidnappings that have justifiably gotten our senior officers' attention, but it would be easier to explain more about it when your folks get here and I can do it all at once."

The server brought their drinks, and since neither was especially hungry after that pizza, they ordered only a small appetizer to share.

When the server left, Owen looked at Selena with his gorgeous blue eyes and said nothing for a long moment. She felt her insides heat as if those eyes were igniting her nearly as much as his lips had. Before she lost herself in their depths she said, "Okay, tell me why you're here."

Shrugging, he took a drink of his beer. He still kept his voice low as he responded. "Not much to say that you don't already know. As a kid, I always loved to see Mounties in their formal red uniforms riding horses and all. I told you about some of my assignments, but most recently I was assigned to the task force investigating those kidnappings I mentioned. That's partly why I was chosen to help form the Canada Alphas—so I could use a different direction to catch the kidnappers."

"Your career sounds amazing," Selena said.

They started speaking again of Canada and what Selena might see here. The rest of their outing was pleasant. More than pleasant. Selena found herself looking into Owen's face constantly, sharing smiles and laughs and banter, almost as if they were flirting.

Which, of course, they couldn't be. Despite that one-time, unforgettable kiss. They were professional colleagues—that was all. Her role was to teach him and his fellow RCMP members what they needed to know and then leave.

Developing any other kind of relationship just couldn't happen.

Sitting across the table from the lovely Selena, Owen now wished they'd found the rest of their crowd and hung out with them.

As much as he was enjoying Selena's company,

he was…well, he was liking it too much. Liking her too much.

Trying too much to remind himself what she was. Why she was here.

How touching her, kissing her, had been way out of line.

But he'd absolutely enjoyed their kiss. He also enjoyed the memory of it now, as he watched those full, sexy lips of hers while she talked and smiled and drank her wine and nibbled their appetizer.

This was unlike him. In all his assignments, he was totally professional. He got along fine with colleagues, sure. Even attractive female ones. But he had always behaved with absolute professionalism.

He had already blown that once with Selena. It couldn't happen again.

She was talking softly now, about her recent assignment, although just loudly enough that he could hear her over the roar of the crowd around them. "Rainey, Lupe and I were in the Seattle area on more of a recon kind of thing. There were some reputed AWOL soldiers hanging out there, around a secluded campground, and the regular army hadn't been able to confirm it. The idea was that the soldiers might be acting the roles of hunters or naturalists or whatever. They might be easier for a wolf to spot." She paused and smiled, raising the ends of those sexy lips slowly. "They were. The assignment was pretty well over when I got a call from my superior officer. So here we are."

"Yes, and I think your presence here will be a particularly good thing. We'd already been planning to form the CAs, but it had to come together even faster than originally thought because of those kidnappings. We—"

He heard a cell phone chime. "Mine," Selena said. She pulled it from her pocketbook and looked at it. "It's my captain. Excuse me." She rose and walked away.

At the same time, Owen's phone rang. He pulled it from his pocket and looked at it. Anthony Creay, his boss.

"Yes, sir?" he answered.

"I hope you're getting your CAs trained well and fast, Owen. There's been another kidnapping."

"But the last one was only last week. There's always been a good month or more before the next one." Owen realized his protest was inane. If there'd been another kidnapping, the criminals' prior MO on the four previous cases was no longer relevant.

"True. They've been so successful that they must be ramping it up. Which is all the more reason that your group is so critical."

Selena returned and sat across from him again, no longer holding her phone. He mouthed *Creay* when she raised her eyebrows in question.

"We're still waiting for some of the Alpha Force members," he said, this time keeping his voice low in case anyone was eavesdropping.

"I heard what you said," she told him in a soft voice. "Tell your boss they'll be here tomorrow."

Across the table his eyes met hers. The mission was about to get under way. And things were about to get interesting.

Chapter 4

They left immediately, at Owen's suggestion, which was fine with Selena. She didn't telephone Rainey, nor did Owen call his CAs. "I'd rather tell them in person to get their tails back to the hotel where they're staying for now so they'll get up early for a briefing, even if your Alpha Force guys haven't arrived yet," he told Selena, and she agreed.

Owen led Selena out the door, but instead of going to the parking lot, they turned left outside and began hurrying down the sidewalk.

"I'd thought the gang would end up at the Yukon, too," he said, "and we could have just talked to them here. But I'm aware of the other bars in town that my group also seems to like. I haven't been downtown much with them, but they took care to introduce me to their favorites."

Several cars drove by under the streetlights, but Selena and Owen were the only ones on the sidewalk outside the bar. The air was cool. Selena was glad she had grabbed a sweater to bring along after partially unpacking her suitcase earlier. She had removed the black wrap when they'd sat down, but now she pulled it on again over her T-shirt.

She was surprised, after sticking an arm through one sleeve, that the other sleeve was lined up so she could easily finish shrugging it on. Owen had grabbed it and held it up for her. Apparently, on top of being a member of the RCMP, he was a gentleman.

"Thanks," she told him, turning enough to glance at him. He nodded in acknowledgment and kept walking.

Evidently more used to the crisp air than she was, he didn't don a sweater or jacket over his gray plaid shirt. It fit well over his black jeans, hugging his chest in a way that suggested his training as a Mountie kept his physique in perfect shape.

West Columbia reminded Selena of countless small towns she'd visited back in the States. The street they traversed, Columbia Avenue, was lined with shops of various types.

There were also a number of restaurants, all with lights on and apparently still open. Selena didn't recognize their names, but they seemed to be an assortment of family-style and gourmet eateries. Some of the aromas wafting out of them, especially the gourmet establishments, filled Selena's senses and made her smile, even though she was far from hungry. Maybe she'd have an opportunity to sample some of the food here before her assignment was complete.

"This seems like a very pleasant town," Selena said to make conversation. She was very aware of Owen at her side. She had the sense he wanted to pick up the pace but had reined himself in somewhat to accommodate her.

He didn't need to. She was quite comfortable walking fast and did so often at home as part of a daily fitness regimen. She ran, too, when she felt like it—in both her forms.

Partly to accommodate him instead, and partly to challenge him, she began walking faster.

He kept up with her with apparently no effort. "I like your speed," he said, sounding not at all out of breath, which didn't surprise her.

"I thought you might." She glanced up at him at her side and caught a glance that appeared somewhat amused—and a whole lot sexy.

She looked away quickly and stepped it up a notch or two more.

The first bar they came to, in the middle of a retail block, was Myrtell's. Selena heard the loud hum of conversation even before Owen opened the glass door, and as they stepped inside, the sound level rose to near deafening, despite her being in human form.

Myrtell's was crowded and smelled of liquor and popcorn and people scents that probably were only somewhat discernible to the patrons here, but were strong and not all pleasant to Selena.

She wasn't about to mention that to Owen, let alone complain. But after they'd both looked around for several minutes and failed to see either Rainey or any of the CAs, Selena was glad when they left.

Once again, Owen allowed her to choose their speed. And once again, she walked fast, though she didn't settle into a run.

The next place—the Wonderbar—was on a side street about three blocks farther than Myrtell's. Its entry was covered by a sign that resembled a theater marquee, and Selena heard the crowd noises emanating from the place nearly as soon as they turned the corner from Columbia Avenue.

As they reached the door, Selena inhaled the aromas

emanating from the Wonderbar. If she had to guess, the patrons here preferred beer over the other kinds of alcohol she had smelled at both of the other bars.

She first heard, then saw, Rainey when she looked inside the door. Her aide was sitting with the four recruits around a moderate-sized round table that held glasses of many sizes, indicating their differences in drinks. Wineglasses sat before Andrea and Tim. Sal had a tall glass in front of him with an amber liquid and ice inside, suggesting a drink with hard liquor—or perhaps it was just a soft drink. Craig and Rainey seemed to fit in better with more of the crowd here since beer steins were on the table in front of them.

Interesting choices, but Selena had no time to do more than give that a passing thought. Owen and she hurried through the door and up to that table.

"Hey, welcome." Sal stood to pull his chair aside to make room for the newcomers. Knowing the young, skinny guy was only nineteen years old, Selena glanced at his amber drink, but she knew that was the legal drinking age in British Columbia. If he had hard liquor in front of him it would be acceptable here, and the scent Selena detected told her it was alcohol.

"Yeah. Where've you been?" Andrea asked. Across the table from Sal, she, too, stood and looked around as if seeking another seat for them, her wide but smallish eyes peering over her prominent nose as she checked out the place.

"Looking for you," Owen said, not entirely truthfully, Selena thought, since they hadn't sought out the rest of the crowd when they first got to the Yukon Bar. "We needed to let you know we're going to hold an update session very early tomorrow morning."

"Then there's been some news?" Rainey was on her feet, too. Selena couldn't help grinning at her aide. Rainey was always eager to jump into whatever assignment they had, and being here with these other shifters seemed to only increase her enthusiasm. She'd pulled a Minnesota Timberwolves sweatshirt on, probably her attempt at a silent joke with regard to the wolf shifters here, including her commanding officer—Selena.

"Yes," Owen said. "We'll tell you about it first thing tomorrow."

"And discuss how we're going to handle things a little later," Selena added, "when the rest of our Alpha Force team arrives."

"Right," Owen agreed. "But right now I'd suggest you head back to your hotel rooms so you can get a reasonably good night's sleep. You have fixings for breakfast at our…site?"

Selena figured he'd avoided saying "headquarters" in case anyone around was eavesdropping. All the crowd she saw seemed caught up in their own conversations— and imbibing. But she appreciated his discretion.

"Yes, we do," Craig said.

"Great. Then get on back to where you're staying now."

"Soon as we finish our drinks," Craig agreed, and the others nodded. Selena suspected they had only recently ordered refills since none of their glasses appeared especially empty. But that was okay. The alcohol might help them sleep better.

"We'll see you in the kitchen of the main house, then, at o-seven…er, seven a.m.," Selena said, quickly getting herself out of military speak.

"Yes, ma'am," Rainey whispered with a sly grin.

Selena wasn't sure whether the RCMP knew US military protocol, speaking or otherwise, let alone followed it. But when she glanced around the table, all the CAs were grinning.

Especially Sergeant Major Owen Dewirter.

"You're staying downtown somewhere, aren't you?" Selena asked as Owen pulled her chair out so she could stand.

Despite being an officer of the law, he didn't always follow traditional etiquette with women. Even so, something about Selena made him want to revert to the old ways he'd learned as a child here in Canada—actions that had supposedly been imported from the mother country of the UK years, even centuries, ago. Odd, he knew. And he didn't want to overthink it now.

But on some level he realized he was hoping to make himself think of his obligatory partner in this program as a lady, not an officer in the United States Army whose rank might be in some ways equivalent to his own in the nonmilitary RCMP, or perhaps even higher. And certainly not as a shapeshifter from whom he had a lot to learn to fulfill his current assignment.

Plus, he got closer to her this way than he otherwise might. Could smell her fresh, almost floral scent—nothing like the scent of dogs or wolves that he might otherwise have anticipated.

In addition, while being polite, he could imagine touching her for other reasons than assisting her in and out of cars or pulling her chair out for her.

Which most likely meant he should start being rude from this moment on.

"That's right," he responded. They left the others behind at the table and wended their way through the bar crowd to the exit door. Once they were out on the sidewalk he continued, "My team and I will move into the house you and your other Alpha Force members will be occupying now once you've trained us and moved on."

"So where are you all living now?"

"Hotels. I'm in one, and the rest of the CAs are in a different one." He'd thought that would help his subordinates bond without worrying too much about being part of a regimented system. That would come in time. And he didn't worry about his command. As soon as the training and the mission started, they'd know who was in charge.

She turned sideways to look up at him. "It would be more convenient for you to stay downtown right now rather than driving me back to the house. I could wait until Rainey is ready to go, then ride with whoever drove her here, or she and I could even walk back to the HQ if she doesn't have a ride. It's not that far."

"In the dark and in tonight's chilly air? No way."

He couldn't help but appreciate her offer, though. She didn't automatically consider him and the CAs her inferiors, who were required to take good care of her in exchange for teaching them.

"All right." She sounded relieved. He liked that, too. He figured she had made the offer because she believed it to be convenient for him, even though she'd hoped he'd refuse it.

They walked back to his SUV in the Yukon Bar's gravel parking lot, and without thinking, he took Selena's arm and helped her into the passenger seat.

Despite the sweater she wore that kept him from touching her skin, he was highly conscious of her warmth. She, too, appeared to notice the contact, since her head turned quickly and her amber eyes captured his for just an instant. "Thank you," she said. He shut the door, then went around to the driver's seat and started off.

He had anticipated struggling to find a neutral topic of conversation on the short drive back to the enclave when he realized he wanted to know everything about this woman—including more of what she really thought about being a shapeshifter. But he didn't really want to bring that up. Not now.

He was relieved when she started the conversation. She sat in shadows in the seat beside him, but the lights outside the vehicle illuminated her enough that he could see her lovely face—and the fact that she was smiling as she watched the scenery while he drove.

First, she commented on the bars they'd visited. "I liked the Yukon best, but I can see why our gang likes the Wonderbar. There's more action there, for one thing."

"True. But I was with them once at the Yukon and they really got into talking about…what they were. Quietly, and using euphemisms, in case anyone was listening."

"Euphemisms like what? Although I might have heard them all. Used them all at different times."

He told her Andrea's description of what they all had in common as being windows through which illumination fell—like the full moon that changed them, he assumed. Did Selena still identify with that? He knew that shifters in her Alpha Force didn't need to wait for the right phase of the moon. He had even seen it, sort of.

His new unit members were also students, ready to learn all they could about the universe. They were animal lovers. And more. And with each description, Owen heard Selena draw in her breath and giggle.

He liked that he could please her like that.

"You enjoyed that conversation, too, didn't you?" she asked, facing him as he waited at a traffic light.

"I liked her ingenuity," he admitted.

"Did you ever think, when you decided to join the RCMP, that you'd find yourself in such an unusual situation?"

He hadn't. Not really. But he had previously become aware that shapeshifters existed, and the experience he'd had suggested that illegal, even violent, situations could result from contact with them.

"No," he said curtly as the light changed and he stepped too quickly on the gas.

He glimpsed Selena's movement beside him, as she was jolted back into her seat.

"Sorry," he added, but didn't explain his discomfort.

"You had a bad experience with shapeshifters, didn't you?" she asked quietly.

Damn, but the woman was perceptive. He would have to watch himself around her.

"No," he said only somewhat truthfully. He realized then that this might be a good time to tell her—and vent a little. "Not me personally. But a short while after I joined the RCMP I had a couple of family members killed in the States—in Minnesota—and others there asked me to come and talk to the local authorities and try to make sense of what had happened. I traveled there, and that's when I learned that one of those killed had been a distant family member by marriage who'd been a wolf shifter. He was shot with a silver bullet while shifted, after he'd killed my blood relative, a third cousin. Despite attempting to dredge out the details and help, I didn't get a lot of information on motive or anything else, other than that it was a family tragedy, and I never did make any sense of it. The cousin who was killed was apparently a prominent business owner in the area, and the details were hushed up so the shop he owned would survive. His wife and kids still own it and we stay in touch at the holidays."

It was something he almost never talked about, and neither did anyone else in the family, except maybe those in Minnesota. But letting Selena know that he genuinely believed in shapeshifters—and why—had seemed appropriate.

"Look, Owen, I understand that it's a difficult topic to discuss, but—"

"Glad you recognize that." He realized he sounded curt, but she apparently got the message and didn't push. In fact, they didn't say much as he continued onward until he reached the houses. She might not be satisfied with his silence, but that was the way he wanted it.

He pulled his car in front of the larger house, where she and Rainey would spend this night and should be joined by the rest of her Alpha Force team tomorrow. They had left the lights on, and the two homes were illuminated.

He saw a half-moon off to the east. Not a full moon. It nevertheless seemed symbolic of what was to occur here.

As he parked, Selena opened her own door. He quickly exited the SUV and hurried around to hold it for her and to reach out for her hand as if to steady her.

"I'm really okay," she said, not touching him and giving him a stubborn look. Her full bottom lip stuck out obstinately. Sexily. "But—"

"You definitely are okay," he said. And then, as if he had planned it—maybe to keep her quiet—he bent down, put his arms around her curvaceous, struggling body and put his lips on hers.

Struggling? No. Maybe for a moment, but then she reacted. Positively. Hotly. She leaned in and placed her hands on his chest, and he relished the feel of her so close, her warmth.

The kiss went on for hours, or was it only seconds?

Didn't matter. Didn't matter that it was inappropriate, or that his body was reacting in a way that made him both uncomfortable and eager all at the same time.

She wasn't the one to pull away. He was, and he regretted it.

"Rainey could get back here anytime," he said breathlessly, looking down into Selena's face.

She looked bemused. And hot. And even inviting.

He declined the invitation. "Let me walk you up to the door," he said, taking her arm once more.

She seemed to realize who and where she was at that instant. Her expression hardened; her cheeks reddened in the pale light.

"No need," she said, pulling away, and he watched as she ran up the porch steps and used her key to enter the house.

Chapter 5

Lupe greeted her enthusiastically, whining as Selena walked into the house and jumping up and down in the kitchen behind the chair Selena had set up as a gate.

The wolflike dog had been alone for a while and needed to go outside for a walk.

Selena needed to go outside, too, to cool off in the Canadian breeze after that kiss. That hot, suggestive, sexy kiss that made her insides so aware that Owen felt like a lot more than a professional contact.

She also wanted to ponder some more, on her own, Owen's brief tale of how he had learned of shapeshifters—and his reason for not thinking much of them. Could she get him to discuss it further with her? He hadn't seemed inclined to do so. And she certainly couldn't fix the situation.

After Selena released Lupe from the kitchen, she cautiously opened the front door and looked outside to make sure Owen was gone.

But his vehicle was still there, parked on the pavement linking the two houses.

Lupe whined—she didn't want to wait. So Selena figured she had better take her dog outside now.

She fastened the woven yellow nylon leash to Lupe's matching collar and picked up a recyclable bag for anything Lupe might leave. "Let's go," she said, smiling at her eager dog.

On the front porch, Selena looked around before closing the door behind her. No sign of Owen. Good. But she'd have to try to hurry since she'd no idea when he might reappear, most likely from the other house.

Lupe seemed interested in going to the area between the two buildings, which was mostly grass edged in neatly trimmed bushes. Needles from the nearby fir trees decorated the lawn.

Lupe pulled gently, her nose to the ground, and Selena followed. Since it was dark outside and the illumination from the lights around the driveway wasn't very bright, this area remained shrouded in shadows. That was fine. Selena stayed alert, all of her enhanced senses attuned to ensure that nothing perilous was around.

Selena detected the scent of some kind of small feral animal, although it was light enough to suggest that whatever it was had come and gone. But that explained why Lupe seemed extremely interested in smelling the grass and its light needle covering. The dog soon produced what she needed to, and Selena scooped it with the bag she'd brought.

That was when she heard a sound other than the branches of the nearby trees blowing in the light breeze and the very distant sound of an occasional automobile.

No, this was soft footsteps on pavement. Lupe heard them, too, since she raised her head, and her pointed, erect ears moved like antennae toward the direction of the sound.

Had Rainey returned? Selena hadn't heard any car noises.

No, it was probably Owen heading toward his car. Selena remained still, listening. There was no reason to believe that whoever it was constituted a threat to Lupe or her.

Lupe pulled her lead and dashed toward the sound. "Wait!" Selena commanded, keeping her voice low. She didn't want the person to hear her, especially if it was Owen.

But Lupe didn't wait. Her leash taut, she kept pulling Selena in the direction of the driveway. She was usually quite obedient. Not now. Did she sense a danger from which she wanted to protect Selena? Or a friend she wanted to greet?

Selena found out in moments as the back-lit figure of a tall, well-built male appeared in the gap between the buildings. Lupe headed toward him, and Selena released her leash.

It was clearly Owen.

Selena followed her dog, knowing she needed to work to get Lupe even better trained here. Yes, she was mostly obedient, emphasis on *mostly*. Alpha Force cover dogs did get a significant amount of training, but they weren't necessarily expected to act as official K-9s who sniffed out explosives or cadavers or anything like that. Their function was to be there for their shapeshifter counterparts so that if anyone saw an animal in wolfen form, they wouldn't be surprised—even if that particular wolf happened to be a shifted human.

Same went for other types of cover animals, such as those for felines or birds or whatever.

Selena knew that the Canadians would soon need to

find cover animals for all of their CAs, including a falcon counterpart for Andrea. But that was far from being her current concern.

"What are you doing out here?" Owen demanded as she got closer.

"Since Lupe's all over you, I'd imagine that's pretty clear. She needed to go out." Selena purposely made her tone sarcastic. That would certainly reduce any further possibility that he'd want to kiss her again, wouldn't it?

"Sure. But…well, even up here, you need to be careful. One reason we chose this area is that we don't know of any problems, but there are no guarantees."

As she got nearer, he wasn't silhouetted now and Selena could make out his features. Handsome features—with his brow knitted in apparent concern.

And that made him look all the more appealing.

She suddenly had an urge to rush toward him and be the one to instigate the next kiss.

Fortunately a noise sounded behind him. An automobile was heading up the driveway. Rainey was probably returning.

That sound also gave Selena an instant to calm herself—and her very human hormones. "I appreciate that," she said. Then, to remind him—and herself—of who and what she was, she added, "You may not be aware of it, or even if you are you might not be thinking about it. But shifters' senses are very much like the animals' they shift into. I heard you come outside the other house probably a lot sooner than another person would, for example. I'll stay wary, but you don't need to worry about me."

"Right." He didn't sound entirely convinced.

Rainey parked the car she had driven—a rental, Selena figured, although she wasn't sure whose—and came running up. "Hey, you two. Three, I mean." She bent to pat Lupe. "I'm ready to go off to bed so I can get up early tomorrow. How about you?"

Selena glanced toward Owen before answering. His gaze was on her, and it was probably a good thing that Rainey remained somewhat in the shadows behind him.

She hopefully couldn't see the very hot, very suggestive gaze that Owen leveled on Selena. But she caught it. And quite possibly she thought the same thing he did.

Yes, she was ready to go off to bed. Alone.

But the idea of sharing it with Owen?

After their earlier kiss, it definitely crossed her mind.

Off to bed. Oh, yeah, Owen had heard that. Thought about it as he regarded Selena. Sexy Selena. Hot Selena, whom he'd definitely enjoyed kissing.

Werewolf Selena.

She and her dog walked with him to his SUV as if she hadn't sensed the gist of his thoughts about bed when Rainey had mentioned it. Maybe she hadn't—although her expression seemed to say otherwise.

No matter. He could always act now as if Rainey's words hadn't triggered his imagination—not to mention a reaction from his most private body parts. Selena had, after all, reminded him earlier of why he wasn't fond of shapeshifters.

"I'll be back here first thing with the rest of the group," he said, slipping into the driver's seat of his SUV. He'd decided to stop in at their hotel to speak with them briefly before heading to his own room that night. "I'll make sure we get here early for them to get breakfast ready for all of us. As Canada Alphas, they've already begun to learn that their duties are diverse, and preparing meals can be among them."

He liked how Selena smiled under the faint lights. He was also amused when she shifted her dog's leash to free up one hand so she could grab hold of the car door.

"My turn," she said, starting to close it.

"Hey, you're a gentleman, too," he teased as he settled into the seat.

"You got it." She slammed the door shut.

But as he turned the key in the ignition, his mind rebelled against what he had said.

Selena was anything but a man, gentle or not.

And her very womanly characteristics just might drive him nuts as he continued to work with her on this assignment.

Once they were all inside the house, Selena went upstairs with Rainey and helped her choose the room she would stay in while they were here. Rainey opted for the one overlooking the front of the house. Selena then left Rainey upstairs and returned to the room that was now hers.

She had already changed into her long-sleeved navy pajamas, washed her face and settled herself beneath her bedcovers when Rainey knocked on her door. "Come in," she called.

Rainey, too, had put her on pj's, a frilly pink outfit that contrasted pleasantly with her dark, curly hair. She grinned as she sat at the foot of Selena's bed.

Selena leaned back on both pillows that were resting against the plain black headboard. "Well, we're here," she said.

"Yep, and I gather that we're really supposed to start

our assignment tomorrow." Rainey paused. "Are you ready to show these Canadian folks what real Alpha Force shapeshifters are all about?"

"That's what we're here for." Now it was Selena's turn to smile. "We'll teach them what being a US shifter— and an aide—is all about."

"And a cover dog, too." Rainey slipped her backside from the bed so she could kneel to pat Lupe, who lay on the floor nearby.

"Exactly." Selena didn't want to kick out her aide, but she did want to try to get some sleep. "So…" she began.

At the same time, Rainey asked, "So did you have fun tonight?"

It was all Selena could do to hide her startled reaction. Surely nothing on her face, in her demeanor, revealed that she'd shared a kiss with the man who was in charge of the Canadian group that Alpha Force was here to help.

No. Rainey must just be making conversation. Wasn't she?

Nevertheless, Selena made herself respond as if Owen was just some ordinary guy whom she didn't find attractive at all—maybe married and twice her age. Or at least that was what she attempted.

"Sure," she said nonchalantly. "I had a drink with Owen at one of the other bars in town before we found you guys. He wanted to know more about what Alpha Force was about, but I doubt he got it from our limited conversation there in public. He, of course, knows that shapeshifters exist and that I'm one of them, but I still have the impression he finds them—us—weird." She wasn't about to reveal to Rainey how Owen had formed his opinion of shapeshifters. "I hope he gets over that enough to work well with his own CAs." That was the truth, at least. "He got a phone call that apparently suggested they'll be needed sooner than anticipated, and he'd better be ready for it."

"Well," Rainey said, "we'll see how he is at breakfast tomorrow. The rest of them, too. I had the impression that they're way different from our Alpha Force members, even though they're shifters. They were fun to be with, sure, but they struck me as being kind of wild kids. Good kids, though. Tim even let me use his rental car overnight. I just hope that giving them more control of their ability to shift will help tame them down."

"Guess we'll have to make sure of it," Selena said. But she was glad she wouldn't be the only shifter there as things progressed. She wouldn't be the most senior, either.

And surely having other Alpha Force members here, like Captain Patrick Worley and Lieutenant Marshall Vincenzo, as well as their aide, Captain Jonas Truro, would also make it easier for her to remember who she was and why she really was here.

And to remember to stay far away from Owen Dewirter except to teach him what she could as an Alpha Force member.

To ignore any attraction she felt for him and, definitely, to make sure she never touched him again, let alone kissed him.

When Rainey left a short while later, and after Selena gave Lupe a good-night hug and settled herself back into bed, she couldn't help rehashing those intentions and told herself she needed to focus on her assignment.

She just hoped she could.

In the meantime, she lay in bed conscious of the quiet

here in the Canadian countryside, except for occasional hoots from local owls.

She mulled over all that had happened over the past couple of days, including Owen's tale of his family and shapeshifters.

She was concerned about what would happen tomorrow, and if Alpha Force—no, if *she*—would be able to do all that was expected to help the CAs start their team and deal with the kidnappings that Owen had mentioned.

Not to mention her concern about her absurd attraction to Owen Dewirter that she needed to find a way to turn off. Permanently.

Owen saw Selena almost as soon as he reached the CAs compound early the next morning.

She was outside again, with her dog, in the crisp early air. He knew that had to be a frequent ritual. Dogs had needs that had to be fulfilled often, especially last thing at night and first thing in the morning, no matter what the weather, no matter what the temperature.

No matter what the dog's responsibilities, such as acting as a cover for her owner.

Under the brightening morning sky, it was easier for Owen to remain less concerned about Selena's safety in daylight. Besides, he wasn't alone. All four of the CAs who needed to be trained and sent into the field were exiting the vehicles behind him.

They weren't trained at all, let alone as his special team—yet—but he figured they'd do something if he needed help.

He waved to Selena as he hurried up the front steps of the house. It was dumb, but he felt glad to see her wave back.

"Hey, sir, er, Owen," Andrea called from behind him. "What are we going to do today?" She, like the rest of them, had dressed in casual clothes—jeans and a sweatshirt.

Before coming here, the CAs had been given a brief amount of preliminary training as Canadian police officers and instructed in some of the formalities. Owen had nevertheless told them that, although he was in charge, informality was fine here.

When he had visited them at their hotel last night, he had briefly described to them part of what they'd be up to today, but it wouldn't hurt to repeat it, drum it into their heads, so they would be ready once the rest of the Alpha Force team arrived to teach them their methods of shapeshifting.

"First thing, I'm going to brief you about our assignment and the update I received last night that I didn't mention to you before. Then the rest of the day will depend on when the other Alpha Force members arrive."

"Got it." She was surrounded by the other CAs on the porch, their gazes all trained on him. Each watched him with concentration, a couple of them nodding.

They all looked interested and eager.

But that didn't mean they'd be able to do the job— especially with all the tweaks that needed to be added to normal, rational, predictable RCMP constable duties. Not that they were the usual RCMP constables.

Turning his back on them, he hurried into the house. Maybe he was just being naive, but he believed that Selena would be the ideal trainer—and not just because she was a shapeshifter. They'd studied her background, and since she'd been a teacher before joining Alpha Force, she should be able to take these young shifters and instruct them on exactly what was needed to fulfill the RCMP's needs here.

That was why she was here—not to create impossible sex fantasies in Owen's mind each time he saw her.

And at night when he tried to sleep...like last night.

He shook off the thought. Heading into the kitchen with the gang behind him, Owen began asking questions before giving orders for breakfast preparation. "Who's good about cooking eggs? Sal? Great. There are some in the fridge along with butter, and the frying pan is in the drawer beneath the stove. Who's our go-to toast guy?" Tim Franzer raised his hand, which left Craig Neverts, Andrea and him. Owen decided to brew the coffee, so he told Craig and Andrea where the items were to set the large dining area table.

"Now, let's get to work," Owen said.

"Need any help?" Selena, along with Rainey and Lupe the dog, had just come through the kitchen door.

"I think we're good," Owen said. But he watched as Selena immediately approached Sal and started helping to cook the eggs.

Was there anything that woman couldn't do? She was a US soldier, a teacher, a cook...and a shapeshifter.

And sexier than any other woman Owen had met.

With all that in her favor, he'd no doubt that she'd be one hot partner in the bedroom.

But that was one scenario he'd never see realized.

He walked over to the large coffeemaker, glad he had something entirely neutral to accomplish.

Something that allowed him to keep his back toward the rest of his cohorts—so no one would be able to notice the bulge at the front of his jeans.

Chapter 6

Selena was glad to keep busy, even though it was a challenge for all the CAs and her to stay out of each other's ways while whipping up their breakfast together.

Finally they had the meal prepared, and all of them found seats around the sizable dining table. She didn't plan it, but Selena found herself sitting beside Owen near the doorway to the kitchen. Not a bad place to be. In fact, the two of them were more or less in charge, so why not join forces for what needed to be said here?

Not surprisingly, Owen said he had a lot to tell them, including information he'd just learned yesterday that they needed to know. But he directed them to start eating first.

Selena wanted to hear Owen speak a lot more than she wanted to eat.

Nevertheless, Owen handed her a bowl so she could scoop out her own helping of eggs. "These look great," he said.

"They *are* great," said Craig, who sat across from them. He had already dished himself a substantial helping and had his fork up to his mouth.

Sal and Andrea were on one side of Craig, and Tim

had a seat next to him. Rainey was beside Selena. It was almost as though the two groups were opponents—except that Owen sat close enough to her to appear to be on her side.

That wouldn't be entirely accurate, though. They weren't enemies, of course, but the differences between them seemed as weighty as the matters they needed to work on together.

Then there was the proverbial elephant in the room, at least as far as Selena was concerned: her totally inappropriate sexual attraction to the man.

Selena ate rapidly, watching the others across the table and listening to their friendly hazing of one another. Even Rainey became the subject of their amusing gibes. How could she stand to be in a whole room full of animals? they'd teased her. Even their commanding officer, Owen, was an animal. A human one. Selena knew he didn't need to shift to become a feral creature.

To Owen's credit, he jested along with them, talking about how he would use his own wild nature to mow down any of those here who dared to disobey him.

But after a few minutes of the revelry, Owen fortunately ended it.

"Okay, everyone," Owen called out. "Let me have your attention." He had finished his eggs and toast quickly and now just held a coffee cup in his large right hand. Despite the prior levity, his deep voice now resonated with authority and seriousness, and although it wasn't extremely loud, he did, in fact, appear to capture everyone's attention.

Selena put her fork on her plate though she wasn't through eating. But she wanted to concentrate on what he said.

"I'm going to start at the beginning," Owen said. "I'll give a quick recap of why those of you who are now part of the Canada Alpha team have been recruited, both to refresh your recollections and to make certain our Alpha Force visitors know enough. Then I'll tell you why what you're about to embark on is crucial to our national security. How you can help save lives."

Selena had been informed of the basics before, but hearing them from Owen, with his point of view and earnest tone, drove home the importance that she'd been told surrounded her mission here.

Yes, the recruits were shapeshifters. How they had been found and recruited into the RCMP was only hinted at, but their ultimate objective was a matter of Canadian national security as Selena knew.

"We're all very pleased to have found each of you and look forward to your justifying the trust we've placed in you." Owen's gaze moved slowly from Sal to Andrea to Craig to Tim. In exchange, they each peered solemnly toward him and nodded.

He then looked toward Rainey and, finally, at Selena. Those eyes of his were gleaming and blue and grave. They didn't turn her on at that moment, but they definitely made her take notice. Made her want to fulfill whatever they commanded.

Which, right now, was apparently just to listen.

"I believe you were told what we need to accomplish, how we got the attention of the US military and why we were let in on the highly secret existence of your Alpha Force, but just in case, here's the story."

Owen took a sip of coffee, then reached toward the carafe that sat on the table not far away.

"I've got it." Selena reached for it and then poured

coffee into the nearly empty cup that Owen held out. She warmed her own, and Rainey's, too, before passing the carafe so the CAs could take more as well.

"Thanks," Owen said. Then he finally dived into the crux of what they all needed to hear. He described the horrific serial crimes taking place in Canada. Family members of some of Canada's most successful business magnates, or even the magnates themselves, had been kidnapped to extort tremendous amounts of money. "There were four prior abductions that we're aware of, and you'll recognize the surnames of the victims—or at least those of you who are Canadian will."

Selena hadn't heard of three of them, but the fourth, Marc Wagnere, was well-known in the States as being the originator of an internet search-engine site that competed easily with Google and others. She'd heard something about the senior guy's illness, but as far as she'd known, that was all that had gotten into the news—not anything about an abduction.

"Of course, this is all confidential information," Owen continued, "and you're not to discuss it with anyone except among yourselves. And now there's another victim."

Before he continued, Selena heard a noise outside. Lupe did, too, since the large, furry dog stood up and barked.

Selena couldn't help glancing at the other three wolf shifters in the room. They appeared both alert and confused, looking from one to the other. She suspected they'd heard the outside sounds as well.

Was there some jeopardy here? No, she knew who had just driven up the driveway to the headquarters.

"Let's pause for a moment, okay?" she asked Owen,

whose hearing probably hadn't been tweaked. "And I think you ought to get someone to brew some more coffee."

"Why?" He looked concerned and not exactly happy.

Before Selena could explain her assumption the doorbell rang.

Lupe barked once more even as Selena hurried from the dining room and down the hall to the front door. She had just grasped the knob when she felt a hand on her shoulder and Owen pulled her away.

"What the hell are you doing?" Owen demanded. "We don't know who's out there. It could be dangerous."

Selena hesitated. She could be wrong. She moved away from Owen's grasp and again approached the door. This time she looked through the peephole viewer.

Sure enough, she saw whom she'd expected to see.

Staying out of Owen's reach, she pulled the door open, then grinned at the men who stood there—her fellow Alpha Force members assigned to this mission. No cover dogs, though. Lupe was the only one on this mission.

"About time you gentlemen got here," she told them with a smile, although they had appeared earlier than expected.

"Easy for you to say," retorted Patrick Worley. "Wait until we tell you all we went through to arrive early."

"Hold that thought," Selena said, "and come inside. We're in the middle of a report on why we're here—and something that just occurred." She was a little annoyed that the last time she'd spoken with Patrick, he'd indicated there was no way they could arrive this early.

Was this an attempt to make a good impression on the CAs, by demonstrating that the importance of this mission to Alpha Force made them pull out all the stops to get here fast?

Maybe. But Selena doubted it would have that effect on Owen.

It certainly didn't on her.

Nevertheless, she was glad to see them.

"Sergeant Major Owen Dewirter of the RCMP," Selena said, assuming all the formality expected of a US soldier on duty, "I'd like you to meet Alpha Force members Captain Patrick Worley, Lieutenant Marshall Vincenzo and Captain Jonas Truro."

As the group shook hands, Selena smiled, feeling all kinds of relief circulating inside her.

Formality be damned. These were people with a job to do—herself included.

A job for which they all needed a briefing.

"Hey, everyone," she said. "C'mon back inside so we can talk."

In a few minutes, they were all seated around the dining room table and Owen first introduced the CAs.

"They're our shifters," he told Patrick, "but I'd imagine you know that."

The senior Alpha Force member nodded. Patrick was a tall man, square-shouldered, with light, cropped hair. His face was long, and he had a cleft in his chin. As with the rest of Alpha Force, Selena was used to seeing him in camos, but today he wore a black hoodie. "I assume you can guess that two of the three of us are shifters as well. That's Marshall and me."

Selena saw no expression on Owen's face at that news, but she made a mental note to warn her fellow Alpha Forcers that though he believed in shapeshifters, he didn't appear to like them much.

Despite his reasons, though, he had been behaving utterly professionally—at least if she didn't count his sexiness and those stolen kisses. She certainly wasn't about to mention any of that to her fellow soldiers.

"I'll explain now why we need Alpha Force's help," Owen continued, "both to teach our people how to shift when there's no full moon, and also to stay aware of who and where they are, and why, which I understand our CAs need help with."

"I'll say," Tim asserted, and the other CAs nodded. Selena nearly grinned at the eagerness on his pudgy face, the way he clasped his hands on the table in front of him. "And let me say that I really appreciate this. I want to help my country, and to do it in a way that will help me, too, in ways I never knew were possible before—"

"Hold that thought," Craig interrupted. "Let's let our commanding officer speak."

"In other words," Owen said, his tone slow and droll, "shut up and listen."

Selena smiled and said nothing.

Chapter 7

"First," Owen said, "let me repeat what I started before and give some further explanation."

He was glad that the Alpha Force team was now fully present. That way, he could be certain they knew the appropriate details, and he would not have to repeat anything again.

He mentioned those kidnap victims' names again and then he went into some detail about the abductions that made Selena visibly cringe. Each victim had been treated horribly, denied sleep and food. A couple had been physically abused—beaten and even whipped.

And all were threatened with death should their ransoms not be paid. Their treatment made it clear that this was not an idle threat, but a promise by their abductors.

"They'd been allowed to speak to their wealthy family members now and then, to encourage them to fulfill the ransom demands. And when the money was eventually paid and the victims released, none had enough information as to where they'd been held. But their physical condition—especially that of the elderly Mr. Wagnere—was terrible. And now... Here's what I learned a little while ago." Owen picked up his phone from the table. "I received a call from one of my superior officers in the RCMP who knows about what we're doing—Anthony Creay, deputy commissioner of general policing services. Selena met him when she first arrived in Canada." He glanced toward the woman at his side.

She nodded. "That's right. I had to prove to him, as well as to Owen, that I was a shifter." Her grin was ironic as she leveled it first on him, then looked from one Alpha Force member to the next. They all grinned, too, as if in empathy. Owen wouldn't have been surprised to learn they'd each had situations where they were with nonshifting humans who didn't believe in their...unusual capabilities.

In some ways, he wished he'd had no reason to believe, too.

But he did believe. And at this moment, that was actually a good thing.

"Anyway, there is a new situation. One we need to move on quickly. Someone near the top of our organization—maybe the RCMP's commissioner or an assistant commissioner—somehow became aware of your Alpha Force. How they did doesn't matter. What does matter is that we've had that rash of kidnappings in Canada, where the victims are either the heads of some of our most esteemed and lucrative companies, often in high tech, or a relative of one of those top executives." He had identified them before, but Owen now added details on the victims and their businesses to further explain the urgency.

"I've heard about some of that," Patrick stated, "but not all." His fellow Alpha Force members nodded.

Owen had no doubt that at least some information about the kidnappings would leak and thereby make it into American news reports, as some had in Canada as well. Many crimes that went on here might not have been as interesting to the neighbors to the south. But these, where high-profile companies that also did business in the United States were involved, might get more attention. Particularly if the stories could be considered sensational. Titillating. Scary and exciting.

And unfortunately these could.

He hazarded a glance toward Selena. Was that sympathy he saw in the slight inclination of her head and a touch of sorrow in her lovely amber eyes?

He looked away quickly. He didn't need the distraction. He had a story to relate.

"Each time, because of who the victim was, the companies they headed anted up and paid some pretty colossal amounts of ransom. Meantime, the RCMP and even some government groups attempted to locate the kidnappers to bring them down—with no success so far. Except that…well, we think we might know their location now and where they go with the people they abduct."

"But you haven't stepped in and arrested them?" Selena asked.

"No, because our investigation has been hampered by that believed location. The victims, after being ransomed and released, say they were kept chained to walls and blindfolded, so they haven't been able to say much about their environments."

"But what's your speculation?" That was Patrick, who had leaned forward at the table. Good. The guy in charge of the Alpha Force group now looked intrigued.

So did Selena, although Owen didn't glance sideways at her this time. But she, too, had turned to face him even more. That he could tell.

"Well, there's an area near the border of British Columbia and the Yukon, miles from the nearest village, where satellite sensors have picked up more activity than usual lately, often around the time of a kidnapping. In fact, there used to be almost no activity at all in that very remote location, and what's there now disappears quickly. The place is impossible to reach except by helicopter or plane—and landing anywhere nearby would be difficult, though possible if we know that really is our target. The camera surveillance we've attempted so far was somehow jammed. We believe the victims are taken underground into caverns, but it has been impossible so far to confirm whether this is the actual location."

"How about drones?" asked Tim, leaning forward with a look of fascination on his pudgy face.

"Yes, we've sent drones into the area, but those that haven't disappeared have been retrieved with mechanical difficulties. We're still not sure what caused the problems, though." Owen moved his gaze around the table, trying to gauge the others' reactions.

They all appeared interested—some, like Tim, more than others.

There was something in Selena's look, though, that suggested she knew what he was driving at. The other Alpha Force members, too, seemed to be sitting straighter, anticipating what he would say next.

"Anyway, here is the current situation. There has been another kidnapping—you might have anticipated that from what I said." Nearly everyone in the group nodded.

"Who is it?" asked Andrea Willburn, perhaps the first time she had talked since the meeting started. She might be of particular use to finding a solution, considering she shifted into a falcon and could potentially do a flyover—but Owen hadn't gotten there yet.

"It's the wife of Rene Brodheureux, the founder and chief executive officer of Xanogistics. Her name is Berte, and she went missing three days ago. Mr. Brodheureux has already received a ransom note via electronics—one of the programs his company developed, by the way, and even so, they can't trace the source. If he doesn't come up with fifty million Canadian dollars within five more days, Berte will be executed."

Xanogistics. Selena believed that everyone who had a computer, tablet or smartphone had heard of the Canadian company. It was in some ways that country's equivalent of Microsoft, known for a variety of consumer-friendly programs.

Xanogistics was so well-known, so successful, that Selena had no doubt its CEO had nearly unlimited resources. He could afford to pay to save his wife.

But he shouldn't have to do that.

Not if there was anything she, or the rest of Alpha Force, could do about it.

"I'm going to guess that the RCMP, or at least those in charge of the Canada Alphas, believe that wildlife can get in and surveil the area where technology can't," she said, looking straight at Owen.

His eyes lit up, and the grin he aimed her way almost caressed her—not anything sexual, she told herself. Certainly not with everyone around. But his look showed a touch of admiration that she'd correctly guessed where he was heading. Or was she just projecting that?

Still, she found herself basking in the gaze as he exclaimed, "Bingo! That's exactly it. The area we suspect supports a lot of different kinds of wild creatures—and they just happen to include wolves and falcons."

"That'll be us, then." Selena glanced to her right as Sal Emarra, who'd spoken, stood and clapped his hands. The young man gazed at his fellow CAs and they all rose and smiled at one another.

Selena glanced at Owen. He was scowling, and his expression wasn't unanticipated.

What he had described was far from a game.

But he said nothing to challenge his CAs' attitudes. Maybe he figured that allowing them to react this way only encouraged them to perform as he needed them to.

Nor did Selena want to spoil their premature celebration by reminding them that their assistance wasn't possible yet. They needed instruction by Alpha Force—and, most important, access to the very special elixir that allowed shifters to choose when they shifted and to keep their human awareness.

Otherwise, if this group simply showed up in the remote area where the abductors were thought to be, they'd have to do so during a full moon, which wouldn't occur for another couple of weeks—beyond the date the ransom had to be paid.

Presumably Rene Brodheureux would have paid to rescue his wife by then, assuming she was still alive.

Plus, the shifters would simply act like any other wolves or falcons in the area—roaming wildly without searching for a way to help any kidnap victim, with no human understanding of who they were or why they were there.

Or, worse, they would be no better than the aircraft sent to learn what was going on and would be unsuccessful, discovered and potentially taken out. So far, the

RCMP apparently had no idea how many suspects there were, how well armed they might be and whether they considered themselves hunters.

Sure, the shifted animals sent in would be equipped with some highly special, new-generation video cameras that should not be jammable like the other equipment that had been tried, but those wearing it would need to recognize where to aim them—which meant the Alpha Force elixir and assistance.

She shot a glance toward her fellow Alpha Force members. Judging by the way they sat unmoving, except for trading glances at one another, their minds were on a similar wavelength.

Owen finally replied to Sal, but it wasn't the criticism she figured he felt. "Yes, we hope it will be you—all four of you. But in some ways a very different kind of you. What we need is not simply for wild wolves and a falcon to converge on the place sometime. We need shifters who know what they are and what they need to accomplish there."

"Like you guys?" This time it was Craig talking. He looked at Selena first, then the other Alpha Force members. "You can do that, can't you? That's what we were told."

Selena smiled, but she let Patrick reply. "Yes, we can do that, thanks to our amazing elixir. And it'll let you do it, too."

"That's fantastic!" Sal exclaimed.

"Yes, it is," Rainey said. "Even just to watch."

Selena was aware that Rainey loved Alpha Force. She even admitted to Selena that she'd once hoped the elixir would help regular humans shift, but she was happy enough, since it didn't, just to work with shapeshifters. And Selena was happy to have her.

"Since we now know that acting fast is crucial—" she looked at Owen, who gave a slight nod of his head, as if he knew just what she was going to say "—I think it's time for us to give our new protégés a demonstration of what Alpha Force is all about."

"You're reading my mind," Owen said. Selena couldn't help thinking about the last time she shifted to prove to Owen and his superior officer that she was, indeed, a shapeshifter.

This time, there were men around who could give an even better demo to Owen and his fellow male CAs, while Selena could show Andrea how it was done.

No need for any sexual implications or awareness that way.

But as Selena continued to observe Owen, his small, cocky grin, which disappeared nearly immediately, told her that he, too, must be thinking about humans going nude before a shift.

In a way, Selena regretted that this time, now that she knew Owen better, she was unlikely to have an opportunity to tease him about what he wasn't about to see.

A short while later, Selena watched as Owen strode out of the dining room behind Marshall and Jonas. She wondered what he was thinking. He was about to actually see a shift, but not hers.

A pang of slight regret pulsed through her, and she ignored it.

She turned back to regard the others remaining in the dining room with her. Patrick was still there, along with Rainey and the CAs plus Lupe, who woke at the sound of slight activity.

Before the three men had left, Selena had stepped to a corner of the room with Patrick for a few minutes.

Selena had first asked Patrick why the other Alpha Force shifters hadn't brought their cover dogs, and he'd responded that they'd chosen not to in the interest of a speedy arrival, notwithstanding the delays they'd encountered thanks to some inclement weather. And there were logistical reasons, too—they didn't have to prepare the dogs or select planes for transport that would be safe for them. Besides, the Alpha Force team here wouldn't be around civilians much, especially not while shifted, so they wouldn't need the cover provided by their look-alike canines in the event they were seen.

Patrick had then given Selena instructions on what she was to do while Owen watched Marshall shift.

"You're our teacher," he'd said. "Time to give this group a lesson on what to expect, especially when Marshall returns to this room."

She had smiled, glad to know her special career skills were about to be put into use here. And now it was time.

She glanced at Patrick, who nodded. His light brown eyes shone a bit and his mouth curved in a small, encouraging grin. If Selena read the expression correctly, he believed in her.

She wouldn't let him, or Alpha Force, down. Not now and not ever.

"Hey, everyone," she said, standing to get their attention. "I'm going to tell those of you who don't know exactly what's about to happen in the other room."

"You mean Marshall's shapeshifting without a full moon and still knowing he's also human?" asked Craig, who regarded her with his dark brows lowered quizzically. "Isn't that what's going on?"

"That's the summary," Selena agreed. "And you'll all experience it eventually, but it's better if you have some detailed sense of the procedure."

"Then tell us," Andrea said enthusiastically, a huge smile radiating beneath her prominent nose. "I can kind of imagine it, but you can tell us with the voice of experience."

Selena laughed. "You could say that." She then looked at Tim, who regarded her with his small eyes wide, apparently also interested and not, fortunately, flirtatious this time.

And then she looked at Sal. The kid had the biggest, most interested smile of all of them.

"Okay," she said. "Here it is. You probably know, or can guess a lot of it, but I'm going to describe what'll happen moment by moment. That way, you'll all know exactly what to expect when your time comes."

Too bad she didn't have photos or even a chalkboard where she could draw illustrations, the way she had when actually teaching classes. But Alpha Force was such a covert military unit that any physical evidence of what it did, even temporary, was frowned on.

It didn't really matter. She just needed to describe it. They'd all see—and experience—what she explained to them soon.

She started out by pointing to Lupe, who had lain back down on the floor. "You all may know that Lupe is my cover dog." At her name, the dog rose and came over to Selena, who petted her. "Marshall's cover dog is Zarlon. They didn't bring him, but if they had you'd see right now what Marshall will look like when he returns to this room. And here's how he'll get that way now, during the day and with no full moon for another couple of weeks."

She described the steps of shapeshifting the Alpha Force way. The shifter's aide, in charge of carrying the very special shifting elixir, would uncap the small bottle and hand it to the person they assisted. That person would drink it. Then the aide would grab the special, battery-operated light that resembled the illumination of a full moon when turned on and aim it toward the shifter.

Then the shift would begin.

"Do I have to describe a shift to any of you?" Selena asked as she looked from one CA to the next. Since they were all shifters, the answer had to be no.

Instead, Sal asked, "What does the elixir taste like?" He looked concerned.

"It can vary since it is always being researched and changed and improved," Selena said. "Mostly, it's mildly citrusy in flavor. Not bad, in any of the formulations I've ever tasted. How about you, Patrick?"

He had been a member of Alpha Force longer than nearly anyone else. "I wouldn't say I'd ever choose to drink the stuff just because it tastes good," he said, "but I've always gotten it down just fine. Now how about telling them—"

"About what happens once the shift is over? I was just getting there." Selena smiled broadly. "This is one of the reasons I just love Alpha Force. And you'll surely love your CA group even more once you've had access to the elixir."

Selena began talking briefly about how shifting had felt to her when she'd been younger and before she had even heard of the elixir and the discomfort while the shift had occurred. And how she'd transformed into full wolf form when it was over.

"And now—now I'm fully aware of all that's happened, all that's around me, as if my mind is still human. But I'm completely in wolf form then. Plus, I have some control over how long I stay shifted. I can choose to shift back at any time, but otherwise the elixir will wear off, depending on the amount I drank, and I'll shift back automatically. Either way, it's wonderful."

"That sounds so amazing," said Andrea, still grinning. "I can't wait."

The door had just opened. Owen walked in first. "Amazing? Oh, yeah," he said. Selena hesitated to meet his gaze. He had now seen not only the result of a shift, but also the shift itself. Was he disgusted?

Would he despise her for what she was and how she got there?

Instead, his expression seemed full of awe. But she couldn't ask him any more now about what he thought, what he felt. And not just because of all the people around.

As he strode through the door, he was swept aside by the large, shepherd-wolf form.

"This," Owen told the CAs, "is Marshall now. And how he got like this? Wow."

Chapter 8

Wow wasn't really a strong enough word for what he'd seen, Owen thought as he watched the CAs look over the canine who'd just entered the dining room with him. Jonas Truro edged up to Owen's side. Owen was glad that Alpha Force had sent two doctors—shifter Patrick and nonshifter Jonas— just in case the shifting of his CAs led to some kind of medical issue.

"You okay with all that?" Jonas asked him softly.

"You mean the…shift? Yeah, I'm fine with it, though it's like watching a sci-fi movie with special effects." *Really* special effects. Owen didn't look at Jonas as he talked. Instead, he watched Selena, who was speaking with his CAs.

From what he had understood those years ago, the shifter who had married into his family had changed like this, yes, but under a full moon. And had turned wild—all wolf with no human characteristics.

If his shift had been like this, into a calm canine, there would surely have been a different result—and his blood family member would undoubtedly have survived.

Fortunately, the shifter and his wife had had no kids.

And Owen hadn't seen any shifting back then at all.

"Now since you all are shifters," Selena was saying, "I'm sure you're not at all surprised that this is Marshall. But what you may be unfamiliar with is what I told you about before. I'm going to give him some instructions that a true canine wouldn't understand—and neither would you while shifted."

Owen grasped what she was saying. But the vision of Marshall's change from a naked man who grew fur while his body morphed into this form... *Wow*, he thought again.

"Yeah, I remember the first time I saw a shift happen," Jonas said to him.

"Me, too," said Rainey, who'd joined them. They were all standing at one end of the dining room by then, away from the table.

"Sci-fi, weird, unbelievable," Jonas continued. "All those thoughts went through my mind. I assume they're going through yours, too."

"You could say that," Owen agreed. And they weren't the only things.

His mind, as well as his gaze, was on Selena.

He had no trouble visualizing her nude. In fact, he'd much too often ached to see her that way. And touch her. And...well, more.

But she was a shifter. She periodically went through the change he had just seen. In fact, she'd done it in that closed-off room before they'd left Vancouver—unseen by him, but imagined just the same.

And despite being amazed by what he had just seen, oddly enough he now hoped to watch Selena do the same thing.

To see her without clothes—oh, yeah. But also to see her go through that incredible process that should be a complete turnoff, yet was somehow stimulating his curiosity. And more.

"Lupe, you come here and lie down," she told the dog she'd traveled with, and Lupe obeyed. Then she turned to the dog-man who'd just shifted and come into the room. "Okay, Marshall, let's first do what regular dogs do. Sit."

Her voice intruding into his thoughts brought him back to reality. Odd reality, to be sure, but he focused on this room. On her.

The canine before her sat. That didn't surprise Owen, nor, apparently, any of the others who circled around him.

"Now get up and slap Craig on his hip with your left front paw," Selena directed.

No regular dog would understand all that, although presumably one could have been trained to make that move on a specific command. Once again, Owen wasn't surprised to see the dog obey.

He again considered how different things might have been in his family if the Alpha Force elixir had been involved.

"Next, I want you, Andrea, to tell Marshall to do something that ordinary dogs aren't likely to understand."

"Great!" The only woman CA was smiling once more. "Let's see." She moved her slender body, clad in sweatshirt and jeans, near him. "Marshall, my phone is in my pocket. Can you sniff out which one?"

The dog nodded, then raised his nose in the air. In moments, he approached Andrea's right side and nuzzled her hip gently. She reached into the pocket on that side and drew out her phone.

"Good job," she said. "Now, I'm originally from Quebec and my area code is four-one-eight. Can you bark that out? I mean, first bark four times, then once, and then eight times."

Marshall obeyed and the CAs applauded.

"This is so cool," Sal exclaimed. "I can't wait for us to try it." He'd knelt on the floor near Marshall and then rose. "Can we do it today?" he asked Owen.

"Tomorrow," he responded. "Right?" He looked at Patrick.

"That'll work," the captain agreed. "And once all you CAs have your first planned shift, we'll really need to get down to work training you for your mission. This'll probably be your last free evening for a while, so you might as well enjoy it."

"Can we party first, tonight?" Sal asked, looking hopefully toward Owen.

"I thought you partied last night," he responded.

"That was just a visit to a bar for a couple of drinks," Andrea said. "I'm up for a real party."

"Especially if it'll be our last for a while," said Tim.

Owen mulled over the idea quickly. That might actually work well to maintain their cover in this town, where they were just supposed to be tourists hanging out for now until deciding to move here.

"Sure," he said. "Let's party."

Selena was glad to plan on partying, too. That meant she would be around the entire group and unlikely to be alone at all with Owen. That was good.

Even though she was dying to ask him what he thought of the shift he had watched.

"Let's start out early evening," Patrick said. "I don't

want the party to last too late. We should all get up early tomorrow morning."

"Fine with me," Owen agreed.

It was also fine with Selena. With all the discussion and shifting, it was now midafternoon, so the party wouldn't start for a few hours.

Except for Rainey, this would be the first night that the other Alpha Force members slept in the house in this small compound. They would all be upstairs except for her, but she would be well aware of them. She needed a good rest to prepare for all that would happen tomorrow.

She'd done some teaching today, but what she and the others would provide as instruction tomorrow was likely to be pretty taxing. As well as a lot of fun. These shifters had much to learn about the Alpha Force elixir and what it could do for them.

And how it could allow them to help their country.

Facing Owen, Jonas asked, "Do you want to watch Marshall shift back?"

"Yeah," he said. "Definitely."

What was his mind-set? Selena wondered, not looking him straight in face. Did he find it fascinating or horrifying? Was he trying to get used to the terrible reality he would need to deal with as the commanding officer of the CAs, or was he actually drawn to it?

She couldn't help hoping for the latter, but suspected the former was the truth.

"Great," she said. "In the meantime, I'll go check out some things on my computer and change clothes. Rainey, you going to town later, too?"

"Absolutely. Looking forward to it. Last night was fun. Are those friends going to join us again?" Rainey's gaze was on the CAs, who'd taken seats on the living room sofas and chairs.

"Friends?" Owen, who hadn't yet left the room, asked.

"Just Craig's girlfriend and my sister," Sal said. "We knew our cover was to be like tourists, so we invited them to come to town for a little while. They joined us last night for drinks but left early."

Worry shot through Selena. Had the CAs' cover been broken? Had Alpha Force's?

"Who gave you permission to ask them?" Owen's voice wasn't loud, but it was strong enough to make his recruits blanch or look down or both.

"Really, sir, it's okay," Craig responded, meeting Owen's gaze briefly before tearing his away again. "My girlfriend, Holly, knows I'm a shifter, even though she isn't. She also knows I'm joining the RCMP but thinks I've found a way to hide what I am, not use it, and that I've met some friends who're doing the same thing. I just told her that the group of us had taken a short leave and were meeting up for a vacation here, and she asked if she could come."

"Same goes for my sister, Yvanne," Sal said. "I told her not to mention to anyone that we're RCMP, and she promised not to. And I figured her being here would only help with our cover here as vacationers. She's rooming with Holly in the same hotel as we are and only staying for a few days."

Owen looked as dubious about the situation as Selena felt. Patrick's expression suggested he, too, didn't like it.

"Well, what's done is done," Owen said. "And yes, you'd better make sure they both party with us tonight so I can check them out. If they're as you say, no harm, no foul. But you both might have compromised the entire mission."

"It's not like that at all, sir," Craig said, his face drawn into a worried frown. "Holly's been my girl for a long time. She's trustworthy. She'd never do anything that could hurt me."

"Same with my sister," Sal said. "I promise."

Selena could only hope that they both knew the women well enough to know that trust was merited.

As they left the room a little while later, Rainey apologized not only to Selena but also to the other Alpha Force members. "Sorry," she said as they stood in the hallway. "They all told me that Owen and the RCMP knew they were coming and were okay with it, or I'd have mentioned those women first thing."

"It should be fine," Patrick said, "since we're all meeting with them tonight. We'll make it clear that it's in their loved ones' best interests not to talk about them, or even visit here, at all."

Selena just hoped they'd understand that lack of discretion could result in nasty consequences for those loved ones—and possibly the rest of them, too.

They had all been in the Yukon's main bar area for nearly an hour now. Owen had helped, on their arrival, to push three tables together for this somewhat sizable party: the five members of Alpha Force, the five CAs including him…and the two outsiders.

Or sort-of outsiders, he reminded himself while taking a long sip of the second bottle of his imported US beer.

The place was crowded and noisy, every table taken.

The TV hanging above the bar was muted but showed a football game being broadcast from the UK—soccer in the US. One of the teams was Manchester United, a huge and global fan favorite.

Owen hadn't paid much attention to the screen or the rival team, though. Instead, he listened to what was happening with this group. His group.

The group he had to ensure remained in sync with one another while one part taught the other what was necessary for its members to fulfill their assignment. Their very critical assignment.

Then there were the other two people who, despite being outside his control, had the potential to blow their whole mission. But he wouldn't panic. For now all he had to do was listen.

Selena, bless her, was doing all the rest.

"So on a scale of one to ten, what's your skill at keeping secrets?" she had just asked Yvanne. Selena's voice was a bit slurred, her head tilted so her light brown hair hung lower on her left side than her right. Owen was rather surprised that the highlights in her hair shone even in the bar's low light—but that was probably a result of its unusual nature. *Her* unusual nature. Her amber eyes, too, gleamed despite the lack of illumination around them.

Of course, most of the man-wolf shifters at the extended table also had similar characteristics, but Selena's intriguing feminine features trumped them all.

And her apparent high brought on by too much alcohol? A pretense. He was sure of it. He had observed what she had actually had to drink, and it hadn't been that much. No doubt she wanted the others to think she'd overimbibed so they'd lower their guard around her.

"I'm quite good at keeping secrets," Yvanne responded. She was apparently Sal's older sister, maybe in her midtwenties to his nineteen years. She was slender, too, and her hair was longer and blonder than his. It, like Selena's, sparkled now and then in the scant light in the bar. "On the scale you mentioned, I'm at least a ten. Maybe higher."

"That's my sister," Sal said. He reached over from where he sat next to her and rubbed her hair in obvious fondness. She responded by making a fist and giving him a brief Dutch rub that made her bro laugh and stand as if he wanted to tackle her. That lasted for only a second, though, before he again sat down and took a swig of beer.

Good show, Owen thought. And since Yvanne, too, was apparently a shifter, he believed what she said—at least with respect to some things. Would she keep silent about her brother having joined the RCMP, and the nature of the unit he was now part of if she happened to figure it out? They'd been told that these two women thought their men were hiding their special abilities from the RCMP, but they might suspect otherwise. In fact, Owen felt fairly sure Yvanne knew the truth, and perhaps the other woman did, too.

He hoped, in any event, they would remain discreet, but he would keep his eyes and ears open.

Selena had already turned toward the other complete stranger in their midst, Craig Neverts's girlfriend, Holly Alverton. Holly was petite in stature but curvaceous. She seemed attached to Craig's left side and was either holding his arm or rubbing up against him. Her eyes were huge and blue, her smile nonstop except when she took a sip of her white wine.

"How 'bout you, Holly?" Selena said, still slurring her words. "You know your boyfriend's…special, don't you?"

Owen knew just what Selena's slight hesitation meant. Did Holly?

"Oh, yes," Holly said, her voice ringing out despite the noisiness of their surroundings. "There's a whole lot that's special about Craig." She snuggled even closer to him, if that was possible.

Craig turned toward her and kissed her cheek, then rubbed his own, with its dark beard shadow, against it. "Holly's pretty special, too," he said.

"But not as special as you," Selena persisted. "Not the same way, at least."

"That's right," Holly said. "I know how very special Craig is." She turned and kissed him back on his rough cheek.

"Then I'd love to hear, on my scale of one to ten, where you fit, Holly," Selena said. "Keeping secrets or not? What's your score?"

"She's great at it, aren't you, love?" Craig said. His glare at Selena was nasty enough that Owen considered intervening.

He must have moved a bit on his chair, since Selena glanced at him, gave an almost imperceptible shake of her head, then returned her attention to Holly, even as she took another sip of beer.

"It depends on the secret," Holly said, her voice more muted now. "There are certain ones, one in particular, that really have to be kept to myself. On that one I'm a ten." The gaze she turned toward Selena appeared almost defiant, as if daring her to guess which one she was talking about.

But Owen knew which she meant. Obviously Selena did, too. Craig certainly did. This time the kiss he gave his girlfriend was right on the lips. A long one that appeared deep and hot and a bit too sexy while in the company of other people.

It made Owen think of Selena. He looked toward her...and found that she was looking at him, too. That made a certain part of him tense up and thicken—good thing he was sitting down. Selena's expression suggested she could see his reaction anyway, or at least anticipate what he was going through.

Did that mean she felt a similar heat, similar attraction, similar...desire? That only made Owen's erection thicken even more.

She took a much longer swig of beer this time—one he believed might actually lead to the intoxication she'd been feigning if she followed it up with many more. When she put her bottle down, she pulled her gaze quickly away from Owen and looked again toward Holly.

"Excellent," Selena said. "Secrets can be a lot of fun, can't they?"

"Definitely," Holly responded, then started to kiss Craig once more.

This time Selena smiled at Owen before reaching again for her beer.

Chapter 9

If only she were as inebriated as she pretended, Selena thought, taking another small sip of her beer while making it appear as though she was swallowing a lot.

Maybe then she'd simply be having a good time without trying so hard to read the thoughts behind every expression Owen leveled at her.

She saw lust in his intense blue eyes beneath lowered brows, or so she believed. Was it true? A touch of amusement and admiration, too. She could understand his appreciation of her attempts to get usable impressions of the two visiting women, a feel for whether either or both were trustworthy with the very important secrets hovering around this group.

That knowledge was critical to the success of their mission. Not to mention Alpha Force's need to remain covert.

The CAs also had reason to keep silent about their nature and Alpha Force's. But outsiders, even with relationships?

She knew better than to believe either woman's assertion of her ability to keep confidences. But at least this way both Yvanne and Holly had to be aware that secrecy was expected of them—as if they hadn't known it before.

"So who'd like another round?" Selena waved her half-full bottle in the air as if it was empty.

"I think we've all had enough," Owen said. He looked not at her but toward Patrick, who was in charge of the US contingent here.

Patrick clearly got the message. He took what appeared to be a final swig from the bottle in front of him. "Agreed," he said. "We have a big day tomorrow."

"We sure do." Sal looked at his sister and grinned. Was he going to talk with her about what was planned for the CAs? Selena figured Yvanne probably knew, at least in general, despite claiming otherwise. From what she'd gathered, Yvanne was a shifter like her brother. Would she be jealous of his upcoming ability to shift at will and keep his human sensibilities?

Maybe. But if all went as hoped, the CAs might even recruit other shifters into their ranks.

Later. If this mission was successful.

Which it had to be. A life was at stake—and maybe more lives in the future.

Selena shot a glance toward Owen. "Well, then," she said, "let's all go back to our quarters for the night so we can get up early."

Soon everyone was standing, their bar tabs were paid and they headed toward the Yukon Bar's exit.

Outside, beneath the glow of the bar's bright neon signage that lit the darkness well into the adjoining street, Selena wasn't surprised to find Owen beside her. He leaned down and said softly into her ear, "Good job."

She ignored the warmth that flowed through her at his approval. "What time are we having breakfast?" she asked. She half hoped he would offer her a ride back to the CAs headquarters, but Patrick had driven one of the vehicles rented by Alpha Force here, so she didn't actually need other transportation.

"Seven o'clock sharp," Owen said. "As soon as we're done we'll do a quick recap, then begin our exercises." His eyes glistened in the light for a moment before he looked toward his group of RCMP members. They all stood together watching him, with the two outsider females behind them. Selena could read the excitement in the expressions of each of them.

"We'll be there right on time," Craig said, his smile huge.

His girlfriend behind him smiled, too, but her expression seemed a bit puzzled, as if she didn't really know why he was so eager to leave her early the next day.

Whether that was real or feigned didn't matter. Tomorrow was going to be a thoroughly enlightening day to the CAs—and possibly to the Alpha Force members, too, as they did their first training of the outsiders.

"Good night, everyone," Rainey said. Her aide slipped beside Selena and faced the others. "Sleep well."

Selena glanced toward Owen again. Did he actually wink at her, or was that just an illusion under the light?

"Yeah," he said, his gaze still on her. "Sleep well." Was that a challenge? Did he assume she'd stay awake all night thinking of him?

Or was that just her own assumption?

He looked away from her then and again faced the CAs. "You'll all need a good night's sleep." With that, he headed down the street while the recruits started off in the other direction.

Where was Owen staying while here in West Columbia?

And why did Selena suddenly want to visit his quarters?

She tamped down her absurd yearning and followed the other Alpha Force members as they crossed the street toward where their car was.

After Selena walked Lupe for the last time that evening, she stepped into her room. She couldn't help the images that bombarded her mind. Images of the first time she'd entered this room, with Owen. Even then she'd sensed something between them.

Shaking off the memories, she plugged her phone's charger into the wall. Just as she did, it rang.

It was Owen. She had programmed his number into her caller ID. "Hello," she said, wondering if he was going to do something to keep her wide-awake after all.

Like saying things that were suggestive and hot and—

"Hi, Selena," he said. "I just wanted to let you know that I've spoken with both Craig and Sal independently this evening. I called each of them to once again underscore the importance of their making sure that Holly and Yvanne keep their mouths shut about whatever they happen to know, even if it isn't much. As it turned out, and unsurprisingly, Yvanne knows it all."

Selena sat down on top of the bed. Lupe came over and laid her muzzle on top of Selena's knee, and she petted the dog's head distractedly.

"And as a shifter she's jealous?" Selena made it a question despite being fairly sure of the answer.

"Yes, but according to Sal, she's concerned for his

safety and won't say anything. Plus, she's hoping to join the CAs in the future."

Exactly as Selena had figured. "So she'll keep her mouth shut for that as much as anything else."

"Right."

"And Holly?" Selena asked. She was a little more of an enigma, but since she apparently knew that Craig was a shifter, she was unlikely to do anything that would harm him.

Unless they were arguing, and that certainly didn't appear to be the situation. Not the way they'd had their hands all over one another at the Yukon Bar.

"From what Craig said, she's fascinated by the fact he's a shifter. Can't wait until they're married and have shifter kids. He vouches for her unequivocally."

"Still...well, even if those two women are perfect, we should nevertheless remain cautious about all the CAs and what they do and who they tell." She didn't say so, but in her mind that included Owen.

She was an Alpha Force member and a shifter. He wasn't—no matter that he was the RCMP member in charge of his newly formed group.

And also no matter that she found him attractive. And sexy.

And way out of her reach. He was Canadian. She was American. He was a high-ranking police officer in the RCMP. She was a lower-ranking officer in the US military.

Most of all, she was a shifter, and he wasn't. If nothing else erected barriers between them, that certainly did.

"You're entirely right," Owen said. "I'll be cautious on my end, and you might remind your fellow Alpha Force members to observe as well as teach."

"Will do," she said, then paused. "Thanks for calling, Owen, and giving me at least some sense of reassurance."

"You're welcome. And like I said before, sleep well. Just remember, though, that I'll be thinking of you." His voice grew lower and hoarser. "And wishing you were here. Good night, Selena."

Before she could say anything else, he hung up.

She fortunately didn't have time to mull over what he'd said and how he'd said it—with that deep, sexy tone. Not then, at least. A knock sounded at her door.

She opened it to find Patrick standing there. "Want to go on a brief patrol with me?" he asked. "I want to shift and walk around this compound to check for any apparent dangers."

A pleased feeling coursed through Selena. He had chosen her over those who'd been with Alpha Force longer, whom he knew better?

"Of course," she said, smiling.

"Since you've been here an extra day, you might have a better sense of what's supposed to be around here."

Well, all right. That made sense, although it burst her bubble a little. Her commanding officer had a rational reason for selecting her above the others. But that still was good. She would get to shift that night. Soon, in fact.

And wouldn't have time to think any more about Owen.

At least not now.

He hadn't meant to add those last comments as he'd said good-night to Selena, Owen thought after hanging up the phone.

He knew he wouldn't sleep. Not yet.

Instead, he decided to take one last drive to the CAs compound now occupied by the Alpha Force members. That included Selena. He wouldn't drop in on her, though, or any of them. He wouldn't even go into the meeting house to make certain it was ready for tomorrow.

He simply wanted to ensure that everything looked okay around that important training area.

Or so he told himself. He wouldn't see Selena, after all. That would be a bad idea.

But he knew she was there. And he hopefully would confirm that she was safe.

As if she wouldn't be, with a whole team of Alpha Force members—her own kind—backing her up...

The drive through West Columbia was fast this time of night. Most of the downtown stores were closed, and the bars that remained open—the Yukon and others—even seemed fairly quiet, judging by the few cars parked along the street. It wasn't long past midnight, but apparently this town went to bed early on weeknights.

A good thing to know, especially considering the types of training sessions the CAs would soon be holding.

Owen drove slowly so no one would notice him. In a short while he turned into the driveway up to the compound.

He stopped there. Maybe it wouldn't be a good idea to drive up the hill. Any Alpha Force members would recognize his car and question his being there.

Even *he* questioned his being there.

He parked along the street in front of a nearby house.

If he walked up the driveway in the dark to check things out, he was less likely to be noticed.

By normal people, at least. But most of the Alpha Force members there had extraordinary senses for humans, or so he'd been told. Plus, the cover dog Lupe, too, might catch his sound or scent.

As a result, he decided to compromise. He wouldn't go all the way to the top of the hill. Instead, as quietly as he could, he would stand at the bottom of the driveway before deciding how far up it he would go, and he would let his own, very normal senses work on seeing and hearing anything that might be even a little beyond usual.

Good thing his sweatshirt and jeans were dark colors. He got out of the car quickly so as not to be illuminated long by its inside lights. He glanced around and saw no movement, no indication anyone was aware of his presence.

After waiting for only a minute or two, he started walking up the hill.

She led Patrick out the back of the house, leaving Rainey and Jonas inside.

Their shifts had been fast and hassle-free, as always. Selena had recalled, while drinking the elixir, how Patrick had accurately described the most recent taste as somewhat citrusy. Then Rainey had shone the bright battery-powered light on her, and now she was in wolf form.

So was Patrick. Together, side by side, they prowled down the porch steps, circled both houses, then entered the surrounding woods.

As before, even when not shifted, Selena heard the sounds of small nocturnal creatures. Scented them as well—mostly rodents and owls. The feel of fallen leaves and pine needles tickled the bottoms of her paws. She turned her ears one way, then the other, still listening. The lights from the houses illuminated the clearing, but not here, beneath the trees.

A sound! A footstep? A human?

It seemed to come from the base of the driveway. Patrick must have heard it, too, since he stopped walking and looked at her. She nodded quickly, and then the two of them, still within the cover of the forest, headed in that direction.

Then Selena picked up a scent. A very familiar, very appealing scent. Human and tangy, not sweaty or menacing or anything that suggested a need to approach and attack.

Owen's scent.

She moved slightly sideways as she continued walking, butting gently against Patrick. They both stopped, and she stared into her CO's pale brown eyes, looking down, then shaking her head slightly. Telling him by motions, not words, that there was no danger.

Or so she believed. They had to check, of course, and so she took the lead.

In moments, as she stood halfway down the driveway, remaining tucked into shadows, she saw him.

At the same time, he saw her. His chin rose, his eyes widened, and she heard him mutter something, although she could not make out the words. Despite her acute hearing, he was too far away, his voice too low.

Was he saying her name?

He had seen her before like this, before they had departed from Vancouver. But even if he might recognize her, could he here, in the darkness?

She wasn't certain. Even so, she walked slowly from

beneath the cover of the trees. She nodded her wolfen head slightly, as if in greeting. Heard Patrick's growl behind her, a warning to be cautious.

She was. That was definitely Owen, and he was no threat to her or to any of the shifters.

Owen remained motionless where he was, except that he, too, nodded at her.

And then he turned and walked back down the hill.

Chapter 10

It was her. Owen was certain of it.

He could think of nothing else as he drove cautiously back toward his hotel.

Certainly wild wolves could have shown up in this area, but he knew better. The animals' demeanors, their actions when they had seen him, had convinced him they were shifters.

Even so, there were three Alpha Force wolf shifters. The two canines he had seen could have been the two males who had come here together. One could even have been the cover dog Lupe, he supposed.

Yet the way the one wolf had looked at him, had appeared to react to him, had seemed to communicate with him…

That had to have been Selena.

He turned onto West Columbia's main street once more.

He was tired but doubted he would sleep well that night.

Not after seeing those two shifted wolves.

Not after seeing Selena.

Of course it had been her. It hadn't just been her

actions that convinced him. He had worked with dogs
at the RCMP police-dog service. Many of the German
shepherds who were part of their canine force resembled
one another, yet Owen had taught himself with no effort
at all to tell them apart.

That canine who had appeared at the edge of the forest near the CAs' enclave had looked exactly as Owen
recalled Selena appeared after she had shifted in the
isolated room in Vancouver. Like Lupe but more aware,
more connected.

He hadn't been close enough, hadn't been at an angle
to confirm it was a female wolf, but if nothing else the
resemblance to Lupe convinced him who it was.

He had anticipated seeing Selena changed again
someday as she helped to train the CAs in his charge.
He just hadn't anticipated it here and now, this night.
But he'd been the one to show up at the enclave unan-
nounced. Why wouldn't she have shifted while anticipating no Canadians would be around to spot her?

She—

Damn. He had overshot the entry to the parking lot
for his hotel. He was overthinking this situation.

As if he could do anything else.

Well, tomorrow would be a big day. The first training day. That was what he needed to concentrate on—
and how vital his team would be in rescuing the latest
kidnap victim and preventing any more.

Pulling into another driveway, he turned the car
around to return to his hotel.

They hadn't talked about it at breakfast. They hadn't
talked about it at all.

Now Selena was in the meeting house's closed-off

study with Rainey and Lupe, sitting on the small sofa while waiting for their morning's assignment to begin.

She was no longer in Owen's presence and wouldn't see him again until sometime later.

Had he known she was one of the wolves he had spotted last night? Somehow she didn't doubt it.

The fact he hadn't mentioned it, had simply acted cordial this morning with everyone else around, hadn't erased the likelihood from her mind.

Would he confront her with it sometime?

Would he simply ignore it because though he might need shapeshifters to fulfill his professional assignment, he didn't especially like them?

Didn't especially like her?

"When can we get started?" Andrea had just hurried into the room and shut the door behind her. As she'd been directed, she wore a loose T-shirt and jeans that could be removed quickly.

Rainey and she were also dressed casually, though Selena had no intention of shifting today.

No, this was the day to start training the CAs.

"Right away," Rainey said, then looked at Selena questioningly, which was entirely appropriate. Selena was her commanding officer.

But for what was about to occur, Rainey was in charge.

"Fine with me," Selena responded, glad her focus was now redirected as it should be. "Rainey's going to be the one who'll help you, Andrea. She's not only my aide—and now yours—but she has also checked with another Alpha Force aide who's worked with our avian shifters." That was Ruby Belmont, whom Selena hardly knew. "As you've probably already been told, there's only one right now, a hawk." Autumn Kater, whom Selena didn't know well, either. "The amount of elixir she takes to cause her change is different from what a shifting wolf takes."

"Should a falcon take the same amount as a shifting hawk?" Andrea asked Rainey, her thick brow angled into a worried frown.

"We'll start with a little less, just in case. But it should be quite similar. Your human weights are around the same, less than ten pounds' difference." Rainey's smile was reassuring beneath her curly, dark hair, and she undoubtedly knew what she was doing. "Are you ready to give it a try?"

"Absolutely!" Any hesitation on Andrea's part had disappeared. She looked excited and ready to go.

Selena remained seated, holding Lupe's collar. Her dog had been present while she and others had shifted into wolf form, but Lupe hadn't seen shapeshifting into other forms. On the other hand, she was a very sweet, fairly calm dog who had never been known to chase other animals.

"Okay, here's what we do." Rainey had gotten a sealed container of the special elixir from the basement refrigerator and brought it into the room along with a wrapped plastic glass. "First, please take off your clothes. We're not sure how soon the process will start after you drink the elixir, so it's better for you to be ready."

That was why there were only women in this room. All the men CAs were in the basement with the male Alpha Force members.

Andrea barely took a minute to strip. Though Selena turned away, the glimpse she got told her that Andrea was as reed-thin as she appeared in her clothes.

Rainey handed Andrea a half-full cup of the liquid.

"Now drink this, not too fast and not too slow." Andrea did so. That was when Rainey removed the battery-powered light from her backpack, turned it on and aimed it at the nude woman. "Now we'll wait," she said.

Selena's shifts always began as soon as the light was focused on her. The same thing happened with Andrea. It worked just fine. Despite the length of her limbs, they began to contract nearly immediately. Her face contorted and shrank as well, and feathers began to emerge from her skin.

Fascinating, Selena thought. But then, she thought all shifting was fascinating. She was just a lot more familiar with the change to and from wolfen form.

Lupe moved slightly beside her, but didn't otherwise react. Selena patted her. "Good girl," she said in a low, fervent voice.

In less than five minutes, it was over. A gorgeous falcon of no more than a few pounds, with a determined stare through golden eyes and a curved, sharp beak, perched on avian legs on the far edge of the sofa that Selena occupied.

"Wonderful!" Rainey exclaimed. "Do you feel okay?"

The falcon's head, covered with mottled gray-and-white feathers, bobbed as if nodding yes. Her throat was white. In a moment, the bird raised her wings and began flying around the room making the sound "cack, cack," as if triumphantly calling out in success.

"I'll take that to mean yes." Rainey smiled at Selena, who could only grin back. "Then let's go out to the living room and wait for the men."

"Good idea." Selena looked toward Andrea, who seemed to be listening despite her flight, and as soon as Rainey opened the door the bird soared through.

The living room was empty when the female contingent arrived there, but Selena was pleased that Lupe soon wasn't the only canine present. In fact, three dogs resembling wolves with different backgrounds, including possibly a shepherd, a malamute and an Akita, loped into the room and sat near one another on the wooden floor. As they panted, their mouths resembled smiles. Not surprising, Selena thought. She wasn't certain which was Craig or Tim or Sal—but at that moment it didn't matter.

What was important was that they had all shifted, without a full moon.

Right behind them came Patrick, Marshall, Jonas... and Owen.

"I see all must have gone well with Andrea," Patrick said, watching the bird soar around the room's ceiling.

"It sure did," Selena said. "And I gather that the wolf-shifting CAs had no problems, either."

"Right," Jonas said.

Selena stole a glance toward Owen. Had he enjoyed watching? Hated it?

Thought about her as the humans morphed into wolfen form?

Wondered about possibly having seen her shifted last night?

Her mind was back on that subject. Maybe Owen and Patrick had already discussed it, since her commanding officer had been shifted and at her side. She wasn't about to ask, especially not now.

"Time for you to give a few instructions, Selena," Patrick said. "You're our teacher, after all. It'll all work better when we do this sometime at night, but for now teach these shifters about their human cognition while in animal form."

Selena had known Patrick would direct her to do this. In fact, they had discussed it last night—once they had both shifted back into human form.

Patrick had mentioned seeing Owen at the base of the hill. He hadn't expressed an opinion or anything else, though.

Now Selena turned her attention to her charges, who'd just had their first experience with a shift brought on by the Alpha Force elixir. She started with Andrea. Selena told her to go and gently alight on Rainey's head.

Her aide laughed. "Good idea, but don't even think about providing me with a bird-poop sample."

The other humans laughed, too. The falcon who was Andrea immediately followed orders and perched atop Rainey's head, then squawked once more.

"Good job," Selena said. "Now see how gently you can fly away. No pulling hair. Next, go perch on Owen's shoulder."

Selena met his gaze with a smile. He looked fine with it. He looked fine, period, in his navy sweatshirt and jeans, his blue eyes sparkling over his aquiline nose and strong chin. Selena kept her expression neutral and pleasant.

No need for him to realize he was stoking her sexually just by being there and being a good sport around shifters.

"Now, if you know what I'm saying and you like your current shift, Andrea, give Owen a kiss on top of his head."

The falcon turned her head and lowered her beak to touch Owen's short black hair. She obviously was cognizant of what she did, since her touch was gentle despite the pointed end of her beak.

Selena let herself sigh softly in relief. She certainly wouldn't have wanted the bird to hurt Owen in any way. But she did want to prove to everyone in the room who had human cognition—which should be everyone but Lupe, who lay on the floor near the sofa—that Andrea knew what she was doing.

"Okay, next I want each of you shifted wolves to do as I say." She told the three canines to stand and turn around, one at a time. Next, they were to sit beside one another, then each stand up on hind legs, turn around and sit again. "Then, if you like being shifted thanks to the Alpha Force elixir and know what you're seeing and doing, I want you to each bark, in this order—Sal, then Tim, then Craig."

They did so, and everyone who still had hands clapped in glee.

The plan had been for this first shift to last for about an hour, and the amounts of elixir had been given accordingly—and so had instructions about how to will themselves to start changing back.

When the hour was up, the groups separated to the locations where they'd been before. As soon as they all were in human form once more, the entire group was to meet back here in the living room.

Selena followed Rainey and Lupe into the study with Andrea flying overhead as the men headed downstairs.

She looked forward to the next part of today's experience.

She'd grown up with a little access to the elixir, having known the family who'd invented its first incarnation, but she looked forward to the delighted expressions she knew would come.

Controlling the change, and one's own mind-set, was

an inevitable and endless thrill. It made all the shifters she knew who experienced it feel overjoyed and eager for more.

Even she still felt it.

And the CAs who'd just had their first such experience…?

Selena knew they'd be jazzed and excited and full of anticipation for the next experience.

That would be a good time, she figured, for the men in charge—Patrick and Owen—to remind them of their underlying assignment and its potential danger.

Owen wasn't certain why he felt so drawn to watching the shifters change, but he did. In both directions, from human to wolf, then back again.

Now the reverse process seemed to take even less time, and he observed the wolves' fur absorbed beneath their skin as the forms of their bodies changed, too, while they lay on the floor.

He heard the Alpha Force members cheering them on, a nice gesture on their part, he thought. Or maybe the two who were shifters themselves believed their kudos somehow helped the others engage in their new shifting processes.

He didn't need to wait down here forever in the cool underground chamber with concrete walls and floor, though. He'd seen what he'd wanted to.

While the three CAs lay on the floor in human form, grinning as they received their clothes from the Alpha Force members, Owen slipped up the wooden stairs into the kitchen.

Selena was there.

She clearly heard him coming up the steps since she

was watching the door when he opened it. She stood near the refrigerator, a bottle of water in her hand.

"How are things downstairs?" she asked, her tone as cool as the drink she held.

"Shifting is... Well, it's amazing," he said, shaking his head as if that action would underscore his words.

That thawed her a little. "You could say that. In fact, you did. I shift often, and I'm still amazed by it, particularly now that I have complete access to that wonderful elixir."

"I wish I could try it sometime." Owen stopped, wondering where that thought had come from. Him, interested in shapeshifting?

Of course he knew the impossibility of that. Not even the magic elixir would give nonshifters the ability to shapeshift.

Selena had taken a couple of steps toward him, as if wanting to soften what she was about to say. The soft, sad look on her lovely face seemed compassionate, even sympathetic. "You know you can't, don't you, because—"

"No, no, I realize that. I'm just expressing my wonder at what you do."

Her eyes widened, and he felt utterly captivated by Selena. He took a couple of steps toward her, too. His arms began to reach out, but then he heard a noise behind him.

He turned as the men exited from the basement.

"Hey, where's Andrea?" asked Sal. "We want to compare notes on our experiences."

"Here I am." Andrea strode into the kitchen from the other side, with Rainey and the dog behind her. "And wow!"

"Exactly," said Craig. "Wow."

Owen realized that his brief time alone with Selena had ended. It was better that way. He had probably said too much already.

He might need the help of Alpha Force for his assignment, might have to work with these CAs in ways he could not possibly have done on his own.

Admiring who they were and what they did was okay, too.

But that was enough.

"Okay," he said. "Let's all get together in the living room and discuss what you experienced."

Chapter 11

Selena wasn't surprised to hear each of the CAs attempt to top one another in their descriptions of their shifts.

The three men were outspoken about how different this felt from their uncontrolled changes under a full moon, when they stalked outside until it was time to change back again, only to await the same scenario the following month.

Then there was today. They'd felt the same discomfort during the change, but it was definitely worth it, each asserted. Tim was the first to talk about it, and he seemed so thrilled, so excited, that he could hardly find the words to describe his experience. Selena couldn't help wondering if his slight pudginess made his shift more strenuous and difficult than the others', but he wasn't complaining. No, he had clearly loved it.

Then young Sal gave his description a try, and he was passionate if not clear about what it had felt like not just to shift, but to realize what was happening. And then to be fully cognizant of who and what he was once the change was complete. "It was so, so, so amazing!" he asserted, giving a fist pump of delight into the air.

Craig was less vociferous but no less enthused. "I

can't begin to describe how it felt," he said, "but I can't wait to do it again. And again."

"My turn!" Andrea interjected. "I'm sure all you guys had a great time. But can you even begin to imagine what it's like to soar and see things and understand them from the air just like you see and understand things now? I can." Her falcon-like face beamed.

Selena felt her own smile broaden. Oh, yes, she understood all of what they described. Well, almost all. She'd never soared while shifted like Andrea did. But the experience, the sensations and the knowledge were all incredible.

She glanced around, seeing similar pleasure on the faces of Patrick and Marshall. Their two aides, Jonas and Rainey, looked nearly as happy. Maybe they felt some kind of empathy while being part of the process. Or maybe they were just nice people, military souls who derived pleasure from doing their jobs well.

Then there was Owen, who she had just learned might be experiencing some kind of envy of shifters. Or not. He had to work with them now, so maybe he was just pretending to cast aside his original feelings about them and to like them.

Yet when she hazarded a glance in his direction, he was looking not at his own delighted CAs, but toward her. She made herself keep smiling, and she nodded a little as if she had said something that he should now accept as true.

"I'm really glad to hear about all this," he finally said, not just to her. "In fact, as you all know, this was just step one. Step two, tomorrow, will involve all of you shifting again and then starting to learn the procedures you will need when you are set loose in the area where we believe the kidnappers are hiding out. We'll decide whether to try it at different times in the day and evening and maybe the night since we don't know when you'll actually need to conduct your mission."

"Sounds great!" Sal exclaimed, then lowered his head and stared up at his CO with inquisitive eyes. "Don't suppose we can do it tonight, can we?"

"No," Patrick interjected from beside Selena on the sofa. "This was a partially new experience for all of you. Your bodies will need to rest. But our experience with new Alpha Force recruits using the elixir indicates that you should all be fine for a new shift tomorrow. Of course, if you have any reactions that feel different from when you shift naturally under a full moon, you should let us know right away."

"Of course," Andrea said, and the expression on her face seemed to indicate she was trying to be serious and professional, but wasn't quite able to hide her continuing excitement and triumph about her falcon shift.

Quiet Tim surprised Selena with his next request. "Since it sounds like we'll be busy at night from now on, at least some of the time, and we can't shift again now, is it okay if we have just one more little party tonight?" He looked at Owen. "It'll help in our cover here as temporary visitors. We'll need to come up with a good story about why we're not partying for a while— nighttime hikes or stargazing in the mountains or whatever—and we can mention that at the bar tonight, just in case anyone's paying attention to us." He sounded rational—and eager.

Selena wasn't surprised at Owen's response. "You make a good case for having some fun tonight, Tim," he said. "Anyone else up for it?"

He looked at her, even as his CAs all issued positive responses. She felt a flush of discomfort redden her face, even as she glanced toward Patrick, then her other Alpha Force comrades. None objected, and she couldn't think of a reason to deny the CAs a final evening of fun before their work notched up to a new level.

"Good idea," she added to the replies.

Good idea or bad, Owen looked forward to what could possibly be their final bar outing while in West Columbia. After all, it might be the final opportunity for fun around here for at least a while. If all went well, his team would learn how to conduct its necessary operations over the next few days and nights, and then they'd finally be deployed for the field assignment for which they had been recruited.

No more partying.

Which would probably be a great idea. If he continued to see Selena only in training ops, maybe he would stop thinking about her in anything but her official role here, as an instructional officer for his shifting CAs.

Entering his hotel room back in town, he dialed his commanding officer for an update on the kidnapping situation.

"Dewirter? Glad you called." Creay's voice sounded tense. "I was about to text you to call me whenever you could, since I didn't know what you might be engaged in at the moment."

"Is there any news I should know about?" Owen studied the wall in front of him as though he could view the faceless, nameless kidnappers. He wanted to strangle them. Did he love billionaires? Not particularly, but he loved his country. And he hated anyone who would harm another person for greed or any other reason.

"Rene Brodheureux received another ransom note. It pretty well followed the last one, nothing new, just a reminder that he has only another four days to pay or his wife will be toast." A pause, then Creay continued, "So how are things going with you?"

"In other words, what's my timing? Things are progressing well, but I'll need at least another couple of days before we can deploy." Owen purposely kept his comments general. Not that he believed anyone was monitoring his calls or Creay's, but he wasn't taking any chances.

"Just keep it moving," Creay said. "Fast. And keep me informed."

"Got it," Owen said. "I'll be in touch again soon."

"Real soon," his boss responded. Then Anthony ended their connection.

Good thing Owen had a party to prepare for, he thought. Otherwise he might focus on the implied criticism from his commanding officer.

Things were progressing, on his part, at a fair speed. He knew that pushing his new recruits any faster wouldn't necessarily make them perform better. In fact, it might discombobulate them enough to send them into a tailspin. He wouldn't do anything that would hamper their ability to do what was asked of them: act like the wild animals they sometimes were, at different times and in different ways than they ever had before.

Good thing they were given clear instructions along with the elixir that allowed them to change better.

Instructions largely from Selena Jennay.

Whom Owen looked forward to seeing again tonight. Partying with…for the last time.

While back in her room a short while later, Selena decided to drive herself to the Yukon Bar that evening. She suspected she wouldn't want to stay as long as the rest of the Alpha Force members. And fortunately, Jonas had rented a second car for the convenience of the Alpha Force members, setting things up so that any of them could drive it when necessary. She called him to make sure her using it that night was okay. It was.

"Is that okay with you, too?" she asked Lupe. Her cover dog wagged her tail as Selena patted her head. She'd feed Lupe now, in any case.

Selena decided to wear one of the few dresses she had brought along on this trip. She'd needed them as part of her cover on her last assignment before she had been told to head to Canada. She hadn't really anticipated having to get dressed up while instructing the CAs about what they needed to know as flexible shifters. Nor had she figured she would wear the camos she wore while on duty at the Alpha Force headquarters at Ft. Lukman on Maryland's Eastern Shore. Instead, she'd spent the past few days in casual civilian clothing. Getting dressed up tonight would be a bit of a treat. She selected her black, knee-length dress that had a silky gray jacket that would fight off the after-darkness chill. It was one of her favorite outfits.

She put it on, then quickly checked her hair and makeup. She wanted to look okay, but the idea was just to be one of the partying gang tonight. She had no intention of trying to look especially good for this group. Not even for Owen. Especially not for Owen. Even if

Linda O. Johnston 125

she felt some attraction toward the man, she certainly didn't want to appear as if she was coming on to him. That would be unacceptable in so many ways.

A short while later, she exited her room with Lupe and met up with the rest of the Alpha Force members, who were congregating in the kitchen.

"Ready to go?" Patrick asked.

"Sure." But Selena let him and the others know she didn't expect to stay long so she was going on her own.

She shut Lupe in the kitchen, then invited Rainey to ride with her into town.

"You look good," her aide said as she slipped into the passenger seat. "You planning on having some extra fun tonight with Owen?"

Good thing Selena was already driving. Otherwise, she might have slunk beneath the seat. As it was, she felt her face redden. "No," she said. "I'm not."

"Well, in case you change your mind, it's fine. You know I'll always take care of Lupe if you happen not to be around. I'll cover for you, too. Say that you wanted a night somewhere nearby on your own before things get more intense tomorrow, whatever."

The car had reached the bottom of the driveway. Selena considered confronting her sassy, sweet aide and telling her that her duties didn't include such impossible silliness—and that she was being awfully presumptuous about Selena's supposed interest in the RCMP leader.

Instead, she realized she appreciated Rainey's promise to go the extra mile for her, even when it was unnecessary.

"That's very nice of you," she said, turning to look at Rainey before heading onto the road. She hadn't paid particular attention to what Rainey was wearing before, but now she noticed that her aide had put on a nice dress, too. Her dark hair seemed even curlier than usual, and she wore more makeup. "But are you the one who has other plans for the evening?"

"Not at all. But I'm like you. I wanted to make some men in our group notice that female Alpha Force members are a force to be reckoned with on their own, too."

Selena laughed. "You'll do a great job with that," she said.

"So will you," said Rainey. "And if you happen to change your mind, you won't even need to tell me about it. I've seen the way Owen looks at you. And your looks back at him? Well, like I said, you don't need to tell me if you change your mind."

Selena found a parking spot about a block from the bar. She and Rainey strode quickly along the barely occupied sidewalks, and Selena was glad to notice the CAs arriving at the door at the same time from the other direction. She didn't see Owen with them, though.

"Hi, you two," Sal said, a huge smile on his face. "I'm ready to party. How about you?"

"Fine with me," Rainey said, pulling ahead of Selena and latching on to Sal's arm.

The other two male CAs waited politely for Selena to enter with Andrea in front of them. The moment she stepped inside, Selena saw that three tables had been pushed together in the center of the room once more. She didn't see Owen there, either. But someone familiar sat on one of the tall stools—Holly. She must have come early to claim their spot.

One of the servers Selena had also seen here before stood right beside Holly. He was a tall guy in a plaid shirt and dark pants like all of them, but with long, light hair that didn't quite conceal his large ears. Holly was looking straight up into his face wearing what appeared to Selena to be a sincere yet flirtatious expression, and neither appeared to notice that the CAs had entered the room.

They didn't seem to notice anything else around them in the bar's dim light, for that matter.

Selena felt, as well as saw, Craig move quickly from behind the group and practically fly around the other crowded tables until he, too, stood beside Holly.

Wondering whether there was going to be some kind of unwelcome confrontation, Selena glanced toward Rainey, and they both turned and hurried to join Craig with the others.

"Hi, Holly." Craig's tone was calm, but he butted up against her side, put his arm around her and regarded the server belligerently. Selena could almost feel his feral wolf nature.

"Oh, Craig, I'm so glad you're here," Holly said, almost gushing. "Boyd and I were just talking about how much fun it is to sightsee around here, especially if you like hiking. There are some trails with spectacular views, and I'd love to visit them with you. We could hire Boyd as a guide, you know." She angled her head now to share a quick kiss with Craig.

Selena hadn't only been watching Craig's reaction. She had wondered how the server—Boyd—would react to having the woman he seemed to have been flirting with do a complete reversal now that her boyfriend had appeared.

At first, Boyd's light brows had risen as if in complete bewilderment about what was happening. But was that real?

Apparently not. Those brows lowered, and his expression became friendly, like a server who wanted a substantial tip. "Right," Boyd responded. "Holly and I have talked about this before. I could show her, and the rest of you, a whole lot of fun things about West Columbia. I know you've got a group visiting here. How long will you be in town?"

Instead of Craig, it was Patrick who answered.

"Unsure so far," he said. He and the rest of the Alpha Force members had just walked in and joined this group, making Selena feel relieved. Her CO was in charge once more, as it should be. "But we'll keep your offer in mind. Now, I'd really like a bottle of that locally brewed Canadian red ale I tried the other night." He looked straight at the server, who nodded.

"I'd like to try it, too," Selena added, and she was glad to see Boyd remove a pad of paper from the pocket in his leather belt and start making notes.

"Gin and tonic," said Craig, sitting down on the stool beside Holly. "Lots of gin. And I'd like it fast." The look he directed toward Boyd was clearly designed to put the server back in his place.

"Right away," Boyd said. "As soon as I get everyone else's orders." His expression was a touch less friendly than before, but Selena felt fairly comfortable that the confrontation had ended.

"Hi, sorry I'm a little late," said a deep and very welcome voice from beside Selena. "I had to respond to a couple of phone calls."

Fortunately, the stool beside Selena had remained empty. Or maybe the others knew where Owen would want to sit. In any event, he slid onto the stool and leaned forward on the table. "I'd like whatever she's having," he told Boyd.

"Let the party begin," responded Selena.

Chapter 12

Owen wasn't happy that he'd missed the earlier interplay between Craig and the server. It was now being
whispered about around the table. He heard the comments, despite the noise in the bar and the fact that his
hearing was the ordinary sort that mortals had, unlike
some of those around him.

He listened closely. He needed to know and understand all the interactions between those in his command
and anyone else they spoke with around here, both to
understand who they were and for the security of their
operation.

He considered ordering Craig to send his girlfriend
back home, or at least away from West Columbia, but
that wouldn't improve his relationship with Craig or even
the other CAs.

Sal might even start to worry that Owen was about
to order Yvanne out of here. The young CA might still
follow rules, but he would undoubtedly feel resentful.
Or at least that was the impression Owen now had of
the eager yet somewhat moody kid. And that might affect his ability to do his job.

Plus, after this encounter, such a move might wind up

making the townsfolk—especially this server—wonder who they actually were if no one around here could interact with them except on a business basis.

As Owen shifted on his stool beside Selena and began nursing his beer, he stayed quiet, watching, listening, thinking—and wondering how things would go tomorrow, when they got down to serious business.

Shapeshifting business. Shapeshifting business that would ultimately help achieve highly important RCMP goals.

Shapeshifting as part of the RCMP. If he'd even considered such a possibility as recently as a few months ago, he'd have thought he was going nuts.

Maybe he actually was—especially since one of those shifters in particular fascinated him, despite all his good sense telling him to back far off.

As he sat there, Yvanne joined them, taking a seat near her brother.

"How did you happen to book rooms in the hotel where we're staying here in West Columbia?" That was Holly talking to Craig, apparently on a subject other than her flirtation or what else might have been going on around here. "It's such a nice place for this town. I mean, there are other good places, but I especially like ours."

Eavesdropping could be interesting, Owen thought. Was this an attempt at seduction, to get the guy with whom she might still need to make peace leave the party with her and go screw in the nice hotel room she shared with Yvanne?

Maybe. Owen didn't look toward her to see whether her expression said even more than her words.

But beside him, Selena made a noise that sounded

half like laughter and half like disgust. Owen turned to see her shaking her head.

Why did that reaction, so similar to what he felt, too, make her seem so sexy?

Or at this point, maybe everything about her seemed sexy to him. He took another sip of his beer, then turned to her.

"How about you? Do you like your quarters here?" he asked her, loudly enough for others to hear.

"They're quite nice," she said. "I'm sure that anyone who moves in there will like them a lot."

Good girl. She was saying something that the CAs would understand—that they soon would move into the residential part of their headquarters, once they'd learned all they needed to from the Alpha Force members. But she said it in a way that anyone listening in would not understand.

"And you?" she continued. "I understand you're staying here in town all by yourself, in a different hotel. Guess you're not as friendly a tourist as you seem." Her amber eyes captured his as if in challenge. One he enjoyed.

"Friendly? Me? Heck, yes. But that doesn't mean I don't want my own space, too."

Space he wouldn't mind sharing with her, under other circumstances. The way her skirt barely seemed to cover her thighs despite the prim way she sat with her legs together on that bar stool underscored his inappropriate interest in her. He couldn't help but notice that she even wore dressy heels instead of the athletic shoes or military boots she'd worn around him before.

Sexy.

All the more reason for him to have space of his own,

where he could retreat not only from those under his command, but also away from Selena.

Not now, though. He let his eyes alight on her as he continued to nurse his beer and glance around the crowded bar, listening to both the Alpha Force members and CAs around him make small talk, as they were supposed to: tourist stuff and how good their beers and other drinks were and why they preferred the Yukon Bar over the town's other drinking establishments.

Every once in a while he joined in the conversation, offering a platitude or general comment that meant nothing but added to their pretense.

He actually enjoyed it, and it appeared that the others did, too. Even Craig and Holly seemed to settle down and return to the same kind of flirting Owen had seen between them previously. That was a good thing.

So was his eye contact with Selena.

Lord, was she beautiful, especially now, all dressed up for the evening out. Her light brown hair was loose, framing her smooth and perfect face. She seemed to be teasing him without saying a word, shooting glances toward him with those intense amber eyes.

What was she really thinking?

Was she goading him nonverbally about the fact that his charges had now shifted during daylight, that they would do even more tomorrow and in the following days so they could accomplish their mission?

Or more likely, about the fact that she, too, was a shifter?

"Everything okay with you?" she finally asked him in a low voice. "You look like you're thinking a lot."

"In other words, I'm not entering into the conversations?"

"Exactly." She smiled. "Care to talk about the weather? Or what's on TV tonight?"

"Not really. How about you? Care to talk about how much you're enjoying visiting Canada?"

"Absolutely!" She seemed to beam and in fact did start describing things she liked about this country—its coolness, the friendliness of its citizens, the remoteness and beauty of some of its towns and countryside.

She stopped after a while. "Your eyes are glazing over."

"I'm enjoying what you're saying, but I'm actually quite tired. And as we've all said, tomorrow's going to be a big day."

Her expression grew sober. "Yes," she said. "It is."

"In fact, as much as I'm enjoying myself, I think I will become a party pooper and head back to my hotel." He stood, hoping his departure would in fact inspire the others to take their leave. "Good night, everyone. See you all bright and early tomorrow."

"Good night, Owen," Selena said as he started to walk away. "Sleep well."

Selena meant it. She hoped Owen would sleep well that night.

She doubted she would.

Yes, the first really major step of teaching the CAs what they needed to know had been accomplished that day. But what would evolve over the next days would be even more important to their assignment.

Her training plans would potentially keep her awake.

So would her darned attraction to Owen. She'd already been wondering what he really thought of her.

Apparently he found shifters intriguing on some level—most likely only professionally, not personally.

That was okay. Or it should be. But in actuality...?

No matter. The fact that her most private human areas warmed and ached when he was around was irrelevant.

But she was curious about him on that personal level. Heck, she even just wanted to know where he was staying, what kind of place he had chosen to remain far from his own subordinates as well as the Alpha Force members.

She'd had enough to drink. She'd had enough talking and bantering and pretending to enjoy the party that would be this group's last—at least the last any Alpha Force members would attend.

It was time to leave.

It was only minutes after Owen had left. She had an idea. A dumb one, yes, but it would help to satisfy her curiosity.

It would potentially even help her sleep that night.

She stood, raised her hands into the air as she stretched and looked around at her coworkers. "Hey, everyone. I'm tired. And like Owen said, there's a lot we're going to do and see tomorrow. I'm going to leave, too. Anyone care to join me?"

She glanced at Rainey. Her aide had been busy chatting with Tim and Sal and Yvanne. Rainey looked at her and gave a small, catlike smile as if she assumed Selena had things on her mind besides heading to the compound to sleep.

Which she did, but not the one Rainey probably thought: seducing Owen. Although the idea did hold a lot of appeal...

But no. What she really wanted was to learn where

Owen was staying. And then she would return to her room—and to Lupe—and go to sleep.

"Okay," she said. "I don't see any takers. I'll see you all tomorrow morning." Then she left.

The sidewalk outside was dimly lit, but she nevertheless saw Owen walking briskly about a block away, in the opposite direction from where the CAs' hotel was.

This was dumb, she thought. But he hadn't told her where he was staying, and she wanted to know.

Carefully, staying in the shadows, she followed him. She needed to keep him within her vision, yet not allow him to see her.

There were at least a couple of small hotels down this street, plus a bed-and-breakfast or two. She'd just watch to see where he turned to go inside and then she'd come back here for her car. An easy plan. What could go wrong?

Owen liked the briskness of the air as he strolled toward the WestColum Hotel, a small, independent place that was a little more elite than the chain hotel where his subordinates were staying. Fortunately, it wasn't much more expensive, and he was paying the difference in price to avoid any issues later.

He was about a block away when he felt someone following him.

He wished, for that moment only, that he had some of those enhanced senses that shapeshifters supposedly had—hearing, for one. He believed he heard footsteps occasionally, but when he stopped, so did they.

He considered turning and looking around but felt foolish. And if he was actually right, that would tell whoever was following him that he knew.

No, he waited and walked…until he reached the outside of his hotel. Then he opened the door to the lobby and slipped inside.

And hurried around to leave through a side door.

Outside again, he waited in shadows.

Sure enough, someone had been following him. Selena.

She stopped on the sidewalk and folded her arms in front of her lovely, curvaceous chest, apparently taking in the exterior of the lobby's building.

Then she pivoted and started to walk away.

That was when Owen made his move. He jumped out at her and pulled her toward the building, into the shadows.

"Okay, Owen, enough," she said immediately. "Did you think I didn't hear or smell you there? Why did you come back outside so fast?"

"Because I knew you were there and I wanted to catch you."

"Why?" she demanded.

"This is why," he replied, and then he pulled her tightly into his arms, lowered his mouth and kissed her.

This wasn't why she had been following him—was it?

Selena could no longer think. All of her consciousness, her being, was drawn into the feel of Owen's hard, hot body against her, his lips moving against hers, tasting and teasing her to open her mouth by pushing gently with his tongue.

She could do nothing but obey.

After a minute that seemed like an eternity, though, she realized that very sexy mouth of his was speaking against hers. "Come inside," he said. "We have no privacy here."

Another bad idea, she knew, yet what could she do but follow him inside? Running off held no appeal.

Owen held all the appeal around here.

When he pulled away, she felt bereft but held his hand tightly when he grasped hers. He used a key card to open the door.

He led her through the lobby and into the elevator. As soon as the door closed, she found herself in his arms, his mouth on hers, involved in a kiss that was like no others she had ever experienced.

A short kiss, though. The door opened again on the second floor.

The hallway was bright and not particularly long. Owen took her hand once more and led her past only a few doors. He used a card again to open the door to room 211. She glimpsed that number for only a second before she was inside the room, the door closed behind her.

The dim light of the tiny entry area was the only light in the room. In it she could see the king-size bed, the typical TV facing it, a desk against the wall...

But it was the bed that garnered her attention. Some of her attention, at least. The rest was focused on Owen, who suddenly pulled her into his arms once more.

"Selena," he whispered against her lips. But that was all he said as his hands began stroking her back. The dress she wore had seemed attractive enough and not especially obtrusive before. Now she wondered how fast it could be removed.

But Owen didn't try. Not yet. Instead, he bent enough to touch the backs of her bare legs, the feeling of flesh on flesh making her moan with desire.

Oh, this was a bad idea. They were professional colleagues, both with official missions to accomplish.

But, oh, it was a wonderful idea. She wanted more.

She wanted Owen.

She felt his fingers trail up her legs, over her derriere, up her back. Was he looking for a zipper? She almost smiled against his mouth. He'd have to back away at least a little to get the dress off. It buttoned up the front.

Meantime, she could start undressing him. But first she wanted to tease him a little. Only a very little since she was already starting to become impatient.

She pressed herself against him, feeling his hardness at stomach level. She wriggled just a bit to get his attention.

"Selena," he said again, this time louder, in a more ragged voice.

"Yes, Owen," she managed to say, moving her hand around to latch on to his buttocks, squeeze them and pull him even closer.

Oh, heavens, she wanted him. And this was taking much too long.

She refused to think any more about how bad an idea sex was with a professional colleague—and a nonshifter. Despite how his arms enfolded her, she stepped back and looked at him as much as she could beneath the dim light.

His gaze was hot. So hot. Those blue eyes of his were molten, his mouth swollen and enticing, his breathing fast.

Selena quickly began doing what she wanted, what she needed. She reached toward him and began unfastening the buttons of his shirt—from the bottom up. That allowed her hands to drop just a bit and press against the hardness beneath his dark slacks.

The feeling, even in her fingertips, made her moan, and she hurried to undress him with trembling hands.

Owen began undoing her buttons as well. His hands on her—first skimming over her breasts, then taking hold of them—left her gasping, and she tried to hurry even more.

Somehow, in mere seconds that somehow felt like days later, Selena realized she was nude—and Owen was close. His shirt and pants were on the floor, but he still wore his shorts. They extended out in front of him enticingly, and she wanted to see, not just feel, the erection they hid.

She moved toward him just as he, too, reached for the last item he wore, and suddenly he was naked.

And gorgeous. Selena had visualized in her mind how he would look, all muscles and sinew, plus a male member that was large and erect and altogether alluring.

"Come here," he whispered, even as he began to touch her most sensitive sensual areas and lead her onto the bed.

She lay down facing him, touching him, squeezing him and pumping gently for her own benefit. He clearly needed no further arousal.

His head bent, and she felt him licking, then sucking at her bared breasts. "Owen." Her voice was husky and needy—and then he pulled away. "Owen," she repeated—and then realized he was moving not completely away from the bed but reaching down to the floor, where he pulled his wallet from his slacks.

He pulled a condom from inside the wallet. Oh, this man wasn't merely sexy. He was responsible.

And she wanted him. Now.

"Let me," she whispered to him. She felt the heat and shakiness of his fingers as, smiling as he returned to face her upon the bed, he handed the condom to her.

She needed no help at all unwrapping it and placing it over his swollen, sexy, captivating member. As she finished, she didn't need to tell him he was ready. He gently laid her back, pulled her legs apart, touched and stroked her there again as if to ensure her moistness, and then he entered her in one slow, enticing motion.

"Selena," he said softly as he began pumping gently at first. "Are you—"

She didn't let him finish, covering his mouth with hers even as she again grabbed at his now-bare buttocks, as if guiding and encouraging him despite his clearly not needing any help.

She reveled in the feel of him inside her, breathing harder with each increasing stroke.

Hearing a loud gasp from Owen, she gave a small scream of her own and followed him over the edge.

Chapter 13

Owen didn't move for a long while. He wasn't sure he could. His energy had been expended in an amazing, earth-moving way.

His head was on a pillow now, and Selena's was pressed into his neck. Her entire naked body remained against his, and he timed his breathing to coincide with hers, fast at first and gradually slowing.

Could he speak? What could he—should he—say now?

And if he moved, would his erection stiffen once more? Even sated as he was, he still found Selena incredibly, enticingly sexy.

She seemed all human now. Did she ever! But he knew her senses were sharper than his. Was what they shared somehow different for her? He couldn't imagine how that might be—such amazing sex even stronger and more intense?

What he had felt had been incredible. Something he would never, ever forget. And would always want to experience again.

Yet would he?

At the moment, he glanced her way and wondered

whether their bareness was uncomfortable to Selena, either because she might feel chilly as her body cooled after their fantastic exercise, or because she might feel uncomfortable with his heated gaze on her lovely, curvaceous and utterly sexy body. "Do you feel okay?" he managed to ask in a raspy voice. "I mean, would you like me to put the covers over us?"

She moved back from him just a little, making him feel a bit odd. "I'm fine, but if you're chilly, I have an idea about how to warm you up." Her voice was a bit hoarse, too, yet it managed to sound teasing.

Did she mean what he thought she did?

As her eyes moved from his, down his body, stopping at his now-relaxed erection, he began to grow stiff again. Really stiff. "I think you're succeeding already," he said.

She laughed, then reached for the body part that gave his feelings away. He drew in his breath as she began stroking it again.

"Hey, you're giving me some good ideas," he said, knowing his eyes were half-closed in ecstasy.

"Then why don't you act on them?" she said.

And he did.

This time, when their lovemaking had ended, Selena found herself unable to concentrate simply on the sensations she had experienced and reveled in.

She inhaled Owen's tangy, salty, all-human-male scent once more. She listened to his deep breathing, thought about how delicious he had tasted as their mouths had met and as she had subsequently kissed other parts of his body.

Clearly, now that they'd stopped for a while and Owen did in fact cover them both with the blanket, she couldn't keep her mind from thinking, rehashing…and wondering.

What would come next? They still had to work together. She still had to help him get his recruits ready for a very important, very covert assignment.

He hadn't mentioned that tonight, but it was surely on his mind—or would soon be again.

So would her similarities to those people, her differences from him. She was a shapeshifter. He was not.

They had made love together, a mutual decision. But now what?

She could not think of this as a bad idea. Not now. Not ever. And yet, it had surely been a once-in-a-lifetime event.

Things were changing tomorrow with the CAs, growing more definite, more intense. She and the other Alpha Force members wouldn't have much longer to work with the CAs before they had to go and fulfill their assignment. And then Alpha Force's job here was done.

As her time with Owen would be done.

That meant she had better make the most of this situation right now, while she could.

Had he been sated? In case not, she shifted beneath the blanket so that she wasn't merely against him, absorbing his body heat. No, she reached for the sexiest part of his body once more.

"Mmm." He clearly was still awake, too. "That feels good."

"Want to feel even better?" Selena asked. She drew in her breath as his hands started moving over her body again, too.

"Sure," he said. "Do you?"

* * *

This time, after yet another bout of incredible love-making, Selena slept. She wasn't sure for how long, but she pulled herself awake.

What time was it?

She couldn't stay here all night. Even though Rainey had promised to take care of Lupe, Selena didn't want to face the other Alpha Force members as she walked in the house in the morning. They'd ask questions she wouldn't want to answer—unless they made correct assumptions, which could be even worse.

Carefully, hoping not to wake Owen, she slid away from him and out from under the covers.

"Selena? You okay?"

"Fine, but I didn't mean to wake you. I need to go back to headquarters. It'd be... Well, it wouldn't be a good thing for anyone to suspect we did what we did. Not while we need to work together."

He didn't say anything at first, but in the dim light she saw him rise, too.

Lord, but he was gorgeous, still nude, with his male member at rest.

She couldn't keep looking at him, though, or she would never want to leave.

"I guess you're right," he said. "I'll drive you back there."

"I left my car near the Yukon Bar," she said. "I can just walk there."

"Not at this hour. Like I said, I'll drive you."

She didn't argue. He had already proved he was a nice guy, a gentleman, as well as possibly the sexiest man on earth. Selena was glad she'd experienced what she had with him.

They both got dressed nearly wordlessly. Selena looked around in the hotel's hallway as they exited his room. No one was there to observe them.

In his car a few minutes later, Owen said to her, "I realize that what we did might not be fully acceptable to our respective employers so we'd best not talk about it—even though I've got an urge to shout about it."

"And we both know how compelling your urges can be," Selena said with a laugh. "No, you're right. That's what I've been thinking, too. But, Owen?"

"Yeah?"

"I really had a wonderful time tonight. I thank you for that experience. I'll never forget it."

"That sounds like you're saying 'Goodbye, it's been real, but it'll never happen again.'"

"I don't know how it could, given our respective positions and how we have to work together." Selena was saying what she had to, but it hurt. She wished she could promise, or even suggest, otherwise.

He pulled his car to the curb right behind her rental. When she reached for the door handle, he bent toward her and grabbed her arm, holding it gently. "Never say never, Selena," he said. "Maybe when this is all over and that kidnapping victim is rescued and the abductors incarcerated, we can get together to celebrate—without the burden of everyone and everything else getting in the way."

"*Maybe* is a good word," she said. "Thanks again, Owen." She opened the door and flicked the key to unlock the rental car so she could drive away at last.

It didn't take Selena long to return to headquarters. Although one small outdoor lamp was lit over the doorway—*Thanks, Rainey*, Selena thought—she saw no lights on inside either building, which was a good thing. Maybe everyone was asleep.

She opened and closed the car door as quietly as possible, not wanting to awaken anyone.

As she had the previous night, she inhaled to see if she could identify any local wildlife that emerged after dark. The same kind of rodent scents were around. Avian, too.

And...was that a lingering human scent as well? Too bad she wasn't shifted to see if she could be certain about it with her enhanced senses and identify whose it might be. She didn't recognize it as one of the Alpha Force members, so it had to be one of the CAs. There was something else about it as well that bothered her a bit. A hint of sharpness to it?

She was probably just tired, maybe focusing on stuff that wasn't real, or wasn't important if it was real. She'd mention it to Patrick in the morning, though, just in case.

Quietly she entered the Alpha Force residence, hoping that Lupe wouldn't start barking like a watchdog. She was well trained, as were all the unit's cover dogs, but she was still a canine whose instincts included protecting the people around her.

Selena detected no noise, fortunately—not until she pulled out a small flashlight from her purse for illumination, walked past the living room and kitchen and headed toward her temporary living quarters. She heard scrabbling nails on the hardwood floor of her room and grinned.

Lupe was being a very good girl, but she had heard her human's arrival.

When Selena opened the door and knelt down, her

arms were suddenly full of the fur of a combined wolf-husky, and her face was dampened with doggy kisses.

"Hi, girl," she whispered. "It's great to see you, too. Want to go out for a minute?" She quickly located Lupe's leash—where Rainey must have left it—looped over the doorknob to the hallway. She attached it to Lupe's collar and they headed back in the direction from which Selena had come.

Outside, Lupe stopped on the porch, her ears raised, her nose in the air as if she was doing what Selena had—but with a lot more skill, with her all-canine senses. She gave a small whine. Was she interested in chasing a mole or whatever other rodent happened to be around?

Or was it something else? Did she also sense that a human had been out here? Was that person still here? If so, there was no indication—no car or light or movement except for the light breeze in the air. And Lupe didn't seem particularly upset, even if she did smell something.

Could Owen have followed her here to ensure she got back all right? It was something he would do, yet he wouldn't have preceded her here—and the first time she perceived the scent was when she had first gotten out of her car. That couldn't have been him.

It was probably nothing. Selena was just overly emotional considering her job here—and the fact she'd just engaged in the most mind-blowing sex in her life.

"Let's go back inside and get to bed," she told Lupe, who had just squatted to relieve herself, and they headed inside.

Owen didn't have to show up for breakfast at the residences that would become his CAs' local headquarters, he thought early the next morning as he exited his hotel. It was entirely his choice.

As he got into his car he remembered that the last time he'd been inside the vehicle, he hadn't been alone. Selena had been with him.

As if he could have forgotten that or anything else about last night.

He pulled out of the parking lot, heading through the now-awakening town toward the CAs HQ. He knew there would still be plenty of fixings for breakfast there, including coffee. There was no place else he would rather eat.

He thought about the day ahead. Since their next exercise wasn't scheduled until late afternoon, he'd allowed his recruits to sleep in. Later on, there'd be an informal Q&A and a general rap session with the CAs about how it had been growing up as shifters and more. A lot of that had come out in their vetting before they'd been invited to become CAs, but Owen hadn't been fully involved in that process, so not everything might have been passed along.

Plus, to work together later without the kind of assistance and supervision they were being provided now by Alpha Force, they should have full awareness of each other's backgrounds.

This was his ostensible reason for showing up early.

His real reason? To be in Selena's presence again. Not that he would even hint about their delightful evening. He just wanted to see her as much as possible while he could.

He arrived and parked and knocked on the door. Rainey answered. "Come on in. Are you here for breakfast? It's cooking right now. Selena got it started early, even though she seemed tired. She said she didn't sleep well last night." The smirk she wore suggested she knew why Selena hadn't gotten a full night's sleep. Would Selena have told her aide about where she'd been, or was Rainey only guessing? Knowing Selena's attitude, as well as her sense of discretion, Owen figured it was the latter.

"Thanks." He followed Rainey down the hall toward the kitchen, but was disappointed not to see Selena there. Marshall stood at the stove, with Jonas beside him.

"She's talking with Patrick in the other room," Rainey said, as if hearing the question in his mind.

"Who? Selena?" He didn't want to acknowledge that he was looking for her. At Rainey's nod he asked, "Anything I can do to help in here?"

"Yeah. Sit down and stay out of the way and stop moping. She'll join us here in a few." Rainey pranced toward the stove and took her place at Marshall's side.

If he was that obvious, Owen thought, he'd better stay far, far away from Selena—especially today.

"It was probably nothing, but I wanted to tell you about that scent last night." Selena had asked Patrick to come into her bedroom to talk so their conversation could remain private. "Since I wasn't shifted, I couldn't tell much about it, but it did seem human."

They stood beside the closed door and Patrick leaned on it. Her CO, in addition to being a high-ranking member of Alpha Force, was a medical doctor, a nice guy and a happily married man. She had heard about how he had come to marry Mariah, who was a noted wildlife reporter. Mariah was off on her own research study now, so Patrick apparently didn't mind being away from home.

"Our circumstances will be different tonight," Patrick said with a worried frown. "We won't be able to repeat your late-night walk around the place. You were just walking Lupe then?"

"More or less. I didn't get to sleep immediately." She left it at that. He didn't need to know that she'd been up and about and elsewhere at the time she would otherwise have gotten to sleep. And—oh, yes—having the best sex of her life.

"Would you recognize that scent again?"

She shook her head slightly. "I'm not sure. It probably was nothing, but I know it's important that who we are and what we're doing here remains covert."

"Absolutely. Well, I'll let all the other Alpha Force members know what you've said and make sure they remain alert. Thanks for letting me know."

"Of course, sir." Even though Alpha Force was a fairly informal unit because of its special nature, she gave him a regular military salute. He laughed and saluted back. "Now, let's go have some breakfast," she said.

Selena preceded Patrick back down the hall to the kitchen. She smelled the sausage and bacon that she had started cooking—good dishes for people with canine aspects to them that made them appreciate meats.

She entered the kitchen's doorway and stopped abruptly as she nearly walked straight into Owen.

Oh, she wouldn't mind feeling that hard body of his against her once more, even this soon. Especially this soon. But it couldn't happen again—and most particularly it couldn't happen when they weren't alone.

"Good morning," she said, taking a step back. "I

didn't realize that any of the CAs would be joining us this early." Good. She sounded cool and professional and totally disinterested. She hoped.

"I woke up early." He looked down at her with only the slightest twist of his mouth that suggested a smile. "Lots on my mind. As far as the other CAs, I told them they might want to sleep in since things are going to get busy later today."

"Well, glad you could make it." That was Patrick, who remained behind Selena. "Maybe we can go over how we want to handle things later. I've got some ideas that could work well to ensure that your guys jump right into their shifts independently—and move things along even more quickly on their mission."

"Great!" Owen truly was smiling now. "The sooner we get them going, the sooner we'll catch these kidnappers and let you Alpha Force people return to your own post."

Selena was certain Owen's words were intended to make the members of Alpha Force feel good—Patrick, at least. And maybe the others.

Well, it should make her feel good, too. It would mean she had fulfilled her own duties here, in Canada. She could go back to Ft. Lukman with her mind clear, ready to take on her next assignment back in the States.

But even so, as she moved past Owen to enter the kitchen, she wished that the mug of coffee she poured for herself had something stronger in it, despite the time of day.

Something that could help her forget her feelings and move on.

Chapter 14

They sat around the nice-sized dining table—the Alpha Force team, plus Owen, with Lupe on the floor.

Selena pretended to enjoy her well-made omelet with its meats and cheeses. It did, in fact, taste good. If she'd only been hungry, she would have liked it even more.

She gave occasional bites to Lupe, who was clearly happy about it.

As her team discussed the training with Owen, she just sat there at first, picking at her food and drinking her coffee, listening. And only glancing now and then toward Owen to show interest and politeness.

She purposely kept off her face any indication of what had occurred last night—and her misgivings about what would happen now between them, even though the answer was indisputable. Nothing.

But her emotions were in an uproar. That caused her to think too much about her last relationship, such as it had been, in which her lover had told his son that shapeshifters weren't real and the whole idea was stupid.

Owen knew they were real, and he needed to use shifters in his position with the RCMP. But what did he actually think of them, deep inside?

Especially now.

Not that they actually had a relationship. Not now and not ever.

Only sex…of the mind-blowing kind.

"Have any of you ever conducted this kind of operation before?" Owen was asking. "I mean, shifting first and then going to surveil an area?"

"I think we all have," Patrick said. "Sometimes we do that as an exercise, essentially spying on humans we don't want to notice us. Sometimes it's special-ops troops who are advised there's a covert military exercise going on near them to see if they can spot anything out of the ordinary and report it to their commanders. Sometimes it's in a regular civilian situation like an office building or a shopping center. But our kind of recon only works well if there are nearby wilderness areas or urban parklands known for containing wildlife."

Owen nodded. "I really want to start talking now about the information I'll need once my CAs start our mission."

"Fine. Let's go over it."

For the next hour or so, as the group finished breakfast, mostly Patrick and Owen talked, with the rest of the group chiming in as they had thoughts or suggestions.

That included Selena. Even though she was the least experienced Alpha Force member, she utilized both her educational and shifting backgrounds to try to anticipate the needs of the CAs.

"When I grew up in a remote location in Wisconsin," she said as they planned how CAs who had already shifted would do recon at the highly suspected area, "some friends and family members who were shifters did something similar, long before I engaged in Alpha

Force tasks after joining about six months ago. We had access to a forerunner of the current elixir, thanks to Major Drew Connell and his family also coming from the same area."

Trying not to be distracted by Owen's intense scrutiny of her as she spoke, she described how, for fun and not for security or rescue of anyone, they had tested their skills.

"We would start as far from the target of our exercise as possible while still being able to use our senses that were enhanced by our shifts. In other words, we stayed camouflaged in the woodlands or mountains while listening and using our olfactory senses to smell people or places or other animals."

She paused to take a sip of coffee, then continued, "We learned all we could before moving in to check things out further, assuming that was the goal of what we were doing. If any of us thought the situation too dangerous after that, or potentially so, had it been real, we all backed off—but usually only for a while, until the situation seemed to improve. Plus, we mostly spread out, avoiding each other's company in the interest of safety. Of course, what we were doing was just a game, so safety wasn't a real issue, but we had fun pretending."

"That's essentially how we do it now in Alpha Force maneuvers, too," Patrick agreed, "but safety is a genuine and vital concern. For your mission, just make sure that Andrea, while shifted to a falcon, is primed to circle somewhat low, or perched in trees to keep an eye on each of your wolf shifters. If a problem arises with one, she can use some prearranged signal to let the others know about it."

"And if a problem happens with all of them?" Owen asked.

"She should have another prearranged signal—as well as a way via the camera and other electronic equipment she'll be wearing to inform you and the other nonshifters on your team."

"The same should be arranged with the other shifters in the event Andrea's in trouble," Selena added.

"Absolutely," agreed Patrick.

Selena stood and got herself more coffee from the pot that remained on the kitchen counter.

Despite how little sleep she had gotten last night, she was certain that the adrenaline in her system from what she had done, and what this combined group was about to do, would keep her awake.

While she stood there, she listened to the conversation. She had no input into this part anyway. It was mostly about logistics—how and when the CA members could best be transported to the area and the best time for them to shift. They didn't yet have any aides to help in their shifting using the elixir, but that was under discussion. For now, Rainey and Jonas volunteered to help out since the timing here was so critical.

The Alpha Force members also stressed the idea of getting cover animals as apparent pets to the CAs in the future—ones who looked like them while shifted. The idea had been mentioned before, but Patrick clearly wanted to impress Owen with how useful cover animals could be. "That helps keep your unit's real purpose covert," he said. "Anyone who's met your team members and their apparent pets will most likely assume they're seeing those pets should they run into one of those members while shifted."

When that part of the discussion ended, Owen asked, "Okay, once we've got our CAs in and they've checked out the critical area and reported, via their cameras, how do we get them out? I assume we won't want to wait until they shift back. In case they're seen, it's better for them to remain in animal form, right?"

"Absolutely," Patrick said. "Especially since there are believed to be wolves and falcons in the area in question, it'll be a perfect cover for them. Once again, it's imperative that planning be spot-on. Make sure there's a meeting point fairly distant from your target area. Wolves can run fast to return there, and it should be second nature for a falcon to zoom in on the destination."

"Great," Owen said.

Selena was about to return to her seat at the table as he stood and walked toward her. Their eyes met, and he gave a small but impersonal smile. "Is there any more coffee?" he asked.

Wordlessly, she reached out for the pot and filled his cup, and they walked together back to the table. Selena hated keeping things so distant, so she said, "I'm sure I'm speaking for everyone here in Alpha Force when I say we're all cheering for you and your CAs and wish you success."

"Hear, hear!" Patrick said, and the other Alpha Force members added their good wishes as well.

The timing couldn't have been better, since there was a noise at the front entry and the rest of the CAs came in.

"Good morning, everyone," said Andrea, the first to enter.

"Is there any breakfast left?" asked Tim.

"Plenty," Rainey said. She rose and led the arriving CAs into the kitchen.

"So what are the plans for this afternoon?" Selena asked Owen. "What time will you have them shift on their own?"

"Probably three or four o'clock. In between, I want to meet with them here by myself, get the latest from my commander and pass it along, as well as discuss more RCMP protocol."

"That'll be fine," Patrick said. "In the meantime, we Alpha Force members will head back to the residence house and do some catch-up of our own."

After the CAs had joined him, Owen again emphasized how important their mission was. "If you're successful, I'm sure you'll have a fantastic career within the RCMP despite the secret nature of your unusual skills."

And if they weren't successful? He wasn't about to discuss that with them. There was no choice. They had to do their jobs, and do them well enough to capture the kidnappers and end their vicious operation forever, as well as to free the current victim unharmed—or as unharmed as possible.

They had to achieve the necessary result, but the world could never know exactly how they'd accomplished it. Secrecy was key. And if it took acquiring cover animals for each of the shifters, so be it.

Since he was in law enforcement, keeping things covert was simply part of his job.

"This is all so cool," Sal said as they discussed the logistics of how everything would be handled. Maybe being a shifter enhanced this young guy's appetite, since he had been nibbling on toast since the omelets had been finished.

Chunky Tim had not stopped eating, either. "You said

that the two Alpha Force aides would continue working with us for now. I thought that once we learned everything about shifting with their elixir, we'd buy a good supply of it from Alpha Force, and the RCMP would be on its own. We'd get our own aides to help in our shifts." He paused. "Maybe even you could do it for now."

Owen had considered it. Maybe, in the future, if he remained the officer in charge of the CAs, he would learn all he needed to and act in the capacity of an aide—or at least be prepared to do so in an emergency. But there wasn't time for him to learn everything right now.

Although Selena was one good teacher. She wasn't an aide, but she would certainly know what the aides did.

He wouldn't mind having her as his tutor in that or in anything else.

But he pushed that thought from his mind. Even if it was appropriate to consider, the circumstances and urgency did not make it feasible for now—if ever.

Craig spoke up. "Are there people in the RCMP, besides you and Deputy Commissioner Creay, who even believe in shifters and would be willing to step in and help that way?"

"We'll work that out in the future," Owen said, sidestepping the question. He wasn't yet certain how every detail would be handled, only that they would be—and it would be considered a lot more important if the CAs were successful on this mission.

They simply had to be.

Perhaps, for now, he should attempt to get at least one more person to act as an aide to help in the CAs shift.

Maybe not. Maybe he was just using the idea as an excuse to keep Selena nearby as this mission was carried out.

As if he had called her, Selena suddenly appeared in the kitchen doorway. She looked amazingly sexy even in her plain T-shirt and jeans—but maybe that was because his mind removed them as she stood there.

She glanced toward him. Did her complexion redden a little as if she read his thoughts, or was that just wishful thinking on his part?

What she said didn't reveal her thoughts to him, either. "I know it's a little early," she said, "but Patrick sent me. He suggested that you shifters get started now so you have more time to get used to not only your physical change, but your mental one, before it's time to go outside and work on your preparations there."

"Are all of you ready?" Owen asked.

"Definitely," said Andrea, and she was the first to rise.

Once again, Andrea went into the meeting house's study to shift, and the male CAs headed for the basement.

This time, though, only the two aides went with them.

So, once more, Selena was in the dining room, this time with Patrick, Marshall and Owen, along with Lupe.

"I guess this is something pretty different for all of you," Owen said. He sat with a bottle of water in front of him on the table, as they all did.

"How so?" Marshall asked. He looked tall even sitting down, and his thick brown hair appeared a little unkempt, possibly belying his composed attitude.

"If shifts are going on near you, I assume you're involved most of the time, either changing or helping, right?"

"You could say that," Patrick agreed. "But I think

we're all okay with doing what's appropriate for any situation. Right, guys?"

"Right," Selena agreed, as did the others. She aimed a glance that was slightly challenging toward Owen. "And you? How do you feel knowing there's a shift going on with your subordinates and you're not even invited to watch?"

"Surprisingly left out. But I look forward to seeing them all later. You, too?"

"Me, too," Selena concurred.

The conversation in the dining room was friendly after that, but no topic was found that engaged everyone.

That was fine with Selena. She didn't really want to talk. Instead she barely listened as the men around her talked sports—primarily football.

About half an hour later, she heard some activity in the hallway outside and saw a flash of dark feathers in the air.

Andrea's shift was complete.

The men near her rose.

"Shouldn't we wait for the wolf shifters?" Owen asked, although he stood, too.

"They should be here shortly," Patrick said. "Surprisingly, most shifts, no matter the species, tend to take around the same amount of time."

They stayed in the dining room, waiting. Within five minutes Selena heard the sound of muffled paw falls from the stairway to the basement.

There was another noise, too. The sound of gagging or retching. *Human* gagging or retching.

What was going on?

Two wolf-dogs entered the dining room and stood there, panting. They somehow looked confused.

Rainey and Jonas came into the room then, too, but they weren't alone. Sal was with them, unshifted. He retched again, although nothing came out.

Rainey's eyes were filled with tears. "Something's wrong with Sal."

Chapter 15

Owen paced the study at the back of the meeting house, telling himself that Alpha Force was experienced and knew what they should do for Sal.

But he couldn't stop worrying. His youngest recruit now lay on the pull-out sofa in that compact room moaning and sometimes gagging. Even though that house hadn't been designated as sleeping quarters, Owen had ensured that the rooms were furnished. This room contained a desk and, fortunately, a sofa that converted into a bed. The surface was covered with a sheet that Rainey had quickly retrieved from the other house. A wastebasket lined with a plastic bag sat on the floor nearby. Fortunately, though, Sal must have gotten everything inside him out already since he was no longer vomiting. But the youngster clearly felt lousy.

It didn't hurt that Patrick Worley happened to be a medical doctor. For humans, yes, but since he was a shifter, too, he had to know about how to cure others like him who were ill.

Owen had assisted in getting Sal to the room, where Patrick had conducted an initial exam on him. "Pulse rate high but probably okay," Patrick had said. "I need to get my bag out of my car to conduct a more thorough exam, although I wish we had some better facilities for this. Will you stay here with him for now?"

Owen had agreed and he was now waiting for Patrick's return. He knew Patrick had arrived here with some large crates in the back of his rented SUV—and that they contained a large supply of the Alpha Force shifting elixir. That had been part of the agreement between the US military and the RCMP—provision of an ample initial supply of that special, secret elixir. Considering that Patrick was a physician, it didn't surprise Owen that he had also brought a medical bag.

"How is he?" Selena's voice startled Owen, whose attention had remained primarily on the ill shifter on the bed. He looked up and saw her in the doorway, the expression on her lovely face as grim as he felt, her hands clasped in front of her.

"Not good. Or at least I don't think so, although Patrick's initial check didn't seem to indicate his life was in danger." That was what Owen hoped, at least, and he wasn't about to say otherwise anyway in front of the clearly ill young man. "Do you know what might have happened to him? Have you seen any other shapeshifters react this way after an attempt to change?"

By using that elixir was what Owen meant, but chose not to say. Then again, it wasn't as if Sal hadn't tried it before.

But from what Owen had understood, the dosage yesterday, meant for only an hour-long shift, had been fairly small. Today's dosage had been more significant since the group had intended to prowl the compound and the surrounding hills, getting used to their ability to achieve cognition while in animal form. This time they were supposed to stay shifted for several hours.

Had that damned elixir, in this higher amount, harmed Sal?

But then, if Sal reacted this way and no one else did, was it him or the elixir that was flawed?

Without knowing for certain, did Owen, as a responsible officer in charge, dare to allow this operation to continue? As far as he knew, the other three CAs had shifted and were out prowling and flying and doing what this exercise was supposed to accomplish.

But were they all okay?

Maybe he should take advantage of Selena's being here now to find out. "Could you stay here with Sal until Patrick returns?" he asked, walking toward where she stood at the door. "I want to go outside and check up on the other CAs."

"I've done that already," Selena said, her expression wry. "I assume you're wondering if the elixir harmed Sal. So do I, and just in case the others were at risk, I went outside with them for a few minutes just to observe. I don't know of any differences, genetic or otherwise, between US and Canadian shifters, but that doesn't mean there aren't any that might mean differences in reaction to the elixir. From what I saw, Tim and Craig were doing just fine as wolves prowling the hills, and the falcon who's Andrea was soaring overhead looking pretty pleased with herself."

"Does that mean only Sal's somehow at risk?"

"I don't know what it means, although I have my suspicions." Selena appeared grim as she looked down and shook her head, her light brown hair gleaming a bit in the artificial light overhead.

"So do I." Patrick's voice sounded from behind her. He entered the room, a large medical case in his hand. "I did a quick online check of our records about your CAs. Are you aware that Tim Franzer comes from a town here in British Columbia? It's Roadwich, and it's only about thirty miles from here. I'll check Sal over a bit more thoroughly now, and if he's okay to travel, I'll take him there. I did some further research on my smartphone and made a couple of calls to some very special sources. An urgent-care clinic in the area isn't only for regular humans. It's for local shifters, too."

"Are there many shifters who live in the area?" Selena asked.

"That's what I gather, and the medical team at that urgent-care clinic also includes shifters." Patrick maneuvered past both Selena and Owen, over to his patient.

Owen stood motionless beside Selena, watching as Patrick listened with his stethoscope to Sal's chest, looked down his throat with a light—causing Sal to gag again—and conducted some more tests.

In a few minutes, Patrick asked Sal, "How are you feeling now?"

"Don't know," he said in a lethargic voice.

"I hope you're well enough to take a ride," Patrick said. "We can get you better help in a little while."

"'Kay," Sal managed to reply, then shut his eyes again.

"Can you help me get him to my car?" Patrick asked Owen.

Owen nodded and approached them immediately.

"What can I do to help?" Selena asked.

"Go in front of us and open doors," Patrick said. "And while we're getting him into the car, tell Jonas what we're up to and that I'd like him to come along."

"Of course," Selena said.

Sal was like a deadweight, Owen thought as, together with Patrick, they nearly dragged him back through the house and out the front door.

As they got him into the car, Jonas joined them, as did Selena. She had a couple of vials in her hand. "Jonas said this was the one Sal drank from," she said, raising one of them. "If the clinic you go to has any way of analyzing contents, I think you should check it out. There's a slightly different color to what's left in the bottom of this one, and a different scent, too, that I can't identify. Maybe you can have someone compare its contents to the little bit left in this one." She lifted the other vial she held.

"You think—" Patrick began, then glanced into the car toward Sal. He took the vials from her. "I'll have these checked. Thanks, Selena."

Then Jonas and he got into the car, too, and drove off down the driveway.

Selena watched the car head down the hill. Then she closed her eyes for a moment, her arms limp at her sides.

Had someone tainted the elixir? If so, was it only one bottle?

Only? One was too many, especially if it harmed a shifter.

And it had apparently harmed Sal.

Or maybe not. Maybe there was nothing wrong with the tonic he had taken. Maybe he simply had some kind of allergy to the elixir taken in normal dosage.

She didn't know. None of them did...yet.

Hopefully Patrick would be able to find out.

"Are you okay?" Owen, beside her, took her arm gently at the elbow. She was suddenly very aware of his presence, his strength, his touch.

She wanted to lean on him, take some kind of support from him.

And yet...if the elixir was tainted, who had done it? Most likely not a shifter.

There weren't many nonshifters here. Two—their aides—were members of Alpha Force.

And then there was Owen.

No. She couldn't—didn't—suspect him of anything. He, more than anyone, was the person who truly wanted a good result here.

She mentally shook herself as she looked at him. "I'm fine," she finally replied to his question, knowing it wasn't true but saying it with enough conviction that she might even convince herself. Or not.

"You don't sound like you are." He paused. "Do you want to stay outside for a while and try to see what's going on?"

"Yes." This time she was actually serious. She wasn't sure if they'd have an opportunity to check out the two shifted wolves or the falcon. But at least that gave Selena a purpose for the moment.

"Do you know where they are?" Owen regarded her with a half smile, as if he was challenging her to use her wolfen senses. Maybe she was just reading that into it, but just in case she smiled back.

She closed her eyes for an instant, listening, inhaling, attempting to discern anything with her enhanced senses that would pinpoint the location of either Tim or Craig.

There! She heard a distant bark of excitement, somewhere within the surrounding woods but up higher in the hills and off to her left. "That way," she said. "Want to go look for them?"

"Definitely."

Fortunately, it was early enough in the afternoon that daylight wouldn't start waning for another hour or longer. Selena led Owen toward a narrow path that rose along the mountainside. The aroma from the surrounding fir trees, and the needles on the ground, sweetened the air around them.

Aroma. Selena hadn't thought about it before, but now she recalled all too clearly the smells she had sensed the other evening. Smells that suggested the possibility of other people up here around the enclave.

But even if someone had come up here, surely they couldn't be the source of any tainting of the elixir. No one in this area knew the nature of the group staying or meeting here. Even if they did, they'd have no idea about the elixir or where it was or how to modify it.

Surely the two outside women, Sal's sister and Craig's girlfriend, didn't know enough to do this, either—and they, of all people, wouldn't want to harm the shifters even if they'd been told too much.

The idea bothered Selena a lot, though. She would mull it over in her own mind, perhaps revealing her concern to Patrick depending on what, if anything, was found about the possibly tainted vial of the elixir he had taken with him.

Their trek, though largely uphill, wasn't a problem for Selena. As far as she could tell, Owen's endurance was fine, too. No wonder. He seemed in really good condition. Plus, she knew how muscular he was...all over.

The recollection made her tingle below the waist, despite where she was and what she was doing here. It also made her wonder if she could manage somehow to experience that pleasure yet again. If so, it would have to be soon, since, whatever happened, this combined group would break up within the next few days and possibly never get together again.

She hoped that Sal was okay, no matter what had caused his bad reaction to the elixir.

And that the CAs were completely successful in their assignment.

"You still okay, Selena?" Owen's voice was strong despite the slight shortness of breath it evinced.

"I'm fine. And you?"

"Doing well. So where are those wolves?"

"They should be—" She didn't finish. Her sense of smell informed her even before her sight and hearing that the two shifted wolves were nearby, in front of them on the path.

In just a few moments they were confronted by two wolf shapes bounding down the path toward them.

She sensed Owen stiffening beside her and was glad that, for this assignment, he didn't seem to be carrying a firearm, although she figured that might be standard procedure for RCMP members. Then again, the Canadian police were far different from the US police forces. Surely, though, they needed ways of protecting themselves.

Both wolves stopped right in front of them. They were the same canines who had left the local compound—Tim, who appeared part Akita, and Craig, with what looked like a hint of malamute in him.

"Hi, guys," Selena said softly. "Just so you know, Patrick and Jonas have taken Sal to some urgent-care facility in Roadwich—your hometown, I understand, Tim."

The wolf bent his head in an apparent nod.

"Patrick examined him first and seemed to think he should be okay, but thought that he needed better facilities under the circumstances to be sure."

A whine issued from one of them—Craig, Selena ascertained. "Anyway, you two go ahead with your maneuvers. I know you're supposed to be surveilling an area as if it was your upcoming target, where you'll be heading soon if all goes well tonight. We'll have to see if Sal is well enough to go with you, but we all hope so."

"That's for certain," Owen added. "Anything you two need?" His tone sounded somewhat tentative, as if he wasn't quite certain how to handle a conversation with shapeshifters.

Selena smiled. "I gather they're fine," she told Owen, "but it's good that you asked. Right, guys?"

This time both wolfen heads bowed in nods.

A sound like "cack" sounded overhead, and Selena looked up. A falcon was circling them.

She waved. "Looks like the three of you CAs have things under control. I think we can head back to the compound and wait for you, but have fun with the rest of your maneuvers."

Both wolves turned and loped back in the direction from which they'd come.

Selena turned toward Owen. "Are you ready to go back?"

"I am," he said, but instead of turning back he gently grabbed both of her arms. His blue eyes seemed to bore into hers. "I can't tell you how amazed I am this time, Selena. With each new good experience with shifters... Well, it's nothing I ever thought could be real."

"Fortunately, that's true of most humans," she said.

"Otherwise my species might be in danger of extinction."

"Not if I could help it," he said. And then his mouth came down on hers.

The kiss was brief but, oh, so intense. Selena threw herself into it, tasting him, thrusting her tongue into his open mouth and taunting his with it.

His body was once again hard against hers. Very hard, in the most vital of locations, which made her gasp and give herself even more to the kiss…and into his arms.

She didn't want to pull away, and yet this wasn't an ideal place for kissing…or anything else.

She pulled away after planting one final kiss on his hot mouth.

"I don't suppose you'd want me to come back to your hotel again tonight…to discuss shifter logistics that might work for the CAs' assignment, would you?" Her voice was soft and uneven. Who did she think she was kidding? Hold a discussion? No way.

And yet the distraction after what had happened with Sal might be exactly what she needed.

So would hot, powerful sex with Owen one final time.

"Sure," he said in a deep, raspy tone. "I think that's one hell of a fine idea."

Chapter 16

As it turned out, though, Selena did not go back to Owen's hotel, nor did he. Instead she tackled the development of ideas to assist the CAs, and that required her immediate focus. She wanted to be too busy to think hard about what had been and what could be.

It was better that way.

She now sat on the living room sofa in the meeting house, with Lupe lying on the floor beside her. Owen faced her on one of the upholstered chairs. No one had talked much, but her mind was preoccupied with worry about Sal and his recovery, plus the shifted CAs. At least it kept her mind from drifting to other things.

Outside in the hills, the plan was that Marshall— who was substituting now for Jonas—and Rainey were to remain at a clearing in the woods. If the CAs had any difficulties, they would go there for help. Once their practice mission ended, likely several hours from now, they would go to that area for any assistance they needed changing back again.

"How much do you actually know about the location the shifted CAs are supposed to observe when they're sent on their actual recon mission?" Selena asked Owen, attempting to treat him like just another coworker instead of a gorgeous, sexy man she'd made fantastic love with...and wanted to again.

"Not a lot." His black brows dipped pensively over his distantly focused blue eyes. "We've gone over the known topography of the area as much as possible with some of the nearest local Mounties, without revealing why we needed the information."

"And?"

"I described as much as I knew to my CAs before they shifted earlier so they could work on the situation to the greatest extent possible today."

"That's what I figured," Selena acknowledged.

With their minds entirely human, despite the shifted configurations of their bodies, the CAs were to head to a target area. Once there, they were to circle that location, to act as if it was occupied by the enemy, without knowing the terrain or how that occupation was accomplished—whether in aboveground facilities or underground or a combination of both.

Since the true nature of their kidnappers' compound was unknown, they needed to act as if any situation was possible so they could report back and discuss how they would act in any scenario.

"The thing is, though," Selena said, scrolling through her smartphone, "I want to do some research now, as best I can. Then, when they report on how things went for them today, maybe what I find can help them when they're actually out there performing their mission."

"I just told you I've already conducted research, even talked to people who know the area." Owen scowled at her, probably thinking she had insulted him for not doing his job adequately.

That definitely had not been her intention.

"Of course," she said, "and I've no doubt you did a good job with it. But the one thing you couldn't have factored in, at least not completely, is how someone who is in falcon or wolf form would view the area."

"That's what Andrea, Craig and Tim are supposed to describe when they return. And, of course, Sal was going to as well." He had sat back on the chair, trying to pretend as if he was relaxed, but Selena read something different in his eyes.

Maybe that was a good thing. It certainly kept them apart, both mentally and physically.

"Yes, and I'm sure the three working there today will do a good job rehearsing it," she said. "But remember this is their first outing after using the elixir and on their own. I'm not with them, of course, but having done similar kinds of operations after the same kind of shift, I might have a different perspective that could help them when they're out there for real later."

This time, Owen did seem to genuinely relax, at least a bit. "Care to explain?"

"Not yet. But I will."

Selena knew the area in question was near the border of British Columbia and the Yukon. Satellite sensors and drones had picked up more activity than usual around there lately—particularly after attempts to locate the kidnapped executives and others had begun. Owen had also reported that there had been trouble with the electronics in the area.

Was it certain they'd been taken there? Not at all. But the location had to be ruled out...or a determination made that it should be the focus of the next rescue maneuvers.

That was what Selena had started looking for, via the internet on her smartphone. She might be duplicating the efforts of Owen or others in the RCMP, but it wouldn't hurt. Even using her fingers to enlarge the aerial views she found, though, didn't provide her with enough information to feel she was doing the best job possible.

She was determined to pursue it. Learning about the target area wasn't her job. Instructing the CAs about their shifts was. But now she had time to fill, and she also realized she might bring a different perspective to the research than the others, as both a teacher and a shifter.

"My laptop is in the other house," she told Owen. "I want to use it for a while to look further into that area. Not that you haven't done a good job, but I think the more information retrieved in various ways, the better for the mission. Okay?"

She intended to do it with or without his approval, but for the sake of maintaining some amity between them she at least asked. If he said no, she'd find another way, perhaps without letting him know.

"Good idea," he said.

"Fine." She rose, and so did Lupe. "We can talk again later. Let me know when the CAs return, and most particularly if Patrick and Jonas return with Sal, okay?"

"Of course."

Snapping Lupe's leash on, Selena headed for the door. Owen didn't follow. She felt somewhat bereft even while telling herself that her leaving now, while they were otherwise alone together, was the best thing for both of them.

Plus, she actually did want to conduct the research she'd described. She exited the meeting house, walked

Lupe for a few minutes, then headed toward the residence where she was staying.

She unlocked the door and went inside. For the past few days, the house had been occupied by a number of her Alpha Force teammates. At the moment, being in this building by herself felt unnatural, but she shrugged it off.

Her concern over what had happened to Sal probably overrode her common sense. Everything here was fine, she told herself.

She headed down the hall to her room, Lupe at her heels. She got her laptop out of her suitcase and set it down on her bed, where she sat and booted it up. Fortunately, possibly in anticipation of staying in touch with the outside world as the CAs operations were going on, they had Wi-Fi available, so Selena could start her online search.

From what she gathered, looking at the border areas between British Columbia and the Yukon, a lot of the territory consisted of stark mountain ranges, with sharp peaks that were often covered by snow and ice. But some locations appeared more temperate, and she assumed they were the ones considered most likely for the kidnappers to be using.

Did Owen have a better idea which areas were key? Most likely, considering the kind of research he had been doing.

Selena hadn't looked up the areas before, at least not past double-checking whether there were wolves and falcons in that area of British Columbia. Fortunately, there were, so the CAs should be able to act undercover, no matter what.

Still, for them to actually be of assistance if the kidnappers had taken their victim to the suspected area,

Selena hoped that the vast expanse had been somewhat narrowed down and further researched. She needed that information from Owen.

Or maybe she didn't. Maybe she had just decided to do this research to get away from him, at least temporarily.

For when she was with him, what she wanted was to really *be* with him. Flesh against flesh.

Lupe suddenly stood and gave a deep woof.

"What is it, girl?" Selena stood, too, leaving her computer on the bed.

When she turned, Owen was there. "Sorry if I startled you," he said, "but I thought we should work together on this. I can tell you what I've come up with for where the shifted CAs should go once they learn what to do. And maybe you can advise me what to tell them even now to enhance their skills in using their new abilities."

"Sounds good—especially since despite all I've heard so far, I wasn't sure where to look for the target locale, let alone zero in on the particular area."

"Great. Working together makes the most sense, then." But when Selena looked into Owen's face, working together didn't seem to be what he was thinking about. Doing other things together was. His gaze was sensuous, and so was the set of his mouth.

She didn't even think about resisting. In moments, Selena was in his arms.

When their mouths met, the whole idea of conducting research on her own to avoid him flew from her mind, even as her hands went behind him and grasped his buttocks to pull him even closer.

His hardness against her was irresistible. "Owen," she whispered against his mouth.

"Good thing we're in your bedroom," he said hoarsely. "Or was this why you came in here?"

Despite herself, she laughed a little without pulling back very far. "Believe me, I came in here to avoid this."

"Nope, I don't believe you." He softened his words by deepening the kiss.

Selena moaned against him, even as her most sensitive body parts warmed and tingled in anticipation. Then she closed her laptop and set it on the floor.

She still reveled in her memories of the last time they'd made love despite recognizing what a bad idea it had been. Having sex with Owen again would be an even worse idea…and it was absolutely foolish to even contemplate it here. They were alone, except for Lupe, but who knew when the others would enter this house once more? It could be at any moment.

"You taste so good," Owen said, backing off just a little to look at her. His hands were still upon her, though, and he moved them to her breasts, making her draw in a ragged breath yet again.

"You taste wonderful, too," she said, "and beings like me can really sense the best of flavors."

She half waited for him to be the one to back off after that. Did he care that she had reminded him who, and what, she was?

Apparently not. He didn't flinch.

"Then what do I taste like to you?" he asked, dipping his head for a quick but heated kiss.

"You taste like hot, delicious sex," she said. "Addictive sex."

"Just my kiss? What if we taste each other's bodies all over?"

Just the thought nearly made Selena have an orgasm. But at least one of them had to remain sane.

That had to be her, or so she told herself.

"It sounds wonderful," she said, even as she let her hand creep beneath his shirt and upward, caressing his warm skin with just a hint of chest hair. "But you're as aware as I am that someone could come in here at any time. As much as I'd like to indulge with you again, we just can't."

"Of course we can." His hands began to play games beneath her T-shirt, cupping her breasts, flicking his thumbs over her nipples outside her bra in a way that made her want to forget everything sensible and strip again and have hot, mindless sex with him once more.

Good thing she retained her senses. Didn't she? "But—"

"Here's what we'll do." He moved his hands away and she felt almost robbed, deprived of the sensation that had made her willing—almost—to defy all logic.

His hands moved lower, and she felt him pull her jeans away from her waist, beyond her hips and farther down, until her jeans pooled at her feet.

"What are you doing?" she began, only to have him cover her lips once more as he pulled her closer to the bed.

"Now you do the same to me. Just take my pants partly off. That way, when we make love, if we hear anyone enter the house we can get dressed again more quickly."

What a good idea, she thought. Or maybe she simply wasn't thinking any longer. It was really a foolish idea, wasn't it?

But she had a desire to play along anyway. She had desire. Oh, yeah.

"I don't suppose you have a way to communicate with Lupe to tell her to bark softly if she hears anyone, do you?"

Selena laughed. "She's well trained, and I look a lot like her while shifted, but we still haven't figured out a way to communicate with our cover animals that way. Maybe someday."

"So we don't add to our delays, I'll take care of this." He pulled back just a little and waved the package containing a condom in front of her. She heard the plastic tear, and only a few moments later Owen was stroking her body in its most sensitive and moist area, making her nearly scream with need. "Are you ready?" he whispered hoarsely.

"Are you?" she countered and reached toward him, feeling how stiff and hard he was beneath the covering of the condom. "I'd say yes."

"Yes," he repeated, and in moments he was inside her, thrusting and breathing hard.

She came nearly immediately. Apparently so did he, for he groaned as he continued to move with determination, but for only another minute. And then he was still.

They just lay there on the bed that was Selena's while she was on this assignment, in this town.

"Not bad for a quickie," Owen said after a long moment.

"Not bad at all," Selena said, but what she thought was how wonderful it had been, maybe because of the risk as well as the intensity.

That was when she heard Lupe, beside the bed, rise to her paws and give a small woof.

"Maybe she did understand," Selena said. "I think we've been warned."

Laughing, Owen responded, "Time to pull ourselves together and get back on your computer."

A minute later, Owen and Selena, fully dressed once more and no longer out of breath, walked slowly down the hall and into the entry area together to see who was there, with Lupe already sniffing at the opening door. Owen wasn't especially surprised to see who came inside.

"Oh." Rainey looked startled as she stopped and stared at them. The curls of her dark hair seemed mussed up by the wind outside, and the lids over her brown eyes were lowered a bit, as if she was in pain. She explained, "I didn't think anyone would be here. I just came back for some aspirin to ward off a headache I've started fighting."

"Sorry to hear that," Selena said. "Can I get you anything?"

"No, thanks. I always carry aspirin in my purse just in case. I'll go upstairs and get some from my room." She started past them down the hallway.

Owen asked, "As far as you could tell, the practice surveillance is going okay with the shifted CAs?"

"Yes, as far as Marshall and I could tell. He's still there, and I'm going back to where he's waiting." Rainey stopped at the bottom of the stairway to the second floor. She turned, and the expression on her face now was both inquisitive and teasing. "I didn't expect you to be here since I thought you two would be in the meeting house waiting to see what happened. Are you...working here?"

She aimed a huge, catlike smile at Selena, who shifted where she stood beside Owen.

"Yes, I wanted to research some things about the target area on the internet, so I came back here for my laptop." She'd been carrying it and now gestured with it. "Owen had already done some investigation, online and otherwise. He came with me so we could compare notes and synchronize what we did."

Owen wanted to hug Selena for keeping her cool. Her response was logical and sound. But he couldn't help thinking that Rainey guessed why they were really here, or at least what she had interrupted. Those brows of hers were raised now as she regarded her boss. "I want to hear all about that…research later." She turned again and hurried up the stairs.

Owen heard Selena slowly let out her breath.

"Guess we dodged that bullet," Owen whispered to her, putting an arm around her and squeezing gently.

"Not with Rainey," Selena said, also softly. "Even though she's not a shifter, I suspect her senses help her to know everything."

Rainey returned back down the stairs a few minutes later, a small pill container in her hand. "I'll just be a minute," she said, heading into the kitchen. "I'll bring a water bottle along with me, too, this time."

Selena hoped it wouldn't be tainted, then chastised herself. She didn't know for certain—yet—if the elixir had been tampered with somehow. And even if it had been, that didn't mean there was a problem with everything stored around this compound.

At least she hoped not.

"Then I'll leave you two alone again," Rainey added,

practically dancing into the kitchen on her well-worn tennis shoes.

Selena said nothing, just shook her head and sent a wry smile toward her aide that Rainey, now with her face in the refrigerator, couldn't see. Selena instead aimed it toward Owen, who remained beside her, where she was seated at the kitchen table with the laptop in front of her. He was grinning, but as Rainey turned back toward them his expression turned into what passed for an irritated frown.

Rainey closed the refrigerator. She followed up her pills with a long draft of water. "Okay, done," she said. "I'll leave you two to your…research." She grinned again.

Selena wondered if her aide's imagination was as much of a headache cure as the aspirin. "Oh, I think we've finished it," she said. "I'm ready to go back to the meeting house to wait for everyone to return there. How about you, Owen?"

"Yes," he said. "I'm looking forward to getting a report from the shifters. And also about Sal."

Selena nodded. "All the more reason to wait where everyone'll know where to contact us," she said. Then to Rainey, who hurried toward the door ahead of them, she called, "I hope everything on the mountain continues to go well and that your head feels better." Selena hurried to partially close the door until she could attach Lupe's leash to her collar. "We're going for a short walk first, before we go back to the other house," she said to Owen. "Want to join us?"

Owen watched as Lupe tried at first to catch up to Rainey as she headed along one of the paths through the forest that led up the mountain. Selena didn't let her, but tightened her grip on the handle of the leash. "This way, girl," she said to Lupe.

Not for the first time, Owen considered how this wolf-dog looked so much like Selena when she was shifted. He had seen her that way.

But he hadn't seen her get that way.

Nor had he, that day, gotten to see Selena completely undressed even though they had made love.

He wanted to see her naked again—before touching her and having more hot, hard sex with her.

"Are you thinking about how I look shifted?" Selena asked. "And whether I do similar things as Lupe?"

Startled, he looked toward her. Her smile was huge.

"In a way," he admitted. "Mostly, I was thinking about how I wished I'd seen you completely bare today." His turn to smile. "Maybe next time."

"But—"

"I know. There might not be a next time. But I can always hope."

She looked away from him. Her lovely face was pensive, even as she watched Lupe lift her nose and smell the air.

"We've talked a lot about times that I get completely bare," she reminded him. "Would you still feel so... interested if you saw me shift? You've seen the guys change, so you know what the process is. It's cool, but it's not sexy."

He hesitated, but for only an instant. And then he responded, "It's you." Her glance seemed to suggest she was startled. And did he see a ray of hope in her expression?

Heck, letting her know he was attracted to her no

matter what her background was fine, but he didn't want to give her any hope that there would be something between them in the future. There couldn't be. They were too different. They had to live in the here and now.

Make love as much as they could…in the here and now.

But to make sure she didn't misunderstand anything on his mind, he grinned at her and said, "And in case you haven't figured it out by now, I'll take any opportunity I can to see you naked, Selena."

Chapter 17

They were back in the meeting house.

Needing something to do while they waited for the return of the shifted CAs—and word on Sal—Owen watched Selena start a pot of coffee for them as he wiped the kitchen counter.

How she could look so lithe and pretty doing such a mundane thing? But he realized why. No matter how inappropriate it was, he was falling for her in more ways than just wanting sex with her anytime, anywhere.

He liked her. A lot. Despite her being a shifter.

Loved her?

He wouldn't go there—even though he had heard that her Alpha Force included a number of couples in which one was a shapeshifter and the other wasn't. How did they get together? How did it work out?

Plus, one of the things he'd gathered was that their kids would most likely be shifters. How would he feel about that?

It didn't matter. None of it did. They had no future. He would just live in the moment while they had professional reasons to be together.

He'd started out not trusting shifters at all because

of his family's experience with the one who'd become a killer. He'd had to start trusting them, at least somewhat, because of his job—but that was all.

A permanent relationship with one—even though that one would be Selena? That couldn't happen.

He sensed Selena step beside him, breaking into his thoughts.

"I know you like it black," she said as she handed him a mug of coffee. He put down the dishcloth he'd been using and accepted the coffee from her.

He smiled at her. "Sounds as if you're getting to know me too well."

She didn't quite hide the look of panic on her face as she quickly turned away.

"I'm getting to know you a bit, too," he persisted. He drew closer to her and, standing right behind her, put his arms around her and pulled her against him. "You like things hard, and sometimes fast, and—"

She pulled away and spun to face him. The expression on her beautiful but pale face seemed taunting somehow, yet sad. "Yes, I guess you're getting to know a part of me, too. But not all." She bent and put her hand on top of Lupe's head. The dog was sitting on the floor, looking up at her. "Right, Lupe?"

"I'll bet she knows the rest," Owen said. *And I'm willing to learn.* But he didn't say that. What good would it really do either of them if he did learn?

Although he hadn't been lying to her. He really did hope he got the chance to watch her shift from human to wolf, at least once.

Maybe it would turn him off completely, shut off any avenue within his mind of wanting to get to know her better.

But he suspected, right now, that it would have the exact opposite effect.

As if she was reading his mind, Selena stood up straight and faced him. "Too bad we need to just wait here for now. Otherwise, I could go downstairs and bring up some of the elixir and one of the magical lights. I could change to look just like Lupe before your very eyes." Talk about taunting him with her gaze—she was a pro at it.

But instead of responding directly, he said, "Maybe we should bring some of that stuff up here, compare the vials to one another to see if we recognize differences. But I think it'll be better to get the results of any testing when Sal comes back with Patrick and Jonas."

"You're assuming he'll come back with them." She crossed her arms and regarded him dubiously.

"Aren't you?"

She relaxed just a little. "Yes, I am, actually. Or maybe that's just hopefulness. I want him to be all right. And I also want there to be a good explanation for his having become ill in the first place."

"Other than tainted elixir?"

She nodded. "You already know how I feel about that. It wouldn't have come from Ft. Lukman that way, but I can't imagine how it was tampered with on the way here or by whom. And—"

Owen's phone rang. Selena stopped talking as he pulled it out of his pocket.

It was Anthony. This wasn't a time scheduled for his superior officer to call. Owen immediately felt his shoulders stiffen, expecting he was not going to like the reason Anthony was contacting him.

He was right.

* * *

Selena watched the expression on Owen's face as he leaned his back against the kitchen counter and scowled as he listened to whoever was on the phone. Who was it? Whatever he or she was saying was clearly aggravating Owen.

In a minute, he pulled his phone away from where he had been clutching it against his ear, looked at it and swiped the screen a few times with his forefinger. "Got it. I'll listen and get back to you with any ideas. But I gather that priority number one is to get the CAs off to the target area fast, no later than the day after tomorrow." Owen paused, then said, "Yes, sir." He pressed the button to end the call.

Selena didn't wait. She wanted to know what was going on.

She knew it wasn't anything good.

"Who was that? Anthony?"

"Yeah. He received a message that he needed to pass along to me. Let's go listen to it." He led her into the dining room and sat down on the chair at the head of the table. She grabbed the seat beside him and just waited, while Lupe settled down once more behind her.

He pulled his phone out again and fiddled with it for a few seconds. Then Selena heard a voice crackle out of it.

It was clearly a disguised voice, probably male, much lower than any vocal range she had ever heard, slow and deliberate and understandable. It said, "Greetings, RCMP. You are running out of time to get that ransom paid. Too bad. We are increasing it now by another million dollars and decreasing the deadline by one day. That means we now expect it to appear in the designated foreign bank account no later than Tuesday. And we might change that again if we decide to. We already spoke with Mr. Brodheureux but decided to contact you, too, this time. You need to understand that you Mounties are not in charge here. We are. And if you pretend to do the impossible because you think that will scare us into giving up or allowing you to capture us, you will be making an even bigger mistake. We are much smarter than the RCMP, and you should never forget that. By the way, Mrs. Brodheureux sends her regards. She wants to make sure her husband gets more of his Xanogistics money together fast...or this will also be her goodbye."

That was the end of the call. Selena just looked at Owen, waiting for his reaction.

"I'm not sure what that meant," he said, "besides the obvious. They're tightening the strings, and Mrs. Brodheureux is clearly in even more danger than before. Anthony said he would discuss the additional ransom demand with her husband immediately, but he also made it clear that the CAs had no more time to rehearse. We may not be ready tomorrow, but the day after has to be it. We can't wait any longer."

"Do you think—" Selena began, then stopped. "What about the rest of it? I don't know the details of the prior kidnappings, but there seemed to be a deeper message in what that man said, don't you think? He was warning the RCMP against doing...what? Something impossible?" She had a sinking feeling she knew what it meant, although maybe she was jumping to conclusions.

Owen's expression was grim and his eyes stared somewhere beyond Selena. "You want my gut reaction? My understanding is that most ransom calls are made directly to the family members. When he said we're pretending to do the impossible, I think he somehow found out that we asked Alpha Force for help, and despite its covert nature he's somehow learned about our unit of shapeshifters. The good thing is that he talked about pretense, so he most likely doesn't know it's true."

"That's what I thought, too." Selena bent her head to look down at her lap.

"Maybe bringing you Alpha Forcers in was a huge mistake." Owen's voice was low despite how brutal his words were.

"No, just the opposite," Selena countered, standing abruptly. "Don't you see? The kidnappers are worried about what you Mounties are doing. Maybe they don't buy in to the idea that you've gotten shapeshifters involved to save their kidnap victim this time, but they know you're doing something. Something that'll end their reign of terror once and for all. And they're worried. Damned worried!"

She realized she was glaring angrily at him, even as Lupe rose and stood beside her, hackles raised as if she attempted to assess whether she should attack.

Selena felt like kneeling and hugging her wonderful, empathetic cover dog, but she wasn't about to move or back down or do anything until Owen recanted what he had said.

No matter how things did or didn't work out for them, Alpha Force was involved now—and so was his troop of newly recruited shapeshifters.

The possibility of complete surprise against the kidnappers might not be feasible any longer. But shifters could still do one heck of a lot more than regular humans to conduct reconnaissance of the suspected location… and then even to assist in the rescue.

Instead of snapping back or once more attempting

to discredit Alpha Force, Owen smiled. It was a dubious smile, but he apparently chose not to continue the argument.

"You're right, of course," he said. "I apologize. But I certainly wasn't expecting to lose the element of surprise when my CAs approached our suspected site. Now they'll need to be extra careful. But they will succeed. They have to. And despite what I said before, they'll have you, and the other members of Alpha Force, to thank for it."

Selena stepped toward him, intending to give him a quick hug to reassure him that his assumption of success would come true. But in moments, she was in a full embrace once more and his lips were on hers.

The kiss reassured her that Owen was upset and concerned, but he wasn't refuting what his unit could do. Nor what hers had taught them.

Even more, it reassured her that, anger and worry be damned, Owen wasn't blaming her...and that he still wanted her.

A noise sounded from the front of the house, and at the same time Lupe stood and ran in that direction.

Selena quickly pulled away from Owen. "Who's here?" she asked him.

Owen guessed correctly, partly because it was too early for the CAs to return from their reconnaissance exercise. The people who had just entered the meeting house through the front door were Sal and those who had gone along to help him, Patrick and Jonas.

Sal was still pale, but he was walking on his own—a good sign.

"Are you okay?" Selena had hurried past Owen and

the others to join Sal in the entryway, her hand on his arm below the short sleeve of his black T-shirt. The strain on his face made him look older.

"I'm fine," he managed to answer, "but I think it'll still be a while before the idea of food sounds good to me. Is Yvanne here yet?"

"No," Owen said, trading glances with Patrick.

"It's okay," the senior Alpha Force officer said. "Sal wasn't in any condition to contact his sister at first, but I promised I would if… Well, he improved very quickly, so I let him be the one to call her."

"She was worried," Sal elaborated, "but I told her when we were on our way back here and said she could come and see me."

"That's fine." Selena sent Owen a look that told him to drop the subject. "Why don't you come here, into the living room?" She held on to Sal's arm, and Jonas took his other one. The aide was also dressed in black, since he was initially supposed to have remained on the mountain as the CAs did their practice recon.

Owen watched them go but stayed back, glad that Patrick did, too. "Is he really okay?"

"He is now." The shapeshifting doctor looked worried, though. His pale brown eyes were narrowed, and Owen half expected him to growl like the wolf he changed into.

"Any idea yet what happened to him?"

"I want to hear, too." Selena had returned to the entry area. Owen looked at her. Her hands were on her hips, and she appeared ready to argue if either man suggested she didn't need to hear whatever Patrick was about to say.

Owen, for one, wasn't about to tell her to leave. To

the contrary, he believed she should know everything that was going on. Analyzing and conveying to others what they, too, needed to know was her job.

"Fine," Patrick said. "Let's go out on the porch. Everyone will need to hear this eventually, but I want to get them together and observe their reactions."

"Why?" Selena's tone had the same edge that Owen figured his would have if he'd asked the same question.

Patrick didn't respond directly. Instead, he turned the latch and opened the front door, then motioned for the two of them to go outside. Selena went first and Owen followed, not wanting her to be out there alone even for a few seconds—not until he knew what was going on and, if necessary, could protect her from it.

Twilight now darkened the sky. The wooden porch was largely in shadow, and so was the open area in front of the two houses, but Owen did not return inside to turn on the light. He'd do it later so the CAs did not need to return in darkness. For right now, though, shadows were just fine.

"Okay, what's going on?" He approached Patrick, who had taken a position in what might be the deepest shadow on the porch near the closed and draped window into the living room. Or maybe he was just listening to what was happening inside. Owen heard voices but could not make them out.

Shapeshifters probably could, even while still looking human.

"Actually, it's too soon to tell." Patrick's expression was ironic and, if Owen read it right, rather frustrated, too.

"Then what do you think?" Selena sounded as impatient as Owen felt.

They all stood there in the growing darkness, which made Owen think of eeriness and midnight and all the stuff kids were taught about things that were supposedly paranormal—like shapeshifters. If he wasn't a trained police officer, he might even feel nervous. Instead, he felt protective. Of Selena.

How weird, under the circumstances, was that?

"Well, we did take Sal to that urgent-care clinic near Tim's former home, where there are clearly shapeshifters living. After a bit of careful discussion on both sides, as well as dropping the names of Tim's family, the doctors there admitted to being shapeshifters, too. We didn't get into details like why we were in the area or what we were doing, but we did ask, and receive, access to the clinic's laboratory. I didn't want them to do any analysis on the elixir since its contents were none of their business, but I wanted a shot at figuring out if anything was actually wrong with that vial."

"And was there?" Owen asked.

"I brought it back with us since we'll need to get a more thorough and trustworthy analysis back at Ft. Lukman," Patrick said, "but our initial thought after a preliminary testing was that it was no wonder Sal had become ill."

"Why?" demanded Selena. "Don't keep us in suspense."

"Have you ever heard of ipecac?" Patrick asked.

"I think so," Owen responded. "Isn't it something that's supposed to make people throw up if they've swallowed poison?"

"Did Sal swallow poison?" Selena demanded. "Did the doctors at that clinic want to give him ipecac?"

"The stuff has been somewhat discredited over the

years as being potentially more dangerous than what it's supposed to help cure," Patrick responded. "But our initial thought, Jonas's and mine, was that somehow ipecac had been added to the vial of elixir."

Ipecac? Selena hadn't really known anything about it before, but now she'd learned a little—how it had slightly discolored the blameworthy bottle of elixir with a hint of pink and how it smelled somewhat bitter.

She still wasn't certain how dangerous the stuff was, although she figured that the higher the dosage, the more damage it could do. Fortunately, there hadn't appeared to be much in the elixir.

Selena was particularly glad that Sal apparently would be fine.

She hoped Patrick would keep her informed as he learned more. In fact, it wouldn't hurt to ask now since Owen, too, would need to know. It was his subordinate who had been affected. Besides, he might need some reassurances that the elixir worked fine and was a good thing—nearly all the time.

Selena only hoped that remained true and that nothing like this ever happened again. Not to the CAs and not to Alpha Force.

"When do you think you'll know for sure if it was ipecac?" she asked Patrick, wishing she could see his expression better in the growing darkness. She'd trained with him some back at Ft. Lukman and had always found him to be a kind and courteous man and superior officer. But his tone of voice now had suggested he was holding back a whole lot of anger—unsurprising, of course.

"This isn't something we have facilities to deal with here," he said, "nor will we want to ship it and let it out of our control. We'll keep the vial refrigerated for now and take it back to Ft. Lukman when we head there."

"Have you told Major Connell about it?" Selena was certain that the officer in charge of Alpha Force would want to know all about the tainting of the elixir—especially since he was the one who had been in charge of its development.

"I called him, of course. He's having the rest of the elixir at Ft. Lukman checked to make sure it's all okay and telling all Alpha Force members out on assignment about it, too. But none of us believe we took it from the post that way when we headed here."

"Then how do you think it got tainted?" Owen asked. A sliver of light shone near Owen from between the curtains inside the living room window, allowing Selena to see his face. He, too, looked grim. And so he should. Sal could potentially have died. The kidnapped hostage, too, if the mission failed because of treachery.

Selena fought the urge to hug Owen in sympathy and understanding. It would have been inappropriate with Patrick standing beside them.

"We don't know," Patrick countered, almost as if he felt Owen was accusing him. Or maybe he really was feeling defensive, defending not only the elixir, but also himself—and Alpha Force. "We will find out, though," he said. "You can count on that."

"Right." Owen's tone didn't divulge whether he was genuinely agreeing or full of irony. Not that it mattered.

Selena decided this might be the time to change the subject or suggest they go inside to check on Sal. But before she said anything, lights suddenly appeared along the driveway.

A car was approaching.

Should they head inside and wait to see who it was? That might be the best defensive move. But because neither man moved, she didn't, either.

The car appeared, not one she had seen before. The light-colored sedan parked right in front of them.

In a moment, two familiar women exited the vehicle—Yvanne and Craig's girlfriend, Holly.

Sal had been permitted to call his sister and keep her updated about his condition. But who had contacted Holly?

Even if Yvanne knew that her brother was a CA, and what the CAs were about, Selena didn't think that Holly was supposed to know any more than that her guy was a shapeshifter.

When were the CAs due back here? What form would they be in? Would Holly still be here?

The day had already proved to be interesting. She had a feeling the evening was about to get even more so.

Chapter 18

"Where is Sal? Is he really okay?"

Even in the dim light, Selena could see the panic on Yvanne's face. Her pale brown eyes glowed as they looked from Patrick to Owen to Selena, stopping on her as if the woman sensed that she was an ally.

"He's inside, back from seeing a doctor with…appropriate credentials." Selena glanced toward Holly as she said that. Craig's girlfriend might know that he was a shifter, but none of the CAs was supposed to talk about the new RCMP team or what its characteristics were. Holly might not know that most of the people here were also shifters. Then again, she might. The main thing was that she wasn't supposed to know the reason they were here.

If she only knew her boyfriend was a shifter, though, Selena wasn't going to be the one to broaden her knowledge.

"That's what he said, but is it true?" Without waiting for an answer, Yvanne headed inside, followed by Patrick.

"Is Craig in there?" Holly demanded. "Is he okay?"

Selena took a moment to consider how to answer—

clearly "no" to question one and "we hope so" to question two. But Owen took that task away from her.

"He's not here. He had an errand to take care of and isn't back yet. I'm sure he's fine." Owen's tone was clearly intended to soothe Holly, and Selena admired him for his kind attitude.

"When will he get back?" Holly persisted. She looked different when not hanging on to Craig. Her large blue eyes seemed accusatory, despite the concern demonstrated by the way she gnawed her full, lipstick-covered bottom lip.

"Possibly not for another hour or so."

Was it getting that late already, or was Owen just trying to keep Holly calm? As far as Selena knew, the CAs were not supposed to end their dress rehearsal until the sky had been dark for at least a couple of hours.

That was because it wouldn't be clear how long they would need to scope out the genuine target area, so they needed to practice all possibilities now. Especially now, since their exercise today would be repeated as reality the day after tomorrow.

The shifted CAs, believing they had another day or two beyond that, wouldn't yet know of that urgency unless they were in the presence of the aides. Owen might have informed Patrick and the aides, though, about the change of circumstances, triggered by that kidnapper's phone call.

Given a choice, Selena would tell Holly to wait for Craig at the hotel where they were both staying—most likely in the same room at times, she figured, despite what Owen and others had been told. But she didn't want to spark any bad reaction from Holly. Even so, she didn't feel comfortable inviting her inside.

Once again Owen handled the situation, and Selena appreciated that about him.

That wasn't all she appreciated about him. Even out here in the dimness, she could see his muscular physique silhouetted against the light. She wistfully thought about the last time they had been alone and kissed and made love.

When would they be alone like that again? Not tonight. Maybe not ever.

Selena shrugged aside her sadness, making sure to paste an interested, unemotional expression on her face.

"Why don't you come inside for a while?" Owen said to Holly. "I can't guarantee when Craig will be back, but you can wait with us for now, although you'll need to leave if we decide to go back to town to wait for him."

That wasn't going to happen, but Selena was glad Owen had left the door open to a way to eject Holly from the area.

Selena let Owen lead the way, ushering Holly inside first, and then she followed.

Selena heard voices as they passed the living room, down the hall from the dining room.

Sal sat at the table with his sister beside him. She was asking questions about what had happened, and he seemed to be responding cagily.

Yes, he had drunk something he shouldn't have and had reacted to it badly. Yes, one of the other people he'd been vacationing here with—Tim—was from a nearby town, so they'd figured out where Sal could get appropriate care.

Never mind that Tim had shifted and been unable to speak and give directions when Sal had become ill.

Sal didn't get into any details about how things had worked out.

Patrick and Jonas were around the table now, too.

"Let's sit down," Owen said to Holly. He pulled his phone from his pocket, and Selena figured he was looking for messages or checking the time or both. "Anyone hungry?"

They decided on take-out Chinese, and Patrick asked Jonas to go to town to pick it up.

While they waited, everyone sat around the table and talked, mostly in groups of two or three. Selena wound up talking to Holly, which wasn't exactly her choice. She had to be careful what she said but kept the subject neutral, on how much she was enjoying this visit.

"Me, too," Holly said. "Of course, I always enjoy myself when I'm with Craig. He's why I came here." As if Selena didn't know that. "He's so special, you know." Selena knew that, too—but she wasn't sure if Holly was referring to Craig's shapeshifting abilities.

"He's a very nice guy" was all Selena said.

"Are you like him—a shifter, I mean?"

Selena felt her eyes widen. She supposed it wasn't too wild a guess that the people Craig hung out with would share that characteristic. But she didn't want to admit it.

"Not everyone here is like your boyfriend," said Owen from across the table. "Even if we wish we were."

Once more Selena could have hugged him. Her status remained vague, and Owen had told the truth.

Jonas arrived a while later with the take-out boxes of Chinese food. If Selena weren't aware of the tension in the room, she might consider this a pleasant dinner with friendly acquaintances.

But she knew better, especially when, each time she

looked at Holly, Craig's girlfriend was glancing at the doorway or checking her cell phone for the time.

Not surprising. In a similar situation, Selena figured she would be doing the same thing.

They were all finishing their meals when Lupe stood and woofed. Selena heard something outside, too.

Were the others back? It was eight o'clock, so it was certainly possible.

Would Andrea, Craig and Tim still be shifted? If so, she needed to get Yvanne and Holly out of there. No matter what they knew or didn't know, the two women did not need to see the others in their shifted forms. That would only add to the questions they probably already had.

Even though Selena wanted to stay here and greet the shifters, no matter what form they happened to be in, she had a responsibility to Alpha Force and, consequently, to the CAs.

"I just thought of something I need to get from my room," she said brightly and stood. "Yvanne and Holly, would you like to come with me? I'd like to show you my room." She'd take them out the back door so they wouldn't pass where the others would be entering.

"No, I'd rather stay here with Sal," Yvanne said, remaining seated.

"And I want to wait and see if whoever's outside there that Lupe's excited about includes Craig," said Holly.

Selena looked toward Patrick to see whether her commanding officer was all right with that or if he had an idea of his own how to get the women out of here at this potentially critical time.

"That's okay," Owen said. "You ladies can stay right

here. But I've got something I need to talk over with you, Selena. Would you come with me?"

Ah, she got it. Owen and she could go meet the others and lead them downstairs, where the CAs could shift back, if necessary.

"Oh, please," Holly said in a sarcastic voice that got Selena's attention and seemed to capture the others' as well. The attractive, fashion-conscious woman apparently had a temper. "Yvanne and I know what's going on. Sal and Craig let us in on it. They also let us know the information could go no further than us, and it hasn't, right, Yvanne?"

"Absolutely." The other woman grasped her brother's arm more tightly. Their family resemblance, with their light brown eyes and shining hair, seemed enhanced here despite Sal's continued pallor. "I'd do anything to keep Sal safe—plus, I'm all for what he and the rest of your group of CAs is up to. I wouldn't do anything to jeopardize it."

"Me, either." Holly was standing now. "Let's go welcome them back. I'd love to learn how things went for them." She glanced at each of them. "You don't need to worry about our discretion."

Really? Selena hoped that was true. But Holly and Yvanne hadn't been hanging out with the CAs 24/7. They'd all already seen Holly flirting with that server at the Yukon Bar—Boyd, was it? Sure, maybe that was just to get Craig jealous, or maybe it was a harmless and meaningless flirtation, but who knew what either of the women had done with the supposedly secret information they'd been given?

Selena looked toward Owen again to see how he was reacting to the two women—and the fact they'd been told more than they should have been by shifters under his command.

Judging by his unreadable expression and the way he failed to meet her eyes, Selena assumed he wasn't happy.

"All right," he finally said in a voice that would have resembled a growl if he'd been a shifter. "Let's go greet them."

Saying nothing more, Owen rose and started toward the front door. He figured the others followed him and in fact heard footsteps as well as whispers he did not try to understand.

Nor did he want to say anything else, not then. He didn't even want to talk to Selena because he figured she would express sympathy or concern, or even anger on his behalf.

As much as he appreciated her empathy, he didn't want it just then or he might wind up venting that anger at her, which would be totally inappropriate.

What he really wanted to do was shake sense into all of his recruits. Or even abort their mission and disband the CAs. But the latter would be self-defeating... and impossible. And against everything inside him as a longtime member of the RCMP.

Yet he had told them all, from the minute they had each been recruited, to keep everything about the CAs and their very sensitive assignment secret. But he'd figured before, and had it confirmed, that Sal would have given at least some information to his shapeshifting sister no matter how much Owen stressed discretion. Even so, that might be okay, given her apparent interest in joining the CAs, too.

He couldn't do anything about the fact that Holly

knew the true nature of her boyfriend. But Craig never should have let Holly know that his spontaneous "vacation" here was with other shifters, let alone that they were joining a special police unit. He wouldn't be surprised if Craig had also revealed to Holly the mission they were undertaking after their training here. Sure, it might seem exciting and glamorous to outsiders, something that might even stoke a girlfriend's admiration that could lead to interesting physical contact. But that mission was vital. And dangerous. A woman's life depended on its success. And to be effective, it needed to be kept secret.

But it was too late to boot out Craig for any indiscretion he might have committed or even to punish him for infringement of RCMP rules. Not now. It was also impossible to retract whatever he had told his girlfriend.

No, for now, it would be better to keep Holly in the loop so he could keep an eye on her, as well as on Yvanne.

Patrick was the first of the group to reach the front door. Good. He could assess the situation, see what form the three shifting CAs who'd been out training were in now.

"Hi," he said quickly. "Welcome back. We're just finishing dinner but left some for you, too. Sal's doing well, and his sister and Holly are here with us."

Good. He was cautioning the others not to start talking about their hopefully triumphant, but possibly less successful, training day, at least for the moment.

"Great," Tim said. "It's been quite an experience, and topping it off with dinner will be awesome." So the trio was in human form. He was thankful for that, at least.

In short order, they fussed over Sal and said their

hellos. Then they all sat around the dining room table, where the new arrivals ate dinner. It was like a family gathering, Owen thought—if you ignored the fact that most of the people here had met each other only a week ago.

But as friendly as everyone was, Owen felt the underlying frustration of nearly all of them. The group who'd just returned clearly wanted to talk about their experiences. The others wanted to listen to them—as long as the two women were excluded.

Owen struggled for a way to get rid of them, at least for now, so they could hold a proper debriefing. He was grateful when Selena stood up and corralled the two outsiders. "Let's go wash the dishes," she told them. "As an extra incentive, I've got some information I want to share with you two about the secret nature of this group that I know you've got only some knowledge of."

Patrick stood, too. "Now, Selena, we—"

"We've got to be realistic," she interrupted. "You two with me?" The two women nodded.

Owen wasn't sure whether he wanted to kiss Selena or strangle her.

But on the whole, he trusted her, and clearly Patrick and the other members of Alpha Force did, too.

Even so, he definitely wished he could hear what she said to them in the kitchen. Too bad he didn't have those extra shifter senses to help him out.

Chapter 19

Selena started gathering the dirty dishes that remained on the table, although some had already been cleared away. She handed a few to Yvanne and Holly to carry while she collected the rest.

Then she led them into the kitchen.

She wasn't quite sure what she would say to them. But one thing she was certain of was that she would do all she could as an Alpha Force member to help accomplish her special unit's needs. Right now one of those needs was for the group in the dining room to rehash all that had gone on that day.

From that, they would have to determine what exercises should and would be conducted tomorrow, the final opportunity before the mission went live.

She put the dishes into the sink, wishing not for the first time that this house had a dishwasher. It would be easier to let the machine do the work.

On the other hand, maybe this time it would be better to do it all by hand. It'd give the group time to debrief.

"Yvanne," she said, "you scrape the plates, I'll wash, and then, Holly, you dry. Okay?"

"If we must," Holly said with a sigh.

"And if you really talk to us the way you said," added Yvanne.

So what was she going to do? Selena wondered about it, but for only an instant.

She was going to tell them the truth.

But it would be a modified and abbreviated version that might actually gain their cooperation.

Was that still too much? She figured she would be able to explain to her CO and get him to buy in to her plan after the fact.

But Owen? This was really his operation, and he had clearly wanted total secrecy.

Secrecy that had already been breached. Surely he had to realize that. But would what she suddenly planned to reveal violate it even more in his opinion?

Would he despise her for it?

The idea made her place her hands in the hot water as if it would give her relief instead of discomfort. If she had to choose one kind of discomfort over the other, getting mildly scalded sounded better to her than garnering Owen's hatred.

But she believed that, with the proverbial cat out of the bag anyway, she might be able to ease the problem, if just a little.

"Look," she said, keeping her eyes on the plate she held over the sink. "I gather that Sal and Craig have most likely told you more than they were supposed to because they love you. I understand that. But did they also tell you that, not only were they supposed to maintain the secrecy of what they're doing, but that it would also be dangerous for them to reveal it to anyone, including those they love?"

"No," Holly whispered from beside her. "What do you mean?"

"The exercise they were on today—well, you might have gathered that it's preparation for something else."

"That's right," Yvanne said. "Sal did tell me that, and that it's something really exciting and important, but you can be sure he didn't tell me more than that."

It was more than enough, Selena thought, but instead of criticizing Sal she asked, "How about Craig, Holly? Did he tell you more than Yvanne just described?"

"No, but I really wanted him to." She paused. "Why is it dangerous for them if they told us?"

"I can't tell you that without violating the secrecy they're sworn to. Suffice to say that no matter what you actually know, and whether they've told you more than they should, you need to understand that Sal and Craig can be in great trouble—life-threatening danger, even— if word gets out about this. You need to promise that you won't tell anyone what you know or even suspect. Got that?"

She looked first at Yvanne, then at Holly. They both wore solemn expressions, and each nodded at her as if providing the promise she had asked for.

Still, she wanted a verbal agreement. "Say it aloud," she said.

"I promise," Holly responded.

"Me, too," said Yvanne. "But this is all so dratted frustrating." She shoved the plate she held against the side of the garbage can as if breaking it might make her feel better. The plate survived, fortunately, and so, apparently, did Yvanne's temper. "I'm a shifter like my brother. I know he was so excited that he was going to get to use that skill in a really special way, but he didn't tell me how, just teased me that I'd envy him because of the way he'd be able to shift from now on."

"And do you envy him?" Holly asked.

"I don't know enough about what he's talking about to be sure, but just being able to use his shifting ability for something special… Well, yes."

"I envy you both, in a way," Holly said. "I love Craig. A lot. We'll marry someday. But I'll never be able to do all that he does, even though he has told me how it feels to shift and be a wolf creature and all that, and our kids should be like him." She moved toward Selena. "You're a shifter, too, I gather. I envy you, too."

"Thanks," Selena said. "There are good and bad things about shifting. Not everyone believes in our ability and some who do fear it. It's generally important for shifters to keep quiet about it because there are those who fear and hate us and would even kill us if they learned we were real. I'm glad you're not one of them, Holly. It sounds like Craig is a lucky man to have you."

And Owen? Selena couldn't help thinking about him in the context of this conversation. He knew shifters were real. From what he'd told her, he had known it for a long time, but his initial experiences had made him despise them, too—until he had spent this week with a new set of shifters.

Good thing she already knew what a bad idea it would be to really let herself go and care for him for anything but wonderful, hot sex—assuming they ever got to be alone together again, which at this point seemed highly unlikely.

Holly could envy her all she wanted, though, as long as she didn't tell anyone.

"Okay," she finally said. "I think I've said all I can, and we need to dig in and finish the dishes."

Owen appreciated Selena's removing the two women from the dining room so tactfully. He and the others needed a summation of what had really gone on today during his CAs' exercise.

Selena's act was worth even more gratitude when he considered that she, too, would want to know the same information he and her fellow Alpha Force members learned. She would hear it later, of course, either from him or the others. But he had gotten to know her well enough to realize her action really was a sacrifice on her part.

She liked to learn as fast as possible, or at least that was the impression she gave. That way, she could work on how to include any appropriate new knowledge in the instructions she provided about shifting.

He listened as his recruits recounted their experiences.

At first, Andrea had waxed eloquent about how well things had gone from her perspective. "If our target area is anything like this, I'll be able to soar like any other raptors present. And Craig, Tim, Sal and I talked before about how I'll communicate by circling right or left or which wing I dip." Her thin face was one huge smile beneath her prominent nose and caused Owen to grin a little, too.

"That's right," Tim agreed. "Andrea succeeded in directing us to a particular clearing, where Craig and I headed. No kidnappers there, unsurprisingly, but we did stalk a couple of squirrels. Didn't harm them, though, since there was no need to." The round-faced guy appeared to attempt to look serious, but he clearly was beaming. "It was so cool to be out there and know we were people on a mission, even though it was just an exercise."

"We conducted an exercise today," said Patrick, who sat beside Owen. "There'll be another one tomorrow. But... Owen, please let everyone know about the phone call the RCMP received." Owen complied, and when he was done Patrick continued. "So you now know why we're stepping up the timing. The actual operation begins the day after tomorrow. Were there any particular things you felt needed some work today?"

"My presence," Sal said. "I want to experience what they did today so I'll be of help during our real mission. Okay, guys?" His youth shone through in his eager expression.

"Of course," Craig assured him. "I especially like those mini video cameras that were strapped around our necks. They're small enough not to be too visible, and it was great having our aides not only monitor what we saw, but also be able to talk to us. But what if we're separated and one of us thinks we need to meet up? We can't exactly talk and tell the aides monitoring us what's on our minds when we're shifted."

"What we often do is also plan ahead where to meet and how often," Marshall said, leaning forward at the table. "But with your specific instructions, you may not be able to do that. You should decide ahead of time where we'll be—your aides—so that'll be the place you return to. You should also determine a signal of urgency for Andrea to give you if things start looking bad from her perspective so you can rejoin us. And likewise, there should be some signal any of you can give to her so she'll know she should inform the others that you should leave what you're doing and all meet up with us."

"Sounds good," Tim said.

"To me, too," Andrea added. "We did a little of that today but it wasn't organized enough. Let me think a bit about what I'll be able to see most easily from the air, and we'll practice it some more tomorrow."

"One thing, though—something I asked before." Craig, at Andrea's other side, had one hand up, palm out. "Even though we shifting CAs appreciate all we've learned from you Alpha Force guys, I thought we were going to be an independent, all-Canadian team to take care of a Canadian problem." He looked at Owen, who nodded, but before he could speak Craig continued, "Then why aren't our aides part of the CAs? Or at least from our country? Will they be soon?"

"That's our ultimate plan," Owen responded quickly and firmly. He was glad he had taken a seat at the end of the table. He was in charge, as he had to be. He had a sense, though, that he was facing some kind of small rebellion from Craig without knowing why. If so, it was bad timing, coming on the heels of his lack of protocol in telling Holly about their group. "For right now," he continued, "we needed not only to get some of the elixir and instructions from Alpha Force, but also to get backup assistance—fast. It's crucial that we rescue that hostage immediately without her being harmed any further. Once this operation is complete, we'll have more time to learn more and train others, including aides, for the future." If they were successful, of course, and didn't have to deal with another kidnapping right away.

Craig apparently wasn't satisfied. He looked Owen right in the eyes and belabored his point. "But we have two great potential aides right here with us." He turned to face the others, starting with Sal. "Your sister, for one. She's a perfect aide since she's also a shifter. She might become one of us later, but for now there's no one better to be there as an aide for us. And my Holly would be an asset, too, because she cares. A lot." He looked toward the far side of the table, meeting Rainey's gaze. "I don't mean in any way to offend you, honest. You've done a great job, and you, too, Marshall. And, Jonas, it was great that you stayed to help Sal. But I love the idea of the CAs and what we can do and also what we can become—starting now."

Owen stood up. "I understand your concerns, and we'll certainly address them," he said in a firm tone that brooked no argument. "But not until after the rescue of that hostage."

"But—" Craig stopped and looked down at the table. "I get it."

Owen decided there and then that if he had had more time he would have booted Craig off their team, or at least suspended him.

But he didn't have time. He needed the full complement of these shifters. Craig's insubordination would have to be dealt with later.

"Now it's time for all of us to turn in," Owen said, maintaining the tone of a senior officer in control. "Tomorrow will be another big day. We'll meet here again early so you all, including Sal, can get in as much practice and training as possible."

He was glad to see the whole group, including Craig, rise and begin the routine of saying good-night. Selena reentered the room just then, too, with the two women who would also accompany the CAs back to their hotel.

She nodded as he gave her a quick look that he intended to convey his thanks.

This day, as good and as difficult as it had been, was finally drawing to an end. He could only hope that tomorrow would be better. It had to be, he told himself. They were running out of time.

Selena was dying to know what had gone on in the dining room while she'd acted as nursemaid in the kitchen to the two visiting women.

Okay, it really hadn't been that bad. But she was glad to see the entire group of CAs get into their cars and head down the hill toward town for the night.

At least she was glad to see all of them but Owen go.

He said good-night to her before heading to his car. He also said good-night to Patrick, Jonas and the rest. Nothing appeared personal between Selena and him, and that was fine.

At least it should have been. But she was well aware that their days with one another were numbered. In fact, tomorrow would be the last one.

She wasn't sure where Owen would be when the CAs were off conducting their designated operation the day after tomorrow. She assumed she and the other members of Alpha Force would hang out here to await the return of Jonas and Rainey. Or perhaps they'd go somewhere else, where Jonas and Rainey would meet up with them when done with the mission. Either way, she doubted she would be with Owen.

She walked Lupe for her last outing of the night and was glad when Rainey joined her.

"Boy," her aide said in a muted tone, "too bad you weren't with us in the dining room. Your buddy Owen

had to assert his power over at least one of his minions—
that Craig. He did a good job of it, too. No wonder you
find him sexy, with all that testosterone and all."

"What?" Selena exclaimed. She wanted to hear more,
but Patrick caught up and started walking with them.

"Did you learn anything from the women?" Patrick
asked Selena.

"Like what?" She watched Lupe squat though she
would have preferred looking into her CO's face to catch
whether his expression was critical.

"Like how much they know besides the fact that the
men they're here visiting are shifters."

"I didn't find out much really, although I tried to. I
still gather they know more than they were authorized
to be told. But whether they know it all—that I can't tell
you. I at least tried to impress on them how important it
was that they stay quiet about whatever they do happen
to know." Selena bent, a plastic bag in hand, to clean
what Lupe had done, then rose again.

"Did they tell you they intend to become the aides to
the shifting CAs?" Rainey asked.

Selena turned toward her. "They didn't mention it. Is
that the plan?" She looked at Patrick.

"It wasn't ours, although it could wind up being the
case. But there's no time to train them for it now. Craig
suggested the possibility, and I was wondering, too, if
the women were already in on the idea."

Selena shook her head. "If so, they didn't tell me. And
yeah, it's a really bad idea, at least right now."

"So they were told," Patrick said. "Owen made it very
clear it wasn't going to happen."

They all headed toward the house, Lupe included.
Selena pondered what the women had told her. But even

though Yvanne and Holly made it clear they were there for their shifting men, they hadn't even hinted that they hoped to wind up as aides.

The idea was potentially an okay one for the future, Selena mused. But not now. Definitely not now.

As she led Lupe to their room on the ground floor, the other Alpha Force members, who'd fetched bottles of water from the kitchen, trooped upstairs.

As she started getting ready for bed, her mind was not on the two women and their future use, but on the recruits who'd be facing their last day of training tomorrow.

Yes, tomorrow was going to be an important day.

But what if it started out with the same kind of problems as today?

She might not be able to ensure it didn't…but she had to try.

Selena hadn't been able to sleep. She'd lain in bed and developed a plan that she intended to accomplish very early in the morning, waking before the rest of the household.

But she could do it now instead—although it would undoubtedly require a follow-up, at least for her peace of mind.

The time was approaching midnight, only an hour since she had headed into her room while the others went upstairs. She could still get a reasonable night's sleep— depending on what she found.

"Stay," she whispered to Lupe as she exited their bedroom. She dressed in a dark long-sleeved T-shirt and black jeans and did not turn on any lights. She did, however, carry a small flashlight in case she needed some illumination to get her where she needed to go.

She wished she could shift now so she could make full use of her sense of smell. But even when she was in human form, that sense was still much better than that of most people. She'd noticed that a lot over time, and it had been proved to her on Alpha Force exercises.

She was glad the other Alpha Force shifters hadn't brought their cover dogs. If they had and they'd heard her open the front door, they might have assumed the roles of watchdogs and barked, alerting their humans that someone was on the move. Fortunately, Lupe was good about following commands—including *stay*—and she would know it was her mistress she heard.

Outside, there was very little light on the cement-covered area between the houses, but the moon was building up to being full soon and that illumination was enough for her. She kept her flashlight in her pocket as she approached the other building, then extracted her key card from that same pocket.

Once inside the meeting house she used her flashlight to get to the stairway to the basement.

And stopped at the closed door.

She had thought she wouldn't need to use her acute sense of hearing much that night, but she had nevertheless heard something downstairs. Who was there?

Someone tainting the remainder of the elixir?

Knowing she should run for help, she wanted to know first what she was dealing with. She reached carefully for the door and pulled it open just a little—and saw that a light was on downstairs.

She was about to turn and hurry out to seek assistance when she realized that those same enhanced senses of hers told her who it was. She smelled the light, masculine tangy scent that had become familiar—and delicious—to her.

Owen's scent.

Really? What was he doing here? Or was it someone else who knew how shifters thought and was attempting to smell like him?

She decided to find out rather than run away. But as quietly as she started down the stairs, it was almost as if Owen had enhanced senses, too—or at least his hearing.

"Is that you, Selena?" he called quietly. "I've been expecting you."

Chapter 20

Selena felt her heart rate accelerate. What did Owen mean?

And was anyone with him…or was she going to be alone with him in this unoccupied house?

She straightened her shoulders as she walked down the well-lit stairway in a manner that she intended to look cool and professional.

"What do you mean you were expecting me?" she demanded. "I didn't know I was coming here until a few minutes ago."

He waited at the base of the stairs, dressed, like her, in black. His smile was anything but nonchalant or impersonal. His gaze rolled down her body, making her tingle with desire.

No. That wasn't why she was here. She had a goal to accomplish this night. She couldn't allow herself to be diverted from it.

In moments, his eyes rose again to capture hers, and his smile disappeared. His abruptly serious expression seemed to rob her of the sexual interest that had permeated all of her only seconds before.

Well, it wasn't completely gone. But she realized that

no matter what he felt, that wasn't what he was about to discuss.

"As good as it is to see you alone in the middle of the night again, that's not what I'm talking about," he said. "I've gotten to know you a bit in the last few days, Selena. I know how dedicated you are to Alpha Force, and thanks to your devotion you're clearly concerned about the success of my CAs' mission. I figured you'd want to check on the condition of your elixir before anyone else drank it tomorrow—and the best time to do that was the middle of the night."

She found herself laughing. "Yes, it does sound like you know me. Is that why you're here, too?"

He nodded. "I wanted to check out the elixir. I was hoping you'd join me. I even planned to call you in a few minutes after I did my initial assessment. I can look at the stuff and even smell it, but I figure you'd be a lot more skilled, with your senses, in confirming whether there are any problems or not."

"You definitely know me," Selena said. Or at least he understood some of the abilities of shifters, even when they weren't in shifted form.

She remained on the next-to-last stair, with Owen facing her at the bottom. She had an urge to reach out, to pull him close and kiss him…but they both had work to do. Instead, she moved sideways and stepped onto the floor.

She looked around. She hadn't been in the basement here before, since the only shifting she had watched in this location was Andrea's, upstairs. The male CAs had come down here for their changes.

There appeared to be only one large room with cement walls and several long, upholstered ottomans where the nonshifting aides could observe their charges as the elixir began to work on them.

They were probably sitting there earlier, too, when Sal started to react to the liquid he had drunk. Selena suppressed an angry shudder. "I see a refrigerator over there." She pointed to a tall metal unit against the wall. "I assume that's where the elixir is being stored."

"Yes, that's where Rainey and Jonas and the others have gotten it from."

They both walked quickly along the concrete floor toward the refrigerator. Owen reached it first and opened the door. Inside were a dozen vials in the shape that had become familiar to Selena since she had joined Alpha Force. All the vials contained clear liquid that had to be the special shifting elixir.

"Let's check them out." Selena reached for two on the top glass shelf. They both had metal screw-top caps that were easy enough to open and close. Maybe from now on Alpha Force should package its elixir differently. She held up the vials before her eyes one at a time with the ceiling light in the background. Both appeared still to be clear.

Next, she unscrewed the caps and inhaled. They seemed the usual mild citrus scent she was used to.

No indication of any kind of contamination, let alone ipecac.

"They're okay?" Owen asked.

"They seem to be. Let's check the rest." She put the two she held back into the refrigerator on one side. Owen removed the rest one at a time and she similarly checked each of them.

All seemed fine.

"Then the one that hurt Sal was a fluke?" Owen asked her.

"Is that what you really believe?"

He pursed his lips. "No, but under the circumstances it's what I hoped."

"We can check them out again tomorrow before any of the shifters drink them, but I know you'll lock the house again now, so it'll probably be fine." Or so Selena said, even though she wished she could be certain.

The house had been locked up before, too, yet a vial had become contaminated. That hadn't happened on its own. Nor did she believe that the supply Patrick and the other Alpha Force members had brought from Ft. Lukman had been tainted there or somewhere on the way.

What was the answer? Did the CAs all have keys to this meeting house? Even if they did, surely none of them would have tainted the elixir—would they?

She wished she knew.

"Too bad your elixir isn't somehow primed to let people know what's happened to it," Owen said, echoing her thoughts.

She laughed nevertheless. "I know you must think of shifters like me as woo-woo kinds of entities, but that idea out-woo-woos everything. A liquid that communicates with people around it? I'll have to relay that idea to our superiors who formulate the tonic and see if they can figure out a way to do it."

"Guess you've opened my mind to possibilities I'd never imagined before."

"Then you've really got an imagination," Selena responded, still smiling. "Got a million dollars? I'll sell you shares in a company that'll make that imaginary elixir."

It was Owen's turn to laugh. "Wish I had that million bucks, but I don't think I'll buy in to your company. Sorry."

He remained standing near her, beside the refrigerator. His expression was lighthearted as he looked down at her. He appeared both boyish and all adult male. All gorgeous, sexy adult male.

Selena knew she had to get out of there. Go to bed, since they'd need to awaken early the next morning for their regularly scheduled breakfast and discussion of what that day would bring—before any shifting took place.

She was tired, and it was the middle of the night.

Yet all she was telling herself was nonsense. What she really wanted was to stay right there with Owen. Throw herself into his arms and take advantage of this completely unanticipated opportunity to make love with him yet again.

She made herself take a step backward. Putting her hand up to her mouth, she feigned a yawn. "Anyhow, it's definitely late. We'd better get to bed."

"My thoughts exactly. How about here?" Owen's tone was low and rough and filled with suggestion that made Selena's insides heat up and churn. She didn't resist when he closed the short distance between them and took her into his arms.

She threw her head back, eagerly awaiting the kiss that came immediately. His lips were hot, his tongue more than suggestive as he pressed his lower body against hers.

She could feel his hardness and could not keep herself from moving her hands from behind him and forward, caressing everything in their path outside his warm clothing—his back, then his buttocks, his hips and, finally, his erection.

His moan made her move even more, one hand finding its way inside the front of his pants until she could grasp his hot stiffness. His readiness made her gasp against his mouth—or was it caused by his hands stroking her similarly, starting with her back and behind, then moving to her breasts?

How did he get her shirt and bra off so quickly without her even realizing what he was doing? Or had her movements assisted him in his efforts?

She had a fleeting thought, as they moved in unison toward the ottomans, that their privacy here might be limited.

But it didn't matter. Not when she easily stripped Owen of all his clothing, too.

Hadn't she believed they would never have this kind of opportunity again?

Was it part of the woo-woo auras around them somehow that they did, just this once more?

Again he had come prepared. In moments, his erection was encased in a condom and she was lying on her back on top of two of the ottomans pushed together against the wall. They were firm and velvety against her bare back, not the best place to make love but certainly adequate.

Selena stroked Owen outside the condom even as he gently pressed his hand against her heated moistness and thrust one finger, then two, inside her.

She wanted to scream out her need. Instead, she once more gasped and said, "Please."

She didn't have to say any more. He adjusted his position and was suddenly inside her, moving and heating her and arousing her even more as she thrust her own body up in a primitive, wonderful rhythm.

She heard him moan her name even as he pounded and pressed harder. "Selena…"

And then she flew over the edge.

Okay, so he had taken advantage of her, here in the silence of the currently unoccupied house.

He had taken advantage of himself, too, Owen thought as he walked behind Selena up the steps to the main floor. As phenomenal as making love with her had been—again—he shouldn't have done it.

The more he made love with Selena, the more he wanted her. But soon they would be in a position of never seeing each other again, even if the CAs' mission was successful. Which it had to be.

When they reached the front door, he reached out for the knob, then stopped. "Okay to open it?"

"You mean you want me to listen and sniff the air to ensure there's nothing or no one out there we don't want to see?" Her tone was wry, but her brilliant amber eyes shone as if she appreciated his acceptance of her. He considered teasing her, lying to her, claiming that wasn't what he'd meant at all. But it had been, at least to some extent. And he did accept her, maybe too much.

Although he still hadn't actually seen her shift…

He had, however, seen her while she was shifted. Watching her in the process would simply give him another reason to see her naked.

Did he really want to see her changing as he had viewed the male CAs actually shifting into their wolf forms?

He well knew the answer was yes, as strange as that seemed even to himself.

"You got it," he told her. "Use all those wolfy senses of yours and make sure we're okay."

He put his arm around her slender, black-clad shoulders as she did, in fact, turn up her nose into the air and inhale. She stood still, and as he watched the concentration on her lovely face, he figured she was listening, too.

In a moment she said, "All seems well, at least as far as I can tell. Time for us to go back to our respective quarters and get some sleep. Tomorrow is going to be filled with one vital exercise."

"That's for sure," he said. But he still didn't open the door. Instead, he pulled her back into his arms and gave her one final, hot, deep kiss for the night, then finally led her outside into the darkness and walked her to the front door of the house where she was staying. There, he gave her another kiss—much quicker and cooler. "See you tomorrow," he whispered.

"No, later today." She stood on tiptoe for a moment and gave him another quick kiss in return, then used her key to enter the house.

Good thing he had parked down the hill so as not to be so obvious about his presence up here. He remained on alert with his human senses as he made his way down the driveway, and the brief walk gave him some additional time to think.

As Selena had not had to remind him, tomorrow was damned important.

Despite not being a shifter, he had special senses, too—more intuition than enhanced bodily senses, though.

His gut told him that they would all have to be particularly careful tomorrow in the last round of exercises.

Would something go wrong?

Not if he could help it.

Despite lying in her bed and hearing Lupe snoring gently on the floor beside her, Selena didn't sleep much that night.

It wasn't entirely because she kept rehashing in her mind her latest round of great sex with Owen. No, she was worried.

She had come here as a member of Alpha Force, and her very special unit had been trusted with a very special assignment.

They had all, every one of them, performed well so far, demonstrating and teaching and advising.

But was it enough?

For it seemed there was something else they had to do, something that hadn't been fully anticipated.

They had to protect their students. Protect them potentially from perhaps the most vital part of what they were contributing to help the CAs—the Alpha Force elixir.

Maybe. Maybe the presence of that ipecac, or another chemical, had been a fluke. An accident. It wasn't present in the remaining vials. Selena was pretty convinced of that.

At least it hadn't been tonight, when Owen and she had been there.

But tomorrow?

Did the Alpha Force team dare to allow the CAs to drink the stuff again, just in case?

Did they dare forbid them from trying it—especially when that could ruin their entire pending mission?

One ugly thought in particular imposed itself in Selena's mind.

What if Owen truly had been waiting for her that night? What if he had fully intended her to be there with him checking out the elixir, to ensure that it was pure and untainted, so she could report that to Patrick Worley and the other Alpha Force members here?

She hadn't actually seen Owen leave this enclave.

What if he had gone back inside the meeting house, down into the basement, and contaminated one or more vials of the elixir that she would, at least theoretically, vouch for tomorrow?

Was that why he had made love with her again—as one hot, major, sexy distraction?

No. Surely not. He couldn't do such a terrible thing... could he?

Or was she convincing herself he wouldn't because, despite all her better judgment, she was falling in love with him?

She wasn't certain. Couldn't be certain.

As a result, she would definitely get up very early in the morning and check out the elixir yet again, before Owen arrived. Or appeared to arrive.

During the rest of the day she would be cautious, too. She loved Alpha Force. She owed it to Alpha Force to do her job right. A life could be riding on the result—that kidnap victim's.

The lives of the shifting CAs, too.

"Oh, Owen," she whispered into the night and heard Lupe's doggy nails on the wooden floor beside her bed as her cover dog stood at her words. She reached over and petted Lupe's soft, furry head. "It's okay, girl. I'm just talking out loud. We'll be fine. I'll make sure of it."

She hoped. And she definitely hoped she would not have to accuse the man she was starting to love of treason against his country.

Owen received a phone call very early in the morning from his superior, Deputy Commissioner Anthony Creay.

The call didn't wake him, though. He hadn't slept well that night. And he wasn't surprised.

He had a lot on his mind, including Selena Jennay... and her many, diverse, amazing assets.

"What's up, Anthony?" he asked after their initial greetings. He didn't rise from bed but just lay there, waiting.

"Another message from our kidnappers," he said. "This one was another warning—and a recorded message from their hostage begging for help. They're trying to ratchet things up as they play games with us. And before you ask, we've again put some of our most skilled technical people on it to try to track down where the calls are coming from, but these guys are smart. The signals are bounced around the entire solar system, or so it seems. In any event, there's some satellite involvement from what I gather, as well as pinging from several different countries all over the world. But some newer-technology drones we had flying in the vicinity where we believe they're hiding did sense some kind of outside human presence within the woods—before their electronics were hacked into this time. The kidnappers might just have some kind of undercover sentry on duty, though, since there wasn't any indication of anyone going to or leaving the site. All the more reason to send in your shapeshifters, since the drones also conveyed indications of wildlife in the area."

"What was the warning this time?"

"Basically the same kind of thing, reminding the RCMP that poor, frantic, screaming Madame Brodheureux will be killed in days unless her loving husband dips into the coffers of Xanogistics really quickly now and pays them off. Oh, and all games must stop and reality is the key, whatever that means."

"It still sounds to me as if they've heard rumors of something like shapeshifters supposedly coming to save their prisoner, don't you think?"

"Yeah, I think. And I also think that, if so, we have a traitor in our midst—one who has to be outed before your actual operation begins tomorrow. Any ideas?"

"I'm working on it," Owen said, and he was. The problem was that he hadn't yet reached any conclusions. Whoever it was had to have knowledge and somehow have the ability to reach those kidnappers. Or perhaps be one of them in a double-agent role here.

Who? And how?

One of his new team? A member of Alpha Force? Either way could be deadly to the CAs.

"Any further information on that shifting liquid?" Anthony asked, changing the subject somewhat. Or not. The likely scenario was that the same person who was in contact with the kidnappers had also tainted the elixir.

"Not yet, although I worked with one of the Alpha Force members to confirm that what we still have here appears pure and workable."

"Let's hope so. Now, keep me informed about today's

exercises as they're undertaken. I'll want to feel sure that tomorrow's a go."

So will I, Owen thought. "Yes, sir," he said. They soon hung up. A good thing.

It was definitely time to start this new day.

Chapter 21

That morning, before they all went to the meeting house for breakfast and to help the CAs prepare for their day, Selena requested a brief session with her fellow Alpha Force members.

Patrick looked at her curiously as they all headed into the sparsely furnished living room—their CO was wearing official camo fatigues. "Something wrong?"

"You mean besides some of our elixirs being tainted yesterday?" Selena had stopped beside the fireplace, Lupe at her side, and stood watching the others. She felt too restless to sit down. Too uneasy, and too eager to accomplish something, anything.

Seeing Patrick's displeased grimace at her sarcasm, she realized she needed to settle down and act like the professional military member she was.

"Sorry," she said. "It's just that I've been concerned about it, as we've all been. I even wound up visiting the meeting house in the middle of the night and going to the basement to do what I could to check the remaining vials."

"Really? By yourself?" Rainey, sitting on the edge of

the sofa, looked hurt, as if she thought she should have been asked to accompany her.

Selena had already gone through several scenarios in her mind and decided to be truthful—to a point. "No, it turned out that Owen was as worried as I was, so we met up there and checked out all the vials. He recognized that I would be better than him in noticing any inappropriate odors, but we both studied the coloration. They all seemed fine. But just so you all know, that's where I'm sneaking off to first thing this morning, too—the basement of the meeting house, and I won't want the CAs to know. I just feel I need to double-check those vials again. Okay?"

What if whoever had contaminated that one vial purposely allowed the rest to remain pure—until this morning? She still hadn't zeroed in on one person she thought was guilty, but that didn't mean whoever it was wouldn't act again surreptitiously despite their keeping closer watch on the elixir. She looked again at Patrick.

"I think that's a good idea," her commanding officer said, "at least for today's final exercises. But you all should be aware I was concerned, too—so much so that I ordered a new supply of fresh elixir to be flown in today. Jonas and I will drive down after breakfast to pick it up at the Vancouver airport. It'll arrive too late to be used today, so your checking out the current supply again is a great idea, Selena. But we need everything to be perfect tomorrow, and if anything goes wrong it won't be because of anything Alpha Force could have prevented."

"Thank you," Selena said as gratefully as if she was the one in charge and would be blamed for any failure. She almost wanted to laugh at herself. But she did feel relieved, not just because she wasn't the only one who was truly worried, but also because there was a probable solution on the way.

She was surprised when Jonas came over, shook her hand and followed it with a hug. And a laugh. "Since when does our newest member consider herself in charge?" he asked.

"Since this new member is a former schoolteacher and learned fast that anything that goes wrong in her classroom is ultimately her responsibility," Selena responded, feeling a lot more lighthearted.

"Okay, let's head on over there," Patrick said, breaking up the emotion-fest, which was fine with Selena. "When we get breakfast going, you can excuse yourself to head for the bathroom or whatever. We'll make sure everyone else remains in view while you run your new assessment, okay?"

"Fine with me." Selena felt immensely relieved, first that Patrick was on her side and, second, that she would in fact get the opportunity to make one more inspection.

She only hoped that Patrick found a way to capture Owen's attention, or at least secure his presence. Not that Selena truly suspected him of anything—or did she? In any case, she'd feel a lot less uneasy if, this time, she remained on her own.

Owen had driven himself back to the enclave alone that morning, parking this time in the area at the top of the hill. He had followed the other CAs, who rode in the rental car driven by Sal. The young man clearly wanted to show that he felt fine this morning.

Was that some kind of indication he had poisoned himself yesterday to remove any suspicion against him about things that might go wrong in the next couple of days?

Highly unlikely. Not that upbeat, enthusiastic kid, right?

Yet at the moment, Owen wasn't ready to dismiss anyone from his list of suspects who could have caused yesterday's incident.

Now he was in the kitchen with his entire group of CAs, who all sat at the table, chatting eagerly about their upcoming day. The two other wolf shifters were priming Sal about what they were likely to see and do in final preparation for undertaking the real thing tomorrow.

"The mountains here are likely a lot different from the ones we'll face tomorrow," Tim was saying. "Less craggy, and maybe even more wooded, is what I've gathered. But we'll rehearse it today as if it was the real thing. Both times, especially tomorrow, the main thing we have to do is remember to act like the wolves we'll be, and prowl, and watch—and help the guys back at our headquarters, who'll be monitoring the video from the cameras we'll be wearing so they can zero in on where the hostage is being held."

Exactly, Owen thought. If only it was that easy.

He wondered when the Alpha Force team intended to join them for breakfast. In the meantime, he and Andrea seemed to be the designated chefs this morning. They were cooking pancakes, easy stuff, quick and filling. That should be enough, along with the caffeine in the coffee he had already brewed, to help stimulate the shifting CAs' energy. Or maybe their adrenaline would be sufficient.

Did shifted werewolves or falcons produce adrenaline?

Heck, he really didn't know much at all about shifters—and here he was, relying on them to lead the way on this highly critical mission.

He nearly pounded the stove with the pan he was holding, the one in which he had just poured pancake batter, but caught himself. His lack of complete knowledge wasn't the only source of his frustration.

He wanted more information about the origin of yesterday's elixir problem. He wanted to feel fully comfortable that tomorrow would be a highly successful day, that the captive would be rescued and the kidnappers caught—or killed.

Speaking of frustration...where was Selena?

As if she had heard him, there she was, along with the rest of the Alpha Force team. They seemed to breeze into the kitchen and take over, as though their confidence in who they were and what they did was secure.

If only he could feel that certain of how things would go.

"Good morning," said Patrick, clearly asserting his position as their leader. He even wore a camouflage uniform this morning, which perhaps was standard for the Alpha Force members on official duty at their own posts. That was fine, as long as he stayed up here and didn't head down the hill to West Columbia, where townsfolk might see him.

Owen assumed he was making a nonverbal statement by his clothes—making sure the CAs remembered who Alpha Force was and what they were doing here.

None of Patrick's subordinates were clad similarly, though. Selena, as usual, managed to make a black T-shirt and jeans look highly sexy. The two aides, Jonas and Rainey, also wore black, but Marshall, though similarly clad, had on deep green clothing.

"Are we all ready for the final exercise today?" Patrick looked around the room at the other CAs, who sipped their coffee and talked softly to each other. Owen wished he had the hearing of a shifter so he could have heard what they'd been discussing. Were they revving each other up for success? Or priming themselves to do what they could, yet potentially fail?

It should certainly help to have the Alpha Force members among them.

"Pancakes? Yum." That was Selena, who joined him at the stove.

"Care to help me cook them?" he asked.

"Sorry. I need to take a potty break, and hopefully you'll be finished cooking by the time I get back here."

Really? Potty break, when she had just arrived from right next door? She didn't look ill or uncomfortable. That seemed like too much information anyway.

Owen had a thought, that what she'd said was intended for everyone to hear. He also had an idea where she was really going when she left the kitchen. Would she go downstairs to the basement alone to give the elixir a final check for the day? He hoped so.

On the other hand, what if she was the person who'd contaminated it? He didn't think so, didn't want to think so, but...

She had been gone a little more than a minute when he decided he wanted to join her if his assumption of where she had gone was correct. He could then observe to make sure she didn't do anything she shouldn't with the elixir. Despite believing his suspicion had no merit, he couldn't be positive.

He sidled up to Andrea, who was whipping up some additional batter in a bowl on the counter. "How about watching this for me? I need to take a short break, too."

"Sure," she said and took his place at the stove.

But before Owen got to the kitchen door, Patrick joined him. "We need to talk," he said. The guy spoke with command, and Owen had a feeling that if he said no, Patrick would find a way to ensure that got changed to a yes, but he decided to try anyway.

"About today's exercise? Sounds like a good idea. Soon as I get back."

"No, now."

"Like I said, I need a break." Owen kept his expression calm but put an edge into his voice.

"You want to do an exercise today, then let's talk now."

That convinced Owen all the more that not only was Selena checking out the elixir again, but her commanding officer was also well aware of it—and didn't want anyone else there.

Did that prove Selena was trustworthy...or that Patrick and the other Alpha Force members were not?

No matter. Owen's superiors had entered into the arrangement with Alpha Force trusting them fully. What reason would they have for turning it upside down? Because they were somehow affiliated with the kidnappers? Because the US wanted to sabotage what the RCMP needed to accomplish and allow the hostage to be murdered for some international purpose he couldn't fathom?

It was possible, but highly unlikely. And if Owen decided to dig in his heels, maybe his CAs would get no more access to the vital elixir.

"Okay," he finally said, holding up his hands in what he hoped appeared like surrender. "Let's talk."

But surrender wasn't really in Owen's vocabulary. He had every intention of finding out where Selena had gone and why.

Selena came into the dining room a short while later, practically panting from being out of breath.

She'd done what she needed to and had hurried as she had checked out each of the dozen vials of elixir one more time.

All had still seemed fine. Even so, she would quietly advise the two shifting aides, Jonas and Rainey, to do a final check of each bottle they had their charges drink.

She trusted them. Both had been members of Alpha Force for a while, both in the role of aides to shifters. They hadn't been responsible for yesterday's problem.

And if it turned out there was a problem today? She second-guessed herself. Well, if so, it might be one of them despite her trust.

Taking a deep breath to calm herself, she smiled as she walked toward the end of the large table, where Patrick sat beside Owen. There was an empty chair across from them. "Sorry for the delay," she said without elaborating. She sat down, and soon pancakes and a bottle of syrup were passed to her.

"Are you feeling okay?" Owen asked her. She looked into his face and found that his strong, dark eyebrows were raised over his intense blue eyes. He looked more amused than concerned, and she had a feeling he knew exactly what she had been up to.

"Oh, yes. I wound up checking something on my

phone and time got away from me." She smiled brightly, knowing she wasn't fooling him.

But neither did he look worried. If he was guilty of something, his handsome face would surely be blank if he didn't appear uneasy. That was a good thing.

Just because she hadn't found any problems, though, she couldn't categorically dismiss him from her suspicions.

"Mmm," she soon said. "These pancakes are great. You made them?" She raised her own brows questioningly as she looked at him.

"Yes," he said, "mostly, although Andrea helped."

"Guess you're a man of many talents." Selena took another bite of pancake, knowing she was both teasing and goading him.

Today was likely the last day they would get to see each other. She hoped that all went perfectly with the CAs' last exercise, and she certainly intended to do all she could to guarantee it. But she also planned to enjoy as much as she could her last interplay with Owen. Especially knowing that getting close to him in any manner from now on would be impossible.

Owen hurried from the basement behind Jonas, who, in turn, was behind the three male wolves loping up the stairs ahead of them.

He had just watched them shift. Once again, he could only marvel at their transformation.

Sal, the last of this line of wolves, had seemed fine this time, fortunately. Because Selena had made sure all the elixir remained untainted? Owen was sure that hadn't hurt. He hadn't yet confirmed his assumption about what she had done this morning, but he felt fairly certain of it.

Was that because he had begun to be able to sense things about her? Maybe, or maybe that was just his wish.

He quickly reached the main floor, where Patrick and Marshall waited in the hallway. Their heads were turned to observe the wolves who'd passed them, heading toward the front door. When they turned back Owen saw the smiles on their faces.

"Andrea's already outside," Patrick said. "Selena and Rainey, too, watching our falcon soar above this place. Marshall and I are just hanging around to see our wolves head out for the exercise, but we've got something we need to do, so we'll be leaving in a few minutes."

"Fine," Owen said, then realized, with Jonas and Rainey again heading into the woods to remain at a designated clearing in case they were needed, that would leave him alone here with Selena.

Thoughts of what they could do alone together made his body start to react, but he tamped down those errant ideas. There was too much they still needed to do, no time to make those thoughts become reality.

It was too bad, but he told himself it was better that way. They'd already said that kind of goodbye to one another.

He was the last to go outside, but he was still able to see the wolves run through the paved area toward the woods, followed by Jonas and Rainey. Selena already stood near the path the wolves took, and she turned to watch as they disappeared among the trees.

Above soared the falcon who was Andrea.

The exercise had begun.

He watched as Selena talked briefly with Patrick and

Marshall. Then the two men crossed the paved area and got into their car.

As they drove off, Owen thought once more about how he was now, once again, here alone with Selena. But instead of considering how best to seduce her, he waited until she joined him near the front door of the meeting house and told her, "Looks like it's just us to finish cleaning up after breakfast."

If anything was a turnoff, it had to be that. But Selena's expression as she regarded him with a warm smile somehow still seemed to convey interest in him.

All she said, though, was "Lucky us. Let's get it over with."

As they walked inside, Selena asked once more what he'd thought about watching the men become wolves.

"I doubt I'll become blasé about it," he said. "It seems incredible every time I watch, even though I know it's real."

She was ahead of him and turned back, as if wanting to see his expression, to try to read his mind about what he really thought about it: "It's definitely real," she said. She preceded him past the living room door and into the kitchen.

The morning's plates and flatware had been stacked in the sink. He moved past her. "I'll wash, you put them into the drainer, okay?"

"Fine."

They seemed to coordinate well with no effort. He remained highly aware of Selena's curvaceous form beside him, taking the soapy objects from him, rinsing them, then sticking them into the dish rack in a very organized manner. He wasn't surprised about that. Selena seemed organized, logical, in all she did.

Was she that way while shifted, too?

He'd seen her as a wolf a couple of times, but only briefly. He would likely never see her again that way or learn more about her in her canine form.

Too bad, especially now, when he really had become interested in shifters. His earlier distrust of them had been replaced by at least somewhat of an admiration. He was glad he was the officer in charge of the CAs— and he hoped he would continue to be after tomorrow.

Would they succeed in their operation?

Would they—

His phone rang. He smiled as Selena handed him a towel and he dried his hands.

When he pulled his phone from his pocket, he noticed immediately that it was Anthony Creay calling. "Hello, sir," he said. "I was going to call you a little later. Our exercise of the day has begun, and—"

"There's been yet another message from the kidnappers," Anthony interrupted. "It didn't make much sense, but this is what it said—'Grab on to today since things will go wrong and tomorrow will be worse.'"

Selena realized that Owen did not intend for her to hear his conversation with his boss, but with her enhanced hearing she couldn't help it.

Not that she tried to avoid eavesdropping.

But what did that message mean?

Was something off about what the shifters were planning today as practice for what would actually occur tomorrow?

Would whatever it was lead to failure the next day?

She had to do something to ensure all went well, no matter what that cryptic message meant.

She knew how the mission at least had to begin, and so when Owen ended his conversation and hung up, his expression distant and grim, she said, "I know what I have to do, Owen, at least for now. And you need to help me."

Chapter 22

Was she overreacting? Or was she using this new twist as a reason to do what she'd wanted to do for days, to learn Owen's true feelings about shifters, about her?

Maybe both. Or neither.

"What are you up to?" Owen's expression was both quizzical and amused.

She feared the latter part would undoubtedly change quickly once he knew what was on her mind.

"I want to learn what's really going on," she told him. "Do my own kind of observation today so we can feel comfortable everything will be as good as possible tomorrow. But as I said, I will need your help."

"Sure," he said, sounding anything but sure. "What exactly do you want me to do?"

"Act as my aide. I'm going to shift."

She watched his expression even more carefully, as if her human sense of vision was effective not only for viewing what was happening around her, but also for delving into someone's mind. Owen's mind. Too bad that wasn't really true.

He said nothing for a few seconds, and his expression was unreadable. Did he hate the idea? Would he find an excuse to say no or just come right out and object? She could conceivably handle a shift on her own—but the test part of this equation was important to her, too.

"Good idea," he said finally, half surprising her. "But you're going to have to let me act as your aide not only for shifting, but also for helping to watch out for you during this exercise."

His reaction was interesting. Sure, she knew he was protective, a worthy member of the RCMP, but this went beyond his duty. She didn't ask how he intended to watch out for her. In reality, if she didn't want his help beyond her initial shifting, she would be able to outrun him and ensure he couldn't catch up or be anywhere near her.

She would have to determine what was the best course of action later.

While she was shifted.

At last. He was finally going to get to watch this lovely, human woman go through the clearly uncomfortable—and incredible—process of shapeshifting.

His wish—one of them, at least—was apparently about to come true.

Be careful what you wish for. The old cautionary expression suddenly invaded his mind.

He shooed it out just as quickly.

It turned out that Selena had been particularly smart. Not that he was surprised, since he'd already been impressed by this woman and her knowledge and teaching capabilities and intellect.

Not to mention her physical assets.

But she had also been wise enough to camouflage what was the final vial of elixir that Rainey and she had

had with them when they had first joined Anthony and him, before he had taken the women here to join his CAs.

It was in the refrigerator in the basement of the house in which the Alpha Force members were staying, hidden in what appeared to be a brand-new carton of orange juice.

He found that out after she told him to follow her back to the other home. There, after unlocking the door, she first knelt and gave Lupe, who had been with them, a big hug, then secured her in the bedroom. Afterward they trekked down to the basement fridge for the precious vial.

Now, in the kitchen, he watched as she peeled the cardboard of the orange-juice container away from the glass vial inside. She stood leaning against the counter near the sink, studying the liquid it contained.

"It looks clear, no contamination." She unscrewed the cap and held it to her nose. "No indication of anything but the usual citrusy scent, nothing like ipecac. Of course, I doubt anyone but Rainey and me knew this was here. But even so, there's no guarantee no one else got into this place to do some damage."

"You still think that's what happened with the contaminated bottle Sal drank." He made it a statement, not a question, because that was his belief, too.

"What else could it be?"

He didn't want to get into the other possibilities again, like some kind of problem at the source or en route. No, it was better to assume the trouble originated here and remain cautious.

Like Patrick was doing by retrieving the new supply of elixir that had been shipped here. The stuff that would be used tomorrow. It was a good idea, and Selena had just informed him that was what Patrick and Marshall were up to.

"Okay," she said. "Time to go back to the other house. I want to shift there, in the basement." She opened up a cabinet and withdrew a plastic shopping bag. "This will be strictly an observational detail on my part, and nothing else should be necessary today. I just figure that by watching who's doing what, I'll be able to give some advice to your CAs about how to act tomorrow during the real rescue operation."

That was probably true, but only in part. He knew that her need to do this had been precipitated by his phone call from Anthony Creay and the additional threat it seemed to contain.

He hoped that the techie team set on tracking down the call's source was successful this time. But since it hadn't been before, he remained dubious.

Having someone who knew what she was doing—Selena—provide the kind of advice she was clearly intending to give could be essential to the success of the CAs tomorrow.

They definitely had to be successful on this first attempt. It might very well be their last.

He watched her seal the bottle again and place it in the yellow plastic bag with a supermarket logo on it. If anyone happened to notice her carrying it, she would simply seem to be moving food from one of the houses to the other.

Another smart move on her part, he thought. But when had she done anything other than act smart?

On their way back to the other house, he wished he had some of her enhanced senses. Would he hear anything beyond the normal breeze in the treetops, an occasional car engine from below the driveway, additional chirps from local birds? Would he smell anything more than the slightly sweet aroma of the surrounding fir trees?

They didn't talk. He had a lot of questions about what she would be looking for…and what her shift really would feel like. But he assumed she was using those enhanced senses of hers to ensure their safety on their hurried walk and did not want to interrupt her.

Once they'd reentered the other house and locked its doors again behind them, Owen followed Selena down the steps to the basement.

He knew the drill. He'd seen it several times now when Jonas had acted as aide to the wolf-shifting CAs. Without Selena having to say anything, he crossed the large, concrete-encased room to the refrigerator. Beside it, on the floor, sat a wooden crate. It contained the special battery-operated lantern that created the light resembling that of the full moon.

That would now be his responsibility: aiming it on Selena's naked body to cause her to shift once she had drunk the elixir.

Did he want this to happen? Yes. Maybe. Would he think differently about her once he actually saw her shift?

No. Maybe. But he was more than aware that she was a shifter. Had seen her already shifted.

And between then and now, he had also had the real pleasure of seeing her naked.

"Okay," she finally said, her tone bright and her face beaming. She was clearly looking forward to this.

Was he? He wasn't sure, but he hoped to make her think so.

"This is great," he said, pumping enthusiasm into his voice. "I'll finally get to see you shift." He held the light but did not turn it on yet. No need until she was ready—meaning naked.

He was sorry to see her expression falter, but for only a moment. "Yep," she said. "So you know, once I'm in wolf form my intention is to follow the same path as the wolfen CAs did. I'm sure I'll be able to use my senses to figure out where they went, and if I have any difficulties I'm sure I'll see Andrea flying above them. At this point, I only intend to observe them, make sure all's okay despite what that call Anthony described to you said. I'll also make mental notes about any suggestions I have for tomorrow. This is simply a way of assuring myself, my fellow Alpha Forcers and you that whatever was claimed in that call was a bunch of horse pucky." She grinned. But then she added, "And in case it's not, I'll do what I can to fix it. That may mean my showing up where Rainey and Jonas are, so it wouldn't hurt for you to head there, too, if you can determine where it is. That would be a good way for you to follow up on your intent to not just observe my shift, but to keep an eye on what's going on."

"I'm sure I'll find them," Owen said. In fact, he was certain, since they'd described their rendezvous location to his CAs yesterday and repeated the information earlier that day. The clearing they described was partway up the mountain, along their initial path—the one Selena would follow.

"Okay," she said again. "Here goes." She stood near him as she removed the clear glass vial from the plastic bag. She placed both on the floor.

She started to strip. First, she pulled her black shirt

over her head, mussing her silvery-brown hair, but she did not attempt to smooth it out. She next kicked off her athletic shoes, pulled off her socks and then stepped out of her jeans. She stood there in her underwear for just a moment, looking at him. Smiling softly at him, as if teasing…and tempting.

In moments, she had removed her bra and panties. Without getting near him or waiting to see if he got closer to her, she knelt, picked up the vial of liquid and drank it all quickly.

"Now," she said, "let's get that light going."

And he did.

Ignoring his initial surge of lust at seeing her naked, he watched as if mesmerized as, in moments, her change began. Her limbs grew thinner, changed shape, even as her lovely, smooth skin started to grow hair. Her eyes, still looking at him, remained the same for a long moment, but the rest of her head began quickly morphing into the shape of a wolf's.

He didn't say anything. Couldn't say anything. Was he completely turned off by what was happening?

Yes—and no. He was as fascinated as he had been when the men changed into wolves, even though this was Selena, the woman to whom he was so attracted. With whom he had made love.

He wasn't sure how long he had been watching, but soon there she was—a sleek, fur-covered, attentive wolf.

She stared up at him with her newly modified eyes, her muzzle in the air, watching him stare back at her.

What had he thought of her change? What was he thinking now?

She couldn't ask. Did not want to ask.

She needed to start moving. She had something to accomplish.

She loped to the stairway and up its steps. At the top she had to wait since she could not open the door. She felt Owen's legs against her side as he reached around her and pushed the door so she could get out.

She again had to wait until he opened the front door, and there he maneuvered around so he was the first to go through.

Ever the gentleman, the cautious police officer, he glanced around before allowing her to exit, looking, she imagined, for interlopers.

She waited just in case, not wanting to intrude on what he was doing, yet even in waiting she was not idle. She moved her ears to listen, again lifted her nose to scent the air.

She sensed nothing of any concern.

When Owen stopped walking she sprinted past him, enjoying her freedom to run unimpeded on four legs, swiftly, to the pathway beneath the trees and into the forest.

She did not wait to see if he followed. They had discussed what he would do before, when they could both speak and negotiate and each comprehend what the other was saying.

He called, "Selena, wait," but she did not obey. She was not a trained pet canine. She was an Alpha Force wolf with work to do.

She ran and ran as pine needles scratched at the base of her paws, sometimes feeling only soft dirt instead. Around her were the aromas and sounds of those trees and, sometimes, their occupants—squirrels, birds of many types, wildlife even she did not recognize since this was not her usual habitat.

Finding a small clearing soon that was void of tree branches in the center, she tilted her head back and looked upward. No falcon soaring there.

She picked up only stale aromas, from when the other shifters had trudged through here, yet she slowed her pace when she started off again because she had sensed a different clearing, the one where the aides waited.

What would Rainey do if she knew her shifting charge was so close and in wolfen form? Selena did not know and did not want to find out.

Another clearing appeared, and this time, when she looked up, Selena did see the falcon soaring in circles.

She stalked more slowly this time, not wanting to startle her shifted counterparts into attacking her as if she was truly a wild wolf, a foe of theirs.

She made small woofing noises to alert them, in a pattern humans might recognize as Morse code even if unfamiliar with what the pattern stood for. In this instance she used dash-dot-dash-dot, then dot-dash.

This was one form of communication she had informed these CAs about, should they need to let another one of their kind know of their presence. It was the pattern for C-A.

She approached, scenting all three wolfen forms near her. They were similar yet different in appearance and in scent, and she knew who was who.

Craig was the closest when she entered their clearing at the top of a mountain, along its far side. They each watched her warily as if anticipating she might not be one of their kind.

She simply sat and watched them, nodding her head.

They soon appeared to accept her, and she observed them start to ignore her and resume the exercise they had been conducting before she'd joined them.

One at a time, they lowered their bodies closer to the ground and slunk to the edge of the clearing. Then they each raised their heads and looked out from among the trees over the nearby valley to the mountain slope just beyond. They scented the air as their ears moved to capture sounds.

As if they were in fact in a similar area, searching similar mountains for signs of life. Human life. Kidnappers and victims.

She found no indication of any problems, any danger, despite the message received by Anthony Creay. Even so, she waited and watched, curious, cautious... and concerned.

Owen had just joined Rainey and Jonas at the clearing, where they waited as backup for the shifted CAs. It had been challenging to locate it, but he had finally succeeded.

The area was small, with several boulders in the center, where they sat and waited and chatted.

They looked up, no doubt to watch for a falcon circling overhead. Owen had seen the soaring bird that was Andrea several times on his way up here when there had been other breaks in the trees, and he couldn't help but marvel. Despite her falcon form, she was actually another person...most of the time.

As was Selena.

Now, joining the aides, he told them he was here to observe, went through the motions of acting normal, as if he hadn't just seen the most incredible situation in his life—watching Selena shift into wolf form.

Yes, he had anticipated everything that had happened during her shift. Hadn't he already viewed the men changing from human to wolf form several times? He'd known what to expect.

But this time, it was Selena. Gorgeous, nude Selena.

"Why are you here?" Rainey asked as she walked over to where he stood by the path. She cast a look over her shoulder at Jonas, who was surveilling the woods. Her dark hair seemed even more a nest of curls than usual, maybe because of the breeze here. "Where is Selena?"

"She's—"

"She shifted, didn't she?" An amused and too-smug smile appeared on the aide's face. Did she know that Owen had made love with the shifter she'd been assigned to assist? He had a sinking feeling she did.

Well, so what? It was over now. *They* were over now, except for working together on this difficult assignment for the organizations they worked for.

"Is she up on this mountain, too?" Rainey asked next when he didn't directly respond to her other question. At least that one he had no issue about answering.

"Yes, she's joining the CAs for now."

"But why?" That was Jonas, who had hurriedly strode over to join Owen. He, too, wore casual dark clothing.

Talking to them forced Owen to focus on what they were saying instead of the vision of Selena and her shift that still occupied his mind.

"My superior officer called about yet another communication from the kidnappers. They made vague references that suggested that they knew we were about to take action against them. They didn't mention shapeshifters but indicated something was going to go wrong with whatever was planned. So Selena decided to shift and come up here to check on the CA shifters. Have you heard anything from them?"

"No," Rainey said, "and that probably means all's well."

"Maybe," Owen said slowly. "But...you know, maybe I should just have called to let you know Selena is here on the mountain, too, so you can watch out for her as well as the others. But right now I think I need to get back to our headquarters and wait for everyone there."

It had just occurred to Owen that it was a vital location that was currently unguarded by either CAs or Alpha Force members. It was probably fine, but he couldn't shake the unease. The kidnappers' threats continued to ring through his mind.

With the shifters up here on the mountain rehearsing what they would do tomorrow, these aides here to be their backup and Patrick and Marshall away from the headquarters picking up new elixir, the enclave was left particularly vulnerable—if the kidnappers had learned of its existence and it was the target of whatever they'd threatened to do.

Someone needed to be there to make sure it stayed secure.

That someone, Owen decided, had to be him.

With some help, perhaps. He would move Lupe to the main meeting house. She could bark if anyone appeared who shouldn't be there—and could act as Selena's cover if she happened to show up.

He headed to the Alpha Force house to get her.

Chapter 23

*E*nough. Selena had been there, with the other shifters, for a while. In this form she had the same sense of time as she did in human form, and it felt like an hour. More than an hour. Too long, especially since all seemed fine in their exercise. Nothing appeared amiss in their rehearsal of how they would best fulfill their assignment tomorrow to observe, to learn, to save a life.

She would not be there with them. Would not need to be. And as it had turned out, she did not need to be with them now to confirm all was going well despite her concerns.

Only, had she not come, she would not be certain of that, especially not this soon.

Now Sal sat with her in the clearing while Craig and Tim prowled nearby, continuing to assess this mock situation. She stood and edged toward Sal, then nudged his side with her muzzle to ensure he knew she intended to communicate with him. When he looked at her and made a noise deep in his throat, she nodded sideways toward the path down the hill.

Then, without waiting for him to acknowledge what she had conveyed, she began walking in that direction.

Toward that other clearing, where the aides waited. Where Owen waited.

Only, when she arrived there, just Rainey and Jonas were present. She stood at the edge of that clearing for a while, observing, expecting to see Owen emerge from the trees on one side or another, but he did not.

Rainey spotted her, though. That was part of her job as an aide, being available as assistance for the shifted CAs—remaining aware of all around her and prepared to act as cover or backup or protection or whatever a shifter might need.

Now Selena needed to know where Owen was. She could not ask that question and in fact preferred that the aides, Rainey in particular, did not even recognize her desire to know.

But Rainey was ever aware. "Selena? Everything okay?" She rushed toward her.

Selena nodded her head. There were times when she was in wolf form that she wanted more than anything the ability to truly communicate with humans. Times like now.

But with Rainey, she did not necessarily need to speak. Her aide knew her well. Perhaps too well.

"I figure you checked on the CAs, right?" Rainey asked her now. "That's what Owen said. Are you looking for him? He headed back to the meeting house to wait."

Now Selena was glad she could not speak. She did not need to acknowledge she was seeking Owen. She merely turned and began loping along the path toward the enclave.

As she neared it, apprehension and concern seemed to speed her up, as if turning her legs to limbs that were even more fleet than a normal, swift wolf's.

Where did the concern come from? She did not know.
She only knew it was there.

As soon as Owen exited the path from the trees he saw an unfamiliar car on the pavement at the top of the hill along with the known rentals. He froze and immediately reached for his service weapon—which he did not have with him.

As a police officer on regular duty he was often armed. But his latest assignment was far from regular duty.

He would have to be cautious checking out who was there, but just because someone had come to the enclave did not mean there was a problem.

Looking around from the edge of the path, where he could duck behind the trees and call for backup if necessary, he observed movement. A person stood at the front door of the meeting house.

He recognized the man who was holding what appeared to be pizza boxes. He was one of the servers from the Yukon Bar. What was his name?

Oh, yeah… Boyd.

He didn't look threatening, especially not if he had brought dinner. But who had ordered it? No one had mentioned it to Owen.

In case it was some kind of ploy, he would continue to be vigilant.

"Hey," he called out as he strode from the trees, "what's going on?"

"Pizza." The guy raised the boxes in his hand. His light brown hair was blowing in the breeze, revealing how his ears stuck out. As Owen drew closer, he noticed that Boyd was frowning, but he wasn't acting at all threatening.

"I don't think anyone here ordered pizza." Owen figured that acting negative would get Boyd to reveal his mental state faster than simply okaying and paying for the pies.

"Yeah. It was called in some time ago. Whoever called said to deliver it now—around three o'clock." Boyd repositioned the boxes so he could balance them on one arm, then reached for his pocket. Owen froze, waiting for a weapon to appear, but instead the guy pulled out a phone and looked at it, probably checking the time.

"Do you know who made the call?" And who, therefore, had neglected to reveal it to Owen and possibly anyone else.

"Craig, I think. He's one of the guys I met at the Yukon. But this stuff was ordered from the pizza shop next door where I work during the day. I don't know if he's staying here, but I was told he hangs out here."

Craig. Why would he have ordered food when he was out for training, especially without telling anyone?

"And did Craig pay for it?" Owen asked.

"No, he didn't." Boyd's voice was suddenly chilly and he stared straight at Owen in the fading daylight. "Is he here? Let me talk to him."

"I'm not sure where he is." That wasn't a lie. Owen had a general idea of where the shifter might be, but he wasn't sure of his exact location. "I'll pay you for it."

"Okay." Boyd seemed to relax. Maybe this was legitimate. But Owen didn't like it.

He'd have to have a talk with Craig later about being responsible, particularly on days when an exercise was scheduled, especially a shifting exercise.

Owen reached into his trousers, pulled out his wallet and drew several bills from it. "Keep the change," he said, then exchanged the money for the boxes.

He didn't go into the house but stood there watching as the guy got into his car and drove off.

Only then, shaking his head, did Owen enter the Alpha Force house.

No! Something was terribly wrong. Selena had had an inkling of it before, but now she was certain of it as she watched the exchange between Owen and the server—Boyd—from the edge of the woods.

She smelled the spicy scent of the food Owen now carried into the house.

If that had been all she smelled, she would not feel so worried.

But the scent of ipecac assaulted her nostrils. Not as strong as the tomato, onions, oregano, garlic and a whole lot of red peppers. Much more subtle, but it hung in the air and nearly made her feel ill.

Or was that her concern, her fear for Owen?

Was the ipecac in the pizza? But the odor did not seem to entirely disappear into the house with Owen.

Then Boyd had some on his body? Maybe. But with his departure, shouldn't the scent have left, too?

Would it help for Selena to go into the house and find a way to warn Owen that all might not be well? That he should not eat that pizza? That he should perhaps call for backup, get her Alpha Force aides back down the hill and into action here, to protect their location... and Owen, too?

She had heard a dog woof when Owen went in. It sounded like Lupe. Owen must have moved her into this

house after Selena had run off in wolf form. That famil-
iar woof was her normal reaction to a person entering
someplace where she was located, but she was trained
well enough not to react as a watchdog unless confused
or specifically given an order to react that way.

But now, suddenly, Lupe barked loudly but briefly.
What was happening? Selena had to find out.

And she had to reassure herself that Owen was un-
harmed...or so she hoped.

Odd, Owen thought. Maybe it was nothing, but it just
didn't feel right. He went straight to the kitchen, not only
to put down the food, but also to let Lupe loose.

He was quite surprised to see Yvanne there, kneeling on the floor and petting the now-quiet wolflike dog.
She was rather dressed up, in a silvery scarf over her
charcoal-colored shirt that matched her slacks and low-
topped boots, and seemed to be getting along famously
with Lupe—two wolves communicating? Yvanne was
a shifter, of course.

Despite being in human form, she did not look prepared to communicate with Owen. In fact, she appeared
a bit startled to see him. She stood up immediately and
faced him.

What was going on?

"Hi," Owen said, assuming as casual a demeanor as
he could despite being on high alert. "What brings you
here?"

"A late lunch," she said. "I was told the exercise being
held today would be over but only those who'd shifted
would be around." Which meant she knew too much, but
he was already aware of that. "Where's Sal?"

"He's not back yet," Owen said. "Did you order the pizza?"

"No, I heard Craig did."

Something definitely seemed off here. Why would Yvanne think only the shifters would be around now? Or was this some kind of ploy on her part? Had she ordered the pizza and decided on this pretense of innocence for reasons of her own?

"You know," he said, "I was just up on the mountain with our aides. Why don't you and I go back there and see if they know what's going on?" He didn't want to leave this woman here alone. He didn't especially want her with him, either, but at least this way he would know where she was and what she was doing, even if she had some kind of nefarious plan in mind. He needed some backup, and the aides could help to watch her while Owen determined what he needed to do next.

"I don't know," she said. "I was told to wait here."

"By whom?" Owen demanded.

"Would you like a piece of pizza while we're waiting for everyone?"

What he would like was some answers. Yvanne was clearly avoiding answering anything directly.

Which made Owen feel certain he wouldn't like the truth.

"Come on," he said. "We're going up to the aides' station. Now." He wasn't certain that was the best solution, but for the moment it was the best he could think of. "We'll come back and have pizza when the rest of the crowd's ready." He hoped that would take some of the onus off his giving her an order.

"Well…" She looked nervous, concerned. Which made Owen all the more certain about their leaving.

He grabbed her arm firmly, but not strongly enough to hurt her. "Let's go."

She had forced herself to stay hidden as she watched Boyd's car drive off.

She saw then that the front door of the meeting house was closed, but she nevertheless heard Owen talking with someone else. There were no other cars up here except for the rentals that belonged to the group. Who was there?

She needed to go inside. Now.

Slowly, stalking along the ground, she drew nearer. Below the strong odor of the ipecac wafted the softer scent of another human beside Owen. That scent soon joined with another. Identifiable. Human.

She knew then who was inside.

She wasn't certain but believed she knew why.

And just in case, she had to find a way to help Owen.

Owen didn't want to drag Yvanne or do anything physical beyond what he had already done to garner her cooperation. He wasn't acting as a police officer in charge here, and even if he'd had his weapon, this wasn't the kind of circumstance in which he would use it.

He was glad, then, that although Yvanne resisted his initial touch, she shrugged off his hand and started moving slowly toward the kitchen door and into the hallway.

And stopped.

"Oh, there you are, Holly." Yvanne sounded relieved.

Holly Alverton stood there, and despite her small

stature she blocked the way Owen had intended to go. A disproportionately large purse was slung over her shoulder. What was she doing there?

What were both women doing here?

"I know this is supposed to be a surprise," Yvanne continued, "and I didn't say anything, but I think maybe you need to let Owen in on it."

"What kind of surprise?" He kept his tone cool even though he wanted to demand an answer. Was this some kind of game? A joke?

This was not the time for either. And the women should not have been here.

"A celebration." Holly aimed her large blue eyes down at the floor. "We know today's just practice for something that will be real tomorrow. Yvanne and I love our shifters and we wanted to do something both to thank them and to wish them luck. We just figured having a pizza party here when they got back would show them that. I ordered the pizzas for Craig. It won't be a long party, though, since we know they'll need their rest." She looked around Owen and into the kitchen. "I see Lupe there, but is everyone else up on the mountain?"

That seemed too nosy a question. She didn't need to know where any of the CAs or Alpha Force members were. He'd already mentioned to Yvanne that the aides were up on the mountain and she could probably guess where the others were, too. But Owen didn't choose to answer Holly.

"I appreciate the thought," he lied, "but since you know things might get a bit more intense tomorrow, you should understand that we really need some privacy here to finish our plans."

"We can't party, then?" Holly looked up at him, a

mournful expression on her pretty young face. But Owen had no desire to placate her.

"Sorry, no. In fact, it's time for you to go." Then, to ease things just a little to encourage them to leave, he said, "If all goes well in our actual job, we'll all celebrate afterward, including you." Maybe.

"Well…okay. I want to take the pizza with us, though. Okay with you, Yvanne?" Holly looked toward the other woman, her expression still hurt.

"I guess."

Holly maneuvered around Owen into the kitchen, Yvanne following. Lupe came up to them, too.

Holly patted the dog, then moved sideways, not toward the table.

In moments, Owen saw that she had taken a hypodermic needle from her purse and, with no fanfare, stuck it into Yvanne.

"Hey," the other woman said, looking confused.

"What the—" Owen began, then stopped.

He found himself looking down the barrel of what appeared to be a Smith & Wesson pistol similar to one of the kinds available to RCMP officers.

Holly no longer looked sorrowful. Determination and glee now framed her face as she raised the gun to his head.

Chapter 24

*S*he heard.

From the back of the house, Selena had been able to listen to some of the conversation that must have been occurring in the hallway.

Holly and Yvanne had planned something that did not sound right, some kind of party.

She heard much more when they all reassembled in the kitchen, and it made her fur stand on end.

"What the hell did you do to her?" Owen demanded. "What was in that needle?"

"Something temporary until I decide on the best way to kill her—more drugs or a gunshot wound like you'll die from soon. I know exactly how to use this gun." That was Holly's voice. Had she drugged Yvanne? "I have to figure out how to make it look like you took one another out."

"Why? What's this all about?"

Owen's voice sounded furious. If only she was in human form and could enter the house at will. But shifting back would take time she didn't want to expend.

More important, her being shifted like this was better. Holly might not expect it.

Yet she might, with so many shifters around.

And she apparently had a gun.

If only Selena could tell Owen she was here. Could have him arrange for Lupe and her to change places.

"This is about your interference in my life. Our lives. You and your damned CAs." *Holly spit her words out loudly enough that Selena needn't have been in wolfen form to hear them.*

But she was. She also had her human mind. Now she needed to employ both. Quickly. To save Owen as well as the mission of Alpha Force and the CAs.

Staying low to the ground, she growled softly, loud enough for Lupe to hear, but not a human.

Lupe responded right away, giving one short bark. It did not, fortunately, sound like a bark of alarm that would tell Holly of anyone else's presence—human or wolf. Or so Selena hoped.

"I haven't had her out since I've been back here," *Owen said. Did he suspect Selena was there? Or was he just looking for an excuse to get to the door?*

"Fine. I'll let her outside."

"She needs to be leashed."

"She'll survive—or not." *Clearly, the nonshifting woman was a bitch of a different kind.*

There was shuffling inside. Selena guessed from the noise that Holly was making Owen accompany Lupe and her to the door. She slunk around the side of the house toward the front.

In moments the back door opened and Lupe ran out. Fortunately, the door closed again before her cover dog reached her side.

Two canines together. Selena was pleased. She wished she could confine Lupe where she would be safe. Alter-

*natively, she wished that she could communicate with
her and order her to the clearing where the aides waited.
Just her presence there would alert them to the trouble.*

*But commanding her cover dog to go there was not
possible, not while she was shifted.*

She needed time. And help.

*One thing she knew she could accomplish in wolfen
form was to run. Fast. And so, making sure Lupe followed, she began dashing as rapidly as she could toward the clearing where the aides waited—two silvery
fleet and cunning canines with a mission.*

Would Owen be alive when she returned?

The question made her rev up her speed even more.

"So what are you going to do now?" Owen asked.

"Stop talking," Holly demanded. "Now."

Owen had attempted to appear scared and obedient
in the face of a weapon. He currently sat on a chair in
the kitchen. Yvanne lay on the floor near him, and Holly
stood against the wall, facing both of them, her gun
pointed straight at Owen's chest.

If he was honest with himself, he would accept that
he was, in fact, a bit scared of this deranged woman. But
his determination to do his job, and ensure everyone else
was able to do theirs, outweighed any fear within him.

He would succeed...or die trying.

He had hoped that by letting Lupe out, he would buy
some time, and maybe the dog would dash off to find
her Alpha Force trainers and get help.

But Lupe was just a dog, not a shifted human. Not
really Selena, despite being her cover dog.

He wished he could at least have one more conversation with Selena. See her again one more time.

Kiss her again.

But that was the least likely scenario of all.

He just hoped she was off assisting his CAs so that, no matter what happened to him now, they would follow their orders, save the hostage and help to bring down the kidnappers.

The kidnappers.

Was this disturbed woman affiliated with them? His mind raced for a connection.

Either way, she'd indicated she was working on a plan to kill Yvanne and him. Would she start shooting the instant she zeroed in on what to do?

One way or another, *he* had a plan. He would disarm her, perhaps emotionally at first. But definitely physically. Somehow.

He took his time about saying anything, then began another attempt at distraction. "That guy Boyd," he said. "When I first saw him here with the pizza boxes, I wondered what he was really up to. You and he seemed to have something going on before, and—"

"I was just using him," Holly spat. "I wanted someone else in town to look interested in all of us visitors, mostly you CAs and the people from the States you were working with. I flirted with him partly to make Craig jealous, but also so the rest of you wouldn't think too much about Craig and me."

"That worked," Owen said, then changed the subject to something of more concern. "I'd still like to know what you drugged Yvanne with. I assume you didn't use ipecac on her or she'd be awake and throwing up. You were the one to taint the elixir with ipecac yesterday, weren't you?"

"Of course." She looked proud about it, if for only

an instant. "I intended to do more today, even brought some more ipecac along." She gestured toward her purse, which she had put down on the floor. "But the stuff that's already here should be enough to deal with what's planned for tomorrow. I'll add more ipecac in a few minutes." She waved the gun at him menacingly. "And you won't be in condition to do anything about it."

He didn't dare focus on how deranged she seemed to be. He needed to focus on distracting her, no matter what her mental condition was. "We're having fresh, untainted elixir shipped here, but I guess you didn't know that. Patrick requested it. Did you know he's supposed to return any minute after picking the new shipment up? That's what they'll use tomorrow, and once they're here and on guard, you're the one who'll not be able to do anything about it."

It was actually an hour or more before Owen expected Patrick and Marshall to return, but he wasn't about to reveal that to Holly.

"Damn." Her blue eyes that had appeared so sweet and innocent before today now looked crazed. She left her post near the wall and began walking toward him. Owen braced himself, preparing to use any kind of offensive action or self-defense move to disarm her, but she didn't get near him. Instead, she approached Yvanne and gave her a light kick.

The other woman didn't move, although she did appear to still be breathing.

"So what did you drug her with?" he repeated again. "Will she survive it?"

"She'd better," the woman spluttered. "She was only supposed to be knocked out for a minute or two, and it's been nearly twenty minutes now, damn her. Okay, I've decided. When she wakes up, she'll shoot you, then be so upset about it that she'll shoot herself in the head. I'll just be walking in and see the end of it." The expression she next leveled on him looked horrified and mournful. The witch was a good actress.

Not to mention a psycho.

He needed to keep her talking, sidetrack her—and, if possible, learn what all this was really about.

"What will Craig think of all that?" he asked.

"He'll be upset. So upset that he'll leave your horrible CAs, or what's left of them, and come home with me so we can get married the way we planned before you and your miserable Mounties interfered."

Now she was facing him again, her gun aimed at his forehead, but she had taken a few steps back once more and was too far away for him to disarm her.

He still needed to keep her talking. "Then you like shapeshifters?"

"I love them. I love Craig, at least. We're going to be married and I'm going to have his children, and they should all be shifters like him. That's why I had to stop this stupid CAs mission and—" She glared at him and ceased talking.

She had to stop the mission? She had made one CA ill with ipecac, but that wouldn't necessarily have prevented the rest of them from proceeding with their assignment.

Owen wondered again if she had something to do with the kidnappers, even indirectly.

Anthony Creay and he had suspected some kind of mole riling the kidnappers even further, driving them to taunt the police and act faster.

Could it have been Holly? If so, how?

He wasn't going to ask her that. Not now, at least.

"You know," he said quietly, "you and I have something in common."

He paused, waiting for her reaction.

"What? Are you mad about what your stupid team is doing, too?" Her tone was scornful.

"No, I believe in the CAs and how they will help our country. But I only realized recently that it was possible for nonshifters to truly care about shapeshifters, and not just be amazed at who they are and what they do."

That seemed to startle Holly, who lowered the gun a bit and stared at him for several long seconds. "You and that Selena? I kind of wondered about the two of you."

"Yes," he said. He knew he wasn't lying now. He'd already admitted to himself that he cared about Selena despite what she was. Or maybe her ability to shift only added to her appeal to him. Could he use this truth to shut this woman down? "I love her. I want to be with her. I think she cares for me, too." He stuck a pleading expression on his face. "She and I need to be together, like Craig and you do. You obviously understand about love with a shifter. If you kill me, what do you think that will do to Selena? Imagine how you'd feel if something really bad happened to Craig."

Oops. He could tell from the change on her face— from confusion and interest to fury—that he'd gone too far. "I do imagine it. I'm sure it'll happen if he stays with your damn CAs. That's why I didn't want him to join at all. I just thought you'd all give up if the kidnappers knew more and told your damned RCMP handlers about it. I didn't think they'd speed things up this way, but—"

"You contacted the kidnappers?" Now Owen was the one to feel fury. He only partially attempted to keep it to himself. "And you thought that would somehow protect your Craig? Did you tell them what the CAs were all about? Are they going to be ready to attack the CAs who come to observe them and bring them down?"

Was that actually a look of contrition on Holly's face? She once more stood with her back against the kitchen wall, but now she seemed to be trembling, from her shoulders to her hands holding the gun. "I…" She swallowed hard and seemed to try to still her hands, but failed. "Did Craig tell you I'm a tech consultant for a cutting-edge Canadian software company?" She didn't wait for his reply before she continued. "I figured out how to send information back, in reverse of how I gathered from news reports that the kidnappers contacted our national police with their demands. I didn't tell them Craig or the others were shapeshifters, honest." As Owen continued to glare at her, she said, "I just hinted that they weren't ordinary people and that, just like I might be using sci-fi-like connections to reach them, the people tracking them down had some offbeat stuff behind them, too. I laughed to confuse them when I hinted even more about the kind of offbeat stuff I was referring to."

Okay. Owen realized he was accomplishing what he'd hoped to at first—distracting this crazy, yet apparently very smart, woman. Maybe even making her feel a little guilty.

But she was still the one who was armed. And now he had even more reason to leave here alive, and fast, to pass this information along to his superiors.

"I—I really do understand why you'd care so much for your Selena," Holly continued softly. "I assume she cares about you, too. I'm really sorry that I have to kill you, but—"

A noise sounded from somewhere in the house.

"No!" Holly screamed, but before she could pull the gun back to aim it at Owen, a silver streak of fur, snarling and barking, leaped into the room and onto her, knocking her over.

"Thanks, Lupe," Owen said, dashing forward to retrieve the gun from Holly's grip.

But then he looked into those brilliant, flashing amber eyes glaring at him as the canine stood on Holly, holding her down.

"Thanks, Selena," he corrected himself with a huge and warm smile.

Chapter 25

It was the day after Selena had used her skills and wiles as a shifter, as well as her strength enhanced by wolfen adrenaline, to help save Owen and bring down Holly.

While Selena had stood guard over the prone, defeated woman, Owen had gotten in touch with his superior with this latest development. Soon, someone even higher up in the RCMP had apparently contacted the nearest police detachment and given them orders, and Selena, changed back into human form, had watched from a back room as Owen had helped them take Holly into custody. Holly now awaited transfer to the national police headquarters in Ottawa, where she would eventually be prosecuted for interfering with an official RCMP operation and more.

And now that critical op the CAs had been training for had begun.

It was midafternoon. Selena waited at the meeting house with the others not directly involved in today's mission. That included Owen; despite his being the officer in charge, he would not be assisting in the field. Alpha Force members Patrick and Marshall were with them, too. And Lupe, as always, remained close to Selena.

Yvanne, recuperating from the mild but potent sedative Holly had injected her with, was also with them. The car she had ridden in with Holly had been parked at the bottom of the hill, and she hadn't yet been ready to drive it, so she had stayed at the headquarters compound. She seemed fascinated, involved and definitely willing to become an aide when the CAs moved forward without the direct assistance of Alpha Force.

Not Holly, of course.

Craig had been astounded—and crushed—to learn the truth about her. When the four shifted CAs had returned from their exercise yesterday and changed back to human form, he had been informed what had happened and the many ways Holly had tried to thwart the mission, including somehow getting in touch with the kidnappers.

"I'd wanted to marry her, too," he'd said sadly, "but I'd no idea she resented it when I agreed to join the CAs. She seemed to like the idea." But clearly the opposite had been true.

Despite what had happened, Craig had pleaded to not only remain a CA, but also participate in their operation the next day, promising that the others could watch his every move and rip out his throat if he did anything wrong. He said he wanted them to feel certain he was one of them and not the traitor Holly had wanted him to be.

His attitude had sounded genuine to Selena and apparently to the others, too, for he was now in the middle of the operation.

The aides who had accompanied the CAs part of the

way and assisted them in shifting had again been Jonas and Rainey. Now those who stayed behind were grouped around the dining room table. Patrick sat in front of the laptop computer he had brought and the others huddled around him.

He had been able to log on to the covert website where the images from the cameras attached to the CAs were being transmitted—the same site being observed by the special RCMP team waiting in the field to thwart and capture the kidnappers. They were apparently intending to simply observe that day, acquire the needed information and most likely move in the next day to complete the rescue. They were stationed as nearby as possible, though, so they were prepared to move in at a moment's notice, if necessary.

Everyone was silent in the room now, intently watching what the cameras picked up.

Selena had chosen a seat next to Owen. She was very aware of his presence, his tension from worrying about how things would go down that day, whether the new team he headed would be successful—or even whether they would survive.

If she had been able to, she would have gripped his hand and held on for the comfort of both of them, for she worried, too.

Instead, she took reassurance from their occasional shared glances of mutual support—and a bittersweet sense that, no matter how things went down today, they might never see each other again.

So far, the mission was going according to plan. Whatever Holly may have been able to convey to the kidnappers, they apparently had no concern about wildlife in the targeted area. Aircraft, including drones, had intentionally been kept away—initially at least. But birds, including one very special falcon, flew overhead.

Three wolves sneaked through the forest and up to the mountainside. To shift, they had used the new doses of elixir that had been shipped to Canada and picked up by Patrick and Marshall yesterday. The older bottles still at this enclave would be taken back to Ft. Lukman and analyzed, but would then be dumped rather than used. Maybe something could be learned from them, or maybe not. In any event, no one wanted to take a chance on possibly tainted tonic.

She watched the video transmission. The Mounties suspected there were security cameras near where the shifted wolves now prowled, since satellite views and drone flyovers had failed because of electronic jamming, but fortunately no one came around now to check out—or harm—any roaming wolves. They soon located the openings to several caves, and with their acute senses of smell and hearing they had determined which one to enter.

Although they could not verbally communicate where they were to those who observed them, they knew to turn their heads slowly and allow the cameras around their necks to pan the area, marking the location. The cameras also had GPS tracking attached, so determining where they were was no problem.

Those cameras had begun showing the walls, floor and ceiling of rock-lined passageways, presumably in mountain tunnels that were not completely dark, implying that someone—the kidnappers?—had installed some kind of lighting. The leader of the wolfen group appeared to be Sal, with Craig in the middle and Tim bringing up the rear.

Selena's head was near Owen's shoulder as she managed to watch the slowly unfolding drama on Patrick's computer.

There! A cavern appeared in front of them, and the sound of human voices was evident. Only one camera appeared to move forward, and in moments a group of people appeared, men in dark sweaters and pants seated on the floor in a circle, talking, and a woman bound and apparently unconscious on the ground against the far wall. She couldn't see her face, but she knew it was Mrs. Brodheureux.

The men appeared angry, nervous, and the talk being recorded suggested panic from being unable to reach their contact after being warned something would occur against them today. The situation appeared critical, the hostage's life in imminent danger.

The camera shots quickly retreated the way the shifters had come, backward at first and then, apparently where the wolves could turn, hurrying forward out of the passageways.

When the wolves were outside and looked up through the trees, the falcon flew overhead, apparently confirming the location.

Twenty minutes later the wolves' cameras showed the arrival on foot of police snipers dressed in protective gear and carrying major weapons. Wherever they'd been deployed from, it couldn't have been far away.

The CAs had succeeded in their part of the operation. The actual rescue and capture had begun.

A week later, Owen returned to the headquarters in Ottawa, where he recapped the successful mission in detail to Deputy Commissioner Anthony Creay. He described where he and the Alpha Force members, other than the aides, had been and how they'd been able to observe what was happening from the shifters' perspective.

When the location had in fact been established and the sniper team rolled in, things became more dicey, but the kidnappers had been subdued—a couple shot, the others surrendering—and, fortunately, the kidnapping victim had been rescued. Mrs. Brodheureux had been rushed to a hospital for examination and treatment and was expected to make a complete recovery.

"Good job," Anthony said, looking over his vast, uncluttered desk. He appeared right at home there, the top button on his standard white shirt undone despite the loose blue necktie overtop and a look of satisfaction on his steely face. "If your CAs weren't so covert a unit, we'd give them a public commendation. As it is, you'll get a private one."

Owen, back on official duty at their headquarters, was also in his usual daily uniform, but his buttons were all buttoned and his tie tight. He relished the praise but felt he had to be honest, both with himself and his commanding officer. "We owe a lot to Alpha Force," he said. "They really helped us get our CAs ready in almost no time, and their special elixir was what made the entire operation possible."

"It makes the entire CA force possible," Anthony said. "So does a continuing relationship with that special US military unit. Are you prepared to work in conjunction with them?"

Was he? Owen wasn't sure.

That would mean seeing Selena again. Or maybe not. She might not be around when he went to their Ft. Lukman for meetings or additional training.

What he really wanted was to work with her. To be with her. But they worked for important agencies within their respective, though adjoining, countries. They might as well have lived a world apart, not across the border from each other.

Not that that could matter. He was a police officer. He did not allow his emotions to rule him.

He regarded his commanding officer and responded. "Of course I'll work with them," he said.

"That's good, since I've set up a meeting. Let's go into our conference room." Anthony rose and headed for the door to exit his office.

Owen followed, feeling his heartbeat increase. What meeting was this? It didn't matter. It wouldn't bring Selena any closer to him in the long run, even if she happened to be there. Which she wouldn't be.

Oh, they'd hugged each other after receiving word that the operation had been resolved so quickly and so favorably. Once Selena had left the area the next day with her fellow Alpha Force members, they had traded a few friendly text messages. They had even spoken a couple of times on the phone, mostly congratulating themselves and each other and their respective organizations. Their farewells had been soft, and Owen had thought he had heard regret in Selena's tone. Maybe he had been imagining it, hoping that she felt even a fraction of the regret that he did about their being so far apart and possibly never seeing each other again. He had later fought the urge to get on a plane and join Selena on the US East Coast to say hi—and to touch her once more, preferably all over.

But the CAs, including Owen, had remained headquartered in the enclave in West Columbia after that, and the shifters had immediately taken over the rooms the Alpha Force members had vacated upon their return to Ft. Lukman, Maryland. To locals, word had been spread that these tourists had fallen in love with the area, and fortunately their respective technically oriented careers as advisers to some companies that did business with the government allowed them all to telecommute to perform their jobs. A sham company was even being set up to act as their future employer.

Discussions were under way about getting the CAs cover animals—three wolf-dogs and a falcon. Plus, they required aides. Jonas and Rainey had promised to return to train them. It appeared that Yvanne Emarra would join her brother, Sal, and the rest of the group as possibly a shifter, an aide or maybe both.

As far as Owen knew, he would remain their officer in charge. It would be worthwhile for him to stay in touch with Alpha Force, since his unit would continue to obtain advice and to purchase the shifting elixir from them, and perhaps engage in joint exercises, or even joint missions, if appropriate.

Was that what this pending meeting was about? A new mission?

He felt his mouth roll up into a huge smile as he walked in and saw Selena sitting at the conference table along with the other Alpha Force members who had been in West Columbia with them. "Hi," he said, intending his greeting to include the entire group. The others also said hello, but he heard only Selena's.

Anthony took his place at the head of the oval table. Owen sat beside him across the table from Selena so he could watch her. Was she glad to be here? Why hadn't she let him know she was coming? Maybe talking to him, seeing him again, was the last thing she wanted.

If so, he would deal with it. At least he would have this chance to say a final goodbye.

The meeting was fairly short. Anthony made it clear that the RCMP appreciated all that Alpha Force had done, as well as its offer to continue to work with the CAs.

Then he dropped the bomb that Owen had not anticipated.

"Sergeant Major Dewirter," he said to Owen, "we know you'll be the primary liaison between our CAs and Alpha Force. There's been some discussion about who from Alpha Force will play a similar role, and the decision has been made, pending your approval, that it be Lieutenant Selena Jennay. Is that acceptable to you?"

Owen felt his eyes widen but managed to keep his grin small and, hopefully, professional. "That's fine with me if Lieutenant Jennay is all right with it."

"Fine with me," she said. "But you should know that part of the discussion has been that I'll need to stay in West Columbia at your facilities the majority of the time so I can work with your group, ensure they learn how to work with cover animals and train nonshifting aides, that kind of thing."

Owen strove to keep his expression neutral as he asked, "Is that acceptable to you?" He would have done anything to jump up, run over to her and give her a huge kiss in the hope that it would make her say yes. On the other hand, it might be the kind of thing to repel her, make her say no instead. Maybe it was a good thing this was a professional meeting. He sat still awaiting her response.

"Fine with me," she said. "In fact—" her eyes glinted with humor "—I'm looking forward to it."

The meeting that confirmed some major changes in Selena's life dragged on for a while. Deputy Commissioner Anthony Creay departed soon after she had agreed to move officially to West Columbia. That left Patrick and Owen in charge, as they'd been on the recent training mission.

Selena had forced herself to listen and participate in the conversation in which a lot of logistical concerns were discussed. Everything seemed cordial, and all of them, including the aides in attendance, continued to congratulate each other on how well the actual mission had gone down.

It appeared that all the kidnappers had been apprehended. Mrs. Berte Brodheureux was deemed recuperated after several days in the hospital. Her husband, Rene, the CEO of Xanogistics, had thanked the RCMP profusely and offered a lot of money to its retirement fund, or to charities it supported if that was not appropriate.

Once the meeting finally ended, the group decided to meet for dinner one final time, as they had previously when working together.

As they walked out of the room, Selena held back. So did Owen. Once the others had left, she looked up at him. His blue eyes were gleaming as he smiled down at her. "You're really okay with this?"

"I am," she said with a smile of her own. She looked ahead of them. The other Alpha Force members had stopped and Patrick was looking back at her. "Sorry, gotta run," she told Owen. "But I'll see you later at dinner."

* * *

It was much later that night. Dinner at a small steak house near the RCMP offices had been fine but relatively quick, and Selena and her fellow Alpha Forcers were in their hotel rooms near the Ottawa airport. They were grabbing a plane in the morning to go back to Maryland. There, she would pack all her belongings, put what she wouldn't need in Canada into storage, then move the rest to West Columbia.

Rainey would join her for now, although she would return to Ft. Lukman once the CAs had suitable aides in place. She'd been thrilled to be able to work with the Mounties for at least a little longer.

But had Selena made a big mistake? Had she said okay too fast because of her dream of getting to know Owen better? He had seemed happy enough about it, but was he just being polite?

Damn. She really wanted to know—since, even though it might not be wise, she had really fallen for him. They would have to remain professional as they worked together, but could they nevertheless develop a real relationship? Or was that something only she wanted?

Before she took any major steps, she needed to talk with Owen. Sitting at the desk in her room—a private one, fortunately, since she didn't want anyone to hear this conversation—she reached for her cell phone.

But before she could press in his number, it rang—and it showed that Owen was calling.

"Hi, Selena," he said when she answered. "I'm downstairs. Can I come up—and are you alone? We need to talk."

"How did you know where I was?" she demanded first.

"I'm a police officer," he replied. "We have our ways." She heard the joking of his tone even though what he said was accurate.

"Yes, you can come up, and yes, I'm alone." And, fortunately, her room was on a different floor from the rest of the Alpha Force members, not by design but now she was glad of it.

She heard a knock on her door only a few minutes later. She looked out the peephole, then opened the door to let Owen in.

He shut the door behind him, and in moments she was in his arms.

His kiss was hot and demanding, his hands holding her tightly to him—and she recalled even more vividly their lovemaking as she felt his hardness against her.

But he pulled back nearly at once. His blue eyes regarded her with even more intensity and desire than she thought he ever had. "Selena, are you okay with this? Moving to Canada and working directly with me and the rest of the CAs, I mean."

"I thought you were asking if I was okay with making love with you while we planned to continue working together." Though she tried to sound teasing, her voice was breathless.

"That, too."

She looked up at him, smiled, then reached to pull his head down to meet hers again. This kiss was even hotter than the last, and she immediately started undressing him, even as he touched her breasts, then lower.

"We'll need to be discreet," she whispered against his mouth. "And remain professional. And not let anyone... Oh—"

He was touching her intimately now, removing her clothes, and she swayed against him.

"And you should remember," she continued unevenly, "I'm different from most women. I'll be shifting some to help your CAs. And—"

"Shut up," he said softly, still smiling as he finished removing her clothes. And as he pulled down the cover and they both climbed onto the bed he said, "I've come to think of shapeshifters as damned special, one in particular. And I want to get to know her a lot better." He paused, his eyes fixed directly on hers. "I love you, Selena."

She drew in her breath. All her concerns about how Owen really felt about her and who and what she was evaporated in that instant.

Her smile broadened even more. "I love you, too, Owen. And I think I'm going to really enjoy living in Canada."

* * * * *

Linda Thomas-Sundstrom writes contemporary and paranormal romance novels for Harlequin Nocturne and Harlequin Desire. A teacher by day and a writer by night, Linda lives in the West, juggling teaching, writing, family and caring for a big stretch of land. She swears she has a resident Muse who sings so loudly, she often wears earplugs in order to get anything else done. But she has big plans to eventually get to all those ideas. Visit Linda at lindathomas-sundstrom.com or on Facebook.

Books by Linda Thomas-Sundstrom

Harlequin Nocturne

Immortal Obsession
Wolf Born
Wolf Hunter
Seduced by the Moon

Wolf Moons

Wolf Trap
Red Wolf

Vampire Moons

Guardian of the Night
Golden Vampire

Harlequin Desire

The Boss's Mistletoe Maneuvers

Visit the Author Profile page at
Harlequin.com for more titles.

SEDUCED BY THE MOON

Linda Thomas-Sundstrom

To my family, those here and those gone,
who always believed I had a story to tell.

Chapter 1

Skylar Donovan was being haunted by the same dream.

Four nights in a row.

An erotic, half awake, half asleep nightmare from which she awoke in tangled sheets, body slick with sweat, with her hand between her thighs.

Looked like nothing had changed tonight, either.

The minute Skylar closed her eyes, the dream returned. Moonlight lit the mountains. Shadows edged that light. And through the dark came the echo of a man's voice: a mesmerizing wordless whisper that was the equivalent of a highly charged sexual invitation.

Her dream guy was there again. Hell, it was impossible to tune him out. The remote Colorado cabin she bunked in had no TV for white noise, and she'd left her headphones behind.

He called to her, and she responded to the raw sensuality in his voice. Though his words weren't clear, his provocative tone left her ready to do something about the effect he had on her, whether he was real or not.

These damn dreams would have topped the charts as the best wet dreams ever...if it were an actual man she lusted for instead of a hallucination. Something her mind had created as a distraction from recent painful events. Everyone knew that fantasy was a notoriously viable way of coping with loss.

Problem was, this nighttime lustfest wouldn't stop. Neither would the questions she didn't dare acknowledge out loud.

Who was he?

What was he?

What would this creature's skin feel like against her? How about his mouth? With a voice so totally seductive, surely the rest of him would be sublime.

Although Skylar knew the difference between dreams and reality, there were no clear-cut definitions here. With her eyes closed, she fell under his spell. His image stuck to her with supernatural glue.

Wide shoulders above a broad muscular chest. Thick torso. Narrow waist and hips. Dark hair worn long. His stance was determined, his face sometimes raised to the star-filled sky. And over everything was an aura of wildness that catapulted things into nightmare territory. Because there wasn't the slightest chance of mistaking her nocturnal seducer for a normal human being. He was, in fact, anything but normal.

He was a magnetic combination of man and beast with a ridiculous twist on the DNA sequencing of two species that couldn't share the same physical space in reality. A unique being with its own name.

Werewolf.

Hell. Yes. Werewolf.

With a presence powerful enough to sift through REM.

Of course these were just dreams. She got that. She wasn't an idiot.

Well, maybe she was. Because...

She was so very hot for the creature that stood on that hilltop and looked like a man at times, though that outline was deceptive. She felt vulnerable when he was around, and slightly out of control. But maybe she was only an eavesdropper, and he waited for someone else. Some*thing* else.

Was the moon his mistress? Wasn't that how things worked for werewolves?

Why, then, was he yanking her chain?

A sudden spike in her heart rate, far beyond the usual range, jolted Skylar's eyes open. Anxious, she rolled over on the mattress and sat up, sweat trickling between her breasts, heart pounding too damn fast.

Tonight was different somehow. This time the voice had seemed closer and very, very real. It left an echo in the room.

Not dreaming now?

To prove that, Skylar slipped from the bed and padded to the window. She moved the curtain, expecting to catch sight of her velvety tormentor, wondering again why she allowed a figment of her imagination to continue to interrupt what should have been a good night's sleep.

She saw nothing out there, but God, had she actually expected to?

Resisting the urge to laugh at herself, Skylar rested her forehead on the cool window glass. Probably she had allowed her mind to supercharge some poor nocturnal creature's cry into something it wasn't. That's all those sounds were.

Not a voice.

She wasn't nuts, just tired, worn out and sleep deprived. She also supposed that these nighttime escapades could be tied to the power of suggestion, caused by the discovery of her dad's cache of items in the attic. That old trunk and the things she found inside it.

Her dad, it seemed, kept dirty little secrets to himself here in Colorado, so far away from his family. And it had taken coming to this remote cabin to go through his things for Skylar to realize she hadn't really known David Donovan at all.

One more glance outside, at the night, and she turned back to the bed. Curling up on the mattress with her knees to her chest, she used her usual abundance of common sense to reason things out.

Maybe dreaming about a supernatural lover merely showcased a healthy need to get past the termination of her relationship with Danny, her ex-fiancé. She had left him a couple of months ago, before actually getting to the altar, and everybody needed time to adapt.

It wouldn't take a professional opinion to point out that the sexy dreams she seemed committed to having could be her mind's way of filling the void made by that kind of change, especially since it was followed fairly closely by her father's untimely death…

The father who, as a famous psychiatrist dealing in other peoples' problems, had, it turned out, sometimes dabbled in his own world of make-believe.

Werewolves were his idea, after all.

Not only had her dad believed those creatures existed, he must have thought they roamed the mountains of Colorado, right outside this cabin's door—which was likely the reason he often retreated here under the premise of needing alone time.

Beasts, for God's sake.

Like the one in my dreams.

So maybe fantasies were contagious and could be inherited, and stumbling on her father's secrets had spawned her own nocturnal reveries.

Skylar pulled the blanket up to her neck. Seconds later, she flipped onto her back, staring at the ceiling of the small rustic bedroom.

"Screw the pity party," she murmured. Because truthfully one thing, at least, was clear. She felt liberated by the empty spot on her ring finger.

Seeking comfort in the lavender-scented feather pillow, Skylar vowed to stick to her plan: finish going through and packing up her father's things and then return to her apartment in Miami, where her wedding dress still hung on a hanger. The dress would have to be returned eventually. If she ran into Danny, she'd just have to deal.

She could do that.

In truth, her life sucked sometimes. No mother, no father and no fiancé...but what the heck? She had three loving sisters and the deed to this cabin.

"Bring it on, sexy nightmare!"

Plumping up the pillow, Skylar blew out a breath and dared to close her eyes. Refusing to behave, her heart spiked again.

Swear to God, she was sure the man in her dreams was out there now, waiting for her. Whispering to her. Compelling her to listen.

And why the hell shouldn't she?

Gavin Harris turned his face to the night wind, catching a whiff of a fragrance completely foreign to the rest of the forest smells surrounding him. It was a sudden sensory bombardment that didn't belong here and was, even as he breathed it in, a detour from his agenda.

Eyes shut, he wrapped his senses around the uniqueness of the rich, sweet scent, separating each component with his fine-tuned wolf senses.

Female, he concluded. *Young, supple flesh. Musky pheromones. Traces of soap and denim*. Tantalizing feminine scents that weren't in any way related to the more monstrous odors he sought tonight, but were oh so compelling.

He shook his head hard to ward off the distraction, and muttered, "Forget it." Investigating the source of these new smells would mean detouring from his objective, which had to remain his greatest priority. He was on watch, hunting his own version of big game.

That objective was an important one. Vital.

But damn...

The rosy feminine perfume floating to him from the cabin in the clearing below him caused a visceral physical reaction similar to being shocked by a cattle prod. All the little hairs on his arms stood up. Tingling nerves made his muscles twitch.

He smelled the woman in that cabin as easily as if she stood in front of him, in person.

And she was alone.

Stepping forward brought the cabin into view through a gap in the trees. Gavin leveled his gaze on the dark windows and inhaled deeply, concluding that the woman down there was the only human in the area at the moment. She occupied a cabin that had been originally been built by old Tom Jeevers, making it smell a whole hell of a lot better than its line of former occupants had.

Something else?

The agitated, tinnier scent of anxiousness wafted to him, adding a second, spicier layer to the woman's floral bouquet. Either she was anticipating something, or was in some kind of trouble. A fight with a companion, lover or husband, maybe, that caused a ruffle in the atmosphere? The long-anticipated arrival of a lover who was late?

"Lucky bastard," Gavin muttered. If she had a husband, that guy would get to smell her every damn day.

With a quick glance up at the sky, Gavin widened his stance, knowing he shouldn't linger too long in the moonlight. Though the moon wasn't completely full tonight, that bugger was close enough to that phase to affect him in adverse ways. All the enhanced senses were just a start.

A quick glance down the length of his body found it not actually foreign, but increasingly unfamiliar as each lunar phase progressed. The extra muscle that he hadn't worked out in a gym to maintain helped to add bulk. His height had stretched a good inch or two above his normal six-one.

His jeans were tighter. Shirts now strained at the seams. The only measurements remaining the same were his feet, slammed into his boots.

Then there was his hair. The tangle of chin-length waves were darker and much longer than he was used to, tickling his ears, making him wonder how long he'd been patrolling this section of the mountain ignoring most of the perks of civilization.

Could it have been two years?

Damn if everything hadn't changed in the span of those years. Out of necessity, he'd pretty much become a loner. And though he patrolled this area of the Rockies regularly, during those past two years four people had died. One of them was the last man to occupy the cabin now emitting a woman's enticing pheromones.

Oh, yes. And within those two years he, Gavin Harris, Colorado Forest Ranger, had regrettably, unforgettably, become a beast tethered by a silver chain to the devilish disk in the sky. *Moon.* As absurd as that seemed.

He closed his eyes again, shook his head. Having a woman down there, so very close, and smelling like heaven, served to highlight his shitload of personal issues.

People who abused the clichéd phrase *no crying over spilt milk* had never experienced their skin turning inside out or their muscles expanding to nearly twice their size in the span of sixty seconds. They'd never felt the pain of fingers splitting open to spring a full set of razor-sharp claws, and a jaw disconnecting bone by bone.

After taking another deep breath, Gavin dropped to a crouch. The sultry smells floating upward from the cabin were disturbing to him for so many reasons. One major problem was that they could easily mask the other, more feral odor he'd been out here searching for.

The woman's presence was trouble, any way he looked at it, and also a reminder he didn't need about the better times in his past. And the woman in that cabin might be in danger out here from bigger, badder things than him.

Who are you? he wondered. *Hasn't anyone warned you about this place? Told you that four deaths in and around the area are four too many, and that a woman by herself might be asking for trouble?*

Determined to let this go, Gavin straightened and half turned. That woman wasn't his problem. He had more serious things to worry about. There was a damn good possibility he wasn't the only monster nearby, and if that theory proved true, odds were less than good that he'd ever see another sunrise.

"Leave her alone. Get out of here. Let her be," Gavin warned himself.

Not so fast...

An additional beam of light drew his gaze.

He turned back.

The cabin's door opened, throwing a narrow strip of yellow across the boards of the covered porch. A figure emerged to stand in that beam, and although the features were shadowy from this distance, Gavin's heart exploded in a flurry of racing beats.

The woman stood in the open doorway as if his thoughts had drawn her out. As if she knew he was there, watching her, and felt his presence.

Seeing her jolted the beast inside him.

He'd been right about this woman. Anxiousness rode the breeze. She was tense, uptight and high-strung, like an animal about to spring.

But she was also small, blonde, and only half-dressed.

Gavin stared at the half-dressed part, and the long, lean, very bare legs that melted into delicate ankles and shoeless feet.

His inner wolf gave a soft, muted whine that scattered when he cleared his throat.

Christ, temptation was a bitch.

So was being a goddamn werewolf.

As for you, woman...

His attention snapped to identify another smell.

Metal.

The woman on the porch had a gun?

Gavin realized with a sudden flash of intuition that the icy chill now ripping through him wasn't due only to the alluring sight of the woman, or the scent of her weapon, but to the thing closing in on them from the mountain.

He must have gauged the strange lure of this area correctly if the prodigal beast he sought returned two days early. Forty-eight hours shy of that next full moon.

"Ah, hell..."

With renewed wariness, he glanced again at the cabin and the beauty on the porch whose white T-shirt highlighted her slender torso, and whose face was hidden by a cloud of fair hair. He already felt protective of her. Felt as though he knew her somehow.

She might have courage enough to try to protect herself, but no gun he knew of would save her if the thing he chased turned its attention her way. He whirled, his boots digging up clumps of dirt. *No time to waste.* If the visitor heading this way was what he hoped it might be, he needed to lead that abomination away from the cabin.

With a final look over his shoulder, Gavin took off at a jog because his gut told him he needed to stop this killer before it claimed another poor soul.

Chapter 2

Although no one showed up to confront her as she stood on the porch, Skylar knew she was no longer alone, and that she wasn't dreaming this time. Not a chance in hell.

Her father's gun felt heavy and cold in her hands. It was loaded, and she knew how to fire, just as all the Donovan girls did. Their father had been diligent about his daughters' self-defense.

That didn't stop the shaking, though. She had to hold the gun with both hands as she faced the unknown. Someone was out there. This was real. And at this time of night, that felt like bad news.

Of course, it could be a lost hiker. Maybe it was her father's crusty caretaker coming by to check on the property, or out for a late-night stroll. But the persistent flush of internal heat told her that those possibilities were false and that someone else was here.

Instead of retreating inside and locking the door behind her, Skylar stood her ground, scanning the night beyond the meager pool of porch light where evidence of a visitor lay in the sudden silence of insects.

Biting her lip hard enough to taste blood, she ventured a call. "Where are you? Who are you?"

The silence was unnerving. She worked at drawing a breath.

"Not going to show yourself? I'm here, waiting." She pointed the revolver at the trees on the hillside, upped her volume. "And I'm not happy about it."

The taunt produced no results, but she couldn't give up. Someone was there, somewhere. What if it wasn't some innocent hiker? Suppose her father's killer had returned?

She had to consider that possibility. She refused to believe that her diligent, first-rate climber dad might have fallen to his death. The conclusion she'd come to, independent of her sisters' opinions, was that if David Donovan had fallen, someone must have pushed him.

"So who are you? Have you come for me?" she said to the quiet night, getting nothing back. No response at all.

"No time for hide and seek," she called out in a last-ditch effort to make contact as she backed up slowly, crossing the threshold in a shuffle of bare feet.

A change in the air made her pause. Moving the gun, she refocused her aim on a point just south of the path up the hillside.

"Best to stay inside," a man's voice advised from somewhere near the closest trees. "And lock the door. It might also be a good idea to leave here tomorrow."

Skylar's heart skidded over one too many beats, leaving her breathless. "Who are you?" she called out.

"Ranger, patrolling the area. There's been some trouble around here."

She waved the gun. "I know that, and I know how to use this."

"Better to move on before you have to use it," he said. "A woman alone is far too tempting as a target."

"How do you know I'm alone?"

"It's my business to know who's in the area."

"You've been watching the cabin?"

"As much as I can, but right now I'm needed elsewhere."

"Where's your car, or whatever rangers use to get around in?"

"Over the hill behind me."

"You run around on foot in the dark?"

"There aren't too many paths worthy of a vehicle around here, beyond the main road."

"I don't need you to stand guard," Skylar said. "Thanks, but you can get on with your business."

"Fine. Just offering a friendly warning. Can't be too careful this far out of town."

Skylar waved the gun again. "I'm well aware of that."

"Well, good night, then," the invisible ranger, if that's what he really was, said.

"Good night," Skylar echoed.

The night air changed again, rearranging itself as though something heavy had been removed and the darkness filled in the vacuum left behind. The result was a powerful charge that left Skylar swaying on her feet.

This could have been her imagination, she supposed as she shrugged off a new round of chills. But one thing was clear. She had no doubt whatsoever that this ranger's voice was the voice from her dreams.

The same damn one.

She'd bet her life on that.

* * *

"You're too far out there," Trish said over the phone the next day in the authoritative tone reserved for bossy older sisters.

"It's temporary, so I don't mind." Skylar rubbed her bloodshot eyes. Ten minutes of sleep while sitting by the window all night, gun in hand, wasn't nearly enough for a clear head.

"I need to get this cabin boxed," she added, like she did every time she spoke with Trish, which was every day. Sometimes twice.

"I'll come and help," Trish said.

"No, you won't."

"Then Lark can visit. She can ask for time off."

"I'd rather choke."

Trish's voice deepened. "Do you know any of the neighbors?"

Like most lawyers, Trish didn't like being crossed or argued with for any reason. As the oldest Donovan sister, Trish would lay out her argument logically and plan on wearing her down with repetition.

Skylar didn't want to go home and didn't want company while she explored the circumstances surrounding her father's death. Unless hell froze over, she wasn't going to share that objective with her sisters and get them all riled up.

Besides, the good Lord only knew what would happen if she were to utter the word *werewolf*, or mention being harassed by someone who hadn't really shown themselves last night. If Trish knew any of that, half of Colorado would be on their way over before the phone disconnected.

Which might not have been such a bad idea, actually, if Skylar's stubborn streak would have allowed it.

"The caretaker for this place lives a couple of miles down the road, Trish. I have his phone number right here."

Trish snorted her disapproval. "Miles? Like that's comforting?"

"I have a gun."

Skylar's announcement preceded a beat of silence over the line.

"You what?" Trish eventually said.

"It was Dad's. I took it from the trunk."

"What trunk would that be?" Trish asked. *Demanded*, really, in her best cross-examination style.

"The one I found in the attic here. It's loaded and I know how to use it. We all do."

Trish sighed unhappily. Trisha Lilith Donovan saw far too many weapons in her job as a prosecuting attorney to be comfortable with any of them. And Trish, as the eldest sibling and the only Donovan kid not named after a bird, felt responsible for the rest of the motherless girls.

"I suppose being engaged to the cop for twelve months also had its perks in the weapons department?" Trish suggested.

Skylar lowered the phone to take a deep breath so that Trish wouldn't hear it. Trish had said "the cop," avoiding the use of Danny's name.

Skylar raised the receiver when she heard Trish calling her name.

"Skye? Skylar?"

"Sorry. I have something cooking on the stove. Can we talk later?"

"You're putting me off. We haven't discussed—"

"Good. Thanks," Skylar interrupted. "I'll call you tomorrow morning."

"Skye, wait. I'm sorry I brought up the cop. Really sorry."

"No sweat. I've moved on, that's all."

"I know, but…"

"It's all right. I haven't been a baby for twenty-three years now. Nor have I ever needed help in making up my mind about something."

"I know that, too. But you will always be my baby sister. You can confide in me."

"I'm all right, I swear. My fiancé was a bastard, and it took me too long to figure that out. I'm off the hook now. That's how I look at the breakup. Possibly it was an act of divine intervention in my favor. I feel relief, if you want the truth. We'll talk again tomorrow. Okay?"

"Oh, all right."

"Bye, Trish."

Skylar signed off before the arguments could start up again, and with them the apologies about things not working out with Detective Danny Parker, who had gotten her close enough to matrimony to actually buy the dress.

But it had never been a match made in heaven, and she'd known that, deep down inside. She'd merely been going through the motions.

Worse, in terms of regrets, was realizing she'd gone along with Danny's little mental abuses, and had been swept up in them, rather than openly exerting her true rebellious personality. That hadn't been like her at all, really. And she hadn't been lying to Trish about the relief.

Palming her cell phone, Skylar checked the screen for calls, half expecting Trish to call back. Then she set the phone on the table. Service was spotty in the mountains, and only seemed to like this small area in the front room of the cabin—a fact that wasn't exactly comforting, she supposed, though Trish didn't need to know that, either.

"And if you knew what else I found in that trunk of Dad's, Trish, you'd send in the tanks," she muttered.

Not only had she found the gun in that trunk, well-oiled and ready to go, it was loaded with unusual ammunition that had to have helped shape her dreams. She was sure that silver bullets weren't the norm for anyone, outside of people chasing their own form of madness.

Glancing up at the ceiling as if she could see through the rough wooden beams, she said, "Neither are they standard in a psychiatrist's medicine bag."

In the past, she would have called Danny to talk about this, but she was on her own now—which left her imagination wide-open. Because shiny silver ammunition, unless merely something a collector might covet, was de rigueur for hunting…

"Werewolves."

Skylar turned toward the window, attuned to the drop in temperature that signaled another day's end. Nightfall wasn't far off.

"Damn it, Trish. I need to find out what our father was up to, and why it might have killed him."

Solving the mystery of her father's frequent disappearances was paramount, as was finding out why he needed so much time away from everyone he supposedly loved.

But hell, Dad. Silver bullets?

In all truth, she had to admit, being in this cabin for a few days by herself, with her dad's things, had caused her more discomfort than seeing Danny's face when she told him the engagement was off.

The men in her life were gone, and she was far too intelligent to imagine that velvet-voiced rangers could have stepped out of her dreams.

As for monsters...

The moon would be completely full in another twenty-four hours, a big deal in werewolf lore, at least in the movies. If the approaching moon was some kind of supernatural stimulant, all werewolves would be affected. If there were such things as man-wolf creatures, her dream lover would be affected, too. And with her dad's gun under her pillow, she'd be ready for anything that dream had to offer.

Chapter 3

Gavin hadn't found the trail of the creature he sought. Although he'd gotten close enough to taste its feral presence, one too many detours had brought him back, time and time again, to stare at the cabin, wishing to see *her*.

He hadn't meant to circle back. He had, in fact, been heading in the opposite direction. Yet here he was again, staring down at the blasted cabin, telling himself, "Don't be an idiot. No one needs a woman that bad."

Obviously, he didn't believe that on some level.

The beast he hunted, which had a fondness for blood and sacrifices, disappeared just after midnight. After following its malevolent stench south, the damn thing vanished into thin air. He'd spent a fruitless night backtracking all over the mountain, and more time searching throughout the day to make sure he hadn't missed anything crucial. Now, once again, darkness wasn't far off, putting him a hell of a lot closer to the phase of the moon that counted.

He eyed the cabin warily, figuring that if his interest in the woman down there kept up, he'd have to chain himself to the Jeep to avoid showing up on her doorstep, in person. The next time he confronted that woman, she might do more than point the weapon in his direction. She might actually pull the trigger.

He thought about that gun, and what it might do to him.

It was possible that he could he survive a bullet at close range, but it would certainly slow him down. When the beast inside him took over, several bullets might be required to make a permanent dent.

In theory, anyway.

He'd only tested his survival skills once, when he was accidentally hit by an arrow fired at him by mistake. That hunter now spent time in a cell.

And by the way...that arrow had been a bitch.

Gavin searched the clearing.

The cabin looked quiet in the evening light, though he knew the woman hadn't taken his advice and hit the road. A ribbon of gray smoke rose from the chimney.

Stubborn streak?

Who in their right mind remained resistant to a ranger's warning, or stepped outside in the middle of the night to face anyone or anything that might be out there?

Not courageous, necessarily. More like impulsive.

Maybe she gets off on danger.

And just maybe he'd make it his business to find out.

Besides, he was ravenous for company, and the smoke coming from the cabin carried the smell of food. If he knocked on the door, was there was a remote possibly she'd invite him in for a bite?

Gavin shook his head, rubbed his eyes.

She shouldn't be alone. The last death out here had been gruesome. Some poor doctor found in a gulley, sliced to shreds. Gavin had an idea about how that might have happened, and that idea didn't include a slippery trail. But he couldn't speak of it to anyone. Who'd believe him?

The doctor who had occupied the cabin died just ten days ago, which made the new occupant's tenancy a quick turnaround. Possibly the woman was part of that man's family.

She'd probably have her pants on today.

Smiling felt strange. So did the compulsion to go down there. He didn't know why this woman's presence was so intriguing to him that his vow of celibacy strained at its leash.

He was way too hungry for everything that cabin had to offer, for anyone's good.

As for women? He hadn't dared to sleep with one since he'd been mauled by a hell demon and his life, as he'd always known it, had ceased to exist. He had no idea how the beast, now an integral part of him, would deal with emotion. He wasn't sure if this nightmare could be passed to others by way of something as insignificant as a scratch or a kiss.

There seemed to be no rule book for werewolves. No manual. Hell, it was possible there were no others like him, and he'd have to continue to play it by ear.

"Sorry," Gavin whispered to the female below, though his insides quaked with a longing for what she could offer that bordered on visceral greed.

He craved warmth and closeness and the freedom to fill his lungs with the perfume surrounding this woman like an aura. He wanted to run his hands over every inch of her, and see where that led. Test himself. Push himself.

But he had a job to do and a vow to fulfill. He'd find the beast that had ruined his life, and take that beast down. "Not her," he said to quiet his inner wolf. "Definitely can't bother this woman."

Want her, his wolfish side protested with a sharp stomach twist.

"Yes. Okay. I suppose I do," Gavin admitted as he started down the hill toward the cabin as if pulled there by an invisible chain.

"Stop right there."

Obliging, the man by the fence stopped at the gate.

Even if she hadn't guessed that her nighttime visitor would return, Skylar's first thought actually would have been *ranger* due to the light green pants and the shirt with a badge on the pocket.

She wasn't sure how she noticed the clothing details though, given her initial surprise over how incredibly attractive the rest of him was and how well he fit her dream guy's stats.

Tall and rangy, his outfit did little to hide masses of lean, well-honed muscle. Other dreamed attributes were there, too: the broad shoulders and narrow waist, the dark brown hair with its loose waves curtaining a chiseled face. From where she stood, it appeared that every body part seemed perfectly balanced and in accord with his beautifully united whole.

Just as she'd imagined.

This was downright uncanny, and maybe even a little scary. Still, while the hunky outdoorsman looked strong, he didn't look primeval. His fingers didn't end in razor-sharp claws, though she seemed to recognize him on whatever level of consciousness telegraphed heat.

Skylar felt her temperature begin to rise. Sensitive spots at the base of her spine tingled—a sign that though he hadn't spoken yet, this guy truly was last night's visitor, in the flesh.

"You've lost your gun," he finally observed.

Velvet. Yes. His voice was like a velvet blanket, the vocalization of his appearance.

Skylar's heart fluttered in her chest.

"Do I need it?" She regarded this guy almost rudely, unable to stop the flood of internal warnings about the impossibility of dreams coming to life.

But she couldn't have made this guy up. He was standing in her yard in the last light of a long day, and was close enough for her to see his face.

She wasn't dreaming now. That face and its perfectly symmetrical features struck her as being way too familiar.

"The apron suits you," he said in a teasing manner that might have been inappropriate since they were strangers outside of her fantastically naughty dreams. Nevertheless, she smiled and ran one hand down the front of the dish towel she'd tied around her waist, glad she had on jeans for this reunion.

Her other hand clutched the gun hidden behind her back.

"I guess you're determined to stay, ignoring the advice of the locals," he went on.

"I have business to conclude here."

"Can I ask what that business is?"

"Cleaning up my father's things. He lived here on and off until recently."

The ranger kicked dirt off his boots and looked down, suggesting that he knew what had happened to her dad.

"I'm sorry for your loss." He glanced up again to meet her scrutinizing gaze.

Nervously, Skylar glanced away. The flutter inside her chest spread to her arms. She gripped the gun tighter so she wouldn't drop the damn thing.

"Were you watching my father, too? He had an accident, they said."

Skylar let the word *accident* hang in the air before continuing. "Was anyone patrolling around here when he died?"

Unable to resist the urge to look at him again, almost as if he requested it, she dragged her focus upward until their gazes connected across the small front yard.

Shudders rocked her with the immediacy of the connection, and she shifted from foot to foot to cover the quakes. He stared back at her with a seriousness that set off more alarm bells. His penetrating eyes were very light against his bronzed skin. Though she was unfamiliar with the dream man's eyes, she was sure these were his.

You're a handsome sucker, I'll give you that.

But how do I know you?

Why have I modeled a dream after you?

If she'd met this guy before, she would have remembered, and yet her treacherous body was responding to him as though he'd stepped right out of her dream and was presenting himself to her now in order to culminate all those pent-up feelings.

While reading body language was a trick both her father and her own classes in medical school had taught her, this situation was different. Meeting his gaze was like sharing secrets without having to speak. It felt weird, and also incredibly sexy in a messed-up way.

"Two of us were on duty that night, but not near here," he said in answer to the question she'd almost forgotten.

"Night?" she echoed. "Dad was hiking at night?"

"I don't know that for a fact," he replied. "Sorry again."

Even in stillness, the ranger seemed to be moving, evidence of the wild streak he harbored. Chances were good he was a loner, preferring to live on the fringes of the city, communing with trees. Weren't all forest rangers born with some kind of special calling for the great outdoors?

How about werewolves?

Glad she hadn't said that out loud, Skylar fisted her free hand in the dish cloth, trying on the word *figment* for size. This ranger, so like the man in her dreams, was quite possibly a figment of her overwrought imagination.

"You don't need the gun," he said in a lowered tone. "Not with me."

Although his blue-eyed gaze held steady, Skylar also noted a hint of weariness in his features. He might have been up all night. He could have been near here the whole time, either guarding this cabin's sole resident, or drawn to her for reasons that went beyond being neighborly. Reasons like sharing unusual dreams or offering genuine condolences in person for her loss.

Fingers tight on the gun behind her back, Skylar smiled. "Do all rangers have X-ray vision, or just you?"

He shrugged. "Merely an educated guess since you showed me the gun last night."

"It's a precaution. After all, how do I know you're what you say you are?"

"You're right to mistrust strangers. That's a good sign."

"A good sign of what?"

"Wariness, where it's necessary. Caution. A healthy respect for self-preservation."

He pulled a small radio from his belt and held it up. "This is how I check in." He spoke to the radio. "Harris here, on the eastern slope."

An answer crackled back from the radio, and Skylar heard enough to make her feel better about believing him. His voice, as he spoke, also made her familiarity with it more unsettling. Disconnecting from the dream was proving to be tough.

Puzzled, she said, "I recognize your voice."

Ranger Harris nodded. "We spoke last night."

It's so much more than that. What though?

"Why did you come back today?" she asked.

"I thought I'd check on you. Make sure everything is okay."

"Do your rounds take in all of the cabins out here?"

"Usually. But very few people are in residence right now."

"I passed four cabins on my way to this one."

"Most folks don't live in them year-round. And those who do have taken off for a while."

Breaking the disconcerting eye contact, Skylar looked to the east. "Because of what happened to my father?"

"Your father had an accident."

"So they say."

Other than offering a brief nod, he didn't react to her remark.

"You're alone out here. I just thought you might like to know we're around," he said.

"Rangers, you mean?"

"Yes."

Skylar crossed her arms over her chest, bringing the gun front and center. If nothing else, she needed the weapon to protect her from herself. This guy's gaze made her feel naked, though he didn't appear to be staring at anything other than her face. Outwardly, he acted like a gentleman, the warden of this place, but the sparks tickling her insides weren't appeased by his surface calm, his coolness or his distance.

Hearing him had set off a chain reaction. Too many of her fantasies were built on that voice. In the flesh, this guy, whoever he was, stranger that he might be, was like catnip to a serial dreamer.

Skylar reached for the flush creeping up her neck, hoping to stop it from reaching her face.

"How did they find him?" she finally asked.

Ranger Harris tilted his head to ponder the question. "Who found my father's body?"

"Hikers, I believe," he replied.

"Near here?"

"On the other side of this hill."

"At night?"

"He was found sometime after sundown, I heard."

Skylar lowered the gun. "He was barely recognizable."

"Then I hope you didn't have to see that, Miss…"

"Donovan. Skylar Donovan."

He nodded.

"No one in my family saw him. His partner at the hospital identified his body, and she believed it best we didn't see him…under the circumstances."

"I'm sorry."

Sorry for what? she thought. *For my father's death? For making me want to forget we're strangers?*

Pressing back a strand of hair that had slipped from her ponytail, Skylar remembered how Danny preferred her hair shorter than she wore it. He hadn't liked her in jeans like the ones she wore now. Her cop had been critical about so many things she liked to do and certainly never would have approved of her being out here alone. *Control freak* would have been a good description of his personality.

She had gone along with Danny's preferences for the sake of trying to appear normal, feel normal, be part of a couple…when she had always known it wouldn't work out in the end.

Her next shiver was in the bastard ex-fiancé's honor.

"Are you okay?" the man across from her asked.

"Yes," she lied. "Anyway, I suppose accidents happen."

"Too often," he agreed.

"Especially in this kind of terrain?"

"The trails are tricky," he concurred. "Moreso when wet."

He hadn't budged from his position near the gate. Skylar wondered if he wanted to but was afraid he'd frighten her. Realizing how nuts it might be to trust him at all, she said, "Would you like something to drink? I've got lemonade."

"Lemonade would be nice. Thanks. It's been a fairly warm day, despite the end of summer, and I didn't take time for lunch."

"Come in, then. We can sit on the porch."

"I'd like that. Mind if I wash my hands?"

"There's a hose by the corner of the cabin, and a bar of soap in a pail."

The ranger opened the tiny gate and closed it behind him. Having him on her side of the fence gave her an unanticipated thrill, despite the fence being no more than hip high and easy enough to knock over with one good shove.

The closer he got, the more her body reacted to him. She wanted to get close to this guy, feel him, smell him. She wanted him down and dirty, filthy hands and all.

That damn dream...

Ranger Harris was a delectable mixture of all the things that made a man a man. Equally rugged and elegant, he moved with the casual, effortless grace of an animal, sinew and muscle seeming to work without the impediment of an underlying bone structure. Predatory animals moved like that. Tigers, lions, cheetahs.

Wolves.

Skylar nearly dropped the gun and fumbled to secure it in her grip. Hell, did she have to distort everything?

This guy, with his badge and radio, was not the creature of her dreams. He wasn't a *creature* at all. Her idea that he could be one virtually screamed of her desire to get over what had happened with Danny. Her imagination was twisting situations to match wishes that were nothing more than a bunch of dangling loose ends.

"There's a towel on the rack," she called out.

"Thanks." He crouched down to lift the hose, his green shirt stretching across his shoulders and threatening to tear at the seams. His dark hair, thick with a slight curl, brushed against the back of his collar when his head tilted forward.

She had always loved hair like that. Hair made for running fingers through. Hair that would tickle bare skin in moments of intimacy, and provide something to hang on to.

Skylar cringed, and gave herself a stern silent reprimand.

I will not take this guy to bed.

No way was she going to indulge in her first one-night stand in the middle of a forest, even if he were willing to take her up on what she was thinking.

That's what her mind said.

Her body told her otherwise. There had been far too many erotic thoughts about rugged men lately to ignore what was right in front of her. And he was interested in her. He couldn't hide that fact any more than she could hide her interest in him. He kept looking her way.

Something came to life within her as she watched him. The sensation wasn't familiar, and was centered so deep down inside her body it mimicked the feel of a rising sexual climax.

Working hard to keep from sliding a hand between her thighs to ease the pressure building there, Skylar withheld a sigh that might have given away her fanciful state of neediness. Everything about this cabin and what happened around it was strange. She felt strange... and very much like the predator here.

How's that for a switch?

"I'll get the pitcher," she said as the internal flares going off reached unbearable levels, threatening to burn her up if left untended. She wanted to rush into this guy's arms. Would he be shocked if she did?

"I'll be right back," she said. Yet she didn't turn away, fascinated by the way the ranger's pants adhered to every line and curve of his masculine, muscular backside. Fully aware of how forceful his thrusts into a woman would be with powerful musculature like that.

The oncoming twinge of greed made Skylar cross her legs. Danny had been in good shape, but this guy was exceptional. Almost too perfect. If she looked harder, would she find proof of a hidden wildness that made perfection an art form? One little slip on his part, and he'd growl? There'd be fur in unusual places and spring-loaded claws on those wet hands?

He was looking at her intently.

She'd forgotten to go for the lemonade.

Cheeks flushed with heat, Skylar tried to smile. "I was wondering if you're working tomorrow night, too."

He turned off the water and got to his feet. "I'm here all week."

"Should be easier to see tomorrow, with the moon full."

"You're right." He dried his hands on his pants, forgoing the towel.

There were no claws on those hands.

"Does the approach of a full moon make animals restless? I think I hear them at night," Skylar said.

Now she was pushing things. She was an idiot.

He came closer than she should have allowed, and faced her squarely. He smiled, but with an expression of sadness. Heartbreaking sadness.

Why?

Whatever she had expected, it hadn't been that.

As he slowly moved toward her, she felt every inch he traveled as if the air between them compressed. When he stopped, they were nearly chest to chest, and she had to look up to see his face.

Liquid lava coursed through her veins, pumping, scorching, flowing fast. Her forehead dampened. Her heart raced. She was hot enough to be combustible and breathing hard. All these reactions confirmed that she hadn't been wrong about one thing. Something was going on between them on a crazy personal level. Their chemistry had been instantaneous and wasn't to be ignored.

Animal magnetism taken to extremes.

Lust at first sight.

Dreams trespassing into the realm of reality.

In that moment, she wanted no backstory or history with a man who spoke of relationships and marriage. No rules governing behavior and no regrets of any kind. This was the man she desperately wanted with an all-encompassing physical desire. His hands on her, for real. His mouth torturing her mouth, right now. His body inside hers, his every move making her writhe with pleasure.

Hell...she wanted to bite and scratch and become the beast. She wanted to dig her nails into him and wrap her legs sinuously around his waist. She wanted desperately to let go and be who she really was inside, without anyone else riding shotgun on her behavior.

Screw the dreams. These fiery cravings were real and pulsing and painfully acute. If she acted on them, she wouldn't wake with her own hand between her legs because this guy would be there to do that for her.

"I've changed my mind about the porch." Her voice was throaty and pitched low.

His eyes kept her riveted, casting a familiar spell. Skylar heard thunder, though the skies were clear. She felt lightning strike her, stapling her to the ground, and yet she was able to move.

Brazenly, she reached for his hand. She brought it to her breast and spread his long fingers over the thin fabric of the blue linen shirt covering her. His heat blended with hers, forcing her heart into a frantic tempo.

Miraculously, his face showed no surprise at this kind

of sexual aggression. Maybe, like her, he'd known what was going to happen. With his free arm, he gathered her tightly to him. Warm lips brushed her forehead with the softness of a sigh.

Why in God's name was she doing this?

Because she felt an unearthly attraction to this man, that's why. No, not just attracted to, *possessed by*, and therefore willing to ditch caution for him, and for what they were about to do.

She looked into light blue eyes that sparkled with curiosity and contained no visible wolfish variation. *Just a man, then. A really sexy man.* One she didn't have to have a future with, only a passing moment of eroticism that would be a culmination of her one-sided bed play.

She brushed off the little alarms going off in the back of her skull in favor of the quakes and the heat of the ranger's seductive nearness. It was hardly surprising that she'd go for this. She needed to take the risk.

This guy wasn't Danny. Danny lacked in some departments and was intimidated by her lust for sex. She had tamped down those lusts the entire time they were together in favor of hiding her wilder side. After being corralled so long, some of those needs were pushing back.

The man holding her stroked her face, sending waves of little shivers through her body. Did he understand what was happening to her or was this blatant offer of female physicality merely every ranger's wish come true?

He moved first, backing up, his breathing as labored as hers. Calmly, he took the gun from her and tucked it into his belt. Then he reached for her hand.

She said nothing, couldn't have managed one word. His touch was electric and uncommonly sensuous.

In silence, he led her up the steps toward the front door of the cabin of secrets, where some of those secrets, scary as they might be, strange as they had become, were about to be shared.

Only then did Skylar whisper a curse and a prayer.

Chapter 4

Secrets.

Desire unleashed.

Gavin had touched this sexy woman and was still standing there in human form. His hand had been on her breast, and that hand had remained his own without altering its shape or hurting her.

So maybe he could do this, he thought. Perhaps in the grand scheme of things that made monsters of men, he'd prevail in something he wanted so badly.

The cabin was small, a one-bedroom affair, so the bedroom wasn't hard to find. Once they reached it, Gavin lifted the woman beside him into his arms. In silence he held her, fearing to speak, afraid to ruin what was going on between them. He was sure she felt as strongly about it as he did.

Her eyes told him so. Big green eyes in a pretty oval face, with a small tapered nose, high cheekbones and beautifully arched brows— —all of those features expressive and showing her impatience.

She looked young and felt light, almost buoyant, in his arms, but she buzzed with energy as she laced a slender arm around his neck and snaked her fingers into his hair, just above the nape of his neck. Heat flared white-hot in the spot she touched, and he held back a groan.

He could not afford to come unglued.

Pulse soaring, body hardening, Gavin checked a growl when her lush pink mouth parted and she ran her tongue over her lips, unconsciously wetting them in a seductive sweep without taking her eyes from his.

Siren.

Seductress.

Put here to tempt him. Push him. Test his limits.

Her exhaled breath smelled like the lemons she'd used to make the drink offered to him, but her lips offered so much more, if he dared to cross a line he'd set for himself so achingly long ago.

Gavin wanted nothing more than to devour that pouty mouth and draw from her a moan. He was close enough to her to do that, yet he didn't kiss her, could not kiss her now, because that level of intimacy was too dangerous and might be too much for either man or wolf to bear.

Already her closeness was tricky. His skin rippled with tension. Nerves were firing, exaggerating his pulse, sending it skyrocketing. These reactions might have been normal when facing a situation like this—a beautiful woman offering herself to him on a warm evening, and out of the blue. But of course nothing about this meeting was normal. He sensed this, and so did the creature he carried inside him.

The wolf was stirring, wanting in on the deal. How far would he get? How much did he dare?

He'd have to put this woman on the bed in order to find out, and couldn't make himself release her. Tight against him, she was safe—a prisoner, his captive. *Christ!* He felt her need melt into him. Her anxiousness called him out, and the wolf inside him twisted into knots, wanting to accept her challenge.

Did this woman feel how fast his heart was beating?

"Kiss me," she said, meeting his eyes, tugging him forward with both of her hands fisted in his hair. "Make it real."

Real? Was that just her way of telling him to get on with it?

Take your time, Gavin.

Don't listen.

The excitement he felt had to be measured. Nothing was to be taken for granted or rushed.

He didn't kiss her. Not yet. One step forward and his knees bumped the mattress. Gavin loosened his grip on the sleek body he wanted to tear into. She was covered in faded jeans and a fitted shirt—a lot of layers to peel back while testing himself.

She felt so damn good, and smelled even better. Her body was slim, taut, pliant. Through the shirt, her ribs were ridges beneath his fingers. In place of curves, she was composed of lovely muted angles.

Gavin liked all of this.

He knew exactly what to do and how to do it, if he dared to press this further and face the consequences of accepting the woman's gracious invitation so close to the full moon.

Not long now and he would become the beast, at least in part. Thank God his mind remained his own and in the driver's seat when that happened. The same couldn't be said for the monster that had savaged him not far from here.

Not far from this cabin.

The woman's hands moved, and Gavin sucked in a

breath. Warm fingers slid beneath his collar in a meeting of overheated flesh.

God. Help. Him.

He had to be cautious, careful, diligent. He had to keep sharp and pay attention when all he wanted to do was lose himself in the woman's succulent body and bury himself inside her, where he'd forget the rest of the world for a brief time.

He wanted that very much.

He set her on the bed. Her arms came away from him, limbs falling, muscles wired. She continued to look at him as if she knew him already, as though this wasn't the first time they faced each other in this way. That should have bothered him, Gavin supposed, but it wasn't the time for reasoning. His hunger was growing, and so far he was okay.

All right.

He sat down beside her on a lavender-scented bed not intended for two. The woman watched him with her eyes wide-open and her lips quivering ever so slightly.

I can do this.

This is what I need.

When she blinked slowly, he felt the loss of her gaze, as if part of him had been torn away. In her eyes he was a man, not a freak.

"Look," he whispered to her. "Look at me."

She did, letting out a breath.

With careful hands, in quick movements, he pulled the shirt over her head and tossed it to the floor. The sight of her creamy ivory bareness made him pause to take stock. She was splendid, flawless, made for him. The back of Gavin's neck prickled with appreciation.

Small, rounded breasts rose from a smooth chest beneath a graceful slope of shoulders. The delicate lace of skimpy blue lingerie covered those breasts, held in place by thin ribbons that ran up and over her shoulders to disappear beneath a tangle of tawny golden hair.

Pressure rose in Gavin's chest and groin as he waited out a moment of incomparable agony. Then he eased those ribbons down, leaving them to cross her fair skin like slender slashes of watercolor shadow.

He closed his eyes, aware of the irony.

He was that shadow.

When she touched him, he jumped. She'd tucked a hand inside his shirt, between the buttons, so that once again their fiery skin met. Gavin fought back a sound he was sure would have fallen somewhere between a groan and a growl.

Her touch spurred him on.

Captivating scents, rich and floral, saturated her skin, the see-through lace covering her and the pillows behind her. He had smelled this fragrance before, from afar, and it was what had brought him here, to her.

Her skin was dewy, soft. A flat stomach stretched to the button on her low-slung jeans. Sharp-edged hip bones raised the denim, highlighting the concavity between them that, wolf willing, he'd get to settle himself into. But that was wishful thinking, and he was getting way ahead of himself.

Lowering his mouth to her breasts, Gavin placed a kiss between them, feeling relatively safe if he stayed away from her mouth. With a spike in his pulse, he absorbed the ungodly pleasurable sensation of the delicate lace against his lips.

He placed a second kiss on the exposed edge of one

rounded breast, knowing this might be pushing things and that he was about to become undone.

Taking his time wasn't going to work. Climbing into bed with her wasn't, either. He was starting to sweat, burning up from the inside out, and his hands were quaking. Maybe she was the wrong woman to try his luck with. He'd never ached for a woman this badly, and he didn't want to lose the connection.

Damn it, how would he explain stopping this now?

She was too exquisite to be a test run for his current predicament. He was rock hard, his body begging to be inside her. That kind of inner turmoil tended to spark the wolf to life.

He felt the wolf rising now in direct proportion to the stiffening of his cock. His throat was no longer his own. He didn't dare make a sound with this pressure building.

In hindsight, he should have known better than to come here, this close to a full moon, for any reason. Being drawn to this woman only made matters worse.

Wildness coated the underside of his skin. Although fur wouldn't burst from his pores tonight, the wolf's drive was what Gavin feared. He couldn't be entirely sure which needs were ruling his desires, his or the wolf's. Surely the wolf's hunger had become his own.

Gavin brushed a stray tendril of gold from the woman's forehead, fighting to remain sane when the wolf desired powerful thrusts and the slapping sounds of bodies fiercely merging. The wolf wanted to bite and bruise and voted for ruined beds, broken furniture and swollen mouths.

Fast. Hard. Take it now. That was the way of the wolf. And maybe also the thoughts of a man who had long gone without.

Be careful.

Keep control.

Gavin's teeth slammed shut when she whispered in his ear.

"Now," she said. "You and me, here, now."

To get a grip on a restraint that was rapidly slipping away, Gavin shut his eyes.

If I do as you ask, I'll never be able to see you again. I'll never look into your eyes again or feel the softness of your skin. You'd know me for what I am, what I've become. My secret would be out.

Those were words he could never say out loud. But the truth was that she didn't want him to stop this. She was trembling and ready to take him on. The look in her eyes explained it all.

She reached for his shoulders, dug her fingernails into his shirt as if to tear away barriers and accept everything he had to give.

Forgive me...

He could try to be a man, and only a man, one more time.

For you.

Pulling her from the pillows, Gavin released the clasp keeping her lacy bra between them. As she fell back, he covered one of her breasts with his hot, breathless mouth.

The wolf swam in his bloodstream, causing his heart to thunder as Gavin drew her in, circling the pink raised tip with his tongue. A lick and a draw and then he bit down lightly, teasingly, sweating with the effort of holding passion back. None of this was enough by far, yet it was clear that he wouldn't get much further if he hoped to maintain some control.

More thunder hammered his skull and beat at him

from behind his ribs. Beneath his belt, his body was demanding this union, though shadows lengthened in the room, darkening the floor. Night was near, and inside of that darkness roamed a monster this woman needed protection from.

Two monsters, actually.

When he looked down, it was to find his shirt hanging open from mid-chest down, with a few buttons missing. The woman beside him was running her hands over his stomach with a touch like hot coals—over his abdomen and halfway around to his lower back. He arched with each incendiary caress, maintaining eye contact, holding his breath.

Her nails grated against his ribs to leave long red grooves. She let out a sultry, sexy-as-hell sigh that shook Gavin to his core. This was her own growl of need and longing, an expectation of the otherworldly boundaries she planned on obliterating with him, and a promise to see this through, whatever he had in mind.

"Who the hell are you?" he whispered as his chest met hers.

Her lips separated, luring him into a kiss, daring him to devour her. And what the hell, he would have done it anyway, damn the beast, damn the curse that mocked his life.

Or so his thoughts went until he heard a distant sound that froze him inches from her, and kept him from taking that beautiful mouth for all it was worth.

The roar echoed in the clearing around the cabin and instantly chilled Gavin to the bone. He hesitated for several agonizing seconds, horrified. "No. Not now. Not yet," he whispered.

The woman in the bed also heard the noise. White-faced and wide-eyed, she sat forward, her heart beating as furiously as his.

"What was that?" she asked.

"Nothing you'd want to meet." Even that much of an explanation seemed to expose too much, Gavin thought.

Damn the timing. He should have known better than to put his mind and energy elsewhere when he was sure the monster had returned.

On his feet in a flash, Gavin reached for the radio still tucked into his belt before deciding against using it. Who would believe him or want to face whatever made that awful roar?

With a graceful swing of one arm, he retrieved the gun from the floor and set it on the bed.

"I'm sorry." After taking one last look at the woman who'd distracted him into nearly forgetting a vow, and with his heart filled with regret for having to pass up what she offered here tonight, he added, "Really sorry."

Then he turned for the door.

She scrambled after him. He heard the sounds of her bare feet on the old wooden boards. "What was that?" she repeated. "Tell me."

"Wolf," he said. "Big one. Badass. Doesn't belong here."

"You have to go after it?"

Her voice kept him hard and hating the separation.

"I have to find that beast before it finds other things to harm," he explained.

"Aren't wolves usual out here?"

Gavin stopped at the front door thinking that people were so damn naive. But though this woman looked bewildered, she didn't appear to be the slightest bit hurt by his hasty withdrawal, and only truly curious about the sound they'd heard. She didn't ask him to explain his abrupt behavior. She was looking at him with hunger dilating her beautiful green eyes.

Grabbing her by the shoulders, Gavin tilted her head back with a small shake. She didn't object, just bit her lower lip hard enough to bring up a droplet of blood with her tiny white teeth.

"Christ!" He wanted her so blessed badly, and to prove it, he kissed her mouth so savagely, she uttered a cry of surprise.

He kept on kissing her, deepening the union of their mouths, devouring all he found, breathing her in, tasting her sweetness. And she met him with the fervor of a storm.

God, yes, she was a storm encased in fragile human skin. But it was okay. He could get away now that he had an excuse. She wouldn't have to see what might happen to him if he stayed.

Unsure of how long the kiss lasted, Gavin finally drew back. He'd done it, kissed her, and felt a kind of weary triumph about that. But he had to go, leave her, take care of this. Although he wanted nothing more than to stay, the monster out there in the dark had torn him apart, injected a beast into his bloodstream and then left him to die. That beast was outside right now, close enough to reach out and touch.

He had no choice here.

"Close the windows and lock the door," he said with his lips inches from hers. "I shouldn't have come here like this. I should have known better than to let it get so close."

He turned to go, torn and hurting.

"What do you mean? What's getting close?" she

called after him as Gavin, broken and unfulfilled, strode across the yard, vaulted the fence and headed for the hillside, leaving perhaps the sweetest night of his life behind.

Chapter 5

Skylar didn't call for the ranger to stop as she stood in the doorway staring at the darkness settling over the mountains. The noise they'd heard hadn't just interrupted her first unplanned one-night stand, it had jangled her nerves.

Harris's haste in getting away from her would have seemed like a slap in the face if it had been for any other reason than going after whatever had made that terrible sound. His disappearance gave her breathing room to contemplate what she'd been about to do—to him, with him.

This whole night had proved a fairly spectacular hiccup in her present situation, and she wasn't all that clear about what she wanted right then—a man or a creature that was more than a man. She wasn't certain that a mere man could have done it for her.

Freud would have had a field day with that information.

So would her big sister.

Trish, as the most stable of the four Donovan sisters, wouldn't appreciate that her sibling was in heat and lusting for a tryst with anyone who came along, let

alone lusting for a werewolf. After a conversation like
that with Trish, there'd be a reservation in a white padded cell and some little blue pills—a scene that hit too
close to home.

Skylar stared outside.

Harris had warned her to lock the door. Yet as far as
she knew, wolves, no matter what size, couldn't handle a
doorknob. So what good would a lock have done to protect her from the animal Harris said he needed to chase?

Reason told her that Ranger Harris had lied, that he
might be hiding something.

Part of her wanted to listen to his advice anyway.
The other newly rebellious part that would have taken
a stranger to bed urged her to follow him and see for
herself what was urgent enough to end their lovemaking session before the real fun began.

The guy had been seriously distressed over the sound
they'd heard. There was no way she'd imagined that. And
though her body, too, was trying to warn her about this
sound, and shudder after shudder rocked her stance in
the doorway, Skylar couldn't let lies and secrets become
an integral part of her new reality.

She was different here. She was letting go of her own
secrets, one by one, and open to taking new risks.

Should she go after the ranger? In the dark?

What if her father had fallen to his death while chasing figures from his dreams?

She wasn't familiar enough with the trails to find
footing or have directional cues without proper sight-
lines. Her cell phone wasn't good for much because the
GPS was almost nonexistent.

As for wanting to jump into the sack with this guy,
maybe she just needed a night with an honorable man

for a change. Harris, at least, ran out on her *before* placing a ring on her finger.

Backing up, Skylar listened hard to Harris's fading footsteps. With him went the rest of the evening's light.

Her heart refused to slow as she backed from the doorway. Confusion reigned. The room dimmed around her, but Skylar didn't reach for a lamp. Seconds flew by, then minutes.

Finally, she shut the door and leaned against it with her eyes closed, picturing Harris's tight, tanned flesh pressed to her bare skin. Feeling, even now, his breath on her face.

Gavin picked up the trail of the monster much more easily than he could have hoped, almost as if the blood-thirsty beast wanted him to.

He didn't know what to make of that, but it was too late to consider anything other than finding his prey. His blood was up. His muscles were seizing. The beast inside him recognized this other beast in an unseemly way.

I'm not like you, Gavin wanted to shout. *I'm no killer.*

But shouting would amount to a calling card and telegraph his presence…if the thing didn't know already.

As he jogged up the steep path, the old thoughts returned, though answers to his questions had never been within reach. If he wasn't like that monster, he had to suppose that the blood passed from beast to beast somehow got diluted in the transfer.

His wounds made him suffer a change, but until he knew more about what had happened to him, he had to think of his cursed condition as a disease.

Hell, the differences between him and his maker had to be studied. He couldn't exact a physical change without a full moon, yet he'd been attacked without one. Feelings inside of him shifted, internal stirrings came and went, but no full transformation happened for him without that commanding silver light. When he did morph, he became a strange mixture of both man and wolf, and not more of one thing than the other.

This damn beast was wolfish, with a lot of something extra added that had no relation to *Homo sapiens*. There was no full moon tonight, nor had there been the night before, which solidified the supposition that this monster either remained permanently furry, or could fur-up at will, with or without the moon's kiss.

So different. Yet I sense you, beast, as though what I've become isn't too far removed from what you are.

Part of that beast truly had become part of him.

Gavin's thoughts kept churning as he climbed the hillside trying to sift through facts, in search of answers.

He'd tried locking himself away to avoid the moon's treacherous call, which only made things worse. Unable to change its form, his body had betrayed him anyway. He'd nearly gone mad with the shakes, unconscious spells, roiling stomach upheavals and bouts of fever. His mind had eventually succumbed to the madness. He'd lost control of his temper, lost his mind to the pain of withholding the transformation and ended up in some godforsaken place on the mountain with no recollection of how he got there or what he might have done while his mind was in a fog.

Lesson learned. It was a freaking sharp-witted curse that developed immunity to thoughtful manipulation.

He had to give in to the physical changes in order to remain in charge mentally. Succumbing to the moon's lure was necessary. As long as he changed shape, he was okay. Keeping as far away from other people as was possible near the full moon had allowed him to weather this out.

He got that now, and guessed that without the wolf-ish form there'd be no survival of this monster's horrific species, hence the absolute need to shift. That furry demon's teeth and claws had created another similar freak, and so that had to be the way the moon's cult passed on. If he stayed in these mountains whenever there was a full moon, he'd be safe enough, he hoped. Others would be safe.

Gavin stopped suddenly, skin chilling, senses wide open.

The atmosphere around him had changed, creating new pressure that was like a punch to his chest. He heard rustling sounds and thought them ludicrous for a monster excelling in stealth, as though the beast were leaving him a trail of breadcrumbs.

There was no mistaking the smell. He knew this monster's scent, having been up close and personal with it. Why was it here? Did it want to finish what it had started two years ago? Finish him off?

Is that why you stuck around?

Gavin's heart rate accelerated. He'd left his weapon in the car before visiting the woman in the cabin. Damn it, he should have borrowed her gun.

The wolf inside him clawed at his insides with nails like talons, sensing trouble. An icy shiver of anticipation ran up his spine.

"Come out."

He spoke at a normal decibel, feeling the presence of Otherness as if it were a bad rash.

"You can't possibly imagine I don't know you're there, or what you are."

More rustling noises came from his right. Gavin slowly turned toward the sound, saw something. Felt something.

The creature he'd sought for so long was here, all right, and standing its ground.

Against the outline of the trees, nearly hidden in the shadow, a huge form took shape. Bigger than anything he could have imagined, the giant specter loomed over the surrounding brush like the main character in a horror movie.

On that fateful night, the thing had moved so fast, Gavin hadn't seen what was coming. But he saw something of its outline now and his inner alarms went off like a string of firecrackers.

This was no mere man-wolf combination. Nor, as he'd guessed, was it anything remotely like him, at all.

Its massive shape left little for Gavin to appeal to, speak to, reason with. Thoughts of getting close to it with any kind of hand-held weapon were absurd. Killing it with a spray of bullets seemed equally as unlikely. He hadn't really expected this abomination to allow him another close-up this soon—he had meant to chase it away from the cabin. Hell, seeing it now, he wanted to run the other way.

No doubt this monster would be faster.

"So here we are," he made himself say to ease a small portion of the fear knotting up his insides. "Should I call you family?"

There couldn't be more than one of these beasts, he hoped, because where'd be the justice in that?

"It had to be you who did this to me. Can you recognize another freak?"

His nemesis didn't move, making this potentially deadly scenario all the spookier.

"What are we to do now, since I can't let you go around killing and maiming people?" he asked, having to talk though this creature could strike at any moment. Talking seemed necessary. He felt like shouting. One more night, and he would have been stronger, at least. He would have had claws and speed and double the muscle. Though his humanness danced on a thin thread of control tonight, there was no full moon to help him.

"I was supposed to protect those people who died. That's my job. Now what? You do whatever the hell you like?" he said. Then he paused to regain the strength in his voice. "If not exactly like you, I'm no longer like them, either. Not like those people."

Like the aftershocks of an earthquake, a series of low growls shook the ground beneath him. Darkness wavered. Leaves rustled. This beast's rumble was terrible, threatening, ominous, but the monster stayed in the shadows.

When Gavin let loose a responding growl, the creature stepped forward on legs the size of a grizzly's. Transfixed, unable to get a handle on the creature's exact size and girth, and fairly sure he didn't want to, Gavin jumped back. This was a damned nightmare.

"Son of a..."

Gavin tried to ignore the tingling in his hands. Angling his head, he heard a crack of bone on bone. Licks of white-hot fire made every joint ache as a wave of lightheadedness washed over him, twisting his stomach into fits. He knew this feeling, recognized these sensations, and they came as a shock.

The beast in front of him was able to call forth Gavin's beast, and maybe even set it free early. Was that because what stood across from him had created him? Blood calling to blood?

Through a slowly revolving whirl of turmoil, Gavin heard his own growl of angry protest. "I'm not like you!"

And though it seemed impossible for anything else to get through the pain and shock of what he was experiencing, something else nipped at his attention, dragging him away from the outrageous situation at hand. Too riled up to put a name to that distraction, and feeling too ill to respond to it, Gavin kept his focus riveted to the beast less than ten feet away from him. He was close enough to hear it breathing. He heard its giant canines snapping, and the memory of teeth like that tearing into him, ripping the flesh from his bones, made his stomach turn over.

This was no werewolf. This truly was a demon. And Gavin's mind warned that he might not be able to get out of this in one piece. Not this time.

When the creature's growls suddenly ceased, the world went deathly quiet with a silence that seemed surreal. Though Gavin's muscles ached to transform and his fingers stung with the threat of popping claws, the grip this specter had on him loosened. It, too, had noticed the distraction, and turned its mind elsewhere.

The enormous werewolf, which could have squashed him like a bug, advanced no farther. After waiting out several hundred of Gavin's thunderous heartbeats, it turned away from him. Uttering a low roar of grumbling displeasure, it drifted away as completely and swiftly as if it had merely melted into the night.

Sounds from behind made Gavin spin around, afraid the creature had reappeared at his back. Lunging forward, taking the advantage, he rushed toward the sound, striking an object hard, taking it to the ground.

His breath whooshed out. His muscles screamed for the strength necessary to do some damage to the thing that had damaged him so very badly.

"This ends here, one way or the other!"

The moment he said those words, Gavin realized it wasn't the beast he'd tackled. The body beneath him was small, fragile, and it squirmed beneath his weight, smelling like soap and the soft fabrics covering it.

Closing his eyes, Gavin fought back an oath. This wasn't the monster. Not even close.

When he reopened his eyes, he found a familiar face looking back. A small white circle of features that were pale enough in the moonlight to be almost transparent.

"What the hell?" was all he managed to say between deep, rasping breaths of mortified relief.

Chapter 6

"You can get off me now."

Breathless from the momentum of the attack, Skylar shook so hard, she stuttered.

Without being able to see Harris's expression in the dark, she felt every racing beat of his heart through the chest pressed to hers.

"What are you doing here?" he demanded.

"Following you."

"I asked you to stay inside."

"About that. I seem to be going through a rebellious streak that makes me impervious to reason. I'm sorry if I startled you."

"Hell, woman, my warning must not have been nearly strong enough to convince you of the danger."

"I was pretty sure you could handle one lone wolf."

"Lone wolf? You have no idea..."

Maddeningly, Harris didn't finish the statement as he fought for his breath.

"I thought you heard me coming," she said. "You were speaking to me, weren't you?"

"I was talking to myself."

"Is that a habit rangers often pick up?"

"Yes." He took some time to go on. "It's not safe here. Not safe anywhere near here. It was foolish of you to ignore me."

"Yes, well, right now the problem is being able to breathe."

Harris only then seemed to realize he was on top of her. Slowly, he backed onto his knees. Seconds later, he offered her his hand and a word of caution. "We have to get you out of here."

Skylar took his hand and let him pull her to her feet. The man was little more than a dim outline in the dark, but she saw him turn his head as if expecting someone else to appear.

Holding tightly to her right wrist, he said, "I can't do my job if people run all over these hills in the dark. There are always a few who think they're above the rules."

Skylar stumbled forward when he snapped his arm. "Meaning I'm one of those."

He didn't challenge her remark.

"Did you find the wolf?"

"No."

He was lying again. She could tell by the way her inner radar was going off.

"I'll go with you to look for it," she suggested.

"You'll do no such thing. You can leave this place as quickly as possible. In fact, I'll take you."

"I don't need a chaperone."

"On the contrary, I have every reason to believe you might."

He began to walk, more or less dragging her with him. "Please listen to me, Skylar. There's a dangerous animal on the loose, and that's no joke. If you're out here,

I'll worry about you. Distractions can make these situations so much worse. Surely you can understand that?"

They slid in a damp patch of dirt on the slope, but righted easily enough. Skylar resolved to pay more attention to her feet. She wasn't going to be the bimbo of horror flicks who always tripped and fell in the scary scenes. She had always been fleet.

She wasn't afraid to be out here with Harris beside her, yet she felt uneasy, and as if they were being watched.

"I think my father might have been chasing a wolf when he died," she confessed, matching Harris's lengthy strides. "If so, then I want to see it skinned."

Harris's sharp intake of air wasn't her imagination. Something out here had bothered him, and bothered him still. He was wired and on edge. He kept looking around.

"I'd like to hear about that, but this isn't the time or place for conversation. You'll have to trust me on this."

"Okay," she said.

The relief in his voice was evident. "Good."

The odd feeling of them not being alone stuck with her on their steep downhill descent until she had to speak of it.

"I think we're being followed."

His response was to utter a choice four-letter word and to walk faster. Skylar wasn't going to argue with him about getting to safety this time. The new presence she sensed was heavy enough to siphon some of the air from her lungs. The night had grown colder, and each breath she struggled to take felt icy after the day's heat.

"Maybe it's a ghost," she whispered.

Harris urged her into a jog.

Thing was, she thought, if ghosts existed, this one

hovering in the woods might turn out to be what was left of her father. But if it was her father, why did the spirit feel so dark? Why was she suddenly afraid?

She let Harris lead her through the night, clinging to his hand. She'd been right. They were being followed, and the man in front of her knew this as well as she did. Clearly whatever he had been chasing out here now stalked them, and it was something Ranger Harris feared.

Halfway down the path, Skylar resisted the impulse to stop and face whatever tracked them. Only then would she confront the awful fear building inside her.

Her guide didn't seem to share her impulse to stop. His hold on her wrist remained unyielding as he led her over rough, unfamiliar terrain ignoring holes and vines as though he saw every detail in the dark.

She couldn't see a blasted thing.

He didn't produce a flashlight, either, seeming to rely on his own internal GPS system. She supposed that rangers had to be familiar with the areas they patrolled and that Harris walked these same paths over and over on a daily basis. All she saw were glimpses of his back, highlighted whenever the moon peeked out from the clouds.

Deliberately, she didn't offer the use of the flashlight she'd used to find him in the first place, now tucked inside her pocket. She was fascinated by how Harris maneuvered and afraid that if she shone that light behind her, the sanity she presently held on to might desert her. She was sure something otherworldly lurked on this hillside.

She thanked God that Harris wasn't the kind of creature she'd almost expected him to be—though the voice he shared with the man in her dreams continued to plague her. He didn't use that voice now, though there were questions that sorely needed answers. Questions having to do with wolves being bold enough to stalk two humans, or if it might be some other Colorado animal. Mountain lion. Bear. Recently escaped homicidal human.

The icy sensation of being tracked didn't ease up as they ran. Traversing the downward path, Skylar felt positive she heard sounds of the creature breathing beyond the two of them.

She kept as close to Harris as possible and his grip on her remained a comfort. But although they had gone a fair distance already, the cabin's porch light didn't appear. Were they lost?

A gravel road suddenly loomed up out of nowhere, noticeable by its ghostly gray color.

"Stop," she said, tugging at Harris's hand. "This isn't anywhere near the cabin. The road to Dad's place is dirt."

"Just a few steps more," Harris urged.

When she saw the car, Skylar remembered what he'd told her about leaving it there. "We're on the opposite side of the hill. Are we driving to the cabin?"

"I'm thinking it might be better to take you someplace else for the rest of the night."

"You heard that stalker, too?"

"What stalker?"

More lies, in the form of withheld information. The rigidity of Harris's arm gave away the fact that he knew much more than he let on.

"Answering a question with a question won't get us very far," Skylar pointed out.

"Maybe not, but my Jeep will."

They reached the car, found the doors unlocked.

"That's all you're going to tell me?" she challenged, facing him over the car's roof.

"I don't want to scare you."

"It's too late for that. Is the rush in honor of a dangerous outlaw on the loose? I have a right to know."

"Would that make you get into this car?"

"I'd just like to know what we're running from."

Harris blew out a breath. "I don't know what it is for sure, okay? I only know that something is out there, and my job is to keep you safe."

The moon was brighter here, away from the trees. Ranger Harris gestured for her to get into the car.

"I'll take you to town, where you can get a room for the night," he said.

"You, too?"

"Afraid not."

Did he sound regretful about that? Skylar wished she could see his face more clearly.

"Should I trust you?" she asked. "We're running from the unknown, but I don't know you, either. Is it wise to get into a car with you?"

"True. I am a stranger to you. But at the moment, I solemnly promise you that I'm the lesser of two evils on this mountain."

Cooperating, Skylar climbed into the vehicle. The worn leather seats smelled like the great outdoors. Like dirt and greenery and Ranger Harris.

She said, "Maybe I should have taken a closer look at that badge on your shirt."

He pulled the badge off and tossed it to her as he slid into the driver's seat. "Be my guest."

Without a doubt, this guy could be infuriating. But what he had tossed her felt like a real badge. She'd seen a few in her time, so this probably meant Harris was one of the good guys.

Skylar closed her fingers over the metal as if it were a talisman to wield against things that went bump in the night.

"Anything you need we can pick up at the store," he said. "I have an account there."

"Does this store have alcohol?"

Harris turned the key and started the engine. "I'm sure it does." After a pause, he added, "We don't have to talk about what happened tonight if you'd prefer that."

"You mean about what chased us, or what nearly took place in my bedroom?"

"Should I apologize for acting on that last one?"

"No." Skylar closed her eyes briefly, listening to the familiar nuances in his voice that fanned her inner heat. "It wasn't your fault."

The car kicked up a spray of gravel as it moved. Skylar felt Harris's attention on her.

"I needed a diversion," she explained.

"From what?"

"The rest of my life."

"Losing your father?"

"That's the most recent blow."

"Then I'm sorry we were interrupted, though it was probably for the best." Harris sounded earnest.

"Yes. For the best," Skylar agreed, leaning sideways as the car made a sharp left turn around a stand of pine trees. "It wasn't really a wolf that made you run out on me, was it?"

Harris glanced in her direction without comment.

They rode in silence after that, which made the bumpy ride more uncomfortable. Eventually it became clear that the man beside her wasn't going to offer anything resembling a decent explanation for what had happened in or around the cabin tonight. Then again, neither could she.

"You might want to pack your father's things during the day and stay in town at night," he suggested some time later.

"Being in town most of the time would be inconvenient."

Again, Skylar felt the intensity of his silent appraisal.

"As a favor to me, then," he said.

"Do I owe you one?"

"If not, you might humor me as the local law enforcement."

Skylar winced. Because of Danny, the words *law enforcement* had a sour ring to them. In essence, she'd gone from one kind of cop to another without thinking. This was far better than the werewolf dream, though.

"Well, I can't jump out of a moving car, so I guess tonight's a done deal," she said.

"Good."

As they rounded another dark curve in the road, the soft glitter of distant lights appeared. Skylar supposed her safety would be assured down there among the masses, if safety was really an issue.

It was that rebel part of her—the part that had sent her traipsing up a mountain path after dark and had given her an appreciation for sensuous dreams, gorgeous werewolves and strangers with seductive voices—that told her to ignore this ranger's plan after tonight and instead find out what the hell was going on.

Her dad had kept secrets, and that hadn't ended well. The man beside her kept things to himself. She had to know who or what was out there, and whether being followed tonight had anything to do with her father's death, less than two weeks ago. She had a hunch that it did.

With good old Donovan perseverance and a dash of stubborn determination, she vowed get to the heart of these mysteries if it was the last thing she ever did.

With or without the man next to her...in her bed.

Chapter 7

Gavin read Skylar Donovan easily and checked his concerns. She was only his business up to a point. After that, his feelings for her couldn't interfere with a task that was too weighty for distractions.

He'd seen the demon. Facing it again, he had survived. And that was one hell of a mystery.

The thing hadn't attacked. If it had scented him and identified him as a Were—one it had created in a bloody mess of poisoned flesh—surely Skylar Donovan's presence should also have piqued its interest. All that succulent ivory skin and her sweet, sweet perfume that right now made him want to look at her instead of the road.

The beast couldn't have missed that.

No beast could have missed it.

Case in point was his own inexplicable longing for her. More than anything, he wanted to stop the car and show her he could maintain some control if he was allowed to have her.

It wasn't only his vow to protect the public that made him want to see to Skylar's safety. It was sheer, unadulterated greed. He wanted to save Skylar Donovan for himself.

She was the sum total of everything he'd lost when that beast attacked him, and so much more. She was lace and perfume, defiance and mystery in a slick feminine casing that escalated his need for those things. He'd be damned if he'd allow the monster to harm one hair on her beautiful head.

Despite this newfound possessiveness, he realized that Skylar really wasn't his to keep. She was human, and he wasn't. Oil and water didn't mix. Neither should wolf and human DNA.

He'd kissed Skylar and wanted his mouth on hers now. Her plush lips were all he thought about when they weren't confronting giant rabid werewolves that by all rights shouldn't exist.

I shouldn't exist, either, as I am now. You deserve better, Skylar.

But maybe she'd been sent here from the heavens as the kind of distraction that would keep him sane and grounded?

Don't look for excuses.

He might be torn apart by the depth of his longing for her, but he had to let this woman go, keep his distance, harness his thoughts and get away from her as soon as possible because his resolve was already weakening where she was concerned, and his energy was needed elsewhere.

The beast had returned. He'd seen it. Instead of taking it down, he'd been seriously unprepared, due in part to Skylar.

"No more kissing."

Though he muttered this softly and to himself, she heard it.

"Is that a promise?" she said.

Grimacing, rubbing his forehead, Gavin felt conflicted. By being here with Skylar he was allowing the monster to get away. By allowing it to get away, he was helping Skylar Donovan avoid the ugly fate that had befallen him.

"Nothing personal," he said to her.

"If you say so."

Lights appeared around them too quickly. Gavin drove the car into the motel parking lot at the edge of town and switched off the engine. They got out of the car without speaking.

She slammed the door.

"Just give them my name." He pointed to the office.

"Ranger Harris has carte blanche here?"

"It'll do unless you run up a tab."

She tilted her head. "You actually have a tab in this place?"

Gavin nodded. "I sometimes need to crash before the long drive home."

"Then you don't live close by."

"Close enough when I haven't been up for several nights in a row. Way too far away otherwise."

Skylar Donovan walked around the car and right up to where he stood. "You're going back out there, aren't you?"

"I'm on duty for another hour or so."

He worked hard to keep his hands to himself, unsure of why he was so attracted to Skylar that he'd want to push the limits of his self-control, or delay his highly charged personal vendetta.

This leggy blonde was just so blessed tempting, the choice seemed tough. It was as if she'd gotten under his skin and nestled there alongside the wolf.

"Does that mean you have to be alone?" she asked.

"Tonight it does."

"Why? Why would you take that chance and go back out there when you know we were followed?"

"It's what I do, Skylar. It's something I have to face and take care of without risking harm to others."

Skylar. He liked her unusual name and liked saying it. Outside of her evident ornery streak, he liked everything about Skylar Donovan that he'd seen so far. Maybe he even liked that stubborn streak.

She might be small, yet she was no shy flower. She was too courageous for her own good, though. She had walked up that mountain alone tonight without being sure of finding him.

Somehow, at that moment, she seemed a lot more than just temptation in tight blue jeans. The delicious scent that had lured him to her in the first place wafted around her like a corona. Golden hair caressed her shoulders in uncombed waves highlighted by shafts of moonlight escaping the cloud cover. The same moonlight that made his forehead dampen with the strain of withholding his wild side.

"So you admit we were followed and have no idea who it might have been?" she asked.

He shrugged to hide the evidence of another unruly spike in his heart rate that pulsed upward and into his jaw. Hell, he wanted to get under *her* skin, seize the moment and take some long-overdue R&R while he could. Surely that was fair after what he'd been through?

When she'd left the cabin, after what had almost taken place in her bedroom, Skylar had tugged on her shirt— the same shirt he'd removed in a fit of passion—without properly stretching it into place. Narrow sections of bare

Seduced by the Moon

skin showed above the waistband of her jeans—smooth, pale and terribly seductive.

No way.

Can't have you.

I've got to go back out there.

All true warnings, but Gavin's body argued adamantly against them, and against reason. Having sampled her, tasted her, felt her beneath his hands, his body repeatedly returned to those sensations as though she'd been imprinted on him. After looking into her big green eyes and finding a shared connection, Skylar Donovan truly did feel like part of his future.

This wasn't right, of course, or normal. She was just a woman he had stumbled upon who'd ended up striking his fancy. Her open-mindedness in terms of sex and lust and freely meeting her own needs had sealed the deal. That was all. He hadn't met anyone like her in a long time.

"Will I see you tomorrow?" She ran her hands over the warm hood of the Jeep the way he imagined her running them over him, and his body responded with a ripple of lustful tension.

With his pulse erratic and a new pressure in his chest, Gavin said, "In the morning I'll be back to take you home."

"Okay. Until then."

When she turned from him, Gavin briefly shut his eyes to block the sight, attempting to keep his distance, keep himself from pulling her back and making a complete fool of himself.

He watched her walk away. Her hips swayed in the fitted jeans he hadn't been lucky enough to get off her. The taut, slender back that had arched passionately during their kiss emphasized a small waist he'd like to en-circle with his hands.

Rebuking himself for staring at her like this, Gavin didn't stop looking. He'd sent her away, and she'd obliged. Her allure might be strong, but he couldn't let it rival the moon's—the moon at that same moment send-ing out signals that he intercepted as clearly as if the giant orb contained a telepathic intelligence.

Tomorrow night he'd change into something that would scare Skylar to death. All thoughts of closeness and intimacy would be a thing of the past if she were to witness his transformation.

In this new reality, however, Skylar had become as potentially dangerous to him as the moon that ruled his shape. She'd become both a distraction and a necessity in no time flat. He had to let her go and didn't want to.

Really didn't want to.

"Definitely no kissing," Gavin said aloud to bolster his willpower.

Over her shoulder, Skylar Donovan smiled. "Don't be too sure about that, Harris. I'm here for a few more days."

Gavin took two steps backward, and then two more, his heart beating out a protest about getting into the car. His fingers curled against his palms. His muscles rippled and twitched. As absurd as it seemed given that he had known this woman for only one day…leaving Skylar Donovan was just about the hardest thing he had ever done.

Skylar heard the car drive out of the parking lot, and her determination to remain independent faltered. In spite of everything she'd been through, she felt forlorn and alone.

Still, she had to admit that Harris's behavior bordered on chivalrous. He was willing to foot the bill tonight at this motel in order to see to her safety, which meant he did believe there might be trouble out there in the dark.

"A civilized ending to a strange night?"

Resigned to her current fate, Skylar gave the motel a wary once-over. It was a standard two-story, U-shaped design from the fifties. The building wrapped around the parking lot on three sides, with all the rooms and doors front-facing, and two sets of stairs leading to the second-floor balcony. Most of the windows were dark. A small blue neon sign pointed to the reception area.

Skylar went inside.

A middle-aged woman with short blond hair, wearing a red fleece vest, greeted her from behind a counter and raised an eyebrow when Skylar mentioned Harris's name. Gratefully, that woman kept what she might have been thinking about a woman showing up in this place on his dime, to herself.

Handing over a key, this receptionist said, "Room twenty-one. That's his favorite," as if being in his favorite room mattered. She then produced an ice bucket and a glass, and looked past Skylar for the missing luggage.

"Will you need anything else?"

"A toothbrush would be nice."

Skylar smiled as though nothing were out of the ordinary about not having a purse or a toothbrush, omitting the explanation of not being able to stop at the cabin for some of life's conveniences because a madman might show up there.

Or a wolf that knew how to open a door.

"Emergency amenities are on the bathroom counter," the woman said, returning the smile with less enthusiasm and leaving Skylar to assume that Ranger Harris had more than one female fan in the area. "The room is on the second floor."

"Thanks."

Skylar climbed the stairs and waited for several minutes before attempting to go inside room twenty-one, which, like the rest of the rooms, overlooked the mostly empty parking lot. Summer was over, so tourists would be scarce. Since no lights were on, she guessed she might have this floor to herself, and dreaded that.

She wished the ice bucket came with a bottle of wine. Suddenly ravenous, she wanted a salad and a steak. This wasn't the kind of motel with room service, though, and since she had no wallet, dinner wasn't in the cards. Her growling stomach would just have to suck it up and deal.

Staring out at the lot, and up at the nearly full moon emerging from the clouds, she felt lost and slightly out of sorts. The cozy cabin stuffed with her father's things made her feel more at home and part of something. Here, in a strange motel without her credit cards or her cell phone, she was cut off and isolated.

"You shouldn't have brought me here, Harris. I've never really been good on my own. Too much time to think."

Her gaze rose from the card key in her hand to the parking lot. "You really shouldn't have left me."

She added wistfully, "Come back."

Her heart kicked out a thump when the Jeep reappeared. Hopping part of the curb, it halted as far away from the building as possible and sat there idling as if the engine were trying to make up its mind about something.

The man inside it sat there, too. Skylar wanted to call out to him. Over the ether, or however such things worked, had he heard her plea? Did he know she was in need of company and felt like screaming?

"Stay," she said, willing Harris to hear her when it was absurd to imagine that he could. "Stay for a while."

The Jeep's engine died. Skylar's heart thundered when the door opened and Harris got out. From across the parking lot he stared up at her over that car door.

She didn't move, just stared back and said softly, "Damn you. Don't make me beg."

The car's door closed silently and the man she knew only by his last name began to walk in her direction, each step renewing Skylar's insatiable longing for company. Harris carried something in his hand. A white paper bag. Skylar smiled, unable to pinpoint what she hungered for most—the food that bag might contain, or the man who'd been thoughtful enough to bring it to her.

No. There really was no question about which thing she wanted most. Her body buzzed with pent-up need for everything Harris had to offer. Without being near to that hillside now, she'd have his full attention if she were lucky.

He didn't return her smile when he reached her. Hoisting the paper bag, he said, "Dinner." But he was quick to catch her expression and what that expression might mean. His hand lowered. His next remark died on his lips.

"Well, damn," he said seconds later.

In a silence filled with racing heartbeats and a rush of adrenaline coursing through her, their eyes met, held. Then he took the key from her and opened the door.

The sound of the paper bag hitting the floor echoed faintly as his body crushed hers to the wall inside the room before the door had fully closed behind them.

Chapter 8

It was a mindless, drowning kiss...deep, passionate, carnal, endless. Eyes closed, and with her fingers wrapped in Harris's thick, silky hair, Skylar breathed him in, absorbed him, became one with the sensations flooding her as his mouth transported her to a place where unadulterated greed reigned and consequences didn't matter.

They went at each other like fiends.

Through some kind of miracle, he'd heard her and returned to help fill the emptiness inside her with companionship, strength and matching ardor. Her prayers had been answered.

She kissed him fiercely in the dark, rewarding him for listening to the words he couldn't have heard. Taunting him with her tongue and teeth, she sucked his lower lip between hers, cupped the back of his neck with shaky hands, only briefly wondering if he did this often, in this room, with other women.

But what the hell. She needed an outlet for the excess energy, and tonight he was hers.

His lips slid to her cheek, her forehead, her right ear, then back to her mouth, his breath enticingly heated.

Strong, warm hands wrapped around her, pulling her from the wall and into a tight embrace that Skylar wouldn't have wanted to escape, even if she could have. If this was to be a union for only one night, and spent with a stranger, her body and her mind were willing.

His hands slipped under her shirt, his sexy, masculine warmth chasing away the chills riddling her lower back. She hadn't been wrong about him being like an inferno, and she found his heat thrilling.

He kissed her with wild abandon as his hands moved up the length of her spine, working their incredible magic. This is what she wanted, what she had always wanted—to give herself over completely and accept everything in return. Strangers had a certain kind of freedom where sex was concerned. Relative anonymity worked in her favor here.

When he paused, allowing her a breath, she shook her head. Through swollen lips she whispered, "Nowhere to run this time, ranger."

Their sense of connection careened through Skylar like a shocking current of wayward electricity. Streaks of fire filled her chest, her belly, ending up as an ache between her thighs, in a place that had never been reached or addressed like this by anyone.

Unable to restrain herself, Skylar jumped into Harris's arms, caught easily by this man who seemed to possess the strength of two. Wrapping her legs and arms around him with her body pressed tightly to his, she said, "No wolf here for us to chase, unless it's you."

Harris, with his devastatingly handsome face and a body like living sin, gave a heavy sigh as he turned for the bed.

* * *

He could have been wrong, Gavin thought as he laid Skylar on the mattress and leaned over her quivering body. Wrong about catching a whiff of something buried inside this woman, far beneath the perfume and outward perfection, that caused both man and wolf to need her so greatly. But his hunger wouldn't be assuaged. Skylar Donovan had become the embodiment of an addiction.

Though he didn't know much about her or her life, he'd already figured out one thing: she was cutting herself loose from old ideas and hindrances, and using him to do it. She also, it seemed to him, had something to prove.

They met here with the impact of two clashing thunder clouds. He couldn't see enough, taste enough, get enough of her. Perhaps this test of his personal limits is what made the affair so dangerously thrilling.

His wolfishness was growing more substantial by the minute, a reminder about how close he was to being moon-whipped.

He hoped that being with Skylar, and the depth of emotion that entailed, wasn't a self-destructive act. He wanted to be here, now. In the darkened room he'd gather the willpower to hold back his inner beast. He'd do anything for this chance at being more like the kind of man he once was.

"Light." Her request was a groan of anticipation.

"Not yet. Feel me. Feel everything, my lovely Skylar, in the dark."

In the light, you might see me for what I am.

He didn't tell her how easily he saw details in that darkness—her face and her expression, if not the color of her eyes. He watched her chest rise and fall, noted the

outline of her breasts beneath her shirt and the hardness
of her nipples. He heard her heart pounding out a crazy
rhythm that mirrored his and laid his hand on her chest
to feel the beat.

Her eyes fluttered shut.

"Yes. That's it." He tugged her shirt over her head,
confronting her sensuous bareness for the second time
that night, and with the determination to see this encounter through.

The question was how much time he could take.

Slow wasn't going to cut it. Neither were lengthy ex-
plorations or the kind of long, lingering foreplay he'd
have given an eye tooth for. He was riled up. His blood
thrashed in his veins, and inside that blood a beast swam
upward, in search of moonlight.

"Can't wait," he groaned, reaching for her zipper, en-
tranced by the sound of that zipper sliding downward
and the thought of what lay behind it.

"Don't." She lifted her hips to help him peel the jeans
off. "Don't wait."

Her shoes hit the floor, along with her pants. Gavin's
fingers hesitated on her flimsy panties. "So fragile and
feminine. These things are made for a man to appreciate before he tears them off."

The lace slipped over her thighs soundlessly, and she
kicked the panties aside. Seconds later, she was off the
pillows and going at him with the hunger of a lioness
in heat.

Pulling him down, she tore at the buttons on his shirt
that were left from their last unscheduled meeting in a
bedroom. Yanking the shirttails from beneath his waistband, she went for his belt buckle.

He helped her with that, wild and ready to burst. Feeling high as he floated on waves of raw sexual greed.

"I can do this." He voiced those words aloud without meaning to, knocking back a rising growl.

"Did you doubt it?" she asked through lips that were for him the highest form of pleasure. "Because I didn't."

On her knees on the bed, her hands flew over his pants, finding the zipper, easing it down. But she wasn't willing to wait for him to undress completely. His bare chest and what lay behind the zipper seemed good enough for her at the moment.

Instead of lying back down to prepare for the entry of his hardness, she again wrapped her arms around his shoulders. Unfurling her long legs, she curled those legs around him, leaving the spot he'd dreamed about entering poised above his pulsing erection.

"Don't stop. Don't wait." She whispered her command in his ear and nipped at his earlobe with her sharp little teeth.

Gavin groaned and spat out an oath. "Christ!"

He lifted her up with his hands beneath her firm, naked ass. In one smooth move, she was on her back on the bed, her thighs open for him, with nothing in the way that might remotely have stopped their joining.

He stretched out on top of her with the tip of his cock against the doorway to what he knew would turn out to be a delight beyond belief. Letting go of his control, he was inside her in a single thrust. He groaned, sighed, cursed silently as the exquisite softness surrounding him threatened to overtake him and give his darker side away.

He let the growl out, and felt better for it. She laughed.

But the lightness was short-lived and only the briefest release from the growing sexual tension between them.

Desiring more friction of skin on skin, Gavin's hands grasped hers. As their fingers entwined, his lover made a soft moan of satisfaction that made his blood boil.

Any touch was going to do it for them—fingers sliding across fingers, palm resting on palm, lips meeting. But Skylar Donovan would have it all, and this was just the start.

When he moved his hips, she responded in kind, grinding against him provocatively, wrapping her molten femininity around him.

Gavin closed his eyes.

Drawing back, he waited…waited while his pulse beat like a drum in this throat and he ached all over with the buildup of the pressure of long withheld needs.

He'd gotten this far, barely. His inner animal was rising, growling, urging him to hurry this along and get to the good part. The part where all three of them would be joined.

Gathering his strength, corralling his body's urges, Gavin thrust into her again. This time she cried out as she reached for him. He remembered the feel of her nails raking his skin the last time they'd been on the verge of intimacy, and the sting of cool air meeting with warm injured flesh. The minor discomfort kept him focused.

He liked it.

His next plunge went deeper into her body. Eyes still half-shut, heart hammering, he repeated the action of pulling back, collecting himself and then burying himself in her plush heat over and over.

Moving faster, harder, he created a rhythm and kept it going, putting all of himself into every move as he stroked her fiery insides until he sensed, felt, absorbed the shudders that rocked her as her body hurled the mother of all sensations forward to meet him.

She let out a groan that became a cry. Arching her back, limbs rigid, she hung on to him, both inside and out. With sharp nails, she scored his back, digging into him as if clinging to the moment in every way possible.

Pain and pleasure merged in a rush of color behind Gavin's eyes. The scent of blood wafted in the air. His blood. But it was only a little, and it somehow fit the degree of intimacy they were sharing.

He ground himself into Skylar Donovan, pelvis to pelvis, hips to hips, his length fully embedded in her wet, flaming heat. And when her orgasm claimed her, he held her there...pinned her there...with Skylar writhing beneath him in blissful agony and the wolf inside him begging for release.

Skylar's voice rang out with a silence-shattering cry. When he could take no more, Gavin groaned and backed up, afraid to let himself go, not knowing where that might lead.

Embroiled in the emotion, spurred on by the fight, the wolf inside him soared through his veins, seeking a way out, a way to share in this taking. But it wasn't time for wolf play.

Skylar belonged to the man.

Chapter 9

Drowsy, Skylar woke to darkness. Still drifting hazily with the slow rhythms of a long overdue sleep, she stretched her legs, wincing at the intensity of the aches stiffening her body. She winced again after discovering the vacant warm spot in the space beside her on the bed.

She was alone.

No. Not alone, her senses told her.

Tired enough to only turn her head, she saw him. Against a thin crack of light, he stood silhouetted at the window in a way that seemed part of a familiar dream. Highlighted by the light of outside electrical bulbs, the man who had fulfilled her sexual cravings several times over stared out the window with his back to her. A guardian. Her incredible protector.

"You're still here."

"Yes." He glanced over his shoulder, his voice igniting her internal furnace in the same way it did every time she heard it.

Though her body tried to rebel against the fatigue making her limbs heavy, it was no good. Real sleep had eluded her for so long, she didn't stand a chance against it.

"Thanks," she whispered, shutting the vision of him off, letting herself, lulled by the presence of her lover watching over her, fall toward the luxury of another forty winks. No dreams interfered with her rest. No call from the mysterious distant male came, because she had found and lain with him.

When Skylar next woke, it was with a start that signified change. She shot her hand out, searching again for warmth next to her. Not finding it, she sat up. Harris wasn't beside her. He wasn't at the window. Without having to search further, she knew he had gone, and that he'd left her recently. Maybe only minutes before. His scent remained strong—in the air, ingrained in her lungs, clinging to her skin. His taste was in her mouth and on her bruised lips.

The pinkish light of dawn streamed in from the gap in the curtains.

Well, okay. He'd disappeared, and she deserved the no-excuses abandonment for both her risky behavior and for wanting more of him than he was willing to give. She had to face facts. Harris had been a heck of a one-nighter, but with the arrival of dawn, that one night was over.

She sat up slowly, her skin cool now that their heat had faded. Her throat felt dry. Her body signaled the needling pains of having been well-used. For all that, she appreciated that Harris had stayed with her until daybreak. The thought of that small consideration was comforting.

"Don't worry," she said with a glance at her chill-riddled nakedness already beginning to show faint purple marks. "I'm not stupid."

Their night of passion had been driven by lust, and nothing more. After the first round of mind-blowing sex, they'd gone at each other like animals, free to explore and be explored. Free to be wild, and hold nothing back. That would have shocked Danny. Her ex wouldn't have been able to cope with the things she and Harris had done. The big bad cop might have wondered how she'd known about half those things.

She had moved on in one hell of a way.

As for her ranger…

It was possible he'd disappear for good now and would send someone else to drive her to the cabin. Maybe that kind of avoidance was for the best. Facing him today would be awkward. What could either of them say? *Thanks for the fuck?*

At the moment, she felt satiated and worn out. Sex and sleep had worked miracles to calm her highly tuned nervous system. Nevertheless, it was too bad she hadn't thanked Harris for the meal she'd ignored in favor of blistering carnal pursuits. She could have used some added fuel now.

The upside of a night with a stranger? Chances were the erotic dreams would stay away now that she'd indulged with a real man who fulfilled the lust quotient. If those fantasies did return, it would prove her overly greedy. In fact, she felt greedy now, with a whole new set of parameters. She wished for Harris to come back and start the circuit all over again—the talented hands, lips, and all the rest.

Listening to the rumble of hunger in her stomach, Skylar sagged against the pillows with her arms crossed over her eyes.

Until the knock came.

"Skylar? Miss Donovan?" a husky female voice said. "Gavin left something for you."

Gavin?

Wrapped in the blanket, Skylar opened the door to find the woman who'd checked her in last night holding a brown paper bag. She wore the same red vest.

Skylar looked at her inquisitively.

"Breakfast." The woman eyed Skylar right back, probably noticing the swollen mouth and nakedness beneath the blanket.

"Ranger Harris left this?" Skylar asked.

The woman shrugged. "Before he left."

Skylar took the bag.

"Don't get your hopes up, hun. It's only a couple of doughnuts. There's coffee in the lounge if you'd care to come down."

"Thanks."

"Don't mention it."

As Skylar started to close the door, the woman said, "He also left the Jeep for you. The keys are under the floor mat. Gavin said he'd get it later and to tell you it's full of gas."

Skylar pressed her back to the closed door and let out a sigh. She'd been right in assuming Harris might prefer to avoid her this morning. At least he'd been thoughtful enough to leave her some wheels so that she wouldn't have to explain about her night in the motel to anyone else on duty with him.

"Aren't we polite?" she muttered. She tossed the bag on the bed and jumped in after it. Two bites into her first meal since breakfast the day before, she silently thanked her lover for this small reward. She'd have to see him again eventually, when he came for the car, and she equally dreaded and looked forward to that.

Thoughtfully, she stopped chewing and lowered the

second doughnut. What if she was being harsh, and there was a positive spin to his actions? Maybe Gavin meant the loan of his car to be read as a promise to her of a future face-to-face meeting instead of avoidance.

Don't get your hopes up. Hopes can ruin a perfectly good memory.

Moving to the window, Skylar searched the parking lot. Spying the beat-up Jeep, she slid down the wall to sit on the floor.

Somehow, *thanks for the fuck* didn't sound as fulfilling or sarcastic as it had moments ago. It sounded more to her like the excuse of two desperate souls dancing around the problem of celibacy and loneliness without knowing how to handle themselves after the night they'd had.

"Who are you, Gavin?"

She posed the question aloud, wanting an answer to that particular question even more than she wanted to finish the food he'd sent. She was determined to banish the coward hiding in the nooks of her own personality. The coward who until last night had kept her true feelings and needs hidden from everyone and who now feared she wouldn't be able to go back to the way things were before.

Uncontrolled sex with the ranger had been exquisitely satisfying. Damn if she didn't want more.

Gavin hitched a ride with the grocer's wife as far as the old logging road, and hoofed it up the dirt track leading to Skylar's cabin.

He'd taken time for a shower, a quick bite and a cup of coffee, courtesy of the motel's overseer, Marian Smith, who'd refrained from asking questions.

He was fairly sure Marian could keep some things private and would do so. If sharing a room with a newcomer got out, it would obliterate the gossip that he'd achieved monk status as far as women were concerned, and turn the tide on incoming dinner proposals.

He didn't need that kind of gossip getting around. Though he'd enjoyed every minute with Skylar, he had almost forgotten about the monster he'd faced, and its odd behavior.

He shook those thoughts off in favor of deciding what to do next.

If he'd been thinking with his head, instead of what lay in his pants, he'd have wondered earlier about the fire in Skylar's old wood stove, which they'd left overnight. The safety of leaving that stove untended should have been a concern. Then again, who could have predicted that Skylar would follow him?

Also, if he hadn't had the run-in with a wolfish demon *and* the fright of Skylar showing up and placing herself in danger, he might have taken more time to get to know her.

Instead they'd skipped past all the "getting to know each other" parts, and delved straight into the realm of really incredible sex. Incendiary stuff. Without a werewolf's one positive perk of nearly miraculous healing powers, he would have had the bite marks from her tiny human teeth to prove it.

But it was a new day, and there were other things on his agenda. Thinking about Skylar any more than he already did would get him nowhere.

He had to find out about that monster.

But first, a couple of stops were necessary. He wanted some background on the Donovans.

Tom Jeevers lived on the road Gavin walked now. The old man rarely left his house, summer or winter, and was listed in Gavin's written log as the caretaker for Skylar's father's cabin.

The old guy, once a great craftsman in and around these parts, had built that cabin with his own two hands before turning his attention to a new spot farther north and closer to the main road. Gavin wanted to question Tom about Skylar's dad. He also wanted to see if Tom might have seen anything strange in the area lately.

Of course, there didn't have to be a connection between the abomination hiding out in the mountains and this particular area, but it seemed to Gavin to be more than coincidental that the creature kept returning here, of all the places it had to choose from in and around the Rockies.

Getting wind of it on the hillside above Skylar's cabin made Gavin extremely wary. Hearing that Doctor Donovan had been found with his face half gone made him warier still. Whether this meant Skylar might also be in danger due to the isolation of the cabin was a further concern. If anything happened to Skylar, he wasn't sure what he might do. Last night seemed to have sealed some kind of unspoken deal between them.

Jeevers's house appeared around the next bend. Made of logs and mortar, with a green metal roof and a large front porch, it complemented the woods surrounding it by blending in.

A long walkway of wood chips led to the rustic house. The intricately carved wood door opened before Gavin set a boot on the steps.

"Ranger," Tom said. "To what do I owe the honor of this visit?"

Gavin smiled. "Wanted to have a chat, Tom. I need some information about the man who bought your other cabin some time back."

"Donovan."

"That's the guy."

"Sorry affair, Harris. He took a nasty fall, I heard. Come and sit. I've got the coffeepot on the stove, and you look like you could use a cup."

Gavin followed Tom into the house, and looked around. Though the place could have used a lighter touch in terms of furniture, and carried a faint scent of dust and strong coffee, the parlor was roomy and pleasant.

Since he'd been here twice before, Gavin made himself at home on a leather sofa covered in an elaborate blanket of Hopi Indian design.

"Black, right?" Tom handed him a steaming mug filled with an aromatic brew.

"Perfect. Thanks, Tom."

Tom settled himself into the chair opposite and crossed his aging legs at the knee. Gavin noted that Tom, a bachelor for as long as anyone could remember, wore clean overalls and a plaid flannel shirt. His gray hair was neatly combed. The image he presented this morning was pretty much the opposite of what most people thought about true mountain men.

"What kind of chat are we having, Harris? An official one or a neighborly exchange?"

Gavin wrapped his hands around the mug, waiting for the coffee to cool. "Both. You know that the doctor's daughter is staying at your old cabin?"

Tom nodded. "Pretty girl. Young. Doesn't look much like her father."

"She's going through her father's things and seems at

a loss over his death. I'm curious about this guy. Is there anything else about the doctor that you can tell me?"

Tom nodded. "He was a serious man, though friendly enough. When he first bought the place, he came around now and then for friendly chats."

"Did he ever mention why he bought the cabin?"

"As a matter of fact, he did mention that once. Said he needed to get away from hectic hospital work from time to time, and that Florida was too humid to spend his downtime in."

Gavin said, "They're from Florida? I didn't know that."

"Miami, if memory serves me right. Can I ask why you're asking about the doc?"

"His daughter has questions about how he died."

Tom nodded again. "Only one of them is here."

Gavin looked up from his coffee. "One of what?"

"The doctor's daughters. There are four of them, he told me, all fairly close in age. No wife, though—at least that's what I deduced from the fact that he never mentioned one."

"His daughters haven't been here before?"

"Not as far as I know."

"Donovan kept mostly to himself, then?"

"I rarely saw him in person after his first couple of years visiting here. He used to go out at night quite often, though. I'd sometimes see him walking down the lane at sundown."

"Was he a fit man, Tom?"

"Fit as a fiddle as far as outward looks are concerned. He was tall, with premature gray hair and a sober face. It looked to me like he could climb the peaks and be right at home."

Gavin sipped his coffee, savoring the heat and slightly bitter aftertaste. "Only he didn't make it home one night."

"No," Tom agreed. "He didn't."

Taking the time to enjoy another sip, Gavin regrouped his thoughts. "I was wondering if you've seen, either recently or in the past, a wolf pack near here, Tom? Maybe you've heard them?"

"As a matter of fact, I have," Tom said. "For the better part of the past three months I've heard howling in the hills. I'm sure you, as a ranger, know that gray wolves disappeared from Colorado when the last ones were hunted and killed in the forties."

Gavin nodded. "I do know that."

Tom went on. "I heard that they've been reintroduced to some states, but not ours. They can travel great distances, though, so they've been expected to get back here eventually."

"And you're hearing them."

"Can't miss them. Even ears as old as mine can pick up their yowling."

Gavin shifted in his seat. "Have you reported this to the other rangers or the wildlife guys?"

"Not yet. But I did hear in town that several years ago a gray male was sighted ten miles from our border, so I assumed he'd made it and brought along his kin." Tom leaned forward in his chair. "Are you checking on those wolves for the Parks and Wildlife guys?"

"Yes, and also for my own curiosity. Skylar Donovan, the doctor's daughter, said something to me yesterday about her father chasing a wolf. She thought he might have been after a wolf when he fell."

"Seems a reasonable explanation for a city man

spending time away from civilization, especially given how close to the road those animals seem to be. Maybe he wanted to see one up close."

"How many of them do you think there might be, Tom?"

The old man scratched his forehead. "Well, there's more than one wolf, for sure. I'm guessing more than two. Each of them has a distinct sound. And I've seen a lot of torn-up animal carcasses around."

Gavin was distressed over that news. He'd been roaming these hills, too, and he'd seen those carcasses for himself. But there were no reports of wolf sightings in the databases he regularly checked. And that was a good thing. If the wildlife guys came in to inspect the area, not only would his search for the monster that put the *Were* in *werewolf* have to be curtailed, he'd have to find someplace else to spend time with his own issues each time a full moon came around.

"So, you're worried for the doctor's daughter?" Tom's question brought Gavin out of thought.

"She mentioned wanting to see that wolf killed, if in fact it played a part in her father's death. I'd hate to see her try to find it. She's alone out here."

"And she's a city girl," Tom said.

Raising his mug to his mouth, Gavin spoke over the rim, "A feisty city girl."

"Maybe I should report the sounds?" Tom suggested.

"Can you postpone that until I take a better look around?"

Tom smiled. "Do you fancy a fur rug?"

Gavin hid a grimace as his internal wolf gave an indecipherable whine. "No. Nothing like that, Tom. If there's a pack, I'll report it. I'd like to see a gray, that's all. I'd also like to make sure the Donovan girl doesn't do anything silly, like trying to hunt the ones you've heard."

He got to his feet with a longing glance at the mug in his hand. "Can I keep this if I promise to return the mug later? I truly believe you make the best damn coffee in the state."

"Sure." Tom beamed. "Stop in anytime for more. I always have a pot on."

"I'll do that."

The old man shook the hand Gavin offered, and smiled.

As Gavin hit the road, his worry doubled. If the old guy thought there was more than one wolf in the area, then more people than himself would be on the lookout for a pack and soon know what roamed here.

He hoped Tom would honor his request to keep the news to himself until Gavin found that big abomination again, this time more prepared to deal with it. Gavin knew he'd have to hustle on this matter before Skylar took it upon herself to return to a forest that hid one of hell's furry minions.

And before he'd have to confess to being one of them.

Chapter 10

"Clutch, gear, gas."

Skylar thanked the heavens that the motel sat on the edge of town, giving her plenty of room for a steep learning curve in stick shifts as she hit the road in Harris's Jeep at a scant thirty miles an hour. Busy Miami streets near her home in Florida weren't made for sticks or four-wheel drive. Florida was all about sleek and flashy convertibles and automatic transmissions. Torn seats and muddy tires weren't allowed.

Things got better as she cruised along, though, and she tried hard to place her surroundings in a landscape that looked totally different in the daylight. Last night her attention had centered on Gavin, and on what followed them from the hillside, with no thought for the road.

Still, her sense of direction didn't desert her. After taking a bend or two, a few miles out from town, she got her bearings.

The first stop on today's agenda was a visit to the caretaker's place. Though her father hadn't mentioned the man, other than jotting down his name and phone number on a note she'd found by the cabin's kitchen sink,

along with the word "watcher," she recalled seeing Tom
Jeevers's house on her drive in from the airport. She
was sure she could find that house now if she took her
time and followed her nose—a saying her father often
used to keep his daughters on track with whatever they
were doing.

And damn…besides missing her father, she'd missed
a call to Trish, who must surely be frantic by now.

"Damn. Damn. Damn."

What she did not need was her big sister coming to
the rescue. She wasn't going to share the contents of
that trunk in the cabin's attic with anyone, especially
after being on the mountain and feeling its heaviness
for herself.

She wasn't going to share Gavin Harris and what
they'd done last night, either. Some things were just too
private and confusing to talk over with a family member who generally, at least on the surface, had her shit
together. All the shit that counted, anyway.

Plus, she still felt confused about her father. Now,
more than ever.

Gavin Harris's rush to get her away from whatever
walked around out there last night had worked. Having
her mind led elsewhere by the way he'd mesmerized her
body made temporarily forgetting the other things easy.
But the eerie feeling of being followed, and of Gavin's
swift retreat from what he might have found on that
mountain, came back to haunt her now.

"Lord, he is talented, though," Skylar muttered as
she stepped harder on the gas pedal, realizing how absolutely absurd it was to crave a man she'd really only
recently met.

At the mere thought of Gavin, the ache between her

thighs throbbed with renewed interest. She would see him one more time to give him back his car.

She looked at her watch. Fifteen minutes had gone by, so the road she needed should appear right about *now*.

Making a sharp turn around a stand of trees, Skylar saw a green mailbox with the Jeevers name painted on it. She pulled into the yard and looked at the house before turning off the engine.

The house looked nice. Well kept. Tidy.

No one came to meet her when she got out of the car. No one answered when she knocked on the door. Undaunted, Skylar walked to the side of the house to find a window to tap on, but the windows were too high in the walls, due to the dramatic drop off of the ground from the front of the house to the back.

The yard behind the house also sloped downward at a steep angle toward the forest beneath it. Skylar shielded her eyes from the sunlight and stared through a lattice of fragrant pine branches, hoping for a better look at the stunning view of the valley. She spotted a small building down there, barely visible beneath those trees.

"Mister Jeevers?" Calling out, Skylar carefully made her way toward that distant building on uneven footing. "It's Skylar Donovan. I believe you knew my father."

Receiving no answer, she hesitated, thinking seriously about going back, and about getting to her own cabin to search for more clues dealing with her father's possible strange mental malady. But she was already here and trespassing on another person's property, so she went on with a nagging suspicion that Tom Jeevers was probably somewhere around, tinkering with the kind of tools most men living apart from town were likely to possess.

She reached the building on the slope. It was small, maybe twenty feet by twenty feet, and made of concrete blocks expertly painted to look like the logs covering the house perched on the slope above it. The roof was some kind of green corrugated metal. There were no windows.

It was quiet under the trees, save for the wind in the branches.

"Mister Jeevers? Are you out here? I'm sorry to bust in like this, but I'd like to talk to you."

Nothing.

Honestly, she didn't belong in another man's backyard.

It was as she turned to leave that she caught sight of the door to the building, open a crack. From the handle dangled a long, thick chain. On the ground beneath the chain lay the broken remnants of a fist-sized lock.

But that wasn't what set her teeth on edge.

Through that small opening in the wall came a putrid smell that triggered her gag reflex. Skylar knew what this awful odor had to be, though she'd never smelled anything like it before.

It was the stench of death.

Gavin found Skylar's cabin's door unlocked and figured she must have left it that way the night before, planning to return.

He went inside.

He looked around, and as far as he could tell, the front room didn't look disturbed. He took the time to look at several landscape paintings hanging in carved wooden frames on the walls and the handful of trinkets strewn on the mantel perched above a fireplace of worn gray river rock that took up one whole corner of the room. There

were no photos or anything of a truly personal nature
that reflected the cabin's last occupant, or his daughter.

Skylar didn't actually live here, though.

The bedroom was another matter. Gazing at the open
bedroom door, Gavin suffered a sudden pang of acute
physical longing for the woman who'd been sleeping
there.

He tossed his head. How would he get any work done
if he missed Skylar already? *Missed* being a completely
inadequate word for what he was feeling. Though he
didn't really know her, he did know every sleek, sexy
inch of her body, having explored as much as possible
with his hands and his mouth before and after discovering its fiery internal depths.

He would never forget being able to get to a place of
such incredible intimacy and abandon so quickly, and
he silently thanked Skylar for getting him through it unscathed. Problem was, now that he'd experienced such
freedom in the bedroom, and with her, he wanted more
of the same.

An endless supply.

His body twitched with the memory of their sometimes rough coupling that had utilized every surface in
the motel room. The wolf remained quiet today, allowing Gavin room for reminiscing because it also wanted
to remember, though that kind of quietness was odd behavior for the wolf this close to a full moon.

Several steps brought Gavin closer to the cabin's bedroom door. Questions appeared in his mind with each
stride. What was Skylar's life like in Florida? What did
she do for a living? Was she a teacher, secretary, CEO,
or a doctor in her own right? He should have found
those things out by now and also should have asked her

why her father might come all this way to play with the wildlife.

Why wolves, though? Why did Dr. Donovan come to this state, and this area in particular? The bad news was that he'd come to the right place for that kind of search.

"Well, all right." The house seemed fine, so there wasn't a sufficient excuse for him to stay. The desire to be in a place where Skylar lived, if only temporarily, couldn't be condoned. Neither could setting one boot inside that bedroom just to get a whiff of any lingering scent.

He'd wait for her outside.

Turning back to the front room, Gavin hesitated as the glint of something shiny, caught in a beam of sunlight coming in the window, captured his attention. Doubling back to the table near the couch, he picked up the object and stared.

"Well, I'll be damned," he said, studying a gold, diamond-encrusted ring nestled in a blue velvet box. There was no mistaking the purpose of a ring like that.

His heart took an unexpected dive that made him want to sit down. Skylar neglected to mention being engaged and hell, he hadn't thought to ask.

Disappointment coursed through him. He honestly believed that theirs might be a connection with the potential for growth, despite his personal issues and everything he'd thought about those issues for the past two years. At least he'd hoped so, against all odds and as ridiculous as that hope might have been.

Placing the ring back where he found it, Gavin straightened. Then he noticed the note paper beneath the box. It wasn't addressed, and he had no right to read what was on that note.

He turned his head to look at the gun resting on the seat of the chair. Skylar must have dropped it there before traipsing after him up the mountainside, thinking to play it safe and keep from accidentally shooting him in the dark.

Thank heavens for that small favor.

Sick over finding the ring, he picked up the gun, an old revolver, gauged its weight in his hand and turned it over. Skylar had said the gun was loaded.

He spun the chamber and dumped the ammo onto his palm. A ripple of shock ran through him. The weapon was loaded, all right. With unusual ammunition. Make that highly unusual ammunition. Bullets made of silver that felt like fire on his open palm.

Silver bullets were meant for hunting a specific kind of animal.

His kind.

Dumbfounded, he stared at a metal that, according to ancient lore, could take down werewolves with a single bullet, though no resources he found provided an explanation for why this might work when other metals didn't.

Some sources believed silver to be like a solid dose of moonlight that, if buried deep within werewolf tissue, would be too much for a beast to take all at once.

Other sources proposed that silver, long used medicinally, would work its way to the heart through the bloodstream, trying to heal a system that could no longer be fixed, taking out both host and wolf at the same time.

Yet there were plenty of arguments citing the silver-bullet theory as being hogwash, and stating that a bullet was a bullet, no matter what it was made of. If struck in the right place, a crucial place, any bullet might take down man or beast. Spots like the head, or a direct hit to the heart...

A beating heart like his, which had already taken a blow from a diamond ring...no bullet necessary.

Gavin reloaded the gun and replaced it on the chair, wondering as he looked to the front door if Skylar knew anything about the special bullets or if she'd merely found the weapon among her father's things without looking closely at the ammo inside it.

He thought back.

"I have a gun," she told him. "I know how to use it."

So, what else did she know about?

Who was the lucky guy with the ring?

He ran a hand through his hair and then pinched the bridge of his nose to ease the ache building behind his eyes as he remembered more of their conversation.

"I think my father might have been chasing a wolf when he died."

New meaning about that struck Gavin with the force of a hammer falling from the sky. This was Skylar's father's gun. These were Dr. Donovan's silver bullets. Chances were that Papa Donovan hadn't been chasing just any old wolf out here if he had purposefully bought those custom bullets. A werewolf had been his target. And there were, as far as Gavin knew, only two werewolves here.

Screeching noises roused him... The sound of a car driven around a tight curve by someone in a hurry.

"Skylar."

Smelling the hot tires with his overworked wolf senses, Gavin headed outside, alerted by the sound of a car door being forcefully kicked open.

She was there, as if he'd conjured her. Skylar faced

him across the small yard, her face as white as parch-
ment paper. "I think Tom Jeevers might be dead," she
said, holding on to the car for support.

Chapter 11

Gavin was by her side quickly, easing her from the car and into his arms. "What? What did you say?"

"At his house. In the back. Bad smell. Really bad."

Gavin held her firmly. "I just came from there. Tom was fine."

"He wasn't there. I found another building."

"What other building?"

"The one behind the house, under the trees."

"The shed?"

Skylar's eyes pleaded with him to believe her. "Get help."

"Okay. You'll come with me," he said. "Get back in the car."

She did as he asked without question or argument and sat quietly as he got in beside her.

"Tell me what happened."

"I don't know what happened."

"You didn't go inside to look for the source of the odor?"

Stricken by that idea, she shook her head. "Not so brave now, huh?"

What was left of Gavin's wounded heart went out to

her. She was seriously shaken. Her tension transferred to him as though a lightning bolt had been trapped in the car with them, with nowhere else to go but back and forth between the two.

"Did you see anyone?" he asked.

"No."

"Are you all right?"

"Out of breath, that's all. Scared for him. For Jeevers."

"Why did you come here, instead of heading for town?"

"I left my phone here, and this was closer."

That wasn't the entire truth. His uncanny connection to her suggested there was more. She must have known she'd find him at the cabin. Maybe she also knew he couldn't have stayed away. He believed that she'd chosen to run to him, instead of in the opposite direction.

Heat continued to flush the skin on the back of his neck. Gavin's forearms tensed as he turned the steering wheel, fighting an impulse to pull over and kiss the woman beside him, no matter how dire the situation might be.

There was no way for this connection, this bond, to be make-believe. Skylar either trusted him or wanted to. By being together, by joining their bodies in an exquisite physical union, and maybe even before that, they'd assessed and discovered each others' worth. One soul sought the other, finding solace in their new companionship.

"You're engaged," he said after using his radio to make a call, though his mind should have been elsewhere.

She glanced at him.

"It might not be a good idea to leave valuable things

lying around where anyone could find them," he added. "I saw the ring. The door was open, if that's any excuse. I wanted to make sure everything was okay since we left in a hurry last night."

The conversational turn didn't seem to unsettle Skylar. She said, "If it still meant something, that ring would be on my finger."

"Must have been a recent decision?"

"Fairly recent, but ancient history now."

"But you brought it here?"

"To send back."

Maybe that was on the note he hadn't read.

"I'm sorry." Gavin heard the relief that gentled his voice, and figured she'd pick up on it, too.

"I'm not," she said, gazing at him.

Gavin pulled the Jeep over with a sharp twist on the wheel. Unfortunately this wasn't anywhere he could have been alone with Skylar, but in Tom Jeevers's front yard.

"Stay here, okay?" he said, hating to leave her.

She nodded.

Out of the car, and with his radio in hand, Gavin strode to the house and knocked. Receiving no answer, he skirted the perimeter, stopping short when Jeevers met him in the back.

"Harris?" Tom said. "Back so soon?"

Gavin lowered the radio. "You're all right, Tom?"

"The question supposes that something might have happened to me in the past hour?"

With a glance behind him at the car, Gavin said, "Good. Glad to see you're okay. Would you mind if I have a look at the building in the back, Tom?"

"Why would you want to see that?"

"I've had a complaint about a bad smell."

Tom's returned gaze was one of surprise. "Bad smell?"

"I'd like to investigate, Tom."

Tom's brow furrowed, adding to the creases already ingrained in his deeply tanned skin. "Well, I suppose it's okay to take you down there now that he's gone."

Gavin tilted his head. "Now that who is gone?"

"Doc Donovan."

"What's he got to do with the building behind your house?"

"He rented it to keep some of his things in."

"You decided not to mention that this morning when we spoke?"

Tom shrugged. "I never saw him use it. As far as I knew, after moving stuff in a few years back, he never came here again."

"You haven't looked at it in all that time?"

"My knees aren't what they used to be, and that hill is steep. There aren't any windows in that structure, and he put a lock on the door. What would I have looked at?"

"I'd appreciate it if you'd show me, Tom. I just need a quick look around."

"All right. I was going to have to bust that lock eventually, anyway, since the doctor is no longer with us. I'd thought to tell his daughter about it while she's here. Hang tight and I'll find some bolt cutters."

As Tom wandered toward the back door of his house, Gavin walked down the slope, only discovering that the little building he'd assumed was a shack was something slightly bigger once he got close to it. The painted camouflage was good. The smell emanating from it was as awful as Skylar had described.

It was an odor having nothing to do with what had been stored here. Something had died.

Gavin tightened his grip on the radio and paused by the door to stare at the dangling chain. The unmistakably silver chain, lightly tarnished with age and weather, and composed of huge interlocking links.

Waves of apprehension washed over him as he reached for the door. He'd made it through a night of sexual gymnastics with a woman, fearing the worst in himself, but he doubted that facing what this building held would be nearly as easy.

Hearing footsteps behind him that he recognized, Gavin pivoted to block Skylar's approach. It just wasn't in her nature to be left behind. He'd have to remember that.

"Do you ever do what's asked of you?" he challenged in a rough voice devoid of any of the kindness his lover might need at the moment after a discovery like this one.

"Hardly ever," she shot back.

"You can't go in there. I won't allow it, Skylar."

"You're going inside?"

"I have to. Tom's okay, and up at the house, so whatever this is requires my attention."

"I think this might have something to do with me."

"Why would that be true?"

"My father has been here. I'm sure of that."

"Why would you think so?" Gavin pressed.

"I just do."

He didn't have time for this. Puzzles would have to wait and so would enigmatic women. This building was surrounded by an atmosphere of violence, and it reeked of death. Skylar had been right about that, too.

"Could be that an animal wandered in and got stuck

when the door partially closed off its escape. Rotting elk carcasses can smell like this as they decompose," he explained, though his crystallizing senses told him a different story.

This was no elk stench. The odor struck a chord that made his inner wolf squirm.

Inching the door open, he held his breath and crossed from the light of day into the building's ominously dark interior.

For once, Skylar didn't move. Between the stench of the place and the expression on Gavin's face, she felt frozen solid. Her muscles and her vocal cords were completely useless.

"Got them," a very alive old man she assumed must be Tom Jeevers shouted from the hill above them.

She watched Gavin back out of the building. He looked to her and then to the man heading their way before again fixing his gaze on the radio clasped in one of the same strong hands that had given her such pleasure. When his eyes found hers, he said, "You'll need to go back to the car."

She wanted to do as he asked. She really did. The chills spreading over her like an icy contagion were the cold fingers of premonition, warning that she might not want to find whatever was in this building. But her shoes were glued to the ground.

Tom Jeevers slid down the last of the slope to stand beside them. He held a large tool she recognized. Bolt cutters.

After taking a lingering look at her, he noticed the lock on the ground and the open door, and made a face.

"There's a light switch inside on the right," he said

to Gavin without introducing himself to her. "Shoulder high. I'll show you."

Gavin stepped back to let the man pass and then followed Jeevers into the building when the lights came on.

With no desire to actually see what that room held, and after hearing muffled exclamations from both men, Skylar swayed on her feet. Passing minutes slowed to a crawl. She put a hand to one ear to stop the ringing sounds about to drive her mad. She wasn't a coward. Was not.

Although neither man emerged from what she currently designated as a house of horror, it was crazy to think that a dangerous fate had befallen them, too. What could they be doing in there? Why were they taking so long?

She wanted to shout out those questions.

Covering her nose with the top of her shirt, she planted one foot in front of the other. Finding the nerve to shuffle forward, she reached the door. Nobody stopped her when she entered. Her fear gave the building a sinister cast, though sinister would have been putting things mildly.

Four steps in, she froze again. Gavin and Tom Jeevers stood in the center of a large open space, unmoving after all that elapsed time, their faces contorted with horror and disgust.

Skylar quickly saw why.

The floor was gray concrete. Walls were padded with extra layers of insulation for soundproofing. Chains with medieval-looking manacles hung from the closest wall, bordering a huge floor-to-ceiling cage that took up most of one corner. The cage's bars gleamed with silver flecks in the light from an overhead lamp. Its door hung open.

Her first impression was that someone had built a torture chamber inside this building behind Tom's house. The awful smell told her that someone had used it.

Strong arms caught her when her legs gave way. Gavin—his pallor as gray as the concrete, his expression grim.

"Tom, can you explain this?" he said.

The older man shook his head. He also looked ill.

"This sits on your property," Gavin said.

With her head pressed to his chest, Skylar felt the rumble of Gavin's voice when he made that charge. His heart was racing. His shoulders continually twitched as if, like hers, his instincts told him to run.

"How could you not know about this, Tom?"

"It wasn't my place to interfere," Tom finally managed to croak. "I didn't have a key. I never saw anyone come in or out."

Aware of Gavin's gaze shifting to her, Skylar raised her chin. Feelings of terror shot through her when she read what lay behind Gavin's intense blue gaze.

"What about your father, Skylar? You told me you knew he'd been here."

She eyed the cage. Her breath squeezed out to form a reply to his question, but another question took precedence. "What kind of animal would that cage hold?"

"A big one," Gavin replied.

"I was wrong. My father couldn't have been here. He would not have allowed this. He was a doctor, and he was kind."

"Could he have discovered this place and been helping whomever or whatever he found here?"

"Yes. That must be it, and why I thought he…" She couldn't finish that sentence, frantic now for a way to explain this scene when her heart and head each maintained different fears.

That cage was built to hold a large animal. A strong animal. For what purpose, though? What about the chains on the walls?

Those chains weren't low, or anywhere near the floor. They'd been attached to the walls with industrial-sized iron rings and placed high up, spread far enough apart to restrain something bigger than a human.

No.

Not that.

She was going to be sick, and fought off a whirl of vertigo. Her father couldn't have found and trapped the kind of creature he'd been seeking because they didn't exist. Even if they did, he could not have kept one here.

He wouldn't have dared.

Unless her father's plan was to keep a dangerous creature locked away from others. Keep it from harming others. Study it closely.

No. That can't be it, either.

Those manacles would eliminate wolves and other typical four-legged predators.

"No," she repeated aloud, helpless to explain this room. Any attempt to address her father's motivations without the facts to back them up might damage his pristine reputation and all the good he'd done. He couldn't speak for himself, and she refused to judge her dad by the way things looked.

She was trembling so hard, Gavin pulled her closer. But she felt a change in him. He was unsure about her now, and about what she'd said about her dad.

She wanted to shout "werewolf" and be done with it. Get that out in the open and let these men decide how crazy she was. But was she crazy? Had her father been nuts, too, or merely a damn good hunter to have bagged a beast? Was there a chance her father's mad mind assumed some other poor animal was a werewolf?

As more awful theories piled up, Skylar dug deep into her thoughts. If her father *had* trapped a werewolf, or any other kind of animal for study, there would be written evidence of that work. She'd have to search to see if such a diary existed in order to find out what had gone on in this dreadful place.

"Charging my father with knowing about or abetting this kind of activity gets us nowhere if all we have to link him to this place is my hunch that he'd been here before," she said.

"He rented this building from Tom." Gavin's voice was as grim as his expression.

"Anyone could have done this," she insisted. "The lock was broken."

Transferring his attention to Tom, Gavin said, "She's right. If Donovan hasn't been here in a couple of years, room for blame is left wide-open."

"We don't know what actually went on here." Tom looked to Skylar as he spoke.

"That smell tells us something did," Gavin said.

Her lover slowly distanced himself from her. His hold on her loosened in a way that suggested he might believe her a part of this, or think that she could have been tainted by her father's deeds.

She spoke again. "What happened to being innocent until proved guilty?"

"Nothing happened to that," Gavin said. "We've all had a nasty shock and we're searching for meaning."

"They might think I did this." Tom Jeevers headed for the door. "I'd better call it in."

Skylar pointed to the radio in Gavin's hand. "Aren't you going to use that?"

"I already have."

That meant others were on their way here.

"I need some air," she said.

Without another word, Skylar left the room. On her own, with only seconds to spare before Gavin might follow her outside and before other members of the law arrived, she leaned against the corner of the building on legs that felt like rubber, allowing the tears of shock and fright and blatant disgust to pool in her eyes.

Wet-faced and shaky, she blinked slowly when a shadow behind her blocked the sunlight. She didn't need to guess who it was.

Chapter 12

"Can we talk?"

Skylar whirled to face him.

"Before the others arrive?" Gavin added.

"I don't know anything about what happened here," she said.

"Then tell me about silver bullets. The bullets in your gun."

She looked at him with her lips parted for a shout she didn't let loose. "I believe the only way you'd find out about that might be called trespassing," she said.

"As I said, I had probable cause to enter your house."

"Such as?"

"Searching the premises for intruders, since we were gone all night."

"Is that all?"

"No. Actually it was just an excuse to wait for you. I wanted to be there when you arrived."

His confession made her look away.

"You have secrets." He spoke softly, not caring to distress her further.

"Obviously, my father is the Donovan who kept secrets," she said.

"Can you talk to me about that, Skylar? Will you?"

"It wouldn't help this case."

"Why not?"

"He was good at what he did and spent his entire professional life helping others. These things…" She waved at the building beside them. "These things aren't indicative of the man I knew. They're far removed from what I know about my father."

"Did he come here to get away from his work?"

"Yes. Dealing with mental patients day in and day out began to take a toll."

Gavin absorbed this news slowly. "He wasn't a general kind of MD?"

"He's a…" She paused before starting over. "He was a psychiatrist."

"At a hospital facility?"

"Yes."

"A mental hospital?"

She nodded. "One that housed patients with extreme mental deficiencies."

Gavin thought he was starting to see a pattern that might lead to answers to some of the problems they faced. But he couldn't yet connect the dots. What he knew pointed to Skylar's father as a suspect in whatever went on behind Tom's house, though at the moment they had no real idea as to what that was.

"We haven't found anything illegal here yet," he said tentatively, disliking that fact. "No proof of illegal activity to go on. For that, more evidence needs to be gathered."

Besides, Gavin inwardly added, if he told anyone of his suspicion that a werewolf might have been caged here, he stood to be laughed out of town.

For him, the chains and silver cages made it a fore-gone conclusion, though. The fact that Skylar's father rented this place from Tom incriminated her good old dad in something unspeakable, as did that gun with the silver bullets.

Silver chains, silver cage, silver bullets.

All this silver business rubbed him the wrong way, as did the picture Skylar painted of her father.

"You do realize that withholding information might prove a fatal mistake?" he said, carefully moderating his tone.

He found it unimaginable that anyone might have trapped that gigantic monster from the mountain here. How the hell could that have been managed? Even if the hunter had used tranquilizer darts made for taking down elephants, the beast would still have to be trans-ported to this location.

And damn it, he was a sucker for the damp green eyes now looking into his. He wanted to kiss the tears from Skylar's beautiful, innocent face. She made him want to believe she knew nothing about her father's intentions.

He brushed the drops of water from her cheeks with his thumbs, allowing his fingers to linger on her too-pale skin.

"If I ask you something personal, will you answer honestly?" Gavin willed himself to keep some emotional distance from the woman who'd taken hold of his soul so quickly and easily.

Long lashes briefly cloaked her eyes. "I'm not sure. Right now I'm not sure about anything."

Gavin lowered his voice. "Did your father have an agenda for those silver bullets, or were they only col-lector's items?"

"I haven't found the answer to that question, though I've been wrestling with it since I arrived," she answered earnestly.

"You knew about the bullets, then?"

"I found the gun and the bullets in a trunk in the attic of the cabin."

Gavin blew out a breath and blinked again, thinking *Holy hell.* Skylar's father might actually have known about the thing in the woods, or thought he did. And that beast might have been right here, either of its own accord or held against its will by Skylar's dad.

Had the elder Donovan actually succeeded in capturing and chaining up the monster Gavin so desperately wanted to find? Could Donovan, at least for a time, have kept that monster captive here behind Tom's house, right beneath Gavin's nose?

Some pieces of this puzzle were lining up, and the pattern he saw suggested that Doc Donovan was a werewolf hunter.

Had the monster managed to get loose and go after its keeper? Maybe Donovan let it go?

Gavin rolled his shoulders as he speculated about the doctor's body being discovered torn to shreds and missing a face. His muscles tensed with the memory of being torn apart on that same mountain.

Theories about revenge would make a horrible kind of sense if life mimicked the pages of horror novels and monsters possessed the ability to think like human beings. Could this be a case of a beast reaping revenge on its tormentor, like in the Frankenstein story?

Wasn't he after the same thing in his own hunt for that big beast? Revenge?

If Skylar's father had succeeded in trapping the creature in this building and it somehow got loose, possibly showing complex thought processes…heaven help the man who'd dared to cage it.

Gavin felt the rightness of his reasoning, but could he prove any of it? Talk about it with anyone? As far as most people were concerned, the only monsters running around hurting other people were low-life human criminals.

If he mentioned any of this, he'd be considered a candidate for Dr. Donovan's mental ward.

"I'd like to know more about your father," he said when the silence had stretched for far too long. "You said he kept secrets. I want to hear what you know about those secrets."

"So you can pin what we've found here on him?" she countered.

Think carefully about what you say next, and how you'll explain what you're about to propose.

"Skylar." Gavin took his hand from her face. "Is it possible that your father believed in the lore of old European legends?"

She shook her head, unwilling to hear more. He could see she resented this kind of personal intrusion.

"Do you have any idea what silver is used for in those legends?" he pressed.

She remained mute, but he couldn't let this go.

"Could your father have brought a wolf here?"

Feeling her mounting tension, Gavin's excitement began to stir. Skylar knew something, all right. She was trying to hide her conclusions from him. Once again, her eyes met his, and the electricity sparking between them scored his soul. The look on her face was sad and lonely and startlingly defiant.

He reached for her without thinking, desiring his hands on her, whether to offer comfort or demand her compliance with his line of questioning. With his cheek buried in her soft, silky hair, he posed the final question, holding her tightly in case she tried to avoid what was coming.

"Did your father believe in werewolves?"

Sirens in the distance broke the silence that followed his question. The woman in his arms struggled to break free, perhaps tortured by what he'd suggested.

She probably thought him crazy for proposing such a thing. Her heart banged in her chest. Small rattling quakes ran up and down the length of her spine. But he didn't let her get away from him, because he was badly in need of her answer.

"Skylar," he said. "Is that why he came to Colorado? To hunt wolves, hoping to capture a special one?"

When she tilted her head back, Gavin noted the fear darkening her eyes. After seeing this place, she'd be afraid to speak further about her father. He didn't blame her, really, especially after he'd mentioned the seriousness of withholding information.

Who would believe it, anyway? he wanted to shout, *Other than me?*

"Werewolves?" Her voice was hardly more than a whisper. "Yes. I think he believed in them."

Skylar's reply set off tiny explosions in his overworked mind. Hell, was Skylar's father at the center of this?

The noise of the sirens told Gavin that two law enforcement vehicles had arrived. He heard doors slam. Calm voices carried on the wind. When Skylar struggled again, he let her go.

"You don't have to be here," he said.

"They'll want to speak with me eventually. Better get it over with."

Skylar set her shoulders and walked past him, looking young and small from behind...and fragile and burdened as she marched to face what came next.

Gavin could have told her this wasn't the end, and that it was only the beginning of the nightmare.

Chapter 13

The interrogation was shorter than Skylar expected. When they freed her to go home, the sheriffs, accompanied by a couple rangers, headed down the hill to see what this nasty business was all about.

She couldn't stay there, near that shed, so she started walking in the direction of her cabin. It was either that or wait for Gavin, who might be some time yet, and would certainly have more questions about her father's secrets.

She was aware that Gavin's thoughts were turning her way, though he was nowhere in sight. The more time she spent with him, the more the bond between them deepened.

It was getting too dangerous to keep holding back some serious family issues. She knew that now. The damn word haunting her was the word Gavin had brought up—*werewolf.*

Is that why he came to Colorado? To hunt wolves, hoping to capture a special one? he'd asked.

Stumbling on a stone bordering the road, Skylar fought off the rise of her temper. Reason told her it would be best to leave Colorado, go home and forget about this place. Put the cabin up for sale with all her father's things in it and move on. Lose the dreams. Lose Gavin Harris.

Pausing long enough to glance over her shoulder, she repeated "Lose Gavin," aloud, testing both the idea and her resolve.

Right then the idea almost seemed doable.

Almost.

Her stubborn streak just didn't agree. Neither did the spot deep inside that wanted his touch so desperately.

What would her father have thought about Gavin, so different from her ex-fiancé? Her dad hadn't liked Danny much. Gavin already showed more stability than the edgy companionship she'd shared with the cop, a relationship that had resembled a positive relationship on only a superficial level. Even after saying yes, she'd known that no woman should settle for superficial when her heart wasn't truly with the program. She'd learned this lesson the hard way.

While Gavin...

Gavin, her handsome, virile lover, kept her on the verge of something she didn't dare name, in a completely different way. He was strong, capable, gorgeous and smart. Around him, she felt safe, but also as if that sense of safety might be temporary, with the future some kind of wild unknown.

The looks. That voice. Hell, yes, she was undeniably attracted to him. Probably too much. He pulled her wildness out and into the open, exposing that side of her. Her shakes and quakes weren't all signs of weakness, but an effort to control the secret longings she felt building up inside.

Yet Gavin had spoken the dreaded word that plagued

her. The word she hated most at the moment. *Were-wolves.*

Confused, flustered, Skylar thought about going back to Tom's house to quiz Gavin about what silver bullets were meant for.

It was going to be a conversation straight from hell.

As luck would have it, she didn't have to turn around or wait long for him to find her. Recognizing the sound of the Jeep's engine, she planted herself in the middle of the road, ready for the next showdown.

One look at her face—the set features, the lips forming a straight line—told Gavin that Skylar wasn't going to jump into the car without an argument.

Too many things left unsaid had created a tension between them that stretched their connection to the breaking point. The accusations he'd made regarding her father might have seemed absurd to anyone else, yet apparently weren't crazy to Skylar.

Why?

Cutting the engine, Gavin got out of the car thinking that if he remained on his side of the vehicle, chances were the woman eyeing him so intently might feel less threatened. Though he wanted to search the trees for the monster able to eat its way out of that silver cage, it was still daylight. He kept his attention on the woman in the road.

"Want a lift?" he asked casually.

"I don't think so." Her voice sounded clipped.

"Want to talk?"

"Do you?" she countered.

"Yes, I do. But why don't I drive you home, and we can leave the talking for later? Get you off the road?"

"You think I don't know what you're dying to say? I can hear your unspoken questions from where I'm standing."

"You've had a shock," Gavin said.

"Understatement," she tossed back.

"Your father didn't necessarily have anything to do with that place."

"Do any of you actually believe that?"

"At this point, and as I've said, any evidence is circumstantial at best. They'll have to go through that place with a fine-tooth comb to dig up more, and that will take time. Please let me drive you home."

She shook her head to reinforce her decision to remain on the road. "You brought up werewolves."

He nodded. "Yes, and you went along with it. I find that not only fascinating, but strange."

"How so?" she challenged.

"You didn't laugh at the word."

"It's not funny."

"No, but it probably should have been funny. That's the point." Gavin rested both hands on the roof of the Jeep. "Are you searching for proof that your father wasn't off his rocker? Because now those law guys are going to try to discover that same thing."

It was clear that some of the fight had gone out of her when she said, "He couldn't have hurt anyone in a place like that."

"You'd be the one to know."

She glanced around uneasily. "You're right. We shouldn't talk here."

"If you don't want to go to the cabin, we can go someplace else."

Gavin waited her out, trying to read in her expression

what she needed at the moment to help ease the shock of seeing that building and imagining what it might have hidden.

"What were you doing at Tom's?" he asked.

"I was going to thank him for watching over Dad's cabin."

"That's all?"

"No," she admitted. "I was looking for information."

"About what?"

"My father, and what he did here in Colorado."

Some of the iron in her tone returned as she added, "Shall I repeat my protest about him not using that awful place?"

"No need. I'm sure no one could believe their father capable of that."

Having successfully defused another potential argument, Gavin waited to see what Skylar might say next. She might want a fight, but he wasn't going to let her have it.

"If my father had lost part of his mind, other people would have noticed. The rest of his family, all of us, would have heard."

"One would think so," he agreed. "Especially if he worked in a hospital where anomalies are noted on a daily basis by people trained to see them."

Skylar's hand moved to the door handle. "I can't explain about the gun."

"Though you admit to knowing what silver ammunition is supposedly for."

Her face fell. "Yes. Wolves. Not just wolves, though. Imaginary wolfish beasts."

Gavin shifted his stance to hide the degree of his surprise.

"Okay," she said. "Believing in werewolves isn't normal behavior. I get that." Looking directly at him, she asked, "Is it?"

Unwilling to answer that question, Gavin blew out a breath. He sure as hell couldn't confess.

"What will those guys in uniform assume when they investigate the room back there?" she asked.

"They will assume that a lunatic has escaped from an asylum."

He was wrong about her face not being able to get any paler. Skylar's shoulders slumped as she opened the door. It took minutes for her to get into car. When she did, she sat as far away from him as possible.

Tonight, he thought, gazing at Skylar with regret and a gigantic knot in his gut. *In a few hours, when the full moon rises and the wolf takes me over, no explanations would be necessary if you were to see me. And that might actually hurt you more than it hurts me.*

Gavin felt the intensity of her heated gaze. For once, he wanted to shape-shift right then and there to put an end to the misery they'd face sooner, rather than later. Get it over with. Let her know that her father might not have been loony.

As if revealing his beast would put her mind at ease.

Chapter 14

The man beside her drove in silence. Skylar wanted anything but distance, but the terrible find had created even more distance between them.

Skylar figured it was past noon. Time had been suspended after her discovery of that shed. She wasn't able to shake off the latest round of chills or ditch the feeling that she was about to step off a cliff.

She kept wondering, as she had for several nights now, if madness might be contagious, because the answer to that particular question seemed more important after today's events. Although she supposed true madness defied the use of logic and reasoning, her brain now hurt.

She refused to link her father to that building behind Tom's house. It just wasn't possible.

When they reached the cabin, she got out first, walked up the steps and turned at the door. "You never got that lemonade."

From a few paces behind her, Gavin said, "Don't you think we're going to need something stronger?"

She gestured him inside. "You're in luck. No self-respecting Irishman with a name like Donovan would fail to know how to stock a bar."

"Funny," Gavin said, pausing on the threshold with a glance in the direction of the bedroom. "I didn't put Donovan and Irish together until you mentioned it."

"Yes, well, we don't really know much about each other, do we? Other than how well our bodies fit together."

Skylar headed for the kitchen, vowing to keep as far away from the bedroom as possible until they did find out some things. She honestly wanted to know more about the man in her front room, even though her body needed more of what he had to offer.

Before this she'd thought of Gavin as a distraction to keep her mind off her father's death and off those exotic dreams about a creature on the hillside. She wasn't sure when that changed, but it had, probably due to Gavin's gallant impulse to protect her from whatever danger he perceived in these mountains.

That, and the incredible sex.

They might have become lovers for the wrong reasons, but did that have to stand in the way of getting to know him better now?

Gavin was at the window when she returned with glasses and a bottle of whiskey. She felt his reluctance to deal with the things needing to be said.

"What are you always looking for out there?" she asked.

"It's habit. My job is to watch for things out of the ordinary."

She handed him a glass when he turned. "Well then, maybe you can fill in a few missing details for me."

She moved the gun from the chair to the table so that

he could sit down if he wanted to. With their attention on that gun, and the silver-bullet issue hanging over them like a dark cloud, Skylar went on. "My first question for you, in what will be a lengthy interrogation, is this—why are you drinking while on duty?"

She hoped her weak smile might break the ice, and watched some of his tension ease. Obviously, he'd expected a more serious discussion after everything that had happened in the past several hours. She was saving that.

"Just a swig to calm the nerves," he said. "I've never really developed an appreciation for this stuff."

"Neither have I." Skylar poured the amber liquid into their glasses. "But what was in that shed would get to anyone."

His nod of agreement caused strands of his hair to fall forward, curtaining his angular cheeks, adding a rugged air to his chiseled beauty that made Skylar's breath catch in her throat.

She knew his outline. She had seen it before, and not just in the motel. In her dreams, the being she had the hots for wasn't merely a man. Was Gavin Harris actually more than he seemed, or had she gone off the deep end again to even consider such a question?

He studied her as if he were attempting to see where this benign conversation might be going. She dared to say what was on her mind, gripping the glass so tightly she feared it might crack. "The moon is full tonight."

His eyes were riveted to hers.

"Will you be going after the wolf we heard out there? Does more light mean that you might actually be able to find it?"

Without waiting for his reply, Skylar poured a few

more drops of whiskey into their glasses, needing something to do with her hands. She took a swig and made a
face as the burn slid down her throat.

"Everything comes back to one word—*wolf*," she
said. "You told me last night that the wolf out there on
the mountain is a special wolf."

Gavin set his glass on the table, breaking eye contact.
"It's a dangerous one, yes."

"Earlier, after discovering a horrible scene at a neigh-
boring house, what came to your mind was again the
word *wolf*. Did my father believe in werewolves, you
asked. Am I to ignore the connection between those
words, or that you brought them up?"

Tiny movements in the muscles of Gavin's forearms
took her attention there, to the smooth bareness exposed
by his rolled-up cuffs. She'd had her tongue on that skin
in the night, and he had believed in returning the favor
in kind. His mouth had traveled over every inch of her,
bringing out far more in her than just shivers of delight.

Steel willpower kept her from looking to the bedroom doorway now.

"Please, Gavin. What have wolves got to do with
any of this?"

Why, in my dreams, are you there?

Gavin moved to stand beside her. Taking the glass
from her hands, he spoke with his mouth inches from
hers. The delicious warmth of his breath raised her pulse
and increased her anxiousness.

"We're speculating about the wolf," he said. "And I'll
admit to being unable to think when I'm this close to
you. All I want to do is take you inside that bedroom,
Skylar. You're like an obsession, or a very bad craving.
But I'll warn you now that you probably don't want to

get to know me any better than you already do because
I'm not permanent relationship material. I'm involved
with the danger around here, and I seek it out. Today,
and especially tonight after the sun goes down, I'll be
absent. I can't protect you if you stay in this cabin."

His words were like a spray of those damn silver bullets. He felt the same as she did and craved her the way
she craved him, yet he'd just clarified his position on
having a relationship without answering her questions.

"Protect me from what?" she pressed. "What do you
think is out there that might hurt me?"

Her heart sputtered when she looked into the eyes of
the man who had freed her from old hang-ups and ta-
boos. Even with all the strange things going on, she'd
have passed up necessary information for one touch of
his hand on her bare back, and for that hand to render
her mindless.

She saw that same wish mirrored in Gavin's blue
eyes, expressive eyes that were flecked with gold, wide-
open, and told her how much he hungered for her.

Maybe she was in need of both wildness and safety
at the same time. Yet Gavin was the one who had been
watching the cabin, and admitted as much. Had her
dreams been some sort of precognition about meeting
the kind of man she needed in order to be the woman
she wanted to be?

Or was something more mystifying going on?

Could dreams affect reality? Be her reality?

His breath on her face stirred her inner restlessness.
His nearness fed the wildness aching to be released.
There was no way to explain how badly she wanted to
be satiated, moved, licked and loved by this man. In

just two days, life had become so much more interesting and complicated.

But the word *wolf* stood between them. And something felt off, if only by a fraction.

Blowing out the breath she'd been holding, Skylar grabbed hold of Gavin's shirt. "Tell me," she whispered. "Tell me why you were watching this cabin, and why you walked into my yard."

"Skylar…" He tried to interrupt. Maybe he wasn't able to follow her thread of thought.

Any minute now she would have to confess that she'd conjured him up out of the stuff of her dreams.

I have to be sure, don't you see?

"How do I know you're you, and not some kind of…" She didn't finish the statement. Wasn't able to. She knew how it would sound.

"We don't have time for this," he protested, his breath mingling with her breath, his lips touching hers when he spoke. "I'm not sure what you're asking."

"I'm asking for the truth and for a starting point that might explain all of this."

"Are you talking about what happened at Tom's?"

"That, and more. This. You and me." She lowered her voice. "And the wolves."

He blinked and set his jaw. Skylar's next thought, as she closed her eyes, was to hope she wasn't dreaming now. Because that would mean the man beside her wasn't real and that she hadn't yet woken from sleep.

"I've never been crazy," she whispered to Gavin as she reached for the buttons on his clean, pressed shirt. "But I feel crazy now."

He didn't protest when she placed her palms against the fabric covering his chest. His skin felt hot through the cotton and pulsed with a heartbeat as hard and fast as hers.

"Please prove me wrong," she said, expecting him to tear himself from her grasp and run the other away. It's what most men might have done. Danny had.

Gavin's hair brushed her cheek when he shook his head. The dark strands felt like satin.

"I'm trying to understand. I'm sorry," he said. But he remained close.

"Werewolves," Skylar whispered. "Tell me why you brought them up."

Her emotions were running rampant. She needed an outlet. Giving in to the lure of his mouth, Skylar pressed her lips to his, finding solace in his taste and his heat. She felt Gavin fight his need to join her on the floor. But another blistering round of sex wouldn't solve anything in the end, and only postpone the answers to these same questions.

Hell, was she awake now?

Her hands glided over Gavin's incredibly taut stomach. She backed up a few inches. "My father had secrets, and I'm asking if you do, too. I need to know if you're part of my father's hidden world, my dream world, or if we're all merely insane."

She paused for a breath. Her hands stopped moving.

He didn't speak, either to explain or condemn, and he didn't touch her back.

She went for broke. "I see you in my dreams. I think I hear you call to me at night. I feel you near me, even when you're not. You've been haunting me since I arrived, when that was ridiculous because I hadn't yet met you."

The man beside her continued to stare, showing no

reaction to what might have been the ravings of a mad-woman.

She rushed on. "That cage had heavy silver-coated bars. You questioned my possession of silver bullets and asked if I knew what they were for. You're thinking that my father may have trapped a wolf in that shed, in that cage, and that it might have been a mythical beast. And because he may have tortured it and the cage is now empty, that animal is not only angry, but could be out there somewhere, loose."

She had one last thing to add, one more long-winded thing to say.

"I might be completely out of line and in need of treatment at the hospital where my dad worked because I'll dare to tell you right now that if that cage held some kind of super wolf of the type you called 'special,' and if you can imagine how it might react to being caged, then you'll understand why I'm beginning to believe that same beast might have killed my father."

She took in a much-needed breath. "And because I might believe that, you must understand why I can't be sure that any of this, including what you and I have done, is more than a fraying filament of my imagination."

Gavin's eyes danced with bright golden flames as he leaned back with his gaze locked to hers. Slowly he began to unbutton his shirt. Pulling the edges open, he let her see all of him from his chest to his belt.

"This is me," he said. "Take a look, Skylar."

His chest was wide. His abs were magnificently mus-cled. Yet he wasn't perfect, and maybe that's why he'd wanted to make love to her in the dark.

Crisscrossing his flesh, stretching from a spot above his heart to his third rib, ran two parallel scars: thick white jagged lines that looked as though they'd been drawn by a child with a marker.

Skylar looked up again to meet his eyes.

"Danger comes with the job, and I've had my share," he said. "This is what I've been warning you about."

The injuries were close to his heart. The scars didn't ruin his perfection, though; they served to bring more attention to the tight golden skin surrounding them.

Dear God, what kind of madness had she let Gavin see?

"Who did this to you?"

"I fought off a wolf," he replied.

No. Her voice sounded faint. "That's why you're going after it."

"That's the reason, yes."

Special wolf. That was his special wolf. Not anything sinister. Just an animal.

"You think it's out there now?" she asked.

"There aren't many wolves around, so there's a good chance it's the one I've been tracking."

He'd been hurt badly, and she'd made him expose that. Skylar wanted to look away, give him space, but didn't. Couldn't. He was so damn beautiful, so masculine and sculpted. This was the body she'd shared herself with last night, and she wanted to do the same now.

She swallowed hard. "Could my father have been killed while chasing that wolf?"

"I didn't know your father or the circumstances surrounding his death. But I do know that once an animal has tasted human flesh and gotten away with it, that animal has to be found and put down."

"Because it will go after someone else?"

"Usually it will."

Skylar let that sink in. Old questions resurfaced, but with a new focus.

"Hypothetically, if a wolf had been kept in the cage in that room and gotten loose, would it be smart enough to want to go after humans? Any humans, and not only the one who caged it there?"

"I don't know. Maybe," he said.

She had answers. Some answers, anyway.

She touched the scars gently, and felt his skin quiver. "Does it hurt?"

"Not anymore," he said, watching her fingers move over him.

Skylar knew he was lying without truly knowing how. With her hand on his bare skin, their bond solidified. By making love and succumbing to their night of passion, they truly had united on an inexplicably deep level.

In her defense, who wouldn't assume that a connection this deep and sudden must be make-believe?

"Somehow," she said, removing her hands, "the scars suit you."

He pulled his shirt closed. "I have to go now. I have to check in."

He had to leave, and she'd have to let him go. Enough truth had been exposed for one day.

Gavin didn't want to talk about being mauled by a wild animal, and she couldn't make him. Nor could she divulge more of her father's secrets, not when she didn't know what those secrets were.

Neither of them was ready to confront the uncanny sense of being fully connected to each other. They were, in essence, still strangers on one level, and yet so much more on another.

And Gavin, just five minutes ago, had made it plain that he wasn't in the market for a serious relationship.

When he turned for the door, she followed him into the yard. The sun was only slightly past its highest point in the sky, so there were plenty of hours to fill before sundown.

He stopped by the gate before swinging it open, looking every bit the handsomely rugged ranger whose presence tugged at her body and her soul.

"Will you take that motel room again tonight, Skylar, if I ask you to?"

"I shouldn't expect you to visit me there?"

"Not tonight."

He sounded regretful about that. So was she.

"A full moon makes animals more restless," he added. "Hopefully I'll find the one I've been searching for."

His sad smile melted Skylar's heart. She wondered what lay behind the expression, if it was a memory of the terrible hurt he must have endured from that animal. Or was it his reaction to the way she'd come unglued in front of him?

"Will you do it, Skylar? Go to town? Stay safe?" He issued the request in that velvety voice she already knew so well, the voice that heated her skin and fevered her insides.

"Yes. I'll go," she lied, hoping he believed her.

Chapter 15

"I've been calling you and am now approaching frantic mode," Trish said when Skylar checked her messages, all ten of them. "If you don't call me back right away, I'm calling the Colorado authorities and booking a flight."

Curled up in the corner of the couch, Skylar punched in her sister's number, hoping her voice would sound normal enough to prevent Trish from making good on either of those threats.

"I'm here, healthy and..." she said when Trish picked up. She had been about to add *sound of mind* to that checklist, when that was pretty far from the truth.

"It's about time," Trish shouted. "Where the heck have you been?"

"The power went out last night. I spent the night at a motel in town and just got back."

"That motel doesn't have a phone?"

"I'm sorry, Trish. I really am. Things happened so fast, I didn't think to call."

"What other things?"

"Everyone here is busy tracking some kind of rogue animal. One of the local rangers came by last night to suggest that with no lights here I might be better off in town."

"Well, glad to hear you exhibited some sense." Trish lowered her voice. "Did you show the ranger the gun you found?"

"As a matter of fact, I did. But they want to capture the animal, not shoot it dead."

"Did they get it?"

"I don't believe they did. I haven't heard about it if they have, anyway."

Silence.

"What kind of animal is it?" Trish eventually asked.

"Some kind of wolf."

"Well, thank God it isn't a bear. Does Colorado have grizzlies?"

"I really don't know," Skylar replied. "In any case, I don't venture far from the yard, except when I have to."

That should just about cover it, Skylar thought. Out-and-out lies had a habit of multiplying.

"Is the power back on?" Trish asked, evidently satisfied with the story for the time being.

"Yep. I'm making tea and about to go through more of Dad's things."

"Find anything interesting yet?"

Hell... Now she was keeping things from her sister, the way their father had kept things from them. This made her uneasy, and it was unfair. Yet she felt the secrecy was necessary if she hoped to keep Trish off her back for a while longer.

"Just the gun I've already mentioned. Dad really didn't have many personal items stockpiled. Mostly clothes, trinkets, a few small trunks, kitchen items, several paintings by local artists and some really strong whiskey."

Trish laughed. "I take it you tried this whiskey."

"I did and couldn't choke it down. Guess I'm not Irish enough for that degree of sensory attack."

"That may turn out to be a good thing, Skye. Sure you don't need help or want company? I've finished with my case and wouldn't mind a break."

"This isn't a task for two, Trish. But I do have a question. Have you ever been here, to this cabin?"

"Nope. I'm pretty sure none of us knew exactly where it was located until Dad's partner at the hospital told us the address. Dad seemed to confide in Dr. James quite a bit. Too bad he didn't do the same with us."

Trish took a drink of something, swallowed and spoke again. "Well, that's water under the bridge, isn't it? I spoke to Dad's partner last night and voiced my concern about you being MIA. She asked if I'd like her to fly out to meet with you and help with Dad's things, and she urged me to say hello to you when you eventually turned up. She'd like to see Dad's cabin and offered to take it off our hands if we sell."

"Great. But really, Trish, this shouldn't take me much longer. I might be home next week, and I'll say hello to Dr. James then. Believe it or not, I'm actually starting to enjoy the scenery and fresh air."

"Truly? How odd for a city slicker," Trish mocked. "By the way, is there anything you'd like me to do here? Take care of your mail? Return some of those gifts before you get back, so you don't have to?"

"Thanks, but no thanks. I'll take care of all that later."

"Skye, you sound…"

"What?"

"Better. You sound better. So okay. I'm just offering to be available."

"And I adore you for that. I really do. Later, then?"

"Later. And please don't scare me again," Trish said before disconnecting.

Setting the phone down, tired of withholding the emotion rolling through her, Skylar headed for the attic, where she'd search those trunks for her father's missing paperwork—paperwork she sincerely hoped wouldn't be there. Especially papers having to do with wolves and keeping living things locked up in cages—sort of like what went on in her father's mental asylum at Fairview, with its comfortably padded cells.

Ah, well, Skylar thought, climbing the narrow stairs to the attic. *This is real. No dream. So what were you doing here, Dad?*

Gavin drove faster than he should have, unwilling to slow down, pressed by the speed of his thoughts. Skylar was behaving strangely. She said she'd heard him call to her at night. What did she mean by that?

If she heard sounds made by the demon in the hills, it meant that the beast had been close to this area for some time, and that he'd been right in guessing it was close.

This whole scene was getting stranger by the minute. Skylar's talk of dreams made no sense, and staying with her hadn't been an option. After seeing that awful room at Tom's and being surrounded by silver this close to the full moon, his nerves were jumpy. Now, he added worry to the mix—worry that Skylar might put her life at risk by going after the wolf she thought her father might have been chasing. Worry that she might find Gavin Harris instead, in his other, less appealing incarnation.

He didn't see how he could go on with his search when he also had to carefully watch Skylar and keep her safe. Skylar Donovan was causing him to rearrange his agenda. She alone had seen his scars, his battle wounds, evidence of his tryst with death. And yet she hadn't found them ugly. Her touch had been unexpectedly tender.

There should have been no scars at all. If the white lines on his chest hadn't disappeared after two years, they likely never would.

He had been branded with the mark of the werewolf. And he still felt the heat of Skylar's touch. Her warmth helped to lessen the old aches. If he closed his eyes, he could almost feel her with him now.

Emotions swirled inside him, casting for a place to land when he remembered how badly Skylar had needed him the previous night without being coy or afraid to show it. With her help, he had prevailed over his fear of the wolf inside him. In loving her, he had successfully compartmentalized his wolfishness.

He had loved Skylar Donovan to within an inch of her life. After their athletic give-and-take, was it any wonder he craved her now, or what he might give for a rematch?

He glanced up at the sky. Only hours remained before sundown, and his hunger for Skylar left him torn. If he lost this opportunity to find the big bad wolf and return the favor of a fight, everyone in these mountains would be in danger for another month or more. Only when a full moon rode the sky could he find the added strength he gained by merging with his wolf. By uniting with his wolf, he'd be able to continue tracking the beast.

And if he lost Skylar in the meantime...

If she were to be harmed...

The human half of him would wither and die.

He stopped the car so abruptly the brakes squealed. Above the sound, the pounding of his heart was audible.

Gavin weighed his options as if he actually had some. Skylar was important to him, but ridding the world of a fanged demon with the ability to create more like it had to take precedence.

Whichever way he looked at this, the woman he had first seen half-naked on her porch was going to be a pain in his backside and get in the way, either intruding physically or in his thoughts.

His hands were, at that very moment, itching to turn the wheel and head back to her. The impulse was nearly as strong as his imminent transformation.

The only way he could see to break the spell he was under would be to present himself to Skylar after dark, coated in fur, and send her running home to Florida. And if he did so, how many people would come after him then, knowing who and what he had become?

Having found the room behind Tom's house, the sheriffs would be on the lookout for anything off base and out of the ordinary.

He was stuck.

Glancing in the rearview mirror, he thought he could almost see that furred-up hell demon's bloody mouth smiling.

There were four trunks in the attic. Since she had already been through the first one, which had produced the gun, Skylar moved on to trunk number two, pressed tight against the back wall.

Standing up in this cramped space wasn't doable, so she crouched on her knees. Light came in through one small window near the eaves, and there was a bulb on a wire overhead.

This trunk by the wall, like all the other trunks, was locked. But the locks weren't going to stop her. She'd opened the first one by applying leverage with a metal garden stake.

"Lock-picking is now officially added to the résumé," she muttered as she stuck the metal stake between the two posts of the small padlock and twisted with all her might.

This one didn't break. Undeterred, she backtracked downstairs, determined to see this task through as quickly as possible. She picked up the gun, already familiar with its dark, cold weight.

In the attic, she carefully aimed at the lock and squeezed the trigger, unconcerned about the potential damage to the trunk.

The blast echoed loudly in the small space, kicking her back a step. The lock was shattered by a specialized silver bullet that might have cost a hefty sum and was a big reminder of the need to see what other kind of secrets this trunk held.

It took both of her hands to open the lid. The trunk was filled to the brim with papers and the kind of notebooks her father often scribbled in.

"Bingo."

Psychiatrists were predisposed to write down everything, in detail, and she'd been counting on this, though she found touching the notebooks difficult. She worried as much about what the notebooks might hold as what they might not.

"Please," she said aloud over the ringing in both ears. "Don't let any of this prove his guilt."

Minutes passed before she gathered enough courage to begin. Reaching for the notebook on top, she opened it to the first page.

Chapter 16

Gavin found cell phone service on the high point in the road, and pulled over. He cut the engine, thinking it safer to keep his research on Skylar's father to himself for the moment, rather than using the computers at any of the ranger substations strung across the area.

He planned to find out everything he could on Dr. Donovan, and why the man's daughter had confirmed Gavin's fears that her late father's activities could have had something to do with werewolves.

Unfortunately, there were a lot of Donovans with the word *doctor* in front of their names when he searched, and he didn't know Skylar's dad's first name. He focused on their home state and hospital facilities housing mental wards.

There were too damn many of those, too. He'd have to narrow the search field.

He typed *Skylar Donovan* and *Florida* into the browser, sure her name wasn't a common one, and sat back to study the screen when the information came up. He'd never asked Skylar anything about herself, other than her relationship to her father and that blasted cabin, and he regretted that now.

But—

"Holy hell," he whispered as he began to read what filled the screen.

What struck Skylar about the first few notebooks was the rather disturbing fact that her father had chronicled the lives of several people in the area, here in Colorado, as if they'd been his patients.

The details her father had put on paper dug deep into other peoples' lives. It was possible he acted as doctor here, too, and helped the locals with their problems. Maybe that was a good thing and the data he collected helped him to recall the sessions.

She didn't recognize any of the names. The symptoms seemed to cover a wide range. Where were these people? Who were they? She'd seen only a few cabins and homes scattered here and there along the route to town, and Gavin told her most of those people had been gone for a while. She skimmed pages as well for the word *wolf* without finding it. She read faster and faster, her stomach feeling queasy, as if some part of her knew what had to be here and what was coming.

Dad...she wanted to shout.

Could a man who liked to plant flowers possess the ability to chain any living thing to the walls in a secret room? Could the same man who kissed his kids goodnight have hidden a dark, sadistic streak?

Final question, Skylar promised herself.

If she was the most like her father out of all of his daughters and was currently in school studying to be a psychiatrist, like him, wasn't she the perfect candidate to understand her father's potential dark side that might have included a belief in werewolves?

She reached for another notebook, opened it and stared at a line scribbled in red ink:

They don't lose their minds. Not completely.

Skylar rocked back on her knees, a strange sense of premonition streaking through her. She forced herself to read on.

I don't know if there might be more than one of them. But the world cannot be trusted to know of their existence. No one else should be deceived, as I was, when the outcome of that deception remains unclear.
    She is my responsibility.
    I do what I can, but she is angry, and I'm tired.
    The goal is safety…at all costs.

Skylar turned the page, found only one other paragraph.

Imprinting remains and the connections seem to change the body at a cellular level. It's as if one soul readjusts its perceptions to include another as part of itself, and each soul leaves a mark on the other. Is this to last forever?

Frantically, Skylar flipped to another page. Was her father writing about the clutches of madness?

Possibly criminals and people already on a downward slide could take advantage of the added strength and inflict real harm on others. Those are the ones the world has to watch for.

There was nothing else. No explanation for those cryptic statements. Skylar tore through several more notebooks and the contents of an unlocked trunk with no luck. There was nothing like the first few paragraphs, which read like a personal confession but didn't actually clarify anything.

More of them?

The world can't know of their existence?

Imprinting?

What the hell did any of that mean, and how had her father been deceived?

Was he writing about an obsession with a patient, or his obsession with…a wolf?

It was too much. And too little. Skylar put her head in her hands and stared at the floor, knowing that her knees wouldn't support her for much longer and that she needed rest almost as much as she needed answers.

Judging by the light from outside filtering into the attic, she could tell that not too many hours had gone by. Returning downstairs meant imagining Gavin with his shirt open, his bareness vivid enough in her memory to be permanently etched there.

She went down the ladder, feeling confused, trying to gather her strength. She looked at the front door, wondering if people could imprint, and bond forever.

Gavin Harris wanted her and wished to keep her safe, but they'd glossed over the dream issue and how he'd managed to step out of those dreams in order to knock at her door.

Chance? Fate? Did precognition actually work

through dreams and random passages in notebooks? She'd been afraid to push for an explanation from Gavin, and her father, who would have known about dreams, was no longer able to help.

Placing the gun back on the table, Skylar went to the window to take in the view, picturing Gavin out there after dark, chasing a wolf bent on attacking humans. If she whispered his name, would Gavin hear her and realize that she needed to find out about the wolf as much as he did? Maybe more?

Would that wolf's body show evidence of having been trapped in a cage? Tortured? Were the articles in that building used for some other purpose?

Had her father been guarding something?

She leaned heavily against the wall, thinking.

She could go to the motel, as Gavin suggested, and get far enough from the cabin to allow herself some peace of mind without thoughts of moons or cages. Gavin would know where to find her. Possibly he would come to her later and they...

They could...

"Obsessed," she said aloud to put an end to the thought of what they'd do together. "Obsessed by a dream and a ranger."

In reality, Gavin was doing his job. The forensic people working on that room behind Tom's house would exonerate her father. Surely other people collected silver bullets for a reason that had nothing to do with killing.

Skylar moved back to the table and picked up her phone. She skimmed through her contacts for her father's partner. Dr. Jenna James. She moved a finger toward the button to place the call but didn't touch it. What would she say to her dad's long-time acquaintance, the person he'd worked beside on a daily basis and spent more time with than he spent with his family?

What kind of message would her call for help send to another psychiatrist?

Pressing the phone to her cheek, Skylar could see through the window that the yard seemed completely normal. Flowers still bloomed in raised beds. Walkways were lined with mulch. Her father had taken the time to garden and keep up this cabin.

Actually, she thought now, *maybe I do need help.* Self-diagnosis wasn't an art form. She'd make that call to Dr. James, just not quite yet.

In the meantime, she'd keep the tarnish from her father's legacy by putting the word *werewolf* to rest. She'd hope for Gavin to find the wolf he sought and take care of it tonight, once and for all. She would call for a ride and go back to town in search of the sheriff's office, to see what else they might have found at Tom's place.

She took a deep breath.

Hoisting the phone, and after glancing again at the gun her father had more than likely kept around just for protection and nothing weirder than that, Skylar placed the dreaded call to Florida—to Fairview Hospital, her dad's former place of business—praying that Dr. Jenna James *wouldn't* pick up on her personal line.

"You booked him?" Gavin asked at the station.

"We've brought Tom in for an interview," Jim Delaney, the sheriff on duty, replied with bureaucratic discretion.

"Can I speak with him, Jim?"

"Professionally, or on a personal matter?"

"Personal."

"He's in room two."

"Is he a suspect for placing any of that stuff in the building behind his house?"

"It is his house, Harris."

Gavin held up both hands. "We've all known him for years."

"Yep. He's a fixture around here. So we'll let him go after one more round."

"Okay," Gavin said, relieved. "I just need a couple minutes."

"Be my guest. Professional courtesy, right?"

"I appreciate the leeway here, Jim."

Gavin found room two and nodded to the officer sitting in a chair outside the door. "Permission granted," he said. The officer nodded.

Tom sat behind a table, looking tired. Gavin sat opposite him. "Hey, Tom. Anything I can get you?"

"A free pass out of here would be nice," Tom replied.

"I'm sure you'll be out of here soon. They need to cross all the t's before opening the door."

Tom sat back, his face a mass of weary lines. "What kind of a person would create a place like that?"

"I'm not here to ask you about it. You're probably tired of addressing that issue, so you can relax. I'd like to talk about something else."

"Such as?"

"Skylar Donovan."

Tom's face sobered further.

"You told me you hadn't met her yet when we spoke this morning. Isn't that right? But you didn't introduce yourself when you met her."

"I was quite busy, as were you," Tom said. "Besides, who else could she have been? They have the same eyes, and the same kind of bearing. I recognized her right away."

Gavin nodded. "She looks like her father?"

"Only somewhat similar."

"If you hadn't met Skylar before, who else in the family have you met? I'm asking because I read some things online a few minutes ago that sparked my interest in the family, beyond what might or might not have happened here."

"I don't rightly know any of them," Tom said. "But I did see a woman with the Doc once, though only from a distance."

"Not Skylar?"

Tom shook his head. "Tall. Reddish hair that was long and wavy. A real looker."

"Where did you see them?"

"On the Doc's driveway when I drove past."

"Then it could have been anyone, I suppose. Maybe even someone stopping by or asking directions."

"None of my business," Tom said. "Nice hair, though. I remember thinking that."

"Do you recall when this was?"

"Had to be over a year ago. I drove that road weekly to Sam Martin's place back then, before Sam passed on."

Gavin stood up. "Well, thanks. Rumor has it you'll be out of here shortly. I'll stop by your place tomorrow to make sure you got home okay."

"I'll put the coffee on," Tom said.

Gavin felt a slight sense of accomplishment as he headed back to his Jeep. Of course, that woman Tom had seen with Skylar's father could have been anyone, but it could just as easily have been a doctor from Donovan's hospital in Miami. Fairview Hospital. According to their online photos, a certain Dr. Jenna James had long auburn hair.

From that photo, Jenna James seemed to be young, and quite stunning. Not at all what he would have expected from a colleague of Donovan's. The woman had a long list of medical initials trailing after her name. But from what he'd found in his search, most of the doctors at Fairview kept out of the limelight and the news, often taking a backseat to Skylar's father, whose full name was Dr. David Donovan. Although Jenna James was a full partner in the directorship of Fairview, her bio was curiously low-key.

He didn't want to think about what the internet had to say about Skylar's personal history. Not yet. He needed time to digest some of what he'd found. For now it was enough to know that, according to some archived newspaper articles, Skylar, just six years old at the time, had lost her mother. She'd inherited a fortune from some other relative at the same time and, along with her sisters, invested a good chunk of that inheritance in the hospital her father had helped build.

And here was the real kicker: Skylar's mother had been a patient at Fairview.

Skylar couldn't have known her mother very well. What did kids remember from when they were six, anyway? Also, he'd found nothing about Greta Donovan's death.

Gavin's list of interesting information about Skylar and her father was growing, but it had to wait. The approach of darkness rustled across his skin like a stiff breeze. His hands kept fisting on their own, fingers curling, forearms cramping. His spine cracked when he turned his head.

It was almost time to find the monster, face it and take that beast down. That was as necessary as returning to Skylar as soon as possible to kiss her, speak with her, take her to bed.

Dreams, she'd said. Dreams and watchers and werewolves.

After today's shock, and after being recently unengaged and orphaned, Skylar would need company and reassurances that things were all right. He planned to give her that. He knew how being alone felt because he hadn't seen his parents since his close call with death in these hills.

He glanced again at the darkening sky. Maybe there was time for him to see Skylar, touch her, hold her one more time.

Just in case.

In case he wouldn't be returning from his meeting with the giant furred-up devil. In case he never got to kiss Skylar Donovan's sweet, succulent lips again.

His Jeep was parked down the street. Having only one hour at most before sundown was cutting things too short. Still, the depth of his need directed his next step.

"I have to see you, Skylar," he said, jogging to his car.

Chapter 17

Thanking her lucky stars to have reached Jenna's personal voice mail instead of Jenna herself, the message Skylar left was short.

"Skylar here, Dr. James. Trisha said you wanted to see my dad's cabin, and that's fine with me. I'll be in Colorado for a few more days and would like to speak with you, just to connect with someone normal. I have a couple quick questions to ask you. You now have my number. And thanks, both for the condolences and for taking care of the things you did for Dad."

She disconnected and lowered the phone.

Speak with someone normal? Did she really say that to a psychiatrist? One bad thing about the current world of non-face-to-face communication was that messages like the one she'd just left couldn't be taken back.

She paced from window to window and across the wooden boards of the porch. Antsy didn't even begin to describe her current state. She searched the sky for a hint of how much time was left until the sun set, unable to shake the idea that if she were to close her eyes, she'd feel insanity's fiery breath on the back of her neck.

The quiet gave way to a sound that paused her pacing. There was a car on the road. Not just any car.

She ran. For him. There wasn't any way to put on the brakes. Gavin was coming back to her, and she wanted him with every fiber of her being.

He stopped the vehicle when he saw her, and stepped out. She stopped three yards away from where he stood, with her pulse thundering.

"What happened?" he asked soberly.

"You came back," she said.

He closed the door and walked toward her, his body sending out an aura of need similar to hers. Bless him, he hadn't returned for any other reason than his desire to see her. She read that in his face.

She was in his arms before he slowed down. She was breathing in audible rasps as she brought her face close to his.

He spoke first.

"I'm not sure what this is." His whisper was hoarse as his lips skated over hers. "I can't seem to stay away, and I don't even care."

He lifted her up with unsteady hands, and Skylar clung to him by wrapping her legs around his waist and her arms around his neck. When his mouth covered hers, heat flashed through her like lashes of flame.

She kissed him back, returned his sensual attack with one of her own, and he groaned with an earthy satisfaction that sounded like relief.

Skylar wasn't sure how they made it to the cabin. She was tuned to him, ready for him, willing to take him on and take him in. If she had her way, the ground would do just fine for what they were about to do and, as always with this guy, the sooner, the better.

Her ranger had other ideas. Holding her tightly in his arms, he put a boot to the half-open door and walked through. That was as far as they got. She was on the floor, on her back, with Gavin's long length covering her and his mouth never leaving hers.

He kissed her greedily, deeply, each move of his mouth a ravenous feasting. Skylar tore at his belt and pants. He kicked off his shoes and helped her remove his clothes, then hers, in the dim, waning light. This time, he allowed her full access to his lean sculpted body, scars and all, because he was as ready as she was for this union.

An inch of space was too much distance between them. Their bare bodies slammed together as if they were two parts of a whole needing to be reunited.

They seemed to be enacting a kind of sensuous war, their actions falling somewhere between an all-out sexfest and hungrily making love. There was no clear-cut delineation of the unevenness of the relationship. Even the edges of the room blurred as Gavin pressed her arms above her head and settled himself between her naked, pulsing thighs.

Then he was inside her with a slick, heated slide that drove a pleasurable groan from her throat. Buried deep inside her, he paused, shuddered and closed his blue eyes.

But he didn't hesitate for long. Before her next breath, he rallied with a quick withdrawal followed by a second perfect thrust of his hips. Straight and true, that plunge touched her innermost need, tickled her core and spawned shuddering intense physical longings for him that Skylar could barely contain.

If she'd thought they had done it all in that motel room

the night before, she'd been wrong. This level of rugged intimacy was new, different and meaningful. This was something else altogether.

Gavin held her in that place where white-hot sensations and riotous emotions met in a kaleidoscope of light and feeling. A place where there wasn't enough air in the world to breathe in and there would never be enough time to keep this up.

Another thrust of his hips and a second hesitation forced from Skylar an outward cry of startled emotion.

Then he moved just once more.

And that was all she needed.

Feelings burst open, ran riot, exploded inside her. She came with a dizzying, room-spinning climax that went on and on until Skylar clawed at her lover with her hands and nipped at him with fierce teeth. But he didn't register any of the damage she inflicted. Her little attacks didn't seem to bother Gavin Harris at all. He was there with her and at the same time curiously absent, Skylar realized when the world eventually stopped revolving.

He shook, holding off his own satisfaction, and the effort took all of his concentration. One giant quake rolled through him after another. Withholding this last bit of himself seemed important to him, as if it were a task to be mastered.

All the while, his vibrant blue eyes stared into hers.

"No," she protested, breathless, hardly able to speak at all and seeing in his expression a hint that he might leave her now. "Don't go. You don't have to. Not tonight."

His sad smile reminded her that she'd only heard him laugh one time, and she longed to hear that laughter now. His muscles were tense, his voice strained. "You have no idea how much I want to stay."

"You're with me right now."

His sadness was devastatingly potent. "I have to go. I'm late already and feel the night closing in."

"But you'll come back," she said hopefully.

The fact that he didn't reply left her anxious.

"You don't have to go," Skylar insisted.

"I do. Please understand that I have to."

"Why? Wolves only come out at night? Is that what you mean? If you have to find one, this is the time?"

"Yes. That's what I mean. The one I seek will be out there."

"To hell with that," Skylar argued. "Being together like this is important to me. You'll never know how much. Tell me I'm not the only one who believes there's something to this. To us."

"You're not the only one. Hell, Skylar. But I've told you. I've warned you about me, and that I also have needs that lie beyond this moment."

"You've told me no such thing, other than to mention revenge against an animal that hurt you and might also have hurt my father."

He touched her forehead with a warm finger and tucked a strand of hair behind her ear—gentle actions, tender moments before a dreaded separation that made the idea of that separation a whole lot worse.

"Then I'm coming with you," she said.

"I can't allow that."

"If there's a wolf or a pack out there, surely other rangers can help us find it," she pressed.

"Us? No. You need to go into town where it's safe."

She stared back at him. "You truly believe that same nasty wolf is still here, and near the cabin, don't you?

That's the big danger you perceive for others and for me. Not some madman, but a damn wolf."

"A man-hater," he corrected, whispering in a way that made Skylar's scalp prickle. "And as dangerous as they come."

He slid off her and braced himself on his elbows without looking away or losing eye contact.

"You're either brave or stupid to go out there if something you consider to be that lethal is on the loose." She spoke her mind without using a filter. "Especially tonight, under a full moon, when everyone is restless."

Skylar felt him stir, and regretted the turn in the conversation. There had hardly been a time when the idea of the wolf hadn't been in the room with her in this cabin, either openly or in hiding.

"Then you'd stop me from taking my best shot at finding it?" Gavin asked.

"I…"

Could she say what she was thinking? Skylar wondered. Or were secrets to remain secrets?

"I don't want anything to happen to you."

His eyes softened, adding fine creases underneath. Seeing that softness tugged at her heart.

"The best way to help me is for you to remain safe, so that I don't have to worry about you. Can you do that, Skylar? Will you get to safety?"

"I said I would."

"You didn't mean it."

She wondered how he knew that.

"So," he began, using her words to further his argument, "does arguing about this make you brave, or stupid?"

She answered that question honestly and the best way she could. "It makes me determined."

"No," he corrected. "I'm determined and have some of the skills to back that up. You are a liability, like..."

He didn't say the rest of what he was thinking, so she did.

"Like my father was, or might have been, being a city man and out of his element here?"

He sighed heavily. "Yes, if he actually was chasing wolves in these mountains."

"How do we find out what my father did or didn't do? What he knew, or believed?"

"We know that he must not have thought what he was doing that last evening was dangerous, otherwise his gun would have been found in his hand, not here in this cabin."

Skylar found the flaw in that reasoning, though it didn't help much.

If her father was delusional and if werewolves had been his target and his reason for being in Colorado, he wouldn't have believed he needed those silver bullets the day he died because ten days ago the moon hadn't been full. No full moon meant no werewolves, supposedly... if Hollywood got that right.

The horrible, nonsensical element to all this over-thinking suddenly left her feeling sick. She'd come full circle back to werewolves.

"My father fell, and there doesn't have to be anything sinister about that tragedy other than how things ended up," she said, testing out her voice and trying to believe that theory.

"Did you think there was something sinister going on?" Gavin asked.

After glancing at the window, she said helplessly, "Yes. But that's my problem."

Yet, she thought, if there was no magic key in the word *werewolf*, why had Gavin brought it up behind Tom's shed? Was he just trying to gauge her mental state?

Wait just a damn minute.

Was there something in the way he was looking at her? Shit. If he wanted to know about her mental state, did that mean he knew something about her mother?

Could he possibly know anything about that?

If he did, would Gavin be wondering if the whole family might be off its rocker? Like the jokes, did he believe that psychiatrists took up the profession because of their own numerous issues?

Damn it, hadn't she, for the past few days, wondered that same thing about her father and herself?

What else did he know?

Had he found out that she studied about psychiatry in a school near Miami? That she'd taken time off to get married, and more time to come here to finish her father's ties to Colorado?

"Skylar?"

She heard her name, and a sound beyond it from somewhere outside. Familiar heat began to battle the onset of chills. Her body convulsed, automatically responding to the provocative quality in Gavin's tone.

Something inside her shifted uncomfortably, in need of more heat.

"Skylar," Gavin repeated with concern.

Through a flutter of her eyelashes, Skylar saw again in fine detail the man so close to her. The wide shoulders above a broad muscular chest. The thick torso, narrow waist and hips. The dark hair, worn long and those brilliant light blue eyes. Every detail about Gavin Harris mirrored what she'd imagined her dream lover would be.

Yet Gavin was only a ranger. A man, not a werewolf.

There were no such things as werewolves.

Holding up a hand, she crawled out from beneath her lover, embarrassed, and no longer trusting her own conclusions because the merging of her dreams and reality continued to mess things up.

There were no werewolves; therefore, either someone had pushed her father over that cliff, or no one had, and his fall was an accident, as officially stated. She would have to accept that and also accept that she'd gone to bed with a stranger because of a dream.

On her knees beside Gavin, she asked with a stern authority, "Do you know about my mother?"

It pained him to answer. She saw that. He didn't really know the nuances of what she was asking, or why, but his answer was important to her.

"Do you know about my family's trouble?" she pressed, looking anywhere but in Gavin's luminous eyes.

"About your mother's commitment, yes," he replied. "I know about that."

Quickly chilling again, Skylar got to her feet and reached for her clothes before turning for the door.

Gavin was beside her. "Skylar, what the hell just happened?"

"I'm going to town like you wanted, if I can use your car."

She wouldn't look at him now, couldn't allow herself to see either the hurt she might be causing or the relief that might show on that face. This man might like to bed her, but he'd gone too far by investigating her family's personal history behind her back.

Gavin Harris, the very definition of eye candy and so unbelievably talented in the sack, might believe that mental illness was not only contagious, but that her father had actually tortured some poor animal in that shed behind Tom Jeevers's house.

And if he believed that, he wasn't worth a damn.

While she...with dreams of moonlight and mountains and the erotic allure of Otherness...

Well...

It came as no surprise that she was a goddamn fool.

When she glanced back at the man holding on to her arm, he looked as perplexed as she felt.

"It's okay." She spoke as she dressed. "It's getting dark. Go. Do your thing. You'll know where to find me."

He let her go because he had no right to keep her back. Besides, what more was there to say when he knew about her mother?

Skylar got to the Jeep quickly and climbed in. When she looked up again, Gavin was nowhere in sight. The gorgeous bastard hadn't even blown her a kiss.

By the time she reached for the keys in the ignition, darkness cloaked the yard. Stars were already starting to appear since there were no clouds.

Her energy was gone, and her queasiness had returned. Swallowing was difficult, her breathing forced. She couldn't stand the idea of getting through another night with her disturbed thoughts, not after veering so far off track. The truth was that she didn't belong here and was sorry she had volunteered to come.

She started the engine, threw the gear shift into Reverse and stepped on the gas. Beyond the dirt driveway, she gunned the car around a sharp bend in the road.

There it was. *That damn moon.* Shining as if it had every right to be the darkly mysterious thing some people presumed it to be. Light streamed across the tree tops, silvery and almost magical, though it only served to highlight a new emptiness inside her.

She felt like closing her eyes to regroup. She could have used a few deep breaths and more alcohol. *Something. Anything.*

She just couldn't go on.

Pulling the Jeep to the side of the road, she cut the engine and sat back. Listening to the quiet beyond the open window, she inhaled air as if she were oxygen starved.

Then she began to pound on the steering wheel with both hands, continuing the tantrum until her hands were sore and throbbing. Giving in to the emotional turmoil eating away at her insides, she slumped forward with her head in her hands.

Chapter 18

It wasn't okay. Nothing was all right, and that was putting things mildly. Whatever Skylar might do next was out of Gavin's hands, yet he hoped her word meant something.

Close one.

Too close.

He now fought to hold on to the human in him. With Skylar tripping his emotional switches, he felt the moon's presence through the roof. That moon called to him right now. *It's time*, the silver seducer whispered. *Don't fight.*

He stood in the front room of the cabin, ignoring that invitation and listening to the sound of the car taking Skylar from him in the nick of time. His blood thickened in his veins. Though moonlight couldn't reach him here, his wolf pounded at him from the inside, seconds away from a major meltdown and about to be released one notch at a time.

Volts of supernatural electricity charged through him, causing a claw to spring from the tip of the middle finger of his right hand. It was, he thought, appropriate, and a stiff universal gesture to the whole ordeal. More claws

followed until all ten fingernails had been replaced, and
his hands could now be considered lethal.

Nowhere to hide.

Angry at the way he'd let Skylar go, he swiped the
razor-sharp claws across the legs of his pants, cutting
through the cloth and into the meat of his right thigh.
Pain was necessary to his thought process. The scent
of the blood trickling from his wound helped to replace
Skylar's seductive perfume.

It's time.

Apprehension twitched his shoulder blades. His
mouth felt dry. The wolf's perceptions came flooding
in on an adrenaline-laced tide to prepare him for action.

He wanted to call Skylar back. Hold her. Comfort her.
Any fool could see that's what she needed. But the moon
could no longer be ignored. His body was about to meld
man and predator, blurring the lines of both, and there
was nothing he could do about it.

He stepped onto the porch with a last look behind.
Vaulting over the steps, he leaped to the ground, doubling over as the wolf clawed its way up his windpipe
and his flesh began to split.

Pain.

An all-too familiar agony.

Christ, he hated this part.

Five seconds passed, then eight, until more muscles got with the program, stretching, rounding as they
molded into larger shapes. His legs quickly joined in,
filling up the extra space in his pants while neck vertebrae separated with a sound like bombs going off.

His ribs cracked apart as they expanded, making his
heartbeat soar in an effort to keep up. The scars on his
chest burned, each one brutally painful, barely tolera-

ble. He covered them with both hands to press back the
sting, trying hard not to drop to one knee.

But he withstood this. He had to. It was always the
same checklist, in the same order: hands, arms, shoulders, hips, legs, back and torso. His face came last, its
delicate bones unhinging before shifting its angles to
rearrange into an alternate pattern without so many rec-
ognizably human features.

As a final insult, a light dusting of hair the consis-
tency of fine fur sprang from his skin. Not thick hair,
or enough of it to cover him completely, yet enough to
leave him slightly shaggier and a little bit like some kind
of throwback to a darker age.

He growled and coughed. Straightening at last, Gavin
gave a loud feral roar. With one more glance to the driveway and the road beyond it, he took off toward the hillside where one creature preferred to rule as if it were the
king of beasts and could do whatever the hell it pleased.

And that, he confirmed with a deep, guttural growl,
just wasn't acceptable.

Skylar told herself that she was stronger than this
and shouldn't condone her jumbled mental state for one
second longer.

She wasn't really invested in any kind of relationship with Gavin Harris after just two strange days. On
the contrary, he'd warned her not to expect a relationship with him at all. A guy couldn't be expected to be
more honest than that, except when it wasn't the truth.

Gavin had lied about this, of course. Every look,
move, kiss told her he wanted more.

The motel in town seemed like a terrible place to
hide out until morning. At the cabin there were several

more things to go through, though the thought of doing so didn't seem as exciting as before.

As for Gavin researching her family...truly, she hadn't seen that coming. The fact that she knew nothing about Gavin seemed much too one-sided now and was a problem she'd have to solve. At least this time, during her hasty exit, she'd remembered to scoop up her cell phone. Finding service was another matter, though, and possibly meant driving until she found reception or heading for the hilltop above the main road where service wasn't blocked by the mountain.

Who would she call?

Trisha would come here to help get the cabin packed up if she asked. Her big sister's presence would also keep Skylar grounded and keep her addiction to Gavin under control, if that's what needed to be done.

An addiction. Yes, that's what this is like.

Every cell in her body urged her to go back to the cabin and follow him or try to pick up his trail.

Some part of her brain refused to be turned away from thoughts about those damn wolves and how her father had ended up.

But Trish was in Miami and hours away when help was needed now and, really, was already overdue.

Though the light on the phone beamed when she tugged it from her pocket, it was a false bit of hope. There were no service bars.

"Damn it."

Skylar reached for the keys dangling from the ignition—Gavin's keys—wondering what kind of man chased away a woman he was so obviously interested in by providing her with the means for escape. No branch of law enforcement she knew of allowed civilians to borrow their vehicles, yet she'd been behind this wheel twice. She understood about his work, and that he had an agenda, but...

She turned her head sharply, senses snapping to alert.

A glance in the rearview mirror showed no cars coming, yet she was sure something passed behind the Jeep in a blur of black-on-black.

Gavin felt exceptionally fleet, though his muscle mass rippled beneath the density of its new heft. This dangerous physical reprogramming left him feeling much the same inside, with different shadings of Gavin Harris on the outside, and a whole new love-hate relationship with his body.

Growls bubbled up from deep inside him with each stride. Though he couldn't speak without human vocal chords, the fierceness of the rumbling sounds he made got his point across just fine. He was angrier than ever and resolute in his determination to see this task through.

Where are you, beast?

Can you hear me?

The moon over his head followed him through the trees with the rapt intensity of a searchlight. If he stopped too long in a place hidden from that icy silver light, he'd shift again in reverse, so he was careful to keep to the open portion of path.

Skylar...

My lover...

He swore. It was best not to think of her. He couldn't be sure about completing this dangerous objective if he kept her in the forefront of his mind.

But some weird fluke of nature allowed him to think he could hear her thoughts, and if she were to call to him again, the way she had the night before, he feared what he might do.

You really shouldn't have left me, she'd said, and he had returned to her, to that motel, as though compelled to do so.

He felt the fear she refused to show. Her disjointed thoughts were increasingly difficult to separate from his. He couldn't get her scent out of his lungs, her taste out of his mouth. One small distraction, like picturing her naked, and he might miss something crucial out here, ending things too quickly in the monster's favor.

He was smart enough to realize that his life had taken a turn for the better the minute he'd laid eyes on Skylar Donovan. After cursing himself and his situation for two long years, barely hanging on to see this task through, all it took for his heart to lighten was seeing her on that porch.

Suddenly a reason to continue living beyond his search for the monster presented itself. There was a reason to live, to protect and to love while he could, in any way he could.

Meeting Skylar had done that.

His senses snapped back to the path. The night smelled like danger and carried an unsettling vibe. Things were too quiet.

Skirting a mound of moss-covered granite, Gavin stopped, curtailing a growl. The monster he sought was here, all right, somewhere close by.

He roared his approval and stood his ground, waiting for the inevitable, daring the creature to find him. But it didn't appear. Its scent grew stronger but then quickly began to fade. Though that abomination's presence clung to Gavin's skin like a second coat of fur, it obviously had other ideas about where to focus its attention.

Gavin jerked his head to the path behind him, fear welling up.

No. Not that.

Not her.

Don't you dare go after Skylar!

He ran, following the scent of wet fur, his heart exploding in his chest, but he didn't get far before his senses screamed for him to stop.

He was hit from behind, hard, and flew sideways. His left shoulder smashed painfully into a tree, but he rebounded quickly and spun around. Ramming was this sucker's MO…

He saw nothing. Not even a leaf moved.

Damn you, beast.

He ventured a step, stood still and upright, and was hurled forward by an unseen force so strong, moving so fast, he didn't even see a hint of it coming.

But he knew what this was. He'd been in this same situation before.

His nerves fired up. His chest hurt like hell from the pounding inside it. His head swam with fear and remembered glimpses of a semi-invisible opponent. He didn't like this game. Didn't appreciate anything about it, or how much stronger the beast was. But he'd be damned if that beast would be allowed to go anywhere near Skylar.

Gavin lunged forward, saw a shadow streak through the brush and gathered himself. As the shadow passed to his left, he leaped again, catching the moving bit of darkness squarely, and hearing its eerie, echoing howl of anger.

The monster turned, lashed out with a lethally clawed,

five-fingered paw. Gavin ducked, but felt the claws part his hair above his right ear. Whirling around, he struck at the beast with both hands, his own anger giving him the strength necessary to tag a moving target.

The beast rallied, swiveled and roared. Using its swinging arm as a bat, it connected with Gavin's stomach, momentarily doubling him over.

But not for long.

Gavin was up on his feet, angry, ready for the next round. Yet all was again silent around him, and there was no monster. It was as if he'd made the whole thing up.

Chapter 19

"Miss Donovan?"

The voice wasn't familiar and, therefore, didn't register as Skylar slammed herself back against the seat wondering what the shadow was.

"It's Tom. Tom Jeevers," the man approaching the window said. "Are you all right? You've been sitting here long enough for me to reach you from the fire access road."

Skylar turned her head, attempting to regulate her breathing. It was only a man, not a people-hating, flesh-eating wolf in the rearview mirror. "Tom?"

"Is there something wrong with the Jeep?" he asked, looking past her. "Where's Harris?"

Feeling silly for imagining she'd seen something, Skylar rallied. "He's in the hills, searching for a wolf."

Tom nodded his gray-haired head. "Sent you to town, did he?"

"Yes."

"And you're heading that way now?"

"I stopped to listen to the night."

"It's a fine time for that," Tom agreed. "Best time to get a walk in, too. With no cars on the road to bother me,

I can think, take my sweet time and breathe. After today, I needed a breather. I don't suppose that you, being from a busy place like Miami, would understand that?"

"I do understand. The quiet takes some getting used to, though," Skylar admitted. "I tend to want to fill it with something, like most city people do."

Tom placed both hands on the door. "Well, I won't keep you."

"Tom?"

He waited.

"Did they find anything today?"

She didn't have to explain what she meant. He said, "Not yet. Not that I know of. I'm just glad they didn't keep me in town. I'm not one for being cooped up after all these years out here."

"I'm sorry." She said this sincerely. "I'm sorry my father had anything to do with that shed."

He nodded and started to turn. Skylar held him up again. "Gavin thinks the wolf out here is dangerous. You will be careful?"

"Oh, don't worry about that. No self-respecting alpha would bother with an old bag of bones like me, I'll bet. I hope Harris catches it, if he's so inclined, though I like to see animals run free, doing what they're meant to do."

"This one hurt him," Skylar said. "I think his search is personal."

"Really? I hadn't heard that." Tom sounded earnest.

"Well, it's none of my business," she said. "So I'll be careful on this road if you will."

Tom stepped back as she got the car running and shifted into gear. He stayed by the side of the road until she pulled out.

Cruising down the road, Skylar watched in the mirror as darkness quickly enveloped Tom Jeevers. She sincerely hoped he was right about that wolf not bothering an old man who, though spry enough for someone in his eighties, probably couldn't outrun a jackrabbit for half a city block.

She drove slowly, deciding how far she'd keep up the pretense of running away before turning back. It wasn't just stubbornness that formed her decision to ignore Gavin's warnings, but a pressurized feeling of absolute necessity. Something was going on out here, and her dad's cabin was part of that mystery.

She drove around one more bend in the curvy two-lane road before jamming on the brakes and white-knuckling the wheel, robbed of yet another crucial breath.

She was not mistaken this time. Something moving very fast had crossed the road, nearly colliding with the Jeep and forcing her to a standstill with her heart again racing.

Deer? Mountain lion? There and gone in a flash?

Seeing no hint of any animal, Skylar rolled up the window and eased the car forward, steering to the right far enough to find room for a U-turn.

She'd go back and pick up Tom, take him home. Her second brief sighting of that animal left her hyped, wary and aware that Tom might not have been the blur she'd seen a few minutes ago. More than one potentially dangerous creature might be on the prowl tonight.

"Gavin," she said aloud, heading back the way she'd come. "Be careful."

The Jeep crawled forward as she rounded the bend. But though she searched, Tom Jeevers was nowhere in sight. Then again, he probably knew these hills well enough to find an alternate trail.

The cabin, on the other hand, was easy to find in the dark. When she climbed out of the car in her dad's driveway, she paused to consider why all the lights in the cabin were blazing.

"How did I know you'd return?" Gavin said from beneath the porch overhang, with a sharp eye on the woman who was the second reason his body battled him mercilessly from the inside out.

"Probably because you would have done the same thing," Skylar replied.

"You're messing with me, Skylar, and putting yourself at risk."

"I have a right to do so, and didn't expect you to be here."

"Which would have made this worse since you'd have been here alone."

"I wouldn't have been here at all," she argued. "I was planning to go after you."

Gavin didn't dare rub his forehead, or lift a hand. The claws pushing against his fingers stung like a son of a bitch. Despite the cover of the porch, the moon still ruled him, and any respite was temporary.

The only other time he had repeatedly shifted back and forth from one shape to another on the same night was right after the attack that had left him hurting.

It was the wolf's turn, and they both knew it.

"It sounds crazy," Skylar said, coming no closer to him than the base of the steps. "And I can't explain it to you or even to myself in a way that makes sense. I have to be here, not in town. I have to help you find whatever is out there."

She waved a hand at the hillside. "It's as though my entire existence depends on this."

"Depends on what, exactly?" Gavin asked.

"I don't know. It's a feeling. A gut feeling that something isn't right, and that I can find out what that is if I try."

"And you think you'll find an answer on the mountain tonight?"

"Yes."

Gavin let a beat of silence pass while he studied her.

"You'll do no such thing," he admonished gruffly, pushing off the wall and fisting his aching hands. His chest was throbbing. Facial muscles tingled wickedly as if they, too, might betray him, shift out of order if necessary, if he didn't get with the program and stay there.

"Help me do this," Skylar said. "Let me go with you."

"I can't allow that."

"Why not?"

"I'm responsible for what could happen to you."

"It's a wolf, Gavin, and I have a flashlight and a gun if you think those things would allow us to find the sucker."

Gavin's throat seized, warning him that he had precious little time to debate this with Skylar and not that many words left. The fact remained that he couldn't lead her, escort her or follow Skylar up the blasted hill. He couldn't take two steps off this porch with her watching.

"Please listen," he began. He had nowhere to go now except to a very bad place. If Skylar started for that path, he'd have no choice but to reveal himself to her. He was out of options and would protect her with his life, no matter what shape he was in. Hell, she might faint if she saw him, and that would be that.

No, he amended right after the thought. Skylar wouldn't faint. She had probably never given in to a weakness like that. *Not you, my fierce lover.*

"I can't take you up there, Skylar." He willed her to accept what he was saying and back down, just this once.

"Then you won't go, either?" she countered.

"It's my search, my fight. Not yours."

Zeroing in on something in his tone, she took a step forward.

"I've read about your family," he said, hoping to deter her from approaching by using the personal information he'd discovered earlier that day. Hoping she would storm off again and let him be.

"I know you've had your share of issues, Skylar, and that your mother wasn't the only Donovan to spend time at Fairview."

He watched her hands and arms go rigid, and he hated hurting her. Skylar's pretty face was set and surrounded by clouds of shiny golden wheat-colored hair that he wanted to run through his fingers. Her lips were bloodless.

"I know you were there also," he continued, coughing to get that out, hanging on to his human shape with the sheerest thread of willpower. Between the moonlight and the woman across from him, his emotions were in upheaval. "And I know you're studying to be a psychiatrist like your father."

"After spending time in the loony-bin to see how the other half live, you mean?" she said.

"How long was it, Skylar? How long were you there, in that Fairview place?" He eased back on the gruffness with that question, and it cost him. Spasms cramped up his throat.

"Didn't your internet search divulge that information?" she challenged.

"I didn't pursue an answer. I thought…"

"One week." Her face was expressionless. "I was there for a week when I was six years old because I wanted to see my mother and wouldn't take no for an answer."

So, your stubbornness isn't anything new, he thought.

"What did you do?" Gavin took an involuntary step toward her, absorbing the pain of his burning thighs and shins that came with his new proximity to the open sky.

"I broke in," she said in an emotionless tone. "Sneaked in, actually, right under their noses, when visiting my dad. Then I tried to let her out."

His brow furrowed as he pictured that. "You tried to get your mother out of the hospital?"

"Yes."

"When you were only six?"

She didn't bother to answer that question, realizing it was a rhetorical outburst on his part.

"Wouldn't that be impossible?" he asked, battling to speak through the tightness in his throat. "And why would you be able to stay there at all? Why would they allow you to stay?"

"They couldn't stop me, Gavin. They couldn't get me out, once I'd gotten in. *She* kept me. Somehow my mother sensed I was near and she fought at the right time to get out of her room. When she found me, she kept me with her, threatening to hurt me if anyone came close with the intention of taking me away."

"Are you saying that no one managed to help you get away from her?"

"After the first round of coaxing and threats and drugged darts, they didn't even try. By then, I suppose she'd built up a tolerance to the drugs. Not wanting to see harm come to me if they pushed too hard, the staff waited out the standoff."

Gavin ran a hand through his hair, fighting off shivers severe enough to visibly move muscle. The moon called but he couldn't respond. Not yet.

"No one would leave a little girl in a situation like that," he said. "They could have shot her with something. Helped you."

She smiled wanly. "I thought of that long afterward. But I believe it became a test. She behaved with me there, as long as they left us alone. I was a calming factor that made her more or less amenable to her daily regimen, such as it was."

"How did you escape?" Gavin's forward momentum took him to the top of the steps.

"She finally let me go."

"And then what?"

"She died."

"Did they...?"

"I don't know if they accidentally had a hand in that."

Gavin closed his eyes, unwilling to imagine the story that Skylar had just told. Or that her father had allowed it.

"I'm so sorry." He shook his head.

"I'm not sorry. It was my goal, and I achieved it. My sisters never saw her there, never knew her. They couldn't even conjure up her face."

"And you can?"

"Yes. I can. I remember her eyes."

His voice no longer sounded anything like him, yet Gavin went on talking. "What about your father and the part he played in this unusual scenario?"

Though the rigidity of Skylar's lean frame hadn't relaxed, she answered him. "I don't remember much about his actions, and I can hardly picture him there. My mother didn't want him near us. He and I never spoke about it afterward, and went on as though my time at Fairview never happened. But I do realize that it had to have been his decision to allow me to stay as long as I did. That for my own safety and hers, he temporarily caved to my mother's threats."

"You don't hold that against him?" Gavin couldn't help but ask.

"Not for one day."

This woman knew nothing of revenge or retribution, then, and Gavin envied her that innocence. She was here to pack her father's things and to find out why he died, without any thought to that other time in her life.

"That was personal information, and not in the news," she said. "How did you access it?"

"I'm tied in to a few special archives."

She fell quiet.

He had started to sweat, the result of his ongoing fight with the moon.

"Skylar, what was wrong with your mother?"

The slow, sad smile that lifted her pale lips as she answered him gave nothing of her feelings away.

"I once heard my father describe her condition as a form of lunacy, but of course that didn't really explain anything. Right after she released me, Dad said my mother's sick mind made her believe she was a…" She swallowed and finished the statement. "A wolf."

The word, and the way she said it, made Gavin bow his head in disgust. Then he wondered if he might be imagining this conversation because out of all the women in the world he could have been attracted to, it turned out to be the daughter of a woman who thought she was a damn werewolf.

Lunacy. Christ! That was an old term applied to sick people who, it was believed, were strangely affected by the moon and in very specific ways. He had looked that term up, as well as all the others he could find relating to the effects of the moon on human beings.

"That's why you thought your father might be chasing wolves," he proposed, looking closely at Skylar. "To conduct more experiments?"

"If that was his plan, he never mentioned it to me or to any of my sisters. The sad fact is that none of us have been close to him for some time. He distanced himself from his family years ago, preferring to spend time at the hospital and here, alone."

"What about that partner you mentioned? The one who identified him after the accident?" he pressed. "Was that person at Fairview when you were?"

She shook her head.

His hands were rising as if he'd reach for her despite his own pressing problem. *Screw the wolf. To hell with the moon.* He hurt for Skylar. He ached for what had happened to her and for what she'd been through. Yet she seemed just as courageous now as she must have been as that six-year-old kid.

He couldn't touch her, didn't dare get closer to her.

Skylar didn't need to experience another inexplicable example of madness from someone close.

"It's not just a wolf out there," he said before thinking about the effect of his statement, or how it might sound to the woman he craved more than the moonlight.

She continued to stare back at him.

Tired of having her call ignored, the moon sent a beam of brilliant light that reached the tips of his boots. His toes tingled, and his shoulders rolled on their own, without any conscious thought on his part to ease the icy needles stabbing him between his shoulder blades.

Have to go. He had to get off this porch and away from Skylar. He was no good for her. She had escaped from that past only to hook up with another goddamn lunatic. How was that for irony?

Gathering himself, Gavin jumped forward, knocking Skylar toward the railing, bending over her and hearing her breath whoosh out. With his face inches from hers and the rest of him already starting to change, he whispered, "Stay here. I'm begging you."

In a single fluid bound, he turned and bolted for the cover of the trees.

Chapter 20

Skylar pushed off the railing and stood up, convincing herself that it didn't matter if Gavin knew about her childhood and the things she'd never told anyone about her mother.

If a lover with the potential for madness in her genes didn't turn him on, well, she'd get over it, and get over him.

She would have thought more of Gavin Harris than that, though…and also that after confessing to him that she never took no for an answer, he'd believe that she would stay away from that hillside tonight.

There was a mystery to be unraveled in these hills, its allure strong enough for her to discount the danger. Getting out there, though, was hard. She felt ill. Her body seemed heavy. Her stomach growled again, protesting the lack of food.

Groping for the wall, she stood up straighter. Still winded from the surprise of Gavin's closeness, she managed to haul herself up the first step, and then she turned to look at the path leading into the trees.

Gavin must have gone that way.

Only an idiot wouldn't get that he didn't want her to follow.

Stay here. I'm begging you, he'd said.

Yet it seemed to her that he was too adamant about keeping her away from that path, and that he might be hiding something, rather than just wanting to keep her safe.

What didn't he want her to see?

Steadied by a couple deep breaths, Skylar climbed the rest of the steps to the front door and looked inside. The gun was on the table where she'd left it. Going in, she picked it up and retraced her steps to the porch.

"Am I certifiable to believe that if I find that wolf, I'll know what Dad was after and what went down?"

Who will answer that question if I can't?

Steeling herself, and with the gun in her hand, Skylar jogged toward the path, hampered by what felt like a two-ton weight on her shoulders and a slight drag in her suddenly aching left leg.

Gavin let his anger rip through a series of growls as his second transformation of the night happened in record time. The shift completed as he hurled himself up the steep, tree-clad slope.

Only a slight hesitation at having to leave Skylar behind marred his stride.

Small nocturnal animals darted out of his way, recognizing the threat. Night birds protested from the tree tops. Somewhere to his right a pair of owls hooted. All this activity showed that the beast he sought wasn't yet in this area, though it wouldn't have gone far. This was its territory, just as it was Gavin's. They both seemed to return sooner or later to the familiarity of home ground.

He reached the granite outcrop without becoming short of breath, and he scrambled to the top of the old stone pile. From there he looked out over the trees below, thinking he saw lights winking near the base of the mountain.

He could not afford to concentrate on those lights.

On top of his granite perch, he roared, waited, dropped to a crouch. No responding roar came.

The monster had not found its way to Skylar's cabin, as he'd feared, though Skylar wasn't safe from its reach.

Skylar.

His heart thudded in response to thinking her name.

Look what obstacles you have risen above to become the woman you are today. But I can't help you find what you seek. Look at me. You crave the love of a dark-haired man, not what I have become.

A sudden sound brought him to attention. It wasn't close, but the birds had stopped chirping.

He leaped from the rock, landed in a crouch with a hand in the dirt and his head lifted.

About time you showed up, beast, he thought, rising slowly.

Skylar stumbled again, not sure what was wrong with her legs. This time she went down, falling to her knees, tripped up by a rock or something else unseen. Her hands and knees stung when they hit the hard ground.

She stayed there a moment, cursing her clumsiness and looking around. The path beside her was lit from above by a potent shaft of moonlight resembling a searchlight. The ground was visible in front of her for five or six feet, but as she breathed in the smell of her surroundings, that ground began to undulate in waves similar to a desert mirage.

Before she could get up, a wave of vertigo hit her. The trees and everything else nearby began to spin as if caught in a cyclone, though not one single leaf fell. Uttering an oath, Skylar didn't make it to her feet.

Hers weren't the only sounds, she realized, taking those night noises as a sign that no evil predators roamed nearby waiting to chew off one of her limbs. There was no other choice but to wait the dizziness out.

The gun was no longer in her hand. She must have dropped it when she fell, and the weapon was difficult to see in the dark. Also, her left foot was bare. She'd lost a shoe, and wouldn't get very far without it.

Don't panic. This will pass.

Problem was, the dizziness didn't fade. The vertigo stubbornly messed with her equilibrium, and made her stomach tighten.

"Damn."

She muttered another stream of choice four-letter oaths that went from bad to worse as a sudden piercing pain between her shoulder blades nearly stretched her flat out in the dirt. Closing her eyes made the world turn faster and tied her stomach into knots. Her forehead dampened from the strain of maintaining her composure as more pain seared behind her eyes.

Her heart beat fast from the shock of the fall and her inability to get up. The thump of her pulse filled her head and her chest, sounding like the drum section in a large brass band.

Soon other body parts caught the beat, drumming, hammering loudly. Her guts heaved up in protest. Her muscles quivered.

Uncontrolled body twitches turned into quakes. Quakes became shudders strong enough to tip her sideways. Having nothing to hang on to, she dug her fingers into the dirt.

She wasn't sure if any illness could strike this fast and this hard without any kind of warning. But the ridiculous dizziness seemed as though it was going to hang on and overtake her here, alone, on the mountain. Her body was betraying her big-time, and just when she needed to get on with her search.

Though impossible to fathom, the pain from her shoulders spread to her back and arms. Nerve fibers caught fire. She couldn't lift her head.

Her hands felt oddly tight and strangely hot. She pulled them from the ground and shook her head in denial. She was hallucinating. Her fingernails weren't really growing and sharpening into points.

Those aren't my hands.

Those hands had claws.

She had to shut her eyes as the fire of fever flashed through her and her stomach again turned over.

What's happening?

She heard a voice, a deep male voice, speaking from somewhere close by as if addressing her silent question.

"Give in," he instructed, his voice a lifeline in a turbulent sea of pain. "Stay calm. As calm as possible. Fighting increases the pain and slows down the process."

Process? What process?

Heaven help me!

"Skylar. Trust me," the familiar velvety voice continued. "And may the devil take me now if I've done this to you."

Fighting to stay conscious, Skylar touched her face,

smelled blood, felt something warm trickle down her cheek. But this wasn't real, she told herself over and over. It was only part of some new dream.

Someone moved beside her, casting a shadow on the ground. Beyond the scent of blood, she recognized this new scent. *Gavin.* Not a stranger. Gavin had found her, and would help.

Strong arms covered her as her ranger's body curled around her body from behind. He tried to lift her up, but his tight hold increased the level of her pain.

She screamed in agony, feeling as if she were being turned inside out. Sizzling blue-white bolts of internal lightning fried her nerve endings.

Beside her, Gavin grunted and swore. She heard the unmistakable crunch of bones breaking. Had Gavin broken his arm in his attempt to lift her? A sickening sound, like wet meat slapping the ground, followed.

Swear to God, she couldn't stand much more.

Fear began to take her over, revving her system for flight. Adrenaline spiked as she cried out again and made an effort to stand. Gavin caught her to him, shaking and speechless, locked in the throes of some kind of physical torment of his own. When his body jerked a final time, he let loose a low rumbling growl that reverberated in her chest as if she'd made it.

And then he hoisted her into his arms, high off the ground. Holding her tight against his chest, he lurched sideways, out of the moonlight.

Chapter 21

"Gavin, I'm sick," Skylar said as he made for a spot deep under the cover of trees that would block the light.

He'd morphed back to his human shape so that she'd recognize him and not be scared. But he wasn't able to maintain that shape.

He hurt like hell.

His arms, wrapped around Skylar, were again furred-up and thick with muscle. His rib cage, pressed to her right shoulder, made nightmarish popping sounds as he moved. The wolf he'd merged with didn't give a fig for decorum and priorities. According to the wolf, Skylar Donovan smelled way too good to let loose.

She shook in his arms, her body contorting every time his did as if mimicking something it was supposed to do, and following his lead.

He chanced a closer look at her.

Skylar's beautiful face was deathly white. Her teeth made bloody indentations on her lower lip. More blood pooled on her cheek, a harsh contrast to her pallor. Long, fair lashes fluttered, and he waited for her eyes to open, dreading that moment, hating it in advance. But she cut him a break for which he was eternally grateful.

Her body pulsed in time with his, one tremendous boom after another jerking them both. She always felt light in his arms, but she was also a weighty part of the same darkness that consumed him.

Out of the moonlight, her blue shirt seemed dull. Her jeans were torn on one knee. He set her down carefully, regretfully, against a tree, and moved away from her, unable to explain any of this to her without a voice.

"Gavin..." she whispered.

But his mind was nearly beyond being able to deal with her rationally. The beast in him wanted her desperately because Skylar was going to be like him. Soon.

Skylar was close to shifting tonight, and wolf recognized wolf. No doubt about it. She was about to shed her skin and become like him for the first time. She was experiencing her first taste of what the moon could do to her, and Gavin, stunned by this, despised himself.

The blame was his. In some way, he'd done this to her. She suffered the consequences of his sleeping with her and being so attracted to her that he put her safety in jeopardy to satisfy a man's physical cravings.

In his defense, resisting her had never been an option. Skylar looked and tasted like the mate he'd feared he'd never find. Both he and his wolf chose her because of needs so intense that nothing could have kept him from her.

She didn't know any of this.

Skylar was innocent.

"Vertigo," she said, exhaling in staggered breaths.

She called this travesty vertigo when in reality what happened tonight was a life sentence of unbelievable pain and torment: of living on the fringes and never feeling normal again.

I am so sorry.

I can't take it back.

Don't you see?

Under the cover of the trees, his body felt as if it were being crushed from within. Imploding with a pressure almost too much to bear. He supposed another shift might kill him this time.

He had to run: get away from Skylar and allow his wolf the room it required. But another monstrous entity also roamed here tonight, and Skylar, weakened and hurting like this, was fair game.

He wasn't the human she expected to see, and yet he didn't dare deny the moon her wicked brand of revelry— the moon that demanded payment for every rebellious transgression, such as denial.

"You won't leave me here, Gavin?"

Without a voice, he couldn't comfort her or shout at her for being so damn stubborn about doing whatever she pleased. How many times had he warned her about staying inside?

Now look, he thought.

"Are you okay?" Her voice shook with concern for him.

Damn it, Skylar. I don't deserve your concern. I did this to you.

He really was sorry. God, he was. He would have given anything to take it back.

You'll be all right for the time being if you stay in the shadows, my beautiful lover, he wanted to say out loud. *Your transformation will be postponed.*

But for how long? She couldn't stay here all night, a prisoner of the moonlight, and he didn't see any way to get her home.

"I heard something break," she said.

Shaking his head was an action she didn't see with the tree blocking her view. And he couldn't manage more. He was very close to giving everything away.

"I'm sorry." Her voice was huskier now. "I think the spinning might be easing up. In a minute I might be able to stand. I can try."

In the silence following her remark, Gavin heard her draw several more rasping breaths. When his wolf whined, the sound emerged as a guttural growl of fury.

"Gavin? What was that?"

He thought seriously about stepping clear of the tree and allowing her to see him. But that wasn't doable. Skylar didn't deserve the knowledge that the man she'd given her body to that very day was a werewolf.

God. Skylar.

She might damn him from this night forward and be justified in doing so. Skylar would surely hate him if she knew he'd done this to her in some way that he still remained ignorant of. Especially since she'd need him more than ever.

No way could he go after the other monster that had done this same thing to him. He wasn't going to let Skylar tackle this transformation from woman to wolf alone. The memory of the trauma of his system rewiring for the first time tormented him still.

Damn moon.

"Something's wrong, isn't it?" she ventured. "You're not okay. What is it? Are you still there, Gavin? Hell, what a pair we are."

Gavin dragged all ten claws down the bark beside him, relishing the minor punishment wood slivers provided. Pretty soon Skylar was going to distrust the silence and come after him, crawling if she had to. He saw no way out of this, but to let her.

And then a ferocious roar, like the sound of a rolling earthquake, shook the darkness around him.

The terrible sound drove Skylar to her feet. Not quite ready to stand on her own, she clung tightly to the tree beside her.

"What the hell was that?"

The sound turned her insides to putty. She felt like death warmed over and was now covered in chills.

If the wolf Gavin chased made that sound, they were screwed. The damn thing howled like an animal on steroids.

"Gavin. Tell me you're here, and that you heard it."

He could have gone, she concluded when he didn't reply, but she didn't think so. She was certain she felt him nearby. That sense of him should have been suspect, she supposed. It was strange how she'd felt Gavin from the start, before seeing him in the garden that night and before ever setting eyes on him, as if she possessed some special kind of ranger radar.

She took a tentative step away from the tree and held out both hands for balance. A second step moved her inches closer to where she thought her handsomely rugged ranger silently waited. Despite whatever it was that kept him from speaking to her.

One more step toward the path that was still drenched in moonlight, and she thought she might make it. But she was broadsided by a moving mass of darkness with the force of a wrecking ball.

Knocked over, but instantly free of the heavy weight of the thing, Skylar rolled to her side and scrambled to her feet. Another roar, this one fainter, yet very close, raised chills on top of chills on the back of her neck.

"Gavin?" she shouted. "Be careful. Something is here."

Snapping her head around, she backpedaled to the tree and pressed her back to it, wishing she hadn't lost the gun. The spinning was gone now and she felt mostly normal, wide-awake and completely alert.

"Damn you," she said to the man so obviously avoiding her. "I know you're there. You can stop this shit, and either pick up my gun or help me find it. I'm fairly certain you can't fight that wolf with your bare hands."

Another growl made her turn to face the trees behind her. Peering into the dark, trying to separate that cloak of darkness from anything that might be hiding within it, she missed the closer threat.

By the time she noticed she was no longer alone beside her tree and that her companion wasn't Gavin, it was too late to scream.

Chapter 22

Some kind of creature faced her, standing upright on two legs and partially resembling the shape of a human.

Stunned by the creature's appearance, Skylar geared up for a sprint, high on adrenaline, wondering how far she'd get.

The thing didn't move. Nor did it attack. It stood there, watching her like the predator it probably was. She sensed something else beyond the entity in front of her, and was too shaken up to want to acknowledge that this creature might have brought a friend.

"Gavin," she said, inching back farther, hoping he heard her and was ready to do some damage to whatever this was.

In response to her voice, the big creature turned its head to look at her, and a fresh round of fear spiked through Skylar that was so potent and senselessly enlightening, she staggered sideways.

Can't be. It's just a mistake. This creature heard me and responded to the sound.

Her gut told her a different story, though, as it clenched. Her body knew what her mind refused to comprehend. She'd sensed this presence, experienced this scenario in her dreams.

No!

This creature couldn't be Gavin. Yet how many times had she questioned the immediacy of her attraction to the ranger, and her feeling that he'd stepped from those dreams and into her current reality?

"Gavin," she whispered, shaken, extremely anxious and again questioning her mental state.

"Gavin, is that you?"

Another roar came from the surroundings in reaction to her voice, but the creature in front of her didn't make that sound. The werewolf turned and stood rigidly with its back to her, its huge body as tense as hers.

Her fear filled the air with a crackling tension that seemed tangible enough to touch before it scattered like spores in the wind. More fear gripped her throat, making speech impossible, stapling her in place though she was desperate to get away.

Brush north of the path rustled. Skylar covered her mouth to muffle a scream. The werewolf—damn it, that's what it was—dropped to a crouch, its body hunched and ready to spring to meet whatever caused the sound.

And if a creature like the one in front of her feared what was out there, how awful must that other thing be?

In a moment of suspended silence, her worst nightmare stepped onto the path and into the moonlight with a full coat of black fur that shone like polished obsidian.

God...

This was a real monster, and as different from the werewolf beside her as the werewolf was from humans.

The world had just come unglued.

The monster's coat rippled in a nonexistent breeze, over a massive chest and long appendages. Nearly twice the size of the creature beside her, its wolf-shaped head perched on a thick, muscled neck. An elongated muzzle protruded menacingly beneath deep-set eyes. Its mouth hung open to reveal a full set of needle-sharp teeth.

Skylar's knees went weak at the sight.

The black beast lifted its massive head and sniffed the air. Those terrible eyes looked in Skylar's direction with an intense focus that pinpointed her location in the shadows.

Skylar shook so hard everything around her moved. *Run*, she told herself. *Try to get away.*

But Gavin...

Was that Gavin in front of her, suited up in his own fur coat and rising to cut off the bigger monster's view of a woman whose legs no longer worked properly?

Neither of the incredible creatures budged in a face-off that lasted minutes. Low warning growls bubbled up from the throat of the one Skylar hoped wasn't actually Gavin, those growls as scary as anything else in this fantastical scene.

Undeterred, the huge black monster remained still, with its head cocked to one side as if it might be calculating a next move or considering her presence. It continued to zero in on her, ignoring the creature barring the way.

And if that wasn't strange enough, under its intense scrutiny, Skylar began to burn with an unfamiliar heat. A burn so hot, it felt cold. She gazed on the scene with a new awareness, as if layers of her senses were being peeled back to reveal a freshly kindled power for seeing what was in front of her.

The darkness around her lightened, dulling shadows

from black to gray. Shafts of moonlight that she hadn't previously noticed dappled the ground around the creature she felt sure stood guard over her, highlighting a musculature that was magnificently alien. But what good would that kind of muscle do against the larger beast?

She didn't want to find out. She had to run, and couldn't. She wanted to speak, though no words came. The black-coated monster didn't move from its circle of moonlight. Only its coat shuddered, catching and reflecting the moonlight each time the beast took a breath.

Finally, the werewolf beside her lunged at the larger creature, kicking up leaves and dirt that flew in all directions. When the dust cleared, Skylar saw only one creature standing. The werewolf she thought might be Gavin was also looking around in disbelief, because no evidence of the black beast remained.

Gavin glanced over his shoulder once at Skylar and then bolted after the monster that had knocked Skylar down and returned, drawn to her like a moth to the flame.

He knew now by the monster's actions that this area was no longer safe for her.

But why hadn't it attacked? Taken what it wanted right there? Surely his own presence hadn't made a difference.

If he could have gotten Skylar out of there that minute, put her in the car and driven straight to the airport, she might possibly have had a chance. But that wasn't an option.

"Not tonight. Not like this. Not for you, Skylar."

Moonlight ruled their shapes. His shape, and soon hers. Gavin again faced the dilemma that was tearing him in two. Find the monster or stay with Skylar. Run after the beast maker, or help a new beast be born.

His pulse raced. As dire as the situation was, he couldn't resist Skylar. As a human female, she'd been a knockout to his senses. With wolf added to the mix, she was a real physical need, an urge heeded by every cell in his body that told him she was his mate and that werewolves mate forever.

He found himself circling back to her. Skylar Donovan was so very important to him.

Needing a voice, he darted beneath tree cover not far from where she still stood, and began the shift in reverse. Listening to the sounds of his body retracting, feeling his skin sucked inward with a sting and a hiss, and nearly unable to breathe, he caved to the pain and pressure that made him utter one last growl.

Halfway through the shift, and with no more time to spare, he moved toward Skylar, his body close enough to human in shape for her to recognize his outline.

"Skylar." He cleared his throat, swallowed back a howl of distress, and began again. "Skylar, we have to get out of here."

Her voice rang with relief. "Oh, thank God. I thought you were gone. I thought…"

"No. I'm here. Listen to me. That fiend touched you. It now knows your scent."

She swayed on her feet with one hand on the tree while she listened to him without interrupting.

"That creature kills and maims, showing no mercy. If it was the same monster your father ran into out here, you can see how easily an accident could happen. If your father chased it, sought it out or knew of its existence, he'd be one of the very few."

Gavin searched for the strength to go on, afraid he might not find it. The pain burning through him was bad, the worst ever, and he had to rise above it.

He backed up, his transition nearly complete, his ears ringing with the mind-numbing pain of far too many shifts and a body currently uncertain of which shape to maintain.

"You don't have to believe me. Trust what your own gut tells you. Do you know what ran you down?"

"Yes," she said without moving, without running to him. "A werewolf. It was a damn werewolf."

Gavin shut his eyes. "Yes."

"And so are you," Skylar said, surprising him when he'd been pretty sure nothing more ever could.

She didn't elaborate. Maybe she couldn't. But she knew.

"There's more." He spoke through gritted teeth, already agonizing over what to say to her next.

"Impossible," she argued, shaking her head, scared to hear anything else. "There can't be more."

Gavin strode forward until he was near enough to catch Skylar if she collapsed, and close enough to fill his lungs with her familiar heady scent. She didn't back away from him. Her eyes searched his as if she saw him clearly.

"You aren't sick," he began.

She cut him off. "I'm better. Fine. We can go home now."

He held up a hand to calm her and shook his head. With a tight check on his emotions, ruled by an aching heart that pained him more than his body did, he said, "You're not okay, Skylar. You have to get from here to there." He pointed down the hill. "And that trip is going to prove more difficult than anything you've ever attempted."

Her green eyes widened. When she brushed strands of golden hair back from her white face, he would have given a year of his life to kiss her fear away.

Dried blood caked one of her cheeks, from where she'd scratched herself with something a whole lot worse than a fingernail. The wolf in him wanted to lick that wound, along with the rest of her, and make her forget they'd started this conversation. The man wanted to console her, ease her into the next phase of her life, and didn't really know how to do that.

"You're not sick," he reiterated, starting over.

It's time. Say it. Do it. Tell her.

"You're like me."

He watched her face crinkle in distaste and sensed her refusal to believe him.

"Do you understand, Skylar?"

She shook her head. "I'm not sure what you are. I know the term because we've spoken the words. And I've dreamed…"

The sentence went unfinished as her mind turned his information over, seeking a recognizable pattern in nonsensical data. Then she looked up and into his eyes.

"Why?" Her voice rattled up from deep in her chest. "Why are you doing this? Talking to me like this?"

"Why aren't you running away?" he countered.

Her eyes never left his. That gaze seemed to touch his soul.

"You don't have to stand here, Skylar, but you do have to accept what I'm telling you as the truth. You've seen what I am. Trust, me, this is not a dream."

She didn't faint, collapse or have a fit. Skylar Donovan presented to him the bold front he'd seen before, and he loved her even more for that strength now. He prayed she wouldn't hate him after this night was over, if she made it through.

"I'm no werewolf, if that's what you're suggesting," she stated adamantly.

"Go ahead, then. Step into the light."

She looked past him, shuddered, and again met his eyes.

"I'll take you," he said. "I'll hold your hand. Hell, Skylar, I'll carry you if that's what you want. But unless we wait until morning, which is a dangerous plan with that abomination hovering so close by, or we slide down the hill on our asses, avoiding the trail and keeping to the trees, we have no choice but to face this."

"Face what?" she asked in such a way that he knew she wanted him to spell it out for her. She wanted to hear her new life sentence without him beating around the bush.

"If you step into the moonlight, you will change." His heart pounded out the beat of his distress. "You aren't human. Not anymore. And if I've caused this, you can use those silver bullets on me and I'll welcome them. But only after I help you through this first shift and if you make it through this night."

Her teeth were chattering. "You're full of shit," she snapped, sidestepping him, walking on unsteady legs toward the moonlight.

She dared to step into that light. Bathed in it, letting its silvery phosphorescence flow over her, Skylar turned to face him with a triumphant look on her face.

Seconds later, she let out a gasp of horror and surprise.

Chapter 23

The threat to Skylar's sanity continued with the sensation of spiders crawling over her face. Spiders quickly became icicles, prodding painfully at her forehead and her cheeks—little jabs, sharp and insidious, here and there.

Standing frozen in the moonlight, the world around her became a tornado of revolving darkness, light and stars. An uncomfortable vibration rumbled deep inside her that began to spread outward and soon took over her arms and legs.

She cried out against the onslaught of pain accompanying that vibration, and fought back with her hands, tearing at her face, her stomach and her hips, fearing this was real and that she wasn't going to wake up.

Her body was in a state of upheaval, getting ready to die one part at a time. That's what this felt like. Dying.

Screams slipped through her lips as the discomfort became real agony that quickly began to escalate. Still, she wouldn't give in, refused to give up her fight. She didn't really want to find the werewolf.

And now...

Now she was becoming one, if Gavin had told the

truth. Her tainted body was being restructured, rewired against her will. Something insidious was short-circuiting her genes to make her like the creature ruining her sleep night after night. Only here, in reality, there was so very little she could do about it.

Not true. Not happening.

In the moonlight she felt naked and terribly, horribly, exposed. Skylar remembered a fleeting explanation her father had given long ago to a child searching for meaning. "Moonlight is poison to people whose genetics are damaged," he said.

How the hell did he know that, way back then?

Profound, deep-seated grief over that memory undermined her determination to stand upright. The last of her energy drained away with the promise of an upcoming shift.

If Gavin was right, she was turning into her father's worst nightmare. Her worst nightmare. Any minute now, she'd be like the thing she imagined her dad had trapped in that cage...and as crazy as her mother. A wolf now resided inside her body, and the moon was that wolf's release switch.

Ready. Set. Go...

Through the whirl of pain she opened her mouth to whisper to the moon, "Come and get me, you bitch!"

And in the end, what will this moon madness produce?

"A she-wolf," the man with the velvet voice supplied from the sidelines, as though he'd heard the question.

Hearing that term from the familiar voice brought on the sweeping undertow that threatened to drag her under. Skylar fell to her knees fighting to stay conscious, only slightly aware of the man yanking her upward.

* * *

Removing her from the light and getting Skylar the hell out of there wasn't going to work, Gavin discovered as he pulled her up from the ground and into his shuddering arms. The only question now was whether being close to her would worsen her pain, or ease her fright when she got a good look at him.

Skylar. He ran a careful hand over her face, traced her quivering lips as his claws extended. His bones screamed bloody murder. The ability to speak disintegrated when there were so many things to tell Skylar, who was well on her way to the kind of breakdown he remembered.

She shook violently because the thing inside her was trying hard to get out. Like Skylar herself, her wolf wouldn't take no for an answer. Nevertheless, the danger of being in the open with a murderous rogue nearby left Skylar vulnerable.

He felt for her, hurt for her and wanted to take back everything they'd done together if that would fix this. He'd go his own way if allowed a do-over. He would leave her alone, and none of this would happen.

The sound of her back hitting the tree sickened him, but she flailed against his protective hold on her arms. Without a voice, soothing her wasn't an option.

Careful not to scratch her with his claws, Gavin readjusted his hold as she thrashed and squirmed. Swearing silently without the pleasure of hearing those oaths, he applied more pressure to her shoulders, pinning her in place with as much force as necessary to restrain her ongoing gyrations.

Skylar, listen.

They were back to the first time he uttered those

words, and he had to settle for thinking them and sending them to her silently with the hope she'd catch on.

*Breathe. Stop fighting. Letting it in is the only way
to survive this.*

Timing was crucial, and time had run out. Above the
noises Skylar made deep in her throat, Gavin sensed
the approach of the moment he dreaded. The beast he'd
sought for so long was on its way back, and he wasn't
ready for a showdown. Skylar wasn't in any kind of
shape to fend for herself, and he'd have to let her go in
order to face the nightmare.

The smell of the abomination was its calling card:
damp fur, aged menace and the iron odor of blood, probably from whatever it ate for dinner. Gavin spun around
and turned his back to Skylar, leaning into her, shield-
ing her and willing her to be silent, though her soft cries
were evidence of her discomfort. He growled his displeasure over the return of such a beast and studied its
approach with a stern, unwavering gaze.

Silently, stealthily, as if floating above the ground, the
stalker moved in without getting too close. It appeared as
a blur of dark between the trees ringing the area where
he and Skylar stood, acting as if it might be content to
toy with the senses of the werewolf it had created.

Gavin didn't buy the delay or the silence. And he sure
as hell wasn't going to be deterred from guarding Skylar.

Anger made his growl a sharp warning. His racing
pulse provided him with a sizzling new adrenaline-
sparked energy.

The delay was in his favor. While the beast lingered
on the outskirts of the area, Gavin hoisted Skylar into
his arms. Though she fought like a wildcat to be free

and face her own demons, Gavin held her as if her life depended on it, since it probably did.

He walked into the light, felt the slap of moonlight sucker punch him and the agony of the accumulated physical strain of winking back and forth between man and Were without fully landing on either choice for long.

Hit over and over again in relentless waves by the pain of the reverse shift he wanted so badly and couldn't manage—the one that would enable him to speak to Skylar again—Gavin ran, slid, leaped down the hillside, utilizing every bit of effort he could dig up and a whole lot of concentrated determination to turn his back on and gain some distance from the abomination behind him.

Time suspended in the effort to reach the cabin. Not certain how he made it to the front yard, or why Skylar's struggles ceased as he hit the porch, Gavin skidded to a halt beneath the overhang.

Safe?

God, were they safe?

His heart stuttered with surprise when the front door opened on its own. He stumbled back in shock. A woman stood in the doorway, a woman he vaguely recognized from bits of data stored in the back of his mind.

Barring the way into the house, she spoke in a low-pitched, authoritative voice that contained the power of a command. "Go on, wolf. I'll take it from here."

Chapter 24

Who the hell was this?

The stranger in Skylar's cabin made him freeze in place.

Go on, wolf?

As if he could leave Skylar, no matter how bad he felt or looked at the moment? This intruder was facing a werewolf as if that wasn't scary at all.

The next reverse shift wasn't going to happen, however much he wanted it to. Possibly a built-in defense mechanism had come into play to keep this woman from recognizing him in the future. Either that, or since he'd abused the whole shifting thing, there might be a chance he'd have to stay in this frigging furred-up shape forever, his human shape lost because it had surpassed the limits of what a human body could endure.

He stood on the porch, holding Skylar for what seemed like eons. He was furious, not sure why this auburn-haired woman didn't run for cover when confronted by a monster. She appeared to be calm and in full control of her wits. Her heart didn't race. She didn't scream or wince. The beautifully constructed face showed no hint of fear or revulsion. When she'd spoken, she'd sounded unemotionally rational.

"I'll take it from here."

Gavin homed in on that, desperate to understand what was going on.

"Why don't you bring Skylar inside and then do what you need to do," the woman suggested, testing his patience. No smile on her lips. No joke. All business.

"We both understand that if she comes inside, Skylar will feel better. Isn't that right?"

Gavin continued to stare without loosening his possessive hold on Skylar. Let his lovely lover go through this alone? *Don't think so. I caused this. It's my fault.*

"If I take the time to explain my presence to you and make introductions, it's going to be worse for her. Do you want that?" the woman asked, looking directly at Skylar, limp in Gavin's arms.

No, damn it. That's the last thing I want.

"Good." She moved aside, making room for him to take Skylar inside.

He wanted to take that step, but couldn't make himself do so, caught in a stranglehold between a nebulous, twisted-gut feeling that told him he needed to do as this woman suggested, and his inability to relinquish his lover.

"Please," the woman said. "I'm a doctor of sorts. You can trust me. I knew her father."

This was a friend of the Donovan family. That's how she knew Skylar's name. Still, how did that make her so inured to his shape?

As he stood there weighing his options, Gavin caught a new scent that made his heartbeat ramp up to a new high.

You're a wolf.

She nodded.

Gavin moved past her into the cabin, accepting that against all odds of finding another moon freak, wolf also tainted this woman's blood. The scent was heady. Different yet unmistakably there. Not only that, she had a full grasp on what the curse meant and how to deal with it, which led him to believe she'd been a werewolf for some time.

Not alone. Not the only one.

"Not by a long-shot," the newcomer confirmed with a blank, expressionless face.

Though the door remained open, the cabin felt cramped and claustrophobic as he laid Skylar on the leather couch. Skylar's face was ash-gray. She seemed short on breath and made wheezing sounds as if her vocal cords were seizing. Noting those things made him feel ill all over again. Sicker than usual.

It will pass, Skylar.

He looked to the auburn-haired she-wolf and added, *Hopefully it will pass.*

Skylar's overwrought body shook the couch. His body shook just as hard, rattling the table beside her. Sweat gathered on his forehead from the effort it took to stand here under this roof without moonlight calling the shots. The damn light outside beckoned to him.

But there was no hint of a transition back to his human form under the shelter of the roof. Not one crack of bone or sting of a claw retracting.

Hell, could he really freeze in this shape? Forever?

"I don't want to tell you what to do," the she-wolf said, coming up beside him, her presence a startling reminder that he might soon have the answers he'd been looking for all this time. "But it's clear you're in trouble and that what you need is out there, in the night."

What I need even more is right here.

Gavin needed to get that point across.

"Skylar needs my help now," she said, reading his thoughts loud and clear in yet another unexplainable anomaly he had no time to question. "Let me attend to her. Trust me to do that."

Gavin couldn't handle another minute indoors. Pain tore through him like a silver-tipped arrow going all the way through.

I can't go.

"You have to, for her," the newcomer said with a solemn finality that Gavin actually believed.

He had to trust this wolf, he supposed, because there was nothing he could do to help Skylar, and he felt so ill.

"I will take care of her," the woman said. "I promise."

The growl he offered in acceptance of her offer emerged as both a thank-you and a threat.

I will be back.

"Tomorrow," she said. "Don't return tonight. It's best she doesn't get close to you while you're like this after you've imprinted. Her body will want a shape she doesn't fully understand how to reach and isn't ready for."

Hellfire, he wanted to shout. *Who could possibly be ready for this transformation or believe it could possibly be a part of reality?*

The woman across from him waved at the doorway.

She's stronger than you think, he added in this strange thought-reading process. *Skylar is strong.*

"Strength will help, but there are no guarantees she'll survive this if the light reaches her now, as you well know. It's up to the body and its willingness to adapt.

Being near me in this human shape will calm her down enough to postpone the transition."

Postpone?

"Wouldn't you have wanted an explanation first, before your first change?"

Yes. No. Hell, how do you know all of this?

"That's a story for another time."

You said "imprinted." What is that? What did you mean? Tell me this one thing.

"You've mated. Found each other. Bonded. Yes? With us, imprinting is a fierce emotion, and it lasts forever. Your wolf senses hers now. That's why you're not changing back, even though you're near me."

He nodded as if that mystical remark made sense because the depth of his feelings for Skylar had been immediate and overwhelming. But did this imprinting business mean that Skylar couldn't escape from him if she wanted to, and vice versa?

"Please," the woman standing beside the door repeated. "You should go."

He had no other option. His body was telling him that. With a relief bordering on madness, Gavin rushed back through the open doorway, hating the separation from Skylar and questioning this stranger's trustworthiness, but he was no good to anyone like this. The she-wolf had arrived in the nick of time to help Skylar, and who could have predicted that?

The situation had changed. There were now four werewolves in this one tiny area—which made him wonder how many more Weres there might be, worldwide.

He had hurt the very person he wanted so desperately. Would Skylar forgive him?

Moonlight welcomed him as if they were the lovers

here. In the open, away from the cabin, the silvery light caressed him with cool fingers, misty palms and chilled lips. That touch dripped over his face, flowed over his shoulders in a beastly, otherworldly cascade of instructions that eased his tremors somewhat.

It's done, then.

He prayed that Skylar was in good hands. He demanded that outcome from the moon. Because the only way to get on with this night was to believe Skylar would survive, and that he would be free to hunt down the creature at the center of their spiraling universe. The monster out here was Gavin's ground zero.

Raising his face to the moonlight, he breathed it in. He opened his mouth, tasted the light on his tongue, swallowed it down as greedily as if it were Skylar's breath.

"I surrender."

With the wind in his face and the light prodding him on, Gavin bolted up the path using all his strength, intending to find the demon whose third generation included the lover he could still feel, phantomlike, in his arms.

"Skylar, can you hear me?"

The question sounded very close and soberly demanding, but nothing was wrong with her hearing. In fact, Skylar heard everything—the clock on the mantel, the stranger's breathing, insects outside, wind in the trees, the drip of a faucet, and louder than all that, the irregular boom of the thunder inside her chest.

She also heard something else with her brand-new, sharply acute awareness: the same mesmerizing call that had plagued her from the beginning, from her first night here. His call. Gavin's voice...so strong and sexy and persuasively clear, it was the voice of a lover whispering her name while on the verge of physical penetration. Like the gasp of sound Gavin made as he slid into her blistering heat.

Gavin.

She opened her eyes, blinked. A woman's face filled her field of vision: a light-skinned angular shape punctuated by high cheekbones and large golden-green eyes. Dark coppery hair with a fringe of bangs surrounded the almost too exquisitely perfect features of a woman in her early thirties.

"You're safe now, for the time being," this stranger said in a voice Skylar easily placed because she had listened to it on a recording earlier that day.

"It's Jenna," that voice said. "I came as soon as I could catch a plane."

Jenna James. Doctor. PhD. Her father's partner. The psychiatrist who worked with her dad at Fairview Hospital and seemed much too young in person to have been a colleague of the famous Doctor Donovan's. This was the female cohort the Donovan siblings had been jealous of for the past few years. Their father's confidant, and closer to him than his real family.

"Why?" Skylar struggled to ask, her voice gruff, her mouth as dry as sand. "Why are you here?"

"Your sister mentioned being worried about you, and that, in turn, worried me."

Skylar vaguely remembered Trish mentioning a conversation with Dr. James, though that seemed so long ago.

"How... How did you find me?"

"I've been here once before and often spoke to your father by phone when he stayed here."

"Then you were the only one who did."

The faint, persistent thrumming in Skylar's skull threatened to drive her to the medicine cabinet. She reached up to cover her ears, remembering the claws as soon as she lifted her hands. But there were no claws on her hands at the moment. The room didn't revolve the way the night sky had.

Her dizziness had waned. She didn't feel quite so sick now, though the shakes continued as did the chills.

"Do you understand what's happening to you?" Jenna asked seriously, in a tone that demanded an equally serious answer.

"No."

Gavin had used the word *wolf*, but that could also have been her imagination, like the claws and everything else going on. Case in point, how could she hear Gavin's voice now if he wasn't here? She believed he was calling her name over and over as he placed more distance between them.

How could she explain to anyone else about what she'd seen out there, or thought she'd seen? Especially this woman, who delved into peoples' minds on a regular basis.

Skylar tried futilely to get up. Dr. James held her down with a firm hand on her shoulder, though there probably was no way Skylar could have managed, anyway. Her limbs just weren't behaving. She felt boneless and unsteady. The knot in her stomach was the size of a plate.

Her dad's partner sat on the low table next to the couch, eyeing her levelly. Jenna James's questions were professional, direct, and got right to the heart of the events that had transpired over the past couple of days.

"Do you realize what your friend is? What he has become?" she asked.

"Do you?" Skylar countered, her voice slightly surer, the ache behind her eyes increasing as she remembered the way Gavin had looked in the moonlight. The Gavin that wasn't Gavin, with added height, molded muscle, and the constant rumble of deep-seated growls he'd used to ward off danger as he carried her to safety.

Gavin was a werewolf, and her dreams weren't just dreams. He had leaped right into her reality as if she possessed the power to make that happen. And he had made sure she was safe before rushing back outside for what? To do what? Hunt another wolf? Be what he needed to be?

What kind of danger lurked on that mountain that made Gavin show such concern for her well-being? The stalker they'd avoided last night? His fear over whatever walked under the full moon tonight had been pronounced and contagious.

While she...

No. She wouldn't think about the claws. If she avoided those kinds of thoughts, maybe they'd go away.

Where are you, Gavin?

"Don't," Jenna James instructed coolly. "Don't call him back. He needs to be away from you tonight. If you care for him, let him go."

If she cared for him? Hell, she thought of nothing else but him. She was possessed. He'd gotten under her skin.

"There's something out there with a dark heart," Skylar explained, clasping her hands and then unclasping them, afraid to look down.

"Yes. I know," Jenna said.

Skylar looked at her. "How could you possibly be aware of anything happening in this place?"

"I'm in on the secret," Jenna replied. "A few of us are. And now, so are you."

Jenna stood up and moved to the windows, checking to make sure all four were closed and covered. Why? Skylar wondered. To stop something from looking in… or to keep her from looking out?

Neither explanation mattered, she supposed. She felt the darkness outside as if some of it had flown in on her wake. Night coated her lungs, producing the rounds of icy chills that arrived without any sign of giving up.

Although four solid walls surrounded her, and Jenna James's cryptic remarks about secrets and about Gavin resonated in the closed space, Skylar felt moonlight seeping through the roof.

She sat up abruptly and turned to face the door, scared, sensing that moonlight wasn't the only thing trying to get in, and this other thing was an entity that ate up moonlight as if it were candy.

"What's happening to me?" Skylar pinned the doctor with a direct gaze that defied the fear building up inside her. "Tell me what you know."

Chapter 25

When her father's partner turned from the window, Skylar put a hand to her forehead without worrying if she might see things like claws on her own hands. It was far too late for that.

Jenna James was here. The woman's pale skin was radiant in the light from the one lamp in the room, as if it glowed from within. Most of her red-brown hair, long, shiny, streaked with gold highlights, was worn pulled back from her face so that every sharp angle on that face was prominent. The problem with Jenna, Skylar realized, was that she looked too alive to be human.

Something else. The psychiatrist's body pulsed in the dim space as if her skin cocooned something living beneath it. This was also the way Skylar felt, with the knot in her gut continually twisting.

Nothing normal about this.

"What are you?" Skylar asked, firing off that question on the tail of the previous request before the doctor could open her mouth to answer.

Jenna's smile seemed wan. "I'm Were, Skylar. A woman and a wolf share this body. Somebody's worst nightmare, I suppose, if they knew. But most people don't."

"I'm guessing my father knew." Skylar's teeth still chattered, but she couldn't clamp them together and talk at the same time, and this was information she needed badly.

"Yes," Jenna said. "David knew."

"About you?"

"After a while."

Skylar thought about the paragraphs in the notebook in the attic. "Did you two have a thing going on?"

Jenna shook her head. "Nothing like that."

"Then why would he come here to chase wolves when you were right next door?"

"I'm not sure he came here to chase them, Skylar. I think your father might have come here to protect them."

"Protect them?"

She really didn't want to be here with Dr. James. She didn't want to speak about any of this, especially to her father's confidante. But this woman had known her father well, and she'd seen Gavin. Seen what he was, what Skylar, on some level, even now refused to believe he could be.

Werewolf.

And since this wasn't a dream and couldn't be her imagination, facing the details of being fully awake became a necessity.

"A Were," she said, testing the word, finding it foreign. "Then you're like Gavin?"

Jenna shook her head. "Your friend and I are enough alike to seem so at first glance."

"You'll need to explain that, but first, tell me why the blinds are closed."

"For your safety. Tonight the moonlight is not your friend, Skylar."

"What about you? If you go outside, will you change?"

Skylar couldn't believe she was asking a question like that seriously.

"I can withhold the desire to shift when I want to, after years of practice."

"Desire?" Skylar latched on to that. "You want to change shape?"

"For me, it's natural, while ignoring and withholding a shift when the time is right isn't."

"But he has to change shape. Gavin has to. He didn't seem able to control it."

"Gavin. That's his name?" Jenna looked to the door he'd exited out of. "Yes. Your friend is new to the trick and has to heed the moon's call or face the threat of being driven mad by the body's push to reshape itself."

Oh, Gavin. It isn't as if you could have told me. I do understand that, at least.

"Why him? Why mad?" Skylar asked. "How are you different, and what am I? Where do I fit in?"

Jenna's voice remained calm, though her expression wasn't truly reassuring. "Your mate was bitten by a werewolf, which made him become what he is. When the virus, passed along through saliva or a mingling of blood, enters the bloodstream, not by choice, but by an act of violence from someone who purposefully passes it on, imagine the surprise of the recipient when the first full moon comes around."

Jenna came closer. "I was born Were. I wasn't bitten by anyone. For me, being Were is a genetic pattern passed down from parents also born Were, just as their parents were before them."

Skylar wanted to throw up. There seemed to be guidelines for becoming a werewolf. There were viruses and people born into families from a secret alternate bloodline.

Why didn't the damn shivering cease? She was chilled to the bone.

She had to speak, had to know more, yet moving her lips seemed momentarily impossible. Rallying, forcing herself to get a grip, Skylar asked, "How far back can all that passing on of the pattern go?"

"As far back as anyone can count, and then further than that. Before the Flood, and the dawn of civilization."

Needing to get to the bathroom or outside to be sick in private, Skylar moved her legs at last, finding them rubbery and useless. She wasn't going to get away from this. Had to face what was happening.

"He didn't lose his mind. Gavin helped me," she said, more frightened in the relative safety of the cabin with this werewolf doctor than she had been on the mountain when she fell. This woman put people in monitored rooms if they sounded crazy, yet was it possible that Jenna didn't hear how nuts she sounded at the moment?

"More," Skylar said shakily. "Tell me more. How many of you are there?" The question rang with the sound of rising panic.

"More than a few," Jenna replied. "Quite a lot, in fact. We have to stay vigilant to keep forms of the virus from diluting further as it's passed on from rogue bite to bite. The world as a whole doesn't know about us. They can't know. So we police ourselves as much as we can."

Skylar doubled over with her hands on her stomach. Her insides were roiling. She spoke without looking up.

"Tell me this. What kind of werewolf would bite another person and make them a werewolf? How does that work?"

"Good guys wouldn't bite. Not for any reason. It's forbidden."

Skylar hated the image that sprang to mind. If Gavin became a werewolf because of a bite, he must have come across a bad guy, and now he had to deal with the strange new direction his life had taken.

She remembered how she'd first seen him up close, in the yard, kneeling by the hose, and how she had absurdly looked for signs that he might be a creature like the one in her dreams.

The thought that there could be such things as werewolves made her wonder if it was possible she could have known what Gavin was before meeting him, and if some people possessed wolf radar. Had her father possessed it, or did knowing Dr. James make him aware of the flaws in nature?

What had he written in that journal she'd read?

They didn't lose their minds.

Gavin had dragged her from the mountain with her safety in mind on two occasions. He did this because he maintained his wits, like Jenna said good guys did. Gavin's human brain stayed in control while wolfish parts took over his body. And once upon a time, he'd been bitten by somebody or something. The scars on his chest could be tied to his ordeal.

"So, what kind of creature did this to him?" she muttered beneath her breath. Who turned him? Was it the stalker she thought she'd heard following them on the mountain? That thing in the trees Gavin had shielded her from?

Could her father have met that same thing?

Damn it, had her father been bitten? Is that what this was all about?

She looked up to find Jenna sitting beside her. Their eyes met. Skylar's stomach whirled.

"Was my dad...?"

Jenna shook her head, seeming to understand her unspoken question. "No. He wasn't one of us."

Okay. All right. Jenna's answer brought a little relief.

"If someone..." She drifted off, staring into Jenna's gold-rimmed eyes before starting again. "If someone were to chase werewolves, it would have to be on a night when the moon is full. How else would anyone recognize a werewolf?"

Jenna held her gaze. "Most Weres require a full moon to shift. All of those possessing diluted blood do."

Skylar remembered a former breakthrough on that line of thinking, and used it now. "Then Dad couldn't have been after werewolves when he died, since there was no full moon at the time. I thought..."

Jenna encouraged her to go on in a warm, sympathetic tone. "You thought what?"

"I thought someone pushed him or hurt him on that hillside."

Would she ever look at this place the same way after tonight? Skylar asked herself. The answer was a resounding no because she was afraid of this night, this room and the next question moving through her mind. So she backtracked, saving that question.

"And," she said, "your conversation with my sister made you worry about me, why?"

"I've been worried about you for a very long time.

Your father didn't want you here. He didn't want you or your sisters anywhere near this place."

"He made that quite obvious," Skylar concurred.

"There was a reason."

"Protecting wolves? You're going with that as an excuse?"

Jenna smiled sadly.

"Gavin didn't bite me," Skylar said. "Yet you both think I'm facing a change."

"You are facing a change."

"Explain to me how that fits in with the rules werewolves have." Skylar rushed on. "If I go out there again, you're saying that I'll shift?"

"Yes. Eventually. You'll meet that fate in what we call the Blackout phase. It's the first rewiring phase of a body's imminent rearrangement. It's best if you don't do that tonight without a full understanding of what's about to take place."

"Why postpone the inevitable, if that's true?"

"Because if Gavin didn't put the wolf in you, we need to know who did, and what that might mean."

Skylar managed to get to her feet, swayed dramatically and sat back down. Her voice was faint. "You do realize how ridiculous this sounds?"

"I do. But I believe you know the truth already."

"I don't know anything." Skylar glanced longingly at the door, wishing Gavin would come through it. "Why is it called a Blackout?"

"The virus changes the body at every level, takes over, forming new neural pathways and messing with cell structure. It's a terrible ordeal, Skylar. I won't lie about that. It causes a loss of consciousness from which some people never awaken."

"Did that happen to you?"

"Yes. For Weres like me, from a family of Weres, it's only slightly easier and more like an awakening, a firing up of the process, rather than a complete restructuring."

Skylar's stomach tightened again, as if something inside her clenched over this knowledge. "Then he went through it." She looked at Jenna. "Gavin went through the Blackout."

"There is no escape clause."

"And I'm going to go through it, though we don't know why. What happened to me out there tonight was just the beginning."

When Jenna nodded, Skylar sensed the woman was hiding something, not willing to tell all.

There was so much more to learn, though. So many questions were in need of answers. The sickness Skylar felt demanded she address the one question nagging at her. The one she couldn't avoid any longer.

It was an awful idea, born of a darkness that could only get worse if the question was answered.

Jenna had admitted to being worried about her for a long time. A call from Trish had brought the doctor here to Colorado the same day. What would make Jenna do that?

She took in a breath and braced herself on the couch, fighting a rising sense of panic.

Opening her mouth, Skylar released the dreaded words, along with a long, exhaled breath.

"Was my mother a werewolf, Dr. James?"

Time seemed to freeze as the silence grew. She had to fill that silence, had to speak the next part of the question and complete the thought. Her lips parted. Sound came out.

"Not just a locked-up delusional lunatic," she said, "but a real, claw-wielding Were?"

Chapter 26

The forest reeked with the smell of Otherness, as though the creature Gavin chased had marked off a specific territory. The problem came from the fact that the area afforded panoramic views of Skylar's cabin through the trees, from all angles.

Gavin faced a second problem. He craved another scent so badly, he nearly turned back at each bend in the path. Her scent. Skylar's. The woman whose essence was imprinted on his soul, according to the mysterious woman helping her.

He spun around and dropped to his haunches, trying to duck the feeling of being too close to the beast, to the kind of danger that could make bloody threads out of a young woman's dewy flesh. It was possible the beast he sought could avoid being found tonight, but what about next month or the month after that?

Had it shown itself tonight because of Skylar's presence, noticing the wolf in her? Did it want a piece?

Gavin refused to ponder that possibility, and yet he realized that the best thing for Skylar would be for her to go back to Florida, removing herself from this threat. If she left, though, was there any way to predict how far the imprinting might stretch to accommodate a long-distance relationship? Would that relationship disintegrate as she traveled away from him, state by state?

What would happen to their connection when Skylar discovered that her new werewolf self was due to something he'd done to her?

Forever. The woman in the cabin said werewolves mated forever. That thought seemed as monstrous as the rest of the werewolf thing, and still there was no getting around it. Nothing was to be done about any of this, except to stick to the original plan, which went so much deeper now that someone else was involved. Someone he cared deeply about.

Someone he ached for.

Gavin straightened and resumed his pace with his senses wide-open and his skull tingling from the effort of not thinking about Skylar. The world had become much more complicated in the past few days and he'd have to deal with it one problem at a time. Safety came first. Hers, and others'. Mostly hers.

This creature could not be allowed to infect anyone else.

Moonlight lit the forest with a clear silvery light that felt like liquid on his skin and tasted like particles of stardust. The light he now dreaded fed his energy, refueling his body with each step he took, but at the same time it stripped his humanity from him, and left him unsound.

As he neared a rock pile forming a ledge overlooking the valley beneath, Gavin stopped, breathing hard, not from physical exertion, but simply to take more scents in. He wasn't alone. Every sense told him that. Red flags were waving in his mind. The air felt dense, thick, in a way even brilliant moonlight couldn't penetrate.

Turning in a slow circle, hands raised, claws long, lethal and ready for the upcoming fight, he let a growl rip that transposed his anger into a sound the monster in the shadows would surely comprehend. Then he growled out an invitation for the damn thing to come out and face him.

Hair on the nape of his neck bristled as his shoulders began to undulate. The scars on his chest, as if recognizing the creature who'd made them, burned once again with an icy-cold fire.

Gavin wished for a voice, so he could to fling oaths at the night. Settling for a low disgruntled roar, he waited, watched, listened, as he studied his surroundings.

He heard it finally…a sound not meant to be an announcement. He spun toward the rocks with his heart pounding.

I might not make it back, Skylar. And I am so very sorry.

Low vibrations punched through his gut as if he'd swallowed an engine idling in neutral. Wildness began to gather and swirl inside him like a volcano about to erupt. His view of the landscape sharpened. Neck muscles stiffened.

Taking down this beast would soften the blow of his own possible demise. He might be a broken man, but as a werewolf, there'd be nothing to stop him now, short of death.

He rolled his massive shoulders, relishing the spark igniting his mounds of muscle. When the sound he both wanted and dreaded came again, he leaped to the rocks, growling a response. *I know you're here.*

Branches moved to his right. Leaves fluttered down.

A spot of shadow began to grow, getting larger by the second, filling the space between the trees.

You really are a monster. The world has no place for the likes of you.

When the beast stepped clear of the greenery, dark-furred, long-muzzled and twice the size of anything Gavin could recall, it stopped long enough for him to get a good long look before ambling forward at a gait that felt to Gavin like death approaching in slow-motion.

"Yes," Jenna said, seated by Skylar, her face showing none of the fear flooding through Skylar at the moment.

Yes?

Had she heard correctly?

Yes, her mother was a werewolf?

Damn it, think back.

She'd been a child when she demanded visitation with her mother. Only six years old. Some of those memories, tucked away because they were too painful to dig up, came back now with the force of an unleashed tide.

Windowless cell. Men in white coats. The hole in the door that food passed through. A mattress on the floor.

More memory, burning like fire...

Her mother's fuzz of dark hair, shaved close to her scalp. The wildness in her mother's gray eyes that came and went, but mostly stayed, scaring a young girl who was determined to stick it out and be with her mom for as long as she could.

Cold concrete floors. Hushed voices. Foul smells. The sense of her mother holding back a raw, raging power.

Skylar repeated her question to Jenna James out of necessity. "My mother was...a werewolf?"

As she waited for a further response, Skylar found

breathing difficult. Because that had to be the right answer, didn't it, and a possible source of her own condition? This doctor had treated patients at Fairview, though not long enough ago to have known her mother.

And if Gavin hadn't done this to her, someone else must have.

Love bites. Nips of her mother's teeth on her hands and arms. Little endearments that didn't seem strange to a child who craved motherly love and knew no better.

Could that have done it? Made her what she had supposedly become?

Faced with this new dilemma, those days inside Fairview's walls became suspect, and the world continued to tilt on its axis.

Like mother, like daughter?

Maybe no bites were necessary, and her mother had passed her the genes? Could having only one wolf parent produce a genetic Were like Jenna?

God...

Had her father known about his wife's condition?

How far back did her dad's information and interest in werewolves go?

She shook so violently, her teeth rattled. When Jenna reached out to her, Skylar warded her off with a stiff raised hand. Jenna knew about her mother, so her dad must have confided everything.

What about silver bullets and metal cages?

Withholding a scream of frustration, Skylar forced herself to speak. "Since we're on the path of truth, I believe I deserve to know more of my own." It took a few tries to get that complete sentence out.

"You do deserve that. But your father made me promise..."

"Promise what?"

"To keep some things from you unless those things became absolutely necessary."

"You don't think that time is now? I've just found out I'm something other than 100 percent human and that my mother wasn't human, either. Neither is my lover or the woman speaking to me. How does that rate as a requirement for needing enlightenment?"

"Your father wasn't sure about you," Jenna said. "He didn't know if you'd ever need to understand."

"He kept my mother locked up."

"For her safety, as well as the safety of others."

"How did he explain that to the rest of the staff? Keeping a werewolf in a padded cell had to have its own challenges. So, which came to my mother first, the wolf or the madness? Or are they one and the same?"

Her voice broke as she went on, recalling things long repressed. "I remember darts. They shot her with darts when they couldn't get close, when she wouldn't let them in. They were careful not to hit me, but there were lots of darts when they finally took me away."

"That would have been medication to calm her down."

"It was barbaric. Would you condone that, Dr. James? If you kept a werewolf in a cell, would you treat it like that? Control it that way?"

Jenna didn't answer that one.

"So, what? Times change? Why aren't you locked away? Why didn't my father go after you?"

"I'm not like your mother, Skylar."

"How do you know? She was beautiful like you. She was lucid at times. What made her so different from you or Gavin?"

She could see the discomfort her question caused in

the woman across from her who probably wasn't much older than Trish. But the questions seemed fair under the circumstances. She had a right to know what to expect.

There were secrets, and then there were secrets, Skylar guessed. Maybe her mother had been stark raving mad on top of being Were and Fairview was the right place to handle that. Yet how was she going to find out without being privy to her own family history?

"Different," Skylar pressed. "Explain that. If not bitten, like Gavin or a genetic werewolf like you, if that's what you mean, what does that leave?"

"A creature that's so much more dangerous," Jenna said, her voice low and gentle. "One that has to be carefully monitored for everyone's good."

Skylar sank farther down on the seat. Damn it, they were talking about her mother as though she'd been possessed by some kind of demented demon.

"So she passed the wolf to me?" Skylar whispered, eyes closing, the last of her energy all used up.

"I think that must be the case."

"And it just happened to show up in me now?" Her staccato voice was as shaky as the rest of her and showing the strain. "Can you even begin to explain that?"

"None of us can," Jenna replied. "Very few of us have experience with anything like this."

Skylar opened her eyes to focus on the woman beside her. She had to know everything, wanted to know…and at the same time didn't want to hear any more. But they had already come this far.

Her voice cracked. "Wouldn't it be easier for me to walk out that door and take it like a Donovan? Face my fate head-on and let my body get on with whatever it's going to do? Prove that all this speculation is true?"

"No," Jenna said adamantly. It was a stern warning, a no-nonsense reply backed by the threat of a werewolf's strength and power. And it made Skylar realize that Jenna James had to be here for a reason that surpassed merely being concerned for a colleague's daughter.

Possibly Jenna was here to monitor her, gauge her, study her since the original Donovan lunatic was lost long ago at Fairview.

And all that was missing from this sordid picture was a tranquilizer dart and a white lab coat.

Chapter 27

Gavin went cold. Numb. Staring at a presence that bridged the gap between heaven and hell by sucking the air and life right out of both. And out of him.

He had a sensation of falling, of the darkness weighing him down, so that thoughts of movement in any direction were impossible. There was no place for other emotions. Fear became an overarching cloud.

He dragged at the air in order to breathe, aware of the need to clear his head. This beast truly wasn't like him at all. If he was its accidental offspring, something had gone terribly wrong with the process.

The thing, creature, monster, abomination, stopped several paces away in a repetition of their meeting earlier in the night, and again the hesitancy seemed strange. Through his stupor, Gavin realized he had to shake off his shock to properly assess this gigantic foe. But all he did was stare.

Again he noted how fur covered its body, with no resemblance to anything human. The dark fur rippled like water over a massive muscle structure each time the creature drew in a breath.

And anything that breathed could conceivably have

its air supply cut off, Gavin thought, hoping for an opportunity to test the theory.

But the outline that seemed wolfish at first look went far past that in scope, outclassing Gavin by at least fifty pounds. Maybe out of self-defense or an act of self-preservation, he hadn't allowed himself to remember details of the complete picture. Yet here those details were, larger than life and twice as nasty.

Watch the mouth and the claws, he warned himself as deep-set eyes stared back at him from red-rimmed sockets. Gavin was surprised to sense a terrifying intelligence gleaming from those eyes, which were a light color. Blue? Green? The creature's eyes were the only evidence of an identifiable humanity in the monster, and for a few seconds they tripped Gavin up.

This wasn't merely a super powerful animal, as he'd first thought. It was a walking, thinking machine—which Gavin figured made it ten times as deadly. And it appeared to be assessing him, too.

The claws were extended and at least six inches long, though the beast's big hands, more reminiscent of paws than Gavin's hands, remained lowered. Its impressive muscle wasn't bunched, which would have suggested it was ready to take Gavin on.

Why are you looking at me? What are you waiting for? What the hell are you?

Gavin's pulse hammered at his insides. He didn't attack or do anything but try to stomach the fear and anxiousness of waiting this out.

The beast across from him sniffed the air and growled menacingly with sounds that raised chills on the back of Gavin's neck. The pain in his chest intensified. His scars continued to burn.

He growled back. *You can't get past me, beast. You'll never get to her.*

He sensed the beast's impatience. Its hunger beat at the air.

Only death will end this. Yours or mine.

Did it laugh at his threat, as if indeed it heard and understood the challenge? Was it anticipating the ease with which it might savor a kill?

The terrible humanlike eyes tracked to the right, looking past Gavin to the gap in the trees that bordered the path. Alerted to the direction of the beast's new focus, Gavin inched sideways to block off the view.

Not going to happen. He growled. *Not tonight. Not ever. Not if I can help it.*

He didn't want to die, and yet he had always been cognizant of the sacrifice he might be asked to make in the line of duty. Still, not making it through the next few minutes wasn't an option he was willing to accept.

The monster roared softly and tossed its wolfish head. Once again it raised its muzzle to sniff the air. Then it stepped closer to Gavin, and though it was only one step, and still a distance from him, it sniffed again as if smelling something on Gavin that it might not have anticipated.

The vastness of the silence around them was chilling. Gavin readied for the fight, raising his claws, demonstrating his willingness to defend that path to the cabin at all cost. He had to force himself to anticipate the beast's first incriminating move. Bile stuck in his throat as he waited.

The giant cocked its head and continued to stare. The second sound it made rolled through Gavin, pulling from him another silent protest.

She's mine. Forever. You did this.

The beast's next roar, louder, more feral, caused a chain reaction. The forest came alive with movement, as if a hurricane had dropped from above, controlled by the creature across from him.

Gavin dropped to his haunches and roared his disgust. His chest heaved. He fought for breath and shook off the searing pain cutting through him from being near his maker. Drawing back his lips, he bared teeth that were so much less impressive than the demon's.

The beast snapped at leaves hurling by as if it were a game. Then, without warning, it sprang. The transition from complete stillness to a moving wall of solid muscle took less time than it took Gavin to blink. The creature was on him before Gavin knew what had hit him, its great jaws open and mere inches from his face.

On the ground, on his back, Gavin felt the heat of its breath, felt its heavy bulk bearing down on him before regaining his wits. By then it should have been too late for him to inflict any real damage on the thing on top of him.

He struck out anyway, his claws parting the thick fur to connect with the monster's ribs. The damn thing didn't even react to the blow. Nor did it finish him off, though Gavin's face was a bite away. Instead, it looked him in the eyes as if seeking something. As its light eyes probed his, a razor-sharp claw touched Gavin's cheek and scratched its way toward his mouth, drawing blood, though the beast seemed to have no sense of that or take notice.

I will kill you, Gavin thought. *Somehow.*

He brought up one knee, rammed it into the beast's thigh as hard as he could, and again went at it with his

claws. The giant, seemingly oblivious to pain, tilted its
head and let out a roar that rattled Gavin's bones.

And then the beast heaved itself backward, lunged to
its feet, and made for the path leading to...

The cabin.

Skylar sat forward, looking to the door and noting
peripherally that Jenna looked there also.

"Closer," Skylar said. "Whatever is out there is getting closer."

Jenna's gaze snapped to her. "Do you know what it
is?"

"I was hoping you did."

"I'm afraid I might." Jenna didn't elaborate.

Skylar tried again to rally and stand. Stumbling sideways, she reached for the rocks surrounding the fireplace
to steady herself. There was no reason to be sick. Werewolves required moonlight to transform, and moonlight
couldn't reach her here. As long as she stayed inside,
she was safe.

Right?

That had to be correct, since Jenna didn't want her
to go outside, and the blinds were closed. Jenna seemed
adamant about remaining indoors.

"What does it want?" Skylar asked.

"I'm not sure." Jenna looked pensive.

"Could it be revenge on whoever resides in this
cabin?"

Jenna turned to her. "Why do you think so?"

"I've seen the cage and the room that contains it. I'm
wondering if my father's interest in werewolves might
have veered off course, and the one he trapped in that
cage got away."

Jenna seemed to stop breathing. Skylar read a lot in that sudden silence, mainly that Jenna didn't know anything about a cage in a room tucked away behind Tom Jeevers's house.

"You told me he wanted to protect wolves, not harm them," Skylar said. "So maybe you can explain how a cage hidden here in Colorado might accomplish that. Tell me you realize that locking up a werewolf didn't work so well when it was my mother."

When Jenna's thoughtful gaze met hers, Skylar saw pain in her expression. "There are things you don't know about that," Jenna said.

"But you do?"

"David confided in me about your mother once he discovered what I am. He wanted information about us and was worried. He had to confide in someone in case—"

"In case he tried the same scenario again and the task killed him?" Skylar used both hands to keep herself upright, sick over having her instincts proved correct. Her father must have captured a Were, and that creature somehow eventually tore the cage apart to make its escape. Maybe her dad went after it, and the creature found him first.

Her mind raced over this conversation with Jenna, sweeping back, moving sideways, leaping ahead to recall what information the doctor had provided either knowingly or unknowingly. One thing stood out. It was Jenna's answer to Skylar's question about how her mother differed from both Jenna and Gavin, and what that revealed.

A creature that's so much more dangerous, Jenna

had told her. *One that has to be carefully monitored for everyone's good.*

Before realizing she'd moved, Skylar found herself across the room and next to Jenna, able to stand without support. While this sudden burst of strength surprised her and raised all the little hairs on the back of her neck, Jenna showed no concern at all, only the discomfort of being the one to break all this bad news.

"Why was my mother considered to be so dangerous?" Skylar asked. "What made her unlike you and Gavin?"

Under the weight of the question, Jenna began to display the first hint of what made her seem a kind of werewolf royalty, if pure bloodlines covered that sort of thing among man-wolf combinations.

Her face became even more angular and set, giving the impression of its having been carved from a slab of marble. Her auburn hair deepened in color and richness, as though the full extent of its color and shine had been purposefully repressed to resemble a normal human's red-gold mane. Jenna stared back at Skylar with eyes flashing gold fire.

Or maybe Skylar just hadn't noticed those things until now.

The effect was stunning and a little scary, and made Skylar take an unconscious step back.

"I've been searching for the answer to that question," Jenna replied. "I spent the past few years trying to understand why your father did what he did to your mother, keeping her at Fairview. When I discovered the truth, or what my pack believes must be the truth, his actions became clearer and made me catch the next plane here."

Pack. Dr. James was the member of a pack of wolves

that were so much more than four-legged animals, and light-years from being human. Not one thing completely, or the other. Altogether different.

Skylar tripped past those thoughts, locking on to what Jenna just said.

"You discovered the truth? And that truth is?"

"Your mother might not have been a true werewolf at all, Skylar."

"What? You just…"

Jenna raised a hand to silence the protest. "I believe… *We* believe your mother might have been a Fenris."

Skylar wanted to shout for the absurdity to stop. Put an end to the ridiculous accusations and all the strange terms that had come her way since arriving in Colorado, threatening to make the world a brand-new place.

But in the really creepy way people were drawn to anomalies and tragedies, unable to help themselves, she repeated the term Jenna used, wondering if Jenna might be making stuff up.

"Fenris?"

"Will you sit down?" Jenna said.

"No. Talk, please."

Jenna said "All right," as if not totally sure about that or where this information might lead. She ran a hand over her forehead as she went on, pressing back her wisp of bangs. "You were thinking your mother was locked up because people thought she was some kind of demented demon."

"I didn't say that out loud," Skylar protested.

"You thought it."

"Are you telling me you can read my thoughts?"

"When the moon is full, all Weres, when lacking voices, can speak through our thoughts."

This news spread like whips of fire through Skylar's mind, enlightening, frightening, changing things. New ideas formed rapidly and she had to follow where they led, because if Jenna was right and Gavin could hear her thoughts, he'd hear her calling to him now.

It meant that the night before, at the motel when she wished for his return, he'd have been aware of those thoughts, too. Nor would he have had to guess what kind of reception he'd receive when he got there.

Knowing of her hunger, he brought food. He came prepared to engage in the kind of wild, abandoned sex she craved while in his arms. And he obliged her desire to have him stay with her until daylight. All when there was no way he could have heard those wishes.

But wait just a damn minute, she wanted to shout.

"How could Gavin have heard me before the discovery tonight that I might be Were?"

"If you were human, he couldn't have," Jenna said.

"Is it possible he felt the wolf inside me without realizing it? Could he have read me without understanding why?"

"That's entirely possible."

Too fast. Too much information is coming in at once.

"Go on." Skylar whispered the prompt, waving a hand, feeling sick again but standing firm. "What the hell is a Fenris?"

Jenna's eyes were soft and empathetic when Skylar looked there. "A Fenris is an animal demon."

What? Her body's shaking tipped Skylar into an open-legged stance.

"Do you want to hear this, Skylar? It gets worse."

"Yes. Damn it, go on."

"If I'm right about this, your mother was an entity not

seen before on earth, or not for generations, anyway. A Fenris comes out of Were legend and is an entity that can appear to be human and also appear in the form of a giant hybrid wolf."

Skylar considered sitting down before she fell, feeling as if she'd been struck by a particularly potent bolt of lightning. Her skin iced over with shock. Her voice pitched an octave higher.

"What do you mean by it *can* appear to be human? A human-wolf combination is what you all are, isn't it?" She failed to include herself in the remark.

"Yes. But we're just that, wolf and human. The Fenris of legend is not human at all, but the offspring of a wolf god."

The shock accompanying this revelation was an almost tangible thing and so dark it covered Skylar with another layer of chills.

Secrets, unknown identities, and the pain and transformations of the body and soul were concepts pushing her beyond her ability to cope. There were too many revelations. The world had gone haywire, taking her down with it, forcing her to either sink or swim.

She laughed with a slightly hysterical tone and then quickly sobered with her attention riveted to Jenna. "You're saying my father married a demon and that union produced four daughters. That my father knowingly carried on with such a creature—not just a werewolf, but something altogether worse—in a way that might now affect his own children. You do realize how ridiculous it sounds? How sick?"

Jenna's reply came swiftly, and as if she'd thought about this before tonight. "He couldn't have known until it was too late. A Fenris must be able to mask what it is for long periods convincingly, until it gets what it wants."

"Which is what? What could a demon want?"

"Offspring."

Skylar's knees threatened to give way, and held her up with only the utmost willpower as she uttered the protest rising from within her. "That's insane!"

Jenna realized this, Skylar knew. She couldn't miss the effect her information was having. Skylar felt Jenna's strong will reaching out to her like an invisible hand helping to shore her up, as if Weres could not only share thoughts, but energy.

"Why not just a werewolf?" Skylar said. "How did you get to Fenris?"

"Gavin's description of the beast fit with the bits of information I found in your father's archives at Fairview. A werewolf would have been easier to deal with when the full moon wasn't overhead. Even a mad one."

"But a demon wouldn't?"

Jenna didn't answer that.

"They had four daughters," Skylar said.

"Two," Jenna corrected.

"Seriously. You think I can't count?"

"Lark and Robyn were adopted," Jenna stated clearly, in a way that defied further argument. "Probably either to further the whole family image or to keep normal kids close to those who might not be quite so normal."

Skylar stared open-mouthed at her father's partner. "How would you possibly know any of that?"

"I checked birth records, just like you could if you dug deep enough."

"Why would you check?"

"Because the children of a Fenris could possess pow-

ers unlike those the Were community is used to and
would need to be watched."

"In cages and padded cells?" Skylar shouted.

Skylar heard little after that because the ringing in her
ears was getting louder by the second. When the alarm
bells grew shrill, she clamped both hands to her head
and muttered in a voice that sounded nothing like hers,
"I'm part demon. That's the charge? My mother was a
demon who seduced my father into a liaison that lasted
a few years before her incarceration in a mental ward?"

She sucked in enough air to go on. "Well, hell. Screw
the body's rewiring process. As the daughter of a demon
and the granddaughter of a god, I might not need help
with my transformation, after all."

She'd said that in full panic mode, sure there was no
way anyone sane could actually believe this nonsense.
Wolf gods? Demons able to take any shape they wanted
to and birth children? Her two younger sisters had been
adopted by her father?

Standing there, listening to this babble, made her feel
less like a demon's child and more like an idiot.

Jenna's hand connected with hers, the Were's long,
thin fingers warm and senselessly calming.

"Skylar, it's okay," Jenna soothed in a voice as mesmerizing as Gavin's, but in a different way. The earnest
compassion in Jenna's eyes gave Skylar the strength to
speak.

"Why didn't he let her go? If Dad knew what she was,
and that being locked up drove her insane, why couldn't
that demon be freed?"

"I'm sure your father discovered his mistake late in
the game. Maybe he didn't realize things fully, even

then. But he took action to prevent it from happening again, to anyone else."

"He married her. He had fallen for her disguise. That's one hell of a mistake. So, after he put her away, why did he allow me to see her at Fairview? What would that prove? You must see that the discrepancies read more like science fiction."

"I don't think he could have known anything about what he was dealing with for quite a while, Skylar. Madness covers a wide range of symptoms and behavior, as you well know from your studies."

Skylar waited for Jenna to go on.

"Your visit must have calmed her. She'd gotten what she wanted in you and Trish. However, she wasn't allowed to see you. Until you went there, she had probably given up. David's paperwork on your mother stopped after you left the hospital. There's no mention of your mother after that, which suggests to me that the discovery about your mother's true identity either came with your visit or soon after."

Skylar fine-tuned her focus on Jenna's face, looking for a hint of the wolf Jenna carried inside her, finding only the gold flash in her eyes.

"You're sticking to this fanciful explanation?" she asked. "Because in all honesty, your theories make me worry about you."

Calmly, Jenna said, "I'm here to help in any way I can, Skylar. David was my partner, but some mistakes are so terribly personal, not even professional friendships can bridge them."

Skylar's spine snapped straight with loathing for the whole idea of demons and wolves. She said insolently, "So, do you have something in mind, now that you're here? Have you brought along a dart or two in case you're right about all this and about me, in case my behavior gets out of hand?"

When Jenna winced at the accusation, Skylar was sorry for the remark. Whether or not these were lies and fantasies, Jenna had done her best to answer some of Skylar's questions.

"I came here to be with you," Jenna explained. "In case you were alone and unsure of what might happen to you here. I thought you might need the company of someone who understands the process and could remain a rock in the bizarre, changing world you as yet know nothing about. I wasn't lying about wanting to help. I didn't know about your lover. And I swear to you now that I would have searched for a way to help your mother if I had been there at the time, no matter what she was."

Skylar's reply sounded very small and faint. "You would have helped a demon as dangerous as you think she could have been?"

If there was a way to do so that wouldn't harm others.

"I believe you," Skylar said. "I believe you're sincere about wanting to help."

How did she know that, though? Was she now reading Jenna's emotions as well as her thoughts? Because doing so meant, proved...

You see? Jenna asked without moving her lips.

And Skylar did see. She was forced to comprehend that Jenna hadn't been lying or making things up. The Were beside her truly believed Skylar's mother might have been a wolf demon in disguise and that somehow this place in Colorado might spark Skylar's first transformation.

"So she died," Skylar said slowly. "My mother died soon after I left Fairview."

"And another one may have shown up here, against all odds," Jenna said.

Pounded by the significance of that and unable to stomach any more bad news, Skylar turned for the door and the moonlight beyond it, hoping to either escape this madness or jump right in with both feet. Being *just* a werewolf was bad enough. Now there was a chance she'd become something worse.

Not much of a choice. Not much of a future.

But either way, good or bad, she had to be sure.

Chapter 28

Gavin ran.

His senses were icy with fear and anger at his inability to stop the beast. The thing moved too damn fast.

There were no sounds of footsteps in front of him on the path, though the scent of malice trailed in the great beast's wake along with the foul odor of wet fur.

Branches tugged at him as he moved. Tree limbs hit him in the face. But he would not slow down. His heart lay in the clearing below, and his lover was in no shape to tackle this kind of nightmare.

He wanted desperately to fight. He would have given anything to avoid what might happen if that fanged thing reached the cabin. He refused to picture it. Fear continued to flow through him, chilling his internal heat, mocking his own tremendous strength.

Darting through the forest, he roared his frustration and swallowed blood from the line the beast had drawn on his face with its claw. He'd gotten away lightly this time. The fact that he could stand, run, breathe, was mystifying.

Why? he asked over and over. *Why did you let me go?*

The area remained quiet, but in that silence his heart

thundered. Gavin tossed his shaggy head as if he'd deny everything that had happened to him up to this point. Everything except Skylar. He'd never wish to take that back.

God. Somebody.

He needed to get to her in time.

Brace yourself for what's coming, little wolf.

Reaching deep inside, finding one more spark of energy formerly trapped by fright, Gavin kicked up his speed. He ran like the wind, his boots eating up the trail.

When the clearing came into view, his heart soared. But he also felt the complications about to happen down there as if being psychic came with the territory.

Skylar. I'm coming. Damn it, hang on!

Skylar didn't stop to wonder how she sensed her second visitor of the night. An acute awareness of this took her over the minute her feet left the porch.

Before she drew her next breath, moonlight found her and she stumbled to her knees, nerves immediately firing like crazy. The feeling was like being lassoed with barbed wire, the iron thorns piercing skin and muscle all the way to the bone.

Crying out, head lowered, she groped unsuccessfully for a steadying breath. Instead, white-hot flames shot across her skin, entered her open mouth, slid down her throat. Those flames got bigger each time she made a sound.

A new vibration of power filled the night, as if moonbeams were lethal. Each bone in her body began to ache, pound and pulse. She needed to get back inside the cabin. This was a mistake. This was madness.

She couldn't get up.

She wasn't alone out here, her senses told her. The scent of the figure standing beside her was one she now recognized. Wolf scent, similar to Gavin's.

"Hush now. It will hear you." Jenna's thigh, covered by soft faded jeans, was a comfort of sorts against Skylar's quaking left shoulder.

By *it*, did Jenna mean the moon?

Skylar coughed, and blood came up. So did something else. The sound Jenna wanted her to suppress emerged as a growl of twisted torment, a throaty rendition of Gavin's earlier wolfish protests. He'd been in pain, she now understood. His shifting damaged him in some way, and she shared that pain.

Searing stabs of it slammed into her with a force so hard, she stopped breathing. Nasty, electrical, nearly heart-stopping, this new form of agony rushed in to take her down.

This was happening. Jenna hadn't lied. Gavin hadn't lied. Given that the story, or as much of it as anyone could comprehend, was true, there had to be a way of fighting back. She would have to be better than the hurting, fragile weakling she appeared to be. Especially if it wasn't just any old werewolf virus ruling her DNA. She might be part demon. *Something far more dangerous...*

Though the full meaning of that freaky status eluded her, Skylar figured that, as the offspring of a wolf god, the chances of the Blackout killing her were slim and odds for survival better than average. The rewiring of her body surely presented nothing more than an obstacle to be mastered. Or so she hoped.

Moonlight flowed over her, and whatever lay nestled inside her paid attention to that. In an attempt to get out, the thing in her gut pummeled her insides until she doubled over with both hands on the ground.

She stared with horror as her fingers sprouted claws, one by one, each of them springing to life faster than the previous one, with pain that was twice as excruciating. Her breath came in agitated fits, her air supply insufficient for any creature, including those tainted with wolf or demon blood.

There was a popping sound near the base of her skull, quickly followed by another. Skylar hissed with each new torment. Between quakes, her spinal column moved as vertebrae began to lengthen and spread apart.

"Can...do...this."

"Yes," Jenna encouraged, though her voice sounded strained. "You can."

Skylar glanced up to find Jenna's attention on the trees and her body rigid with anxiety. Aware of the tension in the air, Skylar pushed her way to her feet, using her hands to claw her way up through the moonlight. Barely upright, she stood, unable to straighten beneath the weight of her body's insufferable demand to change from its human shape into something else.

She managed to lift her head. And there it was, just out of sight—the thing she'd almost seen on the mountain before Gavin had blocked it from view. The thing Gavin had tried so hard to protect her from. This was the bad guy.

Her arm felt heavy when she raised it, though that arm looked much the same as usual. An unnatural sliding sensation in her hip sockets left her feeling sicker, yet she breathed better when upright.

Her wrist came away red when she swiped at her mouth. Blood, from biting her tongue. But the fact that she was standing seemed to be a miracle, and Jenna's concentrated alertness forced her to get a grip.

A new shadow flowed across the path between the trees, getting larger as it neared. Lightning fast, that shadow, merely a blur, reached the edge of the driveway and hurried on to vault the fence.

Jenna didn't stir from her guarded pose. Skylar bit back a scream as that shadow barreled into her. With only a growl of introduction, the shadow became a beast whose thick body pushed her back and up the steps. So scared her ears rang, Skylar fought hard to remain conscious.

She shouted. No sound came out. Her throat seized, squeezing off a howl. Her hands, hanging at her sides, were pinned by the moving mass of muscle, rendering her beginner's claws useless in the face of such a quick attack.

She was through the door and against the wall inside the cabin, trying not to faint, alarmed by the captivity and wondering why Jenna hadn't made one single move in her defense.

It was then Skylar recognized the scent and feel of the beast holding her against the warm stone wall and realized why Jenna hadn't responded. The werewolf beside her wasn't the cause of the trouble ripping through the moonlight. This was Gavin, here with her.

Gavin, the werewolf.

He was huge, angry. His muscles moved like liquid over his tall frame as he growled softly with his face close to hers. She looked right into his blue eyes and found Gavin there.

After making sure she could stand on her own, he said silently, *I guess there are no more secrets.* He brushed her face with his in a tender, loving gesture before rushing back outside.

She was coming unglued. Sanity no longer ruled here, Skylar thought, scraping the wall with a swipe of her claws. The world was in serious trouble…because, with no distinct boundaries in place to protect reality, nightmares were taking over.

Gavin joined the female Were standing as silent as a sentinel in the cabin's front yard, gazing at the trees. She'd obviously sensed trouble brewing without his having to tell her what he'd seen out there. It took him a minute to remember she could read his thoughts.

Not normal, he sent to her. *Not sure what it is or where it came from.*

It followed you? The she-wolf, still in human form, didn't speak out loud.

Other way around. It headed this way and I followed. Can you describe what you saw to me?

Gavin shook his head, unwilling to explain. *Met it before.* He raised his claws. *Gave me these.*

The she-wolf acknowledged that by briefly closing her eyes. When she reopened them, she turned to face him. *Aggressive?* she asked.

Monstrous. Yet it could have hurt me again tonight, twice, and didn't. Why?

The she-wolf named Jenna appeared to contemplate that. She threw a glance over her shoulder at the cabin. Disliking the implication of that look, Gavin shuddered.

Maybe it won't hurt us, he suggested, worried. *Because we're what we are, the thing must realize it's the bane of our existence, but also a relative.*

So, what does that leave to spark its interest here? the she-wolf asked. *Or who?*

Gavin knew damn well who that left. He'd known for some time. The creature had acted strangely tonight when Skylar was on the mountain, its aggressive behavior seemingly at half strength. That beast must have recognized Skylar's scent on Gavin's skin when it sniffed at him quizzically, taken a liking to that scent.

Fresh blood, Gavin thought. *But there goes my theory of Weres being off-limits to Weres, since Skylar isn't...*

Human, the she-wolf finished for him.

He waved his claws at the cabin. *Will she ever forgive me for that? For making her a monster, like me?*

You are not to blame, I promise.

Gavin took that remark in with another skip in his pulse. The she-wolf shook her pretty head as if to ward off arguments and confirm this as fact.

Nevertheless, he couldn't be sure, couldn't see how Skylar's wolf would make an appearance without him putting it there. The guilt over that would kill him eventually if the abomination on this mountain didn't get to him first.

It will fight us for reasons we don't understand, he sent to the other Were, who again gazed thoughtfully at the cabin. He added, *So I hope to hell you're stronger than you look. With two of us in the way, we might have a ghost of a chance of preventing that thing from getting what it wants.*

The next look she gave him was appraising.

I didn't even see it coming, he confessed. *And we both know Skylar won't stay inside for long.*

Taking a step toward the fence, the she-wolf said solemnly, *I know what this is.*

She didn't say what that was, though, and this she-wolf's thoughts weren't so easy to read. Some kind of barrier stood guard over her Otherness, allowing her to project the image of being human, even when in the moonlight and stressed.

Where did this woman come from? Why should he trust her?

Why the hell wasn't she shifting right now?

As I see it, I'm all you've got, was her response.

And she was right. What other option did he have for protecting Skylar from a monster's sudden interest?

He was about to tell the she-wolf that, but didn't get it out. At the fence, her body stilled. With a flick of her head to toss back her hair, she raised her face to the moonlight. Chin lifted, lips parted, she unbuttoned her bronze-colored blouse, slipped her arms free of the silk sleeves, and dropped the shirt. The damn thing fluttered to the ground in slow-motion.

She wore nothing underneath. Naked from the waist up, and with her taut back to Gavin, she kept her focus on the heavens as she reached for the waistband of her pants.

Chapter 29

Skylar stumbled to the open doorway. Panting from the strain of downplaying the pain racking her body, she leaned hard against the door frame with her gaze riveted to a fantastical sight she wasn't entirely sure could be real.

Jenna stood by the fence, completely naked. Her hair was loose now, and radiant in the moonlight. No underwear or tan lines marred the sleek, wiry, silhouette. Her arms were raised, her head thrown back as if she embraced the moonlight and actually welcomed its shape-shifting treachery.

Seconds passed, barely enough time to register that sight, before the sound came of flesh sliding over flesh. The unmistakably sickening pop of bones breaking followed, and then all of Jenna's body parts fluidly made the leap from human to werewolf in unison. In seconds, Jenna simply flowed into her other form, growling just once to externalize the discomfort.

Skylar held what breath she managed to take in. Viewing Jenna's transformation caused a responding reaction in her own body, which had been fighting hard indoors to retain its human origins.

Tugged forward as if by a magnet, her feet soundlessly hit the porch floorboards. Although she didn't get far, both werewolves in the yard turned to look at her.

It was astounding to see them both wolfed up in their alternate shapes. But something loomed in the periphery beyond them—the same dark, dense presence she'd met on the mountain. In her memory she saw its outline, felt its weight.

This required immediate attention, though her focus veered back to the yard where in a truly frightening new rendition of a nightmare, wolf Jenna dropped to her haunches, opened her mouth and howled.

The sound that echoed in the clearing was twice as loud inside Skylar's head. Somehow she recognized this as a multileveled call that was equally an invitation and a warning. Loud, frightening, that howl seemed more terrible than anything Skylar had ever heard.

Her own mouth opened to let out a cry of protest, though the cry didn't happen. Instead, she repeated the sound Jenna made, and her human vocal cords churned out a rolling, growling sound that joined the echo of the other one in the crystal-clear, pure mountain air.

Unconsciously, she moved down the steps and into the yard where moonlight—her enemy, antagonist, torturer—slapped her in the face with a sharp, silvery sting painful enough to make her head fly back, and then immediately, savagely, flowed over a stretch of her bare throat.

A set of hands tore at her shoulders, their claws digging grooves in her flesh. Except this time Skylar wanted no protection, no coddling or signs of personal weakness making her insides heave. She wrenched herself away from Gavin's grip. Standing tall, fending him off with a shake of her head, Skylar waited for whatever would happen next.

The overwhelming pain of several minutes ago didn't make a comeback, yet her claws were there when she looked. She began to heat up inside, her temperature soaring to a combustible degree.

Squirming in clothes that felt way too tight and restrictive, she had a sudden burning desire to be free of all the things binding her to her human outline. She wanted to let go and get this over with. Yet her legs remained her legs, their shape familiar and encased in denim. The brush of her hair against the back of her neck produced the usual tickle.

What the hell? Did a werewolf have to strip to achieve a full-body transformation?

Skylar.

Gavin's anxiety piled on to her own.

"No. Gavin, please. I have to find out what this is like, and what I am."

Bad timing, Skylar. We're not alone.

She gave the trees a sideways glance. "Let it come."

This beast isn't like us. It's more dangerous.

She threw a wary glance to Jenna, now a streamlined rust-colored werewolf with a serious edge, and said, "As dangerous as my mother?"

Jenna's wolfish eyes tracked Skylar in a predatory manner, but no medicated dart gun or syringe glistened in her hand. Gavin was in the dark here about the details. He didn't know what Jenna had revealed about her mother.

He bumped her shoulder to get her attention. *It's bad. Trust me on this.*

Again, Skylar looked to the she-wolf crouching by

the fence. "What is it?" she asked Jenna, pretty damn calmly for the craziness of the situation they faced and the panting, staccato voice she'd spoken with.

They were werewolves, for God's sake. Not just people. Three werewolves stood in this yard. Well, two and a half at the moment since only her claws proved her affiliation with the clan.

The world had just gone to hell. That thought was seconded by a great howl that answered hers from the shadows beneath the trees.

Gavin's automatic response to the sound crashing through the night was to challenge it with a gruff growl tinged with its own hint of darkness.

Behind him, Skylar uttered a gasp of startled surprise. Near the fence, Jenna, the she-wolf, straightened with her head tilted to one side.

The air moved, though the wind had died. Silence gripped the night.

You said you know about it. He directed this thought to the she-wolf, as well as the idea that he was almost as dangerous as anything else that might turn up in the next few minutes. *Is Skylar right? This beast wants revenge for something only it knows about?*

Receiving no reply, he cursed the gaps in his knowledge.

"What does it want now?" Skylar asked in a voice way too steady for a human about to confront the monster they all knew was coming.

Us, he answered, not sure Skylar could hear him through thought.

You, Jenna corrected with a glance to Skylar. *You*

asked for the truth, Skylar, so let's be clear about this one thing. I think it's come for you.

Gavin heard Skylar's teeth snap shut and looked to his beautiful young lover. Even now, his unbridled obsession for Skylar made him want to take her to the ground where he could ease the physical cravings for her that were setting him on fire.

His body hummed with a desire for her made ten times worse by the wolf in him easily recognizing its mate in her. Though she only wielded a set of claws so far and exhibited no other outward signs of an upcoming shift, he sensed the wolf beating at her core, realized that wolf wanted to be free.

Damn it, didn't they all?

He knew he could tug that wolf of hers into being if he chose. Pull it from her with a whisper. Coax it out with a hand on her face. But with the fetid breath of a monster so close by, he knew better than to touch her in any way that might bring more harm.

Skylar stood in the moonlight without swaying. Her face remained ashen, though it glistened with a coat of silver light originating from high above their heads. Her hands were frozen in a raised position, showing off ten lethal claws.

Her gaze moved to him, connecting with his gaze and producing waves of adrenaline that kicked his heart into overdrive. She was thinking she'd be ready for this, yet she had so much to learn.

Here, the she-wolf, suddenly announced. *Look.*

Reluctantly, regretfully, Gavin tore his attention from Skylar, his gut knotting. Following the she-wolf's focus, he found the eyes in the dark that were observing everything in the yard. Those eyes shone with a reddish glow across the short distance between the cabin and the path up the mountain.

He'd seen those eyes up close, firsthand, and thanked the heavens they weren't getting any closer. Boldly, Gavin strode to the gate, where Jenna joined him. Separately, they paced the fence line, their muscles tense and their senses on full alert.

It was Skylar who made the next sound that broke the awkward, loaded silence. She called out to the awful gleam of those eyes, "If you killed him, and he's gone, what more do you need?"

Her voice, full of the fear they all felt, carried. As if it were an invitation too tempting to ignore, the monster Gavin had hunted, chased and thought of with hatred every damn day since the first time he'd encountered it, stepped forward, though not quite clear of the trees.

Its pressurizing effect on the atmosphere reached them in the yard like a bad wind blowing through. Skylar groaned out a whispered "Oh."

The she-wolf, a few paces to Gavin's left, hopped over the fence. Though she didn't go to meet the devil, Gavin considered how brave this Jenna was to close the distance to those trees by even a few measly feet. Although he would have joined her, Skylar's labored breathing, coming in audible starts and stops behind him, kept him from leaving her.

There was no peace to be had with those beastly eyes glaring back at them from the dark. No sense of comfort in his close proximity to the cabin. If he swept Skylar inside again, Jenna might make a stand on her own.

Then again, if they all made it inside, the beast that very likely broken free of the silver cage in the shed would easily tear through a closed wooden door.

I can't picture it, he said. *No human could have captured and trapped this thing. It's too damn powerful.*

Jenna didn't argue or allow her attention to drift. Her concentration possessed an energy all its own.

Skylar made another sound that raised the hair on his arms and made him turn to partially face her. The sound was a word. *Smell.*

With no idea how she could be withholding her shift since beams of moonlight bounced off her in silver sparks—the same moonlight that pelted him and left him voiceless—Gavin thought, *Don't breathe in that bastard's foul stench.*

Her response was quick and unusual. "It's injured."

He was aware of the she-wolf's attention turning their way.

What do you mean? Gavin asked. *Explain.*

"It's been hurt," Skylar said. "Blood and old infections are the cause of the smell."

Gavin wanted to shout "Good!" And he hoped those injuries might eventually claim the damn thing.

Hell. Jenna cursed vehemently several more times, continuously looking from Skylar to whatever watched them from the shadows. *I was right. This thing has come for her and won't wait much longer. Gavin, get Skylar inside. Now.*

Gavin knew better than to argue.

Chapter 30

So, that was it, Skylar thought, allowing Gavin to lead her inside. The directness of Jenna's command brooked no argument from either of them after that final statement.

This thing has come for her.

Mind racing, Skylar looked up from her position at the base of the fireplace, which afforded her a clear view of the door. Gavin stood with his back to it, his body finally retracting, shuddering, compressing back to the man she recognized with an effort that left his dark hair in his eyes and his scarred chest slick with sweat.

She wanted to throw up. She wanted to throw her arms around Gavin but didn't dare. They both had been completely exposed tonight, their secrets shattered, and the shock of those things formed a barrier not easily breached right then.

"Neither of you are anything like what waits in the dark," she said.

Gavin's voice was deep. "Wouldn't your friend know more about that?"

"I'd never met Jenna. Only heard about her."

"No, we're not like that demon," he agreed. "I couldn't intentionally hurt anyone."

"But it can," Skylar said. "That thing can do harm?"

Gavin nodded.

"You know that because you've seen it before. You've met it before tonight," Skylar pressed, needing information in the same desperate way some alcoholics needed a drink. "And before last night, when we were out there."

"I wasn't born like this," Gavin said, standing there, apart from her, trembling.

With sudden comprehension, Skylar made the jump to follow his train of thought. Jenna told her Gavin had been bitten.

"How did it happen?" she asked. "What did that creature do to you? Was it the same one, and can you be sure?"

She could see that Gavin had long avoided the words he spoke now, and see, too, how painful they were for him.

"I was hunting down the cause of a string of animal deaths and reported disappearances," he began, pausing for a breath. "Not only in the wild, but domesticated stock and pets. I tracked drag marks one evening up the hill, following this same path. I was sure the culprit was a mountain lion."

"The path in front of this cabin?" she asked.

"Yes."

"Instead of a mountain lion, you found that thing?"

"Yes."

"You called that creature a man-hater. It left these scars?" She pointed to his chest with a finger ending in a sharply curved claw. Scared to find the claw still there, Skylar dropped her hand and looked away, trembling the same way Gavin did, her body fighting the fever of Otherness.

"I don't know how I survived," he confessed. "For a long time, I wasn't sure I had."

"I'm sorry." Though sincere, her whispered sentiment came nowhere close to covering the horror of what happened to him.

"You've nothing to be sorry for. This had nothing to do with you," he said.

"You might be wrong about that, if it has in fact come looking for me."

Her lover slid a hand over the wall beside him before inching away from the door. "Do you believe that?"

"I'm starting to believe it."

"These—" Gavin pointed to his bare chest where the parallel scars were no longer white and nearly invisible, but a livid, fiery red "—happened two years ago. Long before you came here. How could that thing be waiting for you?"

Although Skylar ached to touch his chest and trace the scars with fingers not sporting the markers of a mythical creature, her claws were a stubborn reminder of how far things had moved past any semblance of being normal.

"My father has been coming here for years. What's happening now must have something to do with that," she said.

"How, though? Who can tell us what's really going on?"

"I can," Jenna said from the doorway, already gracefully slipping back to her human form and unconcerned about ending up naked in company. "But right now we have to get out of here as quickly as possible."

564 Seduced by the Moon

Of course the creature stalking them would have other ideas that probably didn't include allowing them a smooth getaway. Skylar knew that with her own kind of insight as she glanced between slats in the blinds, listening for the groan of the fence being breached. Without seeing anything out there, she felt the nearness of the creature in the same way she'd sensed its closeness earlier, chills and all.

"Too late," she said. "It won't take long for that thing to reach the yard." She looked to Jenna. "Can it hear us?"

"I'm guessing it can." Jenna searched the yard over Skylar's shoulder after catching the blanket Gavin had given her to cover herself up with.

When Skylar backed away from the window, Gavin was there beside her in that quiet way he had of returning to her when least expected and most needed. She found comfort in his body heat and melted into him. His scent was a familiar slice of the heaven she'd been able to sample before this horrid turn of events, and that scent was now an integral part of her.

Gavin, the man-wolf, wrapped his arms around her protectively. "We just need a little help," he whispered with his mouth in her hair. "And some answers."

Skylar looked to the chair, where the gun no longer rested on the seat. She had lost it on the mountain and nearly forgotten about that. "Help in the form of silver bullets?"

Gavin followed her gaze.

"You could have ordered some of those bullets," she said to him. "Why didn't you arm yourself for your next meeting with the thing out there? What kept you from taking this creature down when you could have?"

Gavin said, "That's just it. I didn't have the chance.

Although I've been searching for it, the creature only appeared again a few nights ago after I became aware that you were in this cabin."

He tightened his hold on Skylar and went on. "I've got a special blade reserved for that beast in my back pocket. Firing a gun would have alerted people to the disturbance and brought more rangers in. The potential of the beast harming other rangers seemed too great a risk to take."

He paused again before going on. "I hadn't really ever seen it, and had no accurate idea what kind of enemy roamed out there. The night it found me is a blur. I hit my head when I fell, and couldn't even picture that sucker until…"

When Jenna interrupted, Skylar got the impression Jenna wanted to save Gavin from reliving his ordeal. Jenna said, "So, it knows Skylar's here. That's what we're dealing with now, though we're not really sure why it might be looking for her."

"Revenge for what my father did?" Skylar suggested. "Revenge that didn't end with his death?"

"We have to stop it any way we can," Gavin said, glancing to Jenna. "You know what this is, you said, and you agree that it shows some interest in Skylar. How did you figure that out?"

His tone was authoritative and firm. To Skylar's surprise, Jenna willingly answered those questions.

Still gazing out the window, her dad's partner said, "I think Skylar's father didn't just stumble upon this creature here in the mountains. What I've come to believe is that David might have brought it here."

Chapter 31

Gavin's protest over Jenna's declaration was cut off by the memory of finding the cage in a building that Skylar's father had rented.

"What?" Skylar said in confusion, stinging his right thigh with a scrape of her claw.

He covered her hand with one of his.

Jenna, focusing on the yard, spoke over her shoulder. "It's the only answer that makes sense."

"Make sense to whom?" Gavin countered.

"Your description fits," Jenna said.

"What are you talking about?" he demanded, sensing Skylar's ongoing distress rising to intolerable levels.

Jenna fell silent for several seconds. Then she said to Skylar, as she turned from the window, "I think this beast might be related to your mother."

All the fight went out of the woman in Gavin's arms. No one in the room laughed at the absurdity of that statement.

"You called it a monster," Jenna said to him. "Do you call yourself one? Or me? Or Skylar? Did you label this beast a monster because of what it did to you?" Her eyes met his. "No? Then some part of you realizes this creature is different in very notable ways. I'm wondering what those differences are and if we're actually dealing with something new."

Skylar felt his body stiffen further. Her claws disappeared. "You're thinking my father found another one?" she said faintly, as if the idea was too insane to speak aloud.

"Another what?" Gavin asked, but his question was ignored. The intensity of the energy between the two females in the room grew substantially when Jenna's gaze returned to Skylar.

"It's possible that he did bring one here," Jenna said. "Hell, anything is possible."

"You told me she came out of legend, something not seen in generations, if ever. If that was true, what would be the odds of finding another one like her?"

Picking up on pieces of this conversation, Gavin absorbed the vague details swimming in the minds of both of the females—thoughts of monsters, white rooms and hospitals. Was Jenna suggesting there were monsters at Fairview?

"Maybe this one came for her, and finding her gone, found your father instead," Jenna suggested seriously.

"Then he managed to capture it?" Skylar sounded unsure.

Jenna nodded. "He might have brought it here to hide the creature away."

Skylar didn't seem to have anything further to say about that, but he sure as hell did.

"I think you need to backtrack for those of us not in on the story," he said. "What are we facing here? What are you hinting that thing is—the beast that changed my life with its teeth and claws?"

"Demon." Skylar again spoke faintly, muttering that word as if trying to believe it.

The back of Gavin's neck twitched, not only from hearing that term, but from the shock of more pieces of the puzzle falling into place. The answer Skylar had just given was darkly fantastic, yet if it were true, it explained a lot.

Can it be true?

He turned Skylar around to look into her face, seeing immediately that she believed this might be so. Her eyes were huge, her pupils dilated with fear to a deep, flat black, while the skin surrounding them was so very white.

He wanted to kiss her. He wanted to remove her to someplace safe, where they would never have to confront these kinds of issues again. Until the next full moon.

"Your father came across one of these creatures before?" he asked.

"So the tale goes." She flicked her gaze to Jenna, which let him know that Jenna had been the bearer of that news.

"Something happened to that other one?" he pressed.

"She died. Full of needle marks at Fairview, in a padded room," Skylar explained.

Which didn't really explain much at all. Not to his satisfaction anyway. So he started over.

"You said *she*."

"What the hell do we know about demons?" Jenna said when Skylar's quivering mouth stayed closed. "Except that one of them was able to reproduce."

Horror at this announcement struck a solid blow to his chest as if it were a living fist. Gavin saw how Jenna eyed Skylar and, in return, how Skylar's wolf was about to explode within her as a way of coping with things the human woman couldn't.

His tone was harsh. "A demon held at Fairview produced children, or whatever the hell its equivalent of children would be?"

The room went quiet around this question. Gavin's next one couldn't have been stopped or kept to himself, because that just wasn't possible.

"Where are those offspring now? Could that beast be one of them?"

This would tie in nicely with the whole revenge theory being batted around, he reasoned. Maybe this creature sought to exact its own form of punishment on those responsible for keeping its parent in captivity. Possibly Skylar's father brought that offspring here to hide it or…what?

Who the hell knew what Skylar's father had done in that shed?

"Good reasoning," Jenna said, following his thoughts. "Sound, even. Except for one thing."

Skylar whirled to face Jenna.

But with a tremendous crashing sound, the front door splintered into pieces, scattering wood, hardware, and hinges everywhere.

And the night rushed in.

Chapter 32

All three of them moved at the same time, launching through the bedroom door and using the farthest window to make an exit. Skylar didn't even notice the sharp shards of broken glass from the window she followed Jenna through. Fear made her oblivious to her surroundings and blissfully numb.

They raced for the Jeep, parked on the dirt driveway, but moonlight was in the way. Sprinting through that light was like slogging through ankle-deep mud.

Somehow, miraculously, none of them shifted before jumping inside the car. Maybe the fierceness of their concentration lent a hand, or their incredible speed. Too afraid to look at what might be following, Skylar focused straight ahead, only slightly relieved when she, Jenna and Gavin slammed the doors, as if that would keep a demon out.

Luckily, the keys were in the ignition and all it needed was a turn. Heartbeats filled the tight space when the engine sputtered to life. Gavin stepped on the gas and the Jeep flew forward. With both hands on the wheel, Gavin expertly maneuvered the car in a U-turn, intending to head for the road.

Skylar dreaded speculation that the demon Jenna spoke of wasn't going to let them off so easily after announcing its presence. In her heart, and in her twisted gut, she sensed its intentions, and was too scared to speak.

Flashbacks of memory came—dark shadows passing behind the car the night she drove, seen only out of the corner of her eye and in the rearview mirror. Wolves on the loose, Gavin had said. Nothing about demons seeking revenge. No mention of demons at all.

Inside her, tucked deep, nestled the new fear that her father might indeed have brought one here, as Jenna suggested. The thought became all the more terrible because of what that demon had done to Gavin.

Its behavior would make her dad, in the long run, responsible for the creation of one werewolf, and possibly more that they didn't know about.

Gavin spoke. "I don't know where to go. If that thing follows, we can't lead it to town."

Skylar wished they could go to town. People, in a big group, might be able to tackle a beast. There'd be a chance. Gavin was right, though, and determined as always to protect the community from physical and mental harm. Innocent people not only had to be protected from a raging monster, but the idea of that monster's existence.

Gavin was at that very moment pondering how to keep her safe, and Skylar loved him for that, and for so much more. Someday she'd tell him so. If they survived the night, he'd need to understand how she felt in spite of their short time together.

"I do know," he said, without looking at her. "God, Skylar, I feel the same way."

Jenna interrupted. "Hey, we're not dead yet. Can we make a plan?"

"I'm all ears." Gavin's voice was gruff with emotion. He kept glancing Skylar's way with his hungry blue eyes.

"Now that we've got our breath back, we probably need to realize that I was wrong about running. Going back there might be the only option," Jenna said.

Gavin continued to drive. "I don't think that would be healthy."

"Shall we go in circles, then? All night if we have to? After that, what? For all we know, a demon can be a demon whenever it wants to, with or without a full moon," Jenna argued.

"Whereas I can't be a werewolf without that damn moon," Gavin said. "That's your point, right? A human can't hurt this creature, so we're at a huge disadvantage after tonight?"

He added seconds later, "Jenna, are you able to shift without the moon's shiny silver impetus? Somehow I sense that you can."

"Yes," she replied honestly. "I can and have. It's tough, and it's nothing any Were in their right mind would want to attempt too often. That said, too much adrenaline, too much emotion, can bring on an urge to shift for those born to it."

Skylar heard Gavin's next question in his thoughts before he uttered it aloud.

He said, thoughtfully, "Back there, you said my thinking was sound, except for one thing. Since your advice is to go backward, how about if we start there?"

No explanation came from Jenna.

Gavin thumped the wheel with his palms. "What's so terrible that I can't hear it? Worse than the existence

of werewolves, demons that track humans and the fact
that none of this is myth? Christ, I'm not sure anything
could be worse."

Why are you blocking me from this? he was thinking.

"It's me," Skylar said, and those two little words made
a big impact on the chill ruffling through the car. "I'm
that one thing Jenna was talking about. I may hold the
key to some of this mess."

Gavin swerved to the right, onto the dirt. The tires
kicked up sprays of mountain debris as he put on the
brakes without seeming to give a damn about anything
other than what she'd said.

The car stopped so fast, they all flew forward. Gavin
turned to her, waiting for her to explain her statement.
Skylar saw no place to hide from the confession he
wanted, since he could read her thoughts if he tried.
However, if the answer drove him away, she wasn't sure
what she'd do. A future without Gavin in it presented
a bleak picture... If there was to be any future for her
at all.

She and Gavin were connected, with a bond that had
snapped into place with the first shared look. She would
see him standing at the cabin's gate, and the way he'd
looked at her in that moment, for the rest of her life.
The two feet of distance between them in this car were
two feet too many. She'd have traded anything to be in
his arms.

"I..." Her voice faltered.

Her lover deserved to hear the truth about the dilemma she faced. He deserved to know what Jenna told
her, and that she really couldn't rest until that theory
was proved true or false. Gavin had to understand how

scared she was to tell him any of this, though that's exactly what she must do. Right now.

"You can tell me," he said. "You can trust me, Skylar."

"Okay." She gathered her courage. "Apparently, I could be the child of the demon once housed at Fairview. One of its two children. So unless the beast out there is my big sister, who was in Miami the last time we talked on the phone, the creature on this mountain can't have sprung from my mother's womb, as far as I know. That's something."

Stunned speechless, frozen, Gavin's beautiful eyes were on her. He didn't drop his gaze to search her for signs that this could be true, the way she might have if the tables were reversed—something demonish in her outline that he might have missed. A red gleam in her eyes?

After the shock of her answer began to wear off, his blue gaze softened and he said, "I see."

Just that. *I see.*

They sat opposite each other, trying to make sense of this information when there was no sense to be had. No one cared to offer up a suggestion about how to prove or disprove her statement, or how proving it mattered. An underlying added stress for Skylar was the fact that if the monster followed them, they were easy prey at the moment, parked by the side of the road. Sitting ducks.

But the beast didn't show itself, and that, too, was yet another oddity in a long list.

Gavin eventually turned the wheel and got the Jeep back on the road leading away from the cabin, where under the canopy of trees, moonlight dulled to a dim and distant glow. Out of all the other things he could have chosen to say, he chose this one. "So, you have a sister."

Skylar closed her eyes briefly, thankful to be able to deal with this remark. "Three of them," she said, despite what Jenna had told her about two of them being adopted.

"I don't have any siblings. I haven't seen my parents since…well, you know."

She got that, all right, and said in a rush, "I want to know everything about you before *this*. How you grew up, where you grew up and why you became a ranger. What kind of food you like. What sort of bed you sleep in. Your favorite color. Will I get to hear about those things, or is it too late?"

"I promise you will know all of those things," Gavin said.

Her battered soul required the normalcy of small talk and familiar themes. Her revved-up body craved the werewolf beside her with a nearly out of control passion.

Animal instincts were at work, she supposed, like the ones telling her to run and to howl at the moon. Would Gavin and Jenna let her go if she opened the door? Allow her to find her fate? She didn't think so, and didn't have to read that in their thoughts since it was plainly written on their faces.

Gavin's emotions ran in fiery streaks along her nerve endings. He wanted all those same things and to know her background, too. At that moment they were wounded, desperate souls in search of a good grounding. They were two hungry souls in need of the promise of a good, long future.

It was stupid to imagine the beast wasn't following, though, or watching without showing itself. Did only she feel its breath? Hear its call? Sense it waiting? Was revenge the reason it was after her?

Who'd hurt it, if not her father, in that silver cell?

Did a Fenris reason, think, plan its revenge with intelligence?

Could her mother have been just like it?

God...can any of this be real?

She said, "Stop. Stop the car."

Startled, Gavin again slowed.

"Jenna's right. We need to go back."

"That's nuts," Gavin objected.

"I can't run away. It will never end if I run tonight."

Jenna spoke up. "It's our best bet. Maybe we can capture the demon."

"Capture it?" Gavin repeated. "No. No way. Then what? Keep it locked up? Do the very thing it might be rebelling against?"

"I didn't mean that," Jenna said. "I'd never do that. I meant if we could capture it, we could ask what it wants. Maybe it understands more than we think."

"What if it doesn't?" Gavin asked.

"Do you want it to do more damage? No matter what we like or dislike, would you wish a meeting with that demon on any unsuspecting hiker or summer resident?" Jenna didn't hesitate to tell it like it was. "This is what we do. What my pack and others like us do to keep the peace and keep ourselves safe."

"What do you do?" Skylar asked.

"Whatever it takes to ensure the future and keep the secrets of our species safe," Jenna replied. "As harsh as that may seem to you right now, it's important. Trust me on that."

Skylar got that, no problem. The sticking point continued to be wondering how a demon like this one could have fooled her father and produced children. Her. And

Trish. Then again, maybe her mother wasn't like this one at all. Maybe she was something else entirely.

"Go back," she repeated, tired of the speculation and in dire need of closure. "Please, Gavin. Either take me back to the cabin or let me out right here."

He shook his head as he began a wide turn. "We do this together or not at all."

He looked in the rearview mirror, at Jenna.

"It's not much of a plan, though," he muttered. "So we have about three minutes to make one."

Skylar said, "I just want to see this thing up close and tell it how sorry I am if in fact my family hurt it."

"Then what?" Gavin's frustration showed in his tone. "You're best friends?"

"No." Skylar was deadly serious. "That beast and I acknowledge that we're family."

"You're kidding, right?" Gavin eyed her instead of the road.

"Hate to break it to you, Gavin, but I think she's being sincere," Jenna said.

Chapter 33

No demon waited for them on the road, in the driveway or the yard. Instead of relief, Gavin experienced a flush of new adrenaline that made his muscles dance as he faced the cabin. He had wanted to find this demon for a long time, and when he finally had the chance there were two women by his side with beastly tales of their own to contribute.

Well, not women exactly, though at the moment they were reasonable enough facsimiles.

Every nerve in his body was edgy and on full alert. After switching off the engine, something he didn't really want to do, the night became eerily quiet. Moonlight reflected off the hood of the car and shone through the windshield without reaching his thighs. He noticed Skylar pressing herself against the seat as if that light contained incinerating properties and, in fact, it kind of did.

"It's still here," Skylar said, studying the cabin through the windshield. "Close."

Though he couldn't really determine the truth of that in any tangible way and felt very little beyond the pull of the moonlight waiting for him, Gavin went along with Skylar's assessment.

His breath came in shallow puffs too inadequately timed to keep pace with his racing heartbeats. Instinct told him to get out of the car and find the sucker hiding from them for the moment, but he was too worried about Skylar to open the door.

Jenna made the first move. Tossing off the blanket she'd draped around herself, she stepped out of the car, and with a soft sighing sound again flowed incredibly smoothly into her werewolf form.

Something in the way she did that tugged Gavin into following her lead. Never easy for him, his bone-breaking shift doubled him over. His body convulsed, still fighting the change rather than fully accepting it, but this shift came faster. He rallied in less than a minute.

Jenna growled. Rolling his muscled shoulders, Gavin growled back. From different sides of the car, they focused their attention on the cabin, though neither of them made a move in that direction.

Skylar finally got out of the car and looked at him over the hood. Her eyes met his greedily. Then, without showing so much as a twitch toward a shift in form, she took off toward the cabin on her long human legs.

He went after her with the auburn she-wolf on his heels. Up the steps, across the porch, Gavin chanted, *Slow down, Skylar!*

Her heat was high and her anxiety level through the roof. She'd feel she had more at stake here in facing the beast than they did, when that was far from the truth.

Through the splintered front door, into the living room, they ran. No sign of the monster remained there except for the scattered remnants of that front door, though Skylar paused in a frozen stance, looking over her shoulder at the bedroom.

No demon jumped out at them in the bedroom when they entered it. Gavin supposed that any creature once kept in a cage probably wouldn't like to linger within four square walls.

Skylar spun around to stare at the window they'd broken and used as an exit. Raising her pale face, she sniffed the air—a strangely spooky action for someone in human skin. Then she lunged for the window and dragged herself over the sill. He followed her with Jenna on his heels, not sure what was going on, other than his guess that Skylar was using some kind of special radar to zero in on her prey.

He almost laughed at that thought, fairly close to his limit on patience. The night had been crazy from the get-go, and he felt pumped-up. His thoughts turned to the gun with its silver bullets, which he couldn't have picked up with his wolfish hands anyway, if Skylar hadn't dropped it somewhere on that mountain. He wished things weren't moving so fast and that he could transition back and forth as easily as Jenna. His stamina was already suffering.

Maybe with time he'd become more adept at exchanging one shape for the other.

If he survived.

Outside the cabin, Gavin began to scent the trail the demon had left. By then Skylar was heading for the path leading up the mountain. Other than planting himself in front of her, he doubted anything would stop her from confronting her destiny, and he couldn't fault that wish. In her place, he would have wanted the same thing. He'd need to find the truth.

As he moved after Skylar, he watched her for signs of the moon forcing her to change shape, wondering how she had so far avoided the silvery call that twisted through him.

Higher and higher they climbed: one semi-human demon and her two furred-up companions on a mission that surely would lead to someone's death. He'd be damned if it would be Skylar's.

Gavin's thoughts raced, producing clear images with each breath of moon-filled air. In his mind, he saw the beast, massive, dangerous as hell. But could it be a real demon? Was there any way Skylar's blood could possibly be tainted by a relationship to such a thing?

Then again, if Skylar did have demon blood in her, they were in the same boat. If the beast they were after actually turned out to be a demon, its curse had also fallen on Gavin. That beast's blood had mingled with his, and that's what forced him to change. In that respect, he and Skylar were blood compatible. So again, the question became one of why Skylar wasn't morphing now.

Halfway up the hillside, she stopped, breathing hard, trembling big-time. Gavin closed in, pressing his body to hers possessively. *What do you see?*

She wasn't able to speak, and didn't try. Her eyes held a wild cast and were again black with fear. By her side, Jenna growled an encouraging rumble and continued to survey the area, also having noted the heavy weight of the burdened atmosphere. Jenna's thoughts were clear. She was wishing her pack were here to help.

Skylar surprised them both when she called out "I'm here," as though she perceived something he didn't.

It quickly became obvious she had.

The beast he'd been searching for, the monster that had made his life a living hell, appeared ahead of them on the path as if Skylar had simply conjured it out of thin air.

Or called it to dinner.

The giant beat with life, its body visibly vibrating in the dappled light. This was no bit of overworked imagination, Gavin's gut told him. The fact that he'd met this abomination a few times already didn't dull the effect of this sighting. The thing ahead of them on the path was too big and too otherworldly. Everything about it screamed for him to run.

In that loaded silence, no one moved. The demon didn't advance. Unlike their prior meetings, it failed to circle its prey or even acknowledge Gavin's presence.

It was too busy staring at Skylar.

Her thoughts had stopped reaching Gavin some time ago, replaced by a buzz of static in his ears. Panic gripped him. Jenna stood as though she'd been turned to stone, her unwavering attention on the demon.

"I know what you are," Skylar said to the creature. "And why you're here."

She was fighting to get the words out, squeezing them through her constricted throat.

"You've met my father, I believe. I'm Skylar Donovan, and they tell me I'm the child of one of you."

The red-rimmed eyes across from them were unblinking and remained fully trained on Skylar. Gavin's internal heat flared against the threat, the fires stoked by his nearness to the creature that had made him what he was. But the beast's restraint truly plagued him. Perhaps some demons picked and chose their victims, and then took all the time they needed to attend to that singular objective.

Did this one understand human speech?

When would it pounce?

"I didn't know about you," Skylar went on. "No one I knew did. I'm not sure if my dad hurt you or if someone else might have, but I've come here to tell you how sorry I am for any hand my family might have had in seeing you harmed."

She waved to include him and Jenna. "I don't think I'm like them." Her hand moved toward the moon. "So maybe what they say about me being like you is true. Do you see a connection?"

The beast slid forward, stopped, sniffed with its big head lifted, and then lowered its face until it was level with Skylar's from a distance of five feet.

"Maybe," she said, pushing the limits of Gavin's tolerance for dangerous standoffs, "you knew my mother. Her name was Greta."

Gavin had called this thing a beast and an abomination, but he saw now those things didn't begin to describe what faced them. It had to be a demon that cocked its long-snouted head, straightened to its full and substantial height, and roared with a bellowing blast of anger that sent Gavin and Jenna stumbling sideways. Gavin pulled Skylar with him, his claws embedded in the back of her jeans.

"Do you understand me?" Skylar asked, righting herself, struggling out of Gavin's grasp to face the creature. "Have you come here to hurt me?"

Another great howl went up, filling the area with a harrowing echo. Thing was...that sound hadn't come from the monster across from them.

Thrown off-balance by the sheer surprise of the

sound, both Gavin and Jenna whirled toward this new threat without considering the consequences of turning their backs on a demon.

Chapter 34

Skylar was knocked off her feet and flung to the side, but somehow, with the grace of a cat, managed to land on her feet.

The night filled with the sound of deep, menacing growls and snapping teeth as a great weight descended from behind her, bending her forward and cutting off her air supply.

Face in the dirt, heart pounding at a disastrous rate, she saw shadows darting around her, heard Gavin's burst of exhaled breath and Jenna's protesting yip. An iron-like odor of blood saturated the ground. The lights went out. No. She had merely closed her eyes. The moonlight hadn't gone anywhere.

Coarse, wiry fur smelling of damp, dirty places, brushed across the back of her neck, just above her collar. She shivered and cried out as a scrape of bony claws pierced her shoulder, cutting right through the cloth of her shirt.

A cry went up that wasn't hers, and was immediately answered by another. Dark paws passed in front of her eyes, inches away, scrabbling for traction, attracted to the blood seeping from her wound.

To her right, Jenna was up and moving, encouraging her to do the same. Hunched over, fighting off an on-slaught of swiftly moving bodies, Skylar curled into a ball and rolled away from the nightmare in front of her, only to be confronted with yet another nightmare once she got to her knees.

Gavin, fierce in his werewolf form, pulled animals off her and tossed them aside. Jenna jumped in front of Skylar, growling, doing her share of damage, but not before Skylar saw what those animals fighting Gavin and Jenna were. Wolves. Real ones. No human in them.

They kept coming. Gray blurs with their teeth bared. Some of them called out when Gavin fought through them. Others yowled as if they were not only starved but mad with a rage that knew no bounds. The sight of two werewolves didn't deter them because the smell of blood promised a delicacy too good to pass up.

And maybe they just didn't like what they saw.

Wild animals...

Skylar had time for just that one thought before she was grabbed from behind. Two massive arms closed around her, lifting her off her knees and out of the dirt. The scene in front of her began to fade as she was dragged backward, away from the fight.

She kicked out without connecting with her aggressor. The grip on her waist was tight and growing tighter, a discomfort that made it impossible to cry out.

This is it, she thought. *The beast has found its prey.*

Kicking out again with both legs, squirming as much as she could, Skylar refused to give up. *Not an option.*

She found room to breathe and made a charge. "You...killed...my...father." Those whispered words set the stage for what she was sure was about to happen to her. "He is all I knew. All we had."

More chaos. Dark blurs. Two dark forms rushed at her, one of them lunging for the beast that had her secured. A flash of red that came with the name Jenna jumped on top of the demon, bearing down with her sharp canine fangs. A darker figure with a seductive scent she knew all too well attacked the arms holding her captive with his own wall of moving muscle.

"Gavin!"

The beast loosened its grip and roared its displeasure. Though tough as nails and fighting for a hold, Jenna flew off, discarded with one good shudder. Another fling of its arms dislodged Gavin and let Skylar fall.

Gavin stumbled back and dropped to a crouch, ready to spring again. But, before he got off the ground, the beast was on top of him, growling, knocking Gavin back with a superior speed and strength that suggested to Skylar that this was no fight at all and that the beast that could have snapped them all in half if it chose to.

Yet for some reason, it didn't seem to want to inflict that kind of damage. The monstrosity just sat there, pinning Gavin, roaring over and over as if shouting curses in an alien language.

Why?

Why would such a dangerous creature hold back?

Skylar advanced on the beast, and the beast sprang back so fast, she had to turn her head to find it. Gavin, caught unaware and too riled up to read her body language, leaped in front of her.

One good shove from the beast and Gavin, in all his werewolf glory, backpedaled five or six feet. Another pivot and shove, and Jenna was there next to him, growling with fire in her eyes.

Neither werewolf had time for a replay, though. With a shiver and a long reach, Skylar was again in the creature's grip and being carted away before the werewolves had time to blink.

What the hell was that? Gavin demanded, running for all he was worth after the beast that had taken Skylar.

Fenris.

Jenna was nearly as out of breath as he was, but still faster. He had to kick things up a notch to keep up with her. *If it hurts her, I'll...*

Maybe it won't.

Then what does it want?

I don't know.

Can you find where they've gone, Jenna? We can't be too late. Just please get me there.

Moonlight streaming through pine branches fueled their run. Firing werewolf synapses enabled them to cover ground at an astonishing speed, though Gavin feared it wasn't good enough. The demon stayed well ahead of them, climbing higher and higher up the mountain. Eventually, it would reach the rocks.

Hell. Then what?

His brain turned off the rest of his questions. All his effort was necessary for him to reach Skylar before the demon reached that peak. One slip from up there and there'd be no coming back.

Wait, Skylar. Wait for me.

Did she hear him?

One more bend in the path and the rocks became visible. Crystal veins in the granite made them sparkle in moonlight, which would have been pretty at any other time. They had reached tree line, too high up on the mountain for much to grow.

Gavin saw them immediately. The great hulking creature had Skylar in its grip as it barreled upward, oblivious to the steep drop on its left.

It moved higher, to where the air became thinner, and breathing, for a runner, whether a werewolf or not, was no easy task.

Then it disappeared.

Gavin roared, sucked in what air he could and ran on, hearing Jenna panting behind him. The rocks came into view, and above them, several outcroppings. They had to have run for miles. The elevation was extreme.

Around one more bend, he skidded to a stop, and sensed Jenna doing the same. His heart couldn't have beat any faster. His blood was nearing the boiling point. But he was frozen in place.

Skylar stood on a large rock ledge, with her back to a boulder. Her arms were at her sides, bracing her stance. Her fair hair whipped in the wind, partially covering her ashen face.

The demon, less than a foot away from her, was trapping her there, pacing back and forth and facing her with its great mouth open.

Something inside Gavin went ballistic. Anger turned his vision white, then black, then red. With a running jump, he leaped from rock to rock, growling, furious, no longer caring about anything except reaching Skylar and somehow finding the strength necessary to kick some Fenris ass.

His body responded to the request for strength with

a fresh flush of power. He heard a sound like the crack of lightning, and his legs just took him there.

Landing on the rock several paces from the Fenris, he held up a hand of warning. The demon, its dark fur moving in waves in the wind, turned its big head.

This one is not for you, Gavin said, raking a claw over the scars on his chest. *You've done your share of harm here, and it's time you left.*

The Fenris glared back.

She's not like you. Not really. Look at her. Would you take her away, stop one more breath? She's done nothing to you. Skylar is innocent of anyone else's crimes. Let her go.

Still no response came from the monstrous werewolf that everyone supposed was a demon. In fact, he thought that this thing looked and smelled as if it might have been to hell and back.

Standing firm, Gavin spoke again. *If sacrifice is what you need, then take me in her place. Thanks to you, I'm halfway gone already.*

The Fenris's eyes blinked and then refocused on Gavin. They were light eyes. Red-rimmed, but light in color. Gray? An intelligent gleam backlit them, making those eyes seem way too human. This was a trick. Had to be.

The demon moved, appearing next to Gavin before Gavin's next breath. No werewolf could possibly move that fast. Jenna and Skylar had been right. Just when you thought the world couldn't toss up anything worse, it coughed up worse by the bucketful.

Gavin.

This was Jenna, taking advantage of his current thoughtful state.

Gavin. Please back away. Slowly. No fast moves or threats.

He shook his head. *This ends here.*

Maybe not the way you think it will, Jenna said. *Listen to me. Trust me. Back away now.*

Not happening.

He watched Skylar, using the rock to brace herself, and said to her, *No, my lover. My love. I won't let it hurt you.*

Still visibly quaking, Skylar pushed off from the stone. When the creature's head turned toward her, she looked into that face, into those eyes. Then Skylar swayed and put a hand to her forehead. Gavin heard her say "No," and "Can't be."

Gavin. Jenna called him again. The adamancy in her voice prickled.

His attention was riveted on Skylar. His gaze covered every detail of the body he already knew so well, sure he must be missing something. Though Skylar's fear buzzed like electricity in the air, her face no longer reflected that same level of fright. Her features seemed to have softened into a look he'd witnessed while staring down at her in bed, with his naked body pressed to hers.

What the hell is going on? he demanded.

It knows her, Jenna said. *Recognizes her.*

Gavin's growl of protest stuck in his throat. *Skylar?*

Skylar ignored him, intent on remaining upright as she searched the Fenris's face. Gavin heard her say to the beast, "He kept you in a cage. I can't imagine what that must have been like. God. Was it because you're so dangerous and willing to hurt others?"

Was the damn thing talking to her in return? Gavin

didn't hear anything else. But Skylar was too close to that demon...and to the edge of the ledge she stood on.

His anxiety made him inch forward. Skylar didn't notice. *Keep it busy,* he sent to her, not stopping to consider if the beast could hear him.

Her focus didn't waver. Looking at the Fenris, she said, "He didn't do that to hurt you. I knew him to be kind, so hurting you couldn't have been his intention. He must have brought you here to protect you. Maybe he kept you caged in order to protect others. And to protect us."

Gavin saw her knees begin to weaken. He watched Skylar sag back against the stone, and he stepped forward, intending to reach her. It was Jenna, still furred up and incredibly strong, who held him back.

When Skylar closed her eyes, he wanted to shout, but no sound emerged. Her chest expanded as she sucked in a breath, made a sound like a stifled sob and pushed herself back up, bringing herself closer to the demon. She was face-to-face with the abomination, and Gavin couldn't stand one minute more.

But then Skylar spoke to her captor, in a voice teeming with barely contained emotion.

"Oh, God. Is it you?" she said.

Chapter 35

Is it you?

Skylar's heart seemed to clench inside her chest as the question she asked echoed in and around the rocks. She wasn't sure this was happening.

This wasn't a joke. No mistake. She had to speak but couldn't find a pattern of words to confront the images racing through her mind of white coats, white rooms, a mattress on the floor and food that had to be eaten with bare hands from disposable paper trays.

How could she have missed the signs now lining up?

Why hadn't she recognized this presence, even from afar?

Finding her breath, she spoke slowly, precisely, trying desperately to control her emotions.

"He told us you died."

Noise from the periphery didn't matter to her. Her lover was there, waiting, fighting his need to help when Jenna kept him from doing so. Gavin was trying desperately to understand what was going on. Her father's partner, a good woman and a fierce she-wolf, also waited. But there was no way to explain this, no way to really comprehend that it wasn't just a Fenris she faced here.

This was her mother.

She felt like sitting down. Falling down. The discovery was overwhelming. She felt herself sinking.

"What do I need to do?" she asked the demon that had long ago taken human form. And though this creature might have deceived her father, she had also shielded six-year-old Skylar from medicated darts.

This same being had wanted to be with her child as badly as that child wanted her mother. It was all there in the demon's eyes. Recognition. Familiarity. Frustration. Confusion. Untapped emotion.

"I'm here," Skylar said. "You know me."

The demon tossed her head and looked to where Gavin and Jenna stood.

"You made him," Skylar confirmed. "You made Gavin a werewolf. Is that what it's like? You sometimes lose control and become the thing you fight against? That's the behavior that made Dad keep you away from others?"

The demon's attention, drawn by Skylar's speech, came back to her.

"Did you hurt Dad?"

The demon backed up, taking several small steps at a time, its eyes still on Skylar.

"Stay," Skylar said with a pleading tone. "Please. I'll find a way to take care of you."

She stumbled forward with both hands outstretched, her new claws obvious in the moonlight. The Fenris stood very still for a few heartbeats, as if waiting for Skylar's touch, but it didn't allow the contact.

"He brought you here, didn't he? He kept you here so that no one would find out about you. So that I wouldn't find you again," Skylar said.

She resisted another step, both drawn to and repulsed by the creature in front of her. The creature whose blood ran in her veins.

The Fenris's eyes blinked slowly. Its mouth moved as if it wanted to speak.

"I'm sorry," Skylar said. "I'm sorry for everything, and that if you had a plan for your future here, among humans, it couldn't have worked very well."

The Fenris lifted one massive paw, turned it over invitingly but then retracted the gesture. She sliced her chest open with a four-inch-long claw, and let a drop of blood drip from her fist.

"If you changed once, can you change again?" Skylar asked, understanding what the creature meant by the display of blood. Maybe they weren't one, or exactly alike, but that blood belonged to them both.

The Fenris knew who Skylar Donovan was.

"Can you be her? The mother I saw? I know about the moonlight, and what it does."

The beast in front of her suddenly flickered, as though it had never been solid in the first place. An outline appeared. It was a waifish, slender woman with dark hair and a gaunt face that stood in the Fenris's place for seconds only, but long enough to make Skylar's eyes fill with tears.

They were tears of loss, confusion, fear of the past and of the future. Tears of longing for the mother she never really knew and now might lose, though that mother wasn't human.

"Please," she whispered, taking another step, the tears falling unchecked down her cheeks.

But the image of the woman quickly disappeared,

replaced by the massive body of the Fenris, a frightening creature that so few people knew anything about.

The Fenris made a keening sound, deep in her throat, that made Skylar snap upright.

"No," she said. "Please don't."

With one more toss of her head, one more blink of her light eyes and an accompanying howl of pain, the creature turned. And with a great leap into the air, the Fenris soared from the rock into the valley beneath, not to any escape route this time, but to her death.

Gavin was there in a flash, afraid to touch Skylar though he wanted to, ached to. Skylar was teetering on the brink of the rock the Fenris had leaped from. He said nothing because what was there to say?

Skylar had called that demon *mother*.

That couldn't be right, but Skylar was still in danger.

I'm here, he said, over and over, softly, tenderly, afraid to find cover and change back to his human shape. Afraid to move away from Skylar.

It was a long time before she looked his way: an interminable, unendurable number of minutes. When her eyes registered his presence, there was so much pain in them, he choked back a response.

Speaking was difficult for her, but she said in a voice that cracked, "Sorry."

Gavin fisted his hands to keep from grabbing her as she went on. Another foot backward, and she would fall.

"That's what I carry in me," she said. "At least in part."

The tears glistening in her eyes broke his goddamn werewolf heart.

Hell, so do I, he said, daring just one small step forward. *Maybe that was fate, too, for those who believe in that kind of thing. Maybe I'll be the best person to understand you. I'm willing to try.*

He tracked every tear that ran down her cheeks.

"She didn't do it on purpose," she explained. "She didn't intend to hurt you. She'd been caged, and she got loose. She didn't want to go back there."

There was a further hitch in her voice. "What will happen to me if I inherit that tendency for danger?"

You won't. You're half human, and it turns out that half is a good one. You've been strong enough to keep the changes at bay.

"She could have killed me with one swipe of her claws, Gavin. She wasn't dead. All those years, she was alive and living like this. And now she's gone."

I know. Skylar, I know.

"The myths are wrong. She wasn't a monster. She died for me. She gave her life to save me from having her in my life. I saw that in her. She didn't kill my father. He did his best to keep her safe from others and from herself. She knew that. He must have slipped, fallen."

She turned to face the drop to the valley. "When I look back, I see the things my father did to protect us. We knew how to use guns. He introduced me to Danny, a cop, possibly assuming that kind of relationship might offer me a greater defense in case I needed it. He distanced himself from us so that we wouldn't come here, where he...where he tried to take care of her."

It's over, Gavin said softly.

Skylar's eyes met his. "Really, it's only the beginning."

We'll face whatever comes our way.

"Our way?" she repeated.

Can you finish your school work here? Close to here? Would you regret leaving Miami? I'd like you to stay here with me. I need you to stay.

"Will you two get a room?" Jenna said, appearing beside them in her human form wearing little more than a very sober expression. "You're making me crave my guy, and it's a long flight home. And yes, my Matt is like us. That's important and saves a lot of trouble and heartache."

Jenna's tone was light in an attempt to ease the blow Skylar had received. They all realized this and silently thanked her for it, though he felt Skylar's pain as if it were his own and knew she wouldn't truly get over this for a long, long time, if ever. Such was the way of darkness once it had gotten a foothold.

And he shared her feelings because they had imprinted, bonded, connected, as two halves of a pair.

A lot of questions still needed answers. Questions like how her mother's human-like form could have lasted long enough for her to be married and have children. And when Skylar's father had found out what his wife really was. How he'd taken that shock.

Questions about how a Fenris got here in the first place and met David Donovan, and whether that meeting was chance, or somehow preordained.

How had this Fenris recognized her daughter?

What the hell was a Fenris, really?

How would that kind of blood affect Skylar?

None of those answers would be coming now, not without a lot of research. Maybe they were the same questions Skylar's father had needed answered for the sake of his own peace and sanity. Still, it had to be clear to Skylar that her father had loved her. He had loved his daughters enough to leave them in order to keep them safe. And to protect them from the truth.

Gavin needed a voice, so he could tell Skylar these things. A real voice. The longing to hold Skylar beat at him mercilessly.

We have all the time in the world to search for what answers we can find, he said. *This is the place for you. Here. With me.*

Skylar's heart began to slow, syncing its beats to his heart. He guessed the shock of all this might never wear off.

You might have faced a demon, Skylar, but I'm not going to let you face the future alone.

Her life had taken a strange turn, as his had. He understood about this. He knew.

There are no more secrets. You don't have to be afraid.

"I'm going below to search the valley," Jenna said. "Just to be sure. To ease my mind." She glanced over the ledge. "I'll meet you at the cabin, where I hope there'll be a stiff drink waiting. These Colorado nights are too damn cold."

Gavin closed the distance to Skylar, reached out to her and held tightly to his half human, half something else lover.

She allowed him to carry her, probably because she was shaky and emotionally depleted. But both of them knew she didn't really need this kind of treatment, so it made having her in his arms feel even more special.

Back under the cover of the trees, Gavin set her down. He willed himself back to a form more conducive to sharing with her the depths of his love for her. And whether he was human or werewolf, most of those things bordered on being X-rated.

They both needed to vent some emotional steam.

Pressing her to the tree with his partially bare body, he realized that talking wasn't necessary after all. Having Skylar all to himself, body, mind and soul, was. Selfishly, unabashedly, he craved her full attention.

He wanted her to know how much he cared, and that he would always be there for her. With her.

His mouth hovered over hers, seeking the perfect place to land, waiting to see if she could even respond. His hands covered hers, linking their fingers in a lover's knot. *Will you go for this, my love? Do I have the right to demand anything right now? So soon?*

His hips ground against hers suggestively, in an unconscious gesture. He'd thought he might lose her. God, if he had...

He couldn't stall his longing to possess her. Nothing that had happened tonight had dulled that desire.

He anxiously waited for her to make a move with his heart dancing inside his chest. Finally, Skylar's lips parted. Her mouth met his with a breath that was blissfully hot and slightly salty from the tears she'd shed.

He accepted that kiss, relished it with relief and a raging hunger. When that wasn't enough to assuage his beastly cravings, his hand moved to her zipper, her hand moved to his, and the jeans came down.

Long legs—the first thing he'd noticed about Skylar—wrapped around him, bringing her damp, fiery heat too damn near to his aching erection. She wanted this as much as he did. She needed this, too.

"Foreplay," he muttered. His fevered lips devoured

hers as his hands lifted to settle her into place. "I swore to you that we'd have some."

"First thing you have to know about demons," she whispered back, sliding down over him and pausing to utter a throaty curse as he helped her along, "is that we don't understand that word."

Skylar was willing herself to move on, for now, and using him to do it. Gavin was all for that.

With tears still shining in her eyes and her body needing an outlet for pent-up emotion, Gavin stroked her, each movement reaching her core, where her wolf, or whatever the hell had taken up residence there, accepted him willingly.

Hearing Skylar's throaty cry was like a release. He felt the internal quakes that rocked her, and he moved inside her blistering heat like the madman he was, wanting all of her and vowing to take care of the little wolf demon in his arms for as long as that infernal imprinting thing lasted...plus a hundred years.

And then, when she cried out, he joined her in one long, satisfied exhaled breath. Filled with the hope and promise of finding peace for the first time in a very long while and a bright new future with the woman in his arms, Gavin closed his eyes and whispered Skylar's name.

* * * * *

THE WORLD IS BETTER WITH

Romance

Harlequin has everything from contemporary, passionate and heartwarming to suspenseful and inspirational stories.

Whatever your mood,
we have a romance just for you!

Connect with us to find your next great read, special offers and more.

f /HarlequinBooks

🐦 @HarlequinBooks

www.HarlequinBlog.com

www.Harlequin.com/Newsletters

HARLEQUIN®

A *Romance* FOR EVERY MOOD™

www.Harlequin.com

SERIESHALOAD2015

HARLEQUIN®

A *Romance* FOR EVERY MOOD™

JUST CAN'T GET ENOUGH?

Join our social communities
and talk to us online.

You will have access to the latest
news on upcoming titles and special
promotions, but most importantly,
you can talk to other fans about your
favorite Harlequin reads.

Harlequin.com/Community

 Facebook.com/HarlequinBooks

Twitter.com/HarlequinBooks

 Pinterest.com/HarlequinBooks